# Operation: Genocide

Yvonne Walus

Visit Yvonne online:

www.YvonneWalus.com

# STAIRWAY⹀PRESS

An Armchair Adventurer book
STAIRWAY PRESS—SEATTLE

Cover Design by David Zampa PensiveDragon.com

**www.stairwaypress.com**
1500A East College Way #554
Mount Vernon, WA 98273

# Pretoria, South Africa—One Year Earlier

PROFESSOR ADELBRECHT OF the Biotech Research Agency for Vital Operations felt bile rise to his mouth as he watched one of the government's highest ranking officials wipe red stickiness off his fingers and extract cotton balls from his large, protruding ears. The whop-whop of the ceiling fan added a bizarre sense of ordinariness to the scene.

"I'm listening," the minister said. The cotton balls fell into the waste paper basket with an ominous absence of sound.

Adelbrecht talked fast.

"Brilliant. You sure it'll work?" The minister's question hung heavy in the sizzling African air.

The professor's mouth went dry. "Yes."

*If genocide is really what you want.*

"This office has full confidence in you and your team. We understand the Ebola virus was both an unfortunate and unforeseeable accident."

Spoken like a true politician, yet the professor felt the atmosphere in the room turn as thin as the ground under his feet.

"That's correct, Minister."

"Right. What guarantee do we have this new virus won't go ape-crazy?"

"With all due respect, Minister, Ebola was transmitted through *any* personal contact. The new virus we're proposing will be contagious only via sexual relations. Nothing else."

"So an infected maid will still be able to cook for you, but won't pass the virus on?"

"Hundred percent correct, Minister."

*Assuming you don't sleep with her. But that was illegal, forbidden by the Immorality Act.*

"Goes without saying that this discussion never took place."

"Yes, Minister."

"Even the Prime Minister doesn't know about this project."

*Like hell he didn't.*

"The limousine is at your service, Professor. The driver will take you wherever you desire."

Relief washed over him. He started rising from the sofa, ever the obedient puppet.

"Oh, and Professor?"

"Yes?"

The Minister With No Official Portfolio rose, his shoulders blocking out the sunlight of the summer day outside.

"This is your final warning." Suddenly, he didn't sound like a politician anymore. "Mess this up, and you'll wish you were dead."

# Chapter 1—Saturday Night

IF IT LOOKS like an elephant and walks like an elephant, it's an elephant, thought Captain Trevor Watson.

For some reason, though, the higher powers within the South African Police weren't buying the wisdom.

He stood at the entrance to the rich man's garage, the smell of car fumes still tarnishing the night air. He scanned the confined space.

"This exactly how you found it?" he asked Jones.

The pimply constable stood to attention. "Yes, sir."

To the left side, a Ford Cortina with a teddy bear on the back seat. A silver BMW to the right. An expensive status symbol car for him, a practical one for her, Watson noted. That in itself said something about the dead man. A garden hose extended from the Beemer's exhaust to the driver's side window.

They had all the garage doors open now, airing out the interior before proceeding with the investigation.

"Your thoughts, Constable?"

*Let the youngster learn on the easy ones.*

Jones shrugged. "Looks like a suicide to me."

"Right." Did to Watson too, but obviously the brigadier had a different take on it to call him when he wasn't up on the rotation. Watson knew better than to complain. After last week's crap-out session, his job was hanging by the proverbial thread, except in his case the thread was thinner than a hair and more brittle than a dry twig from a thorn tree.

Officially, he'd been in the right. A white property owner had the legal right to shoot a black burglar, provided a warning shot had been fired first. The way some policeman worked, they would fire that warning shot themselves when they arrived at the crime scene and found only one spent cartridge. Some policemen, but not him. A week ago, Watson had been called out to a shooting scene: one dead burglar, one shot fired. Only one shot. Instead of fixing up the scene after the fact, he had chosen to obey the letter of the law, arrest the white homeowner for culpable homicide. The result? The guy who shot the burglar without warning got off with a smack on the wrist. Watson, given the history of his employment in the South African Police, came out with excrement stuck to both boots.

Remember whose side you're on, Watson, the brigadier's words kept ringing in his ears. One false move. Just one, and you're finished. I'm watching you.

So. Saturday night, and he'd been pulled out of bed to investigate *yet* another suicide. *Yet* another white middle-aged guy whose life of luxury had blown up in his face. Watson remembered the outline of the man's sprawling mansion, eyed the BMW, tried to understand. No go.

"Word has it, he's some sort of big shot. That right?" Jones swatted at his forearm, brushed off the dead insect. "Bloody mozzies."

"Far as I know, the victim hasn't been positively identified yet. Both cars and this residence, though, are registered to a scientist doing classified work for the government. That's why all sorts of trip wires sounded the alarm the moment the call came in."

"Live by the sword, die by the sword, hey, Captain?"

Watson waved a mosquito away from his own arm. Shook his head. "It's not as though the victim..." his memory was still sluggish from the sex marathon he'd had only half an hour before, "this Gordon Pretorius..." He paused, found his train of thought. "Not as though he died of poison, or a bomb explosion, or whatever it is government scientists create in their labs."

Annette Pretorius sat in her bedroom, facing her dressing table. Her gaze bounced off the freshly polished mirror and the bottles on the dust-free surface without taking them in. The words of the typed note she'd found behind the BMW's windscreen wiper flashed in her memory.

BURN ALL THE FILES, OR YOU DIE, TOO.
DON'T TELL THE COPS.
YOU HAVE TILL MONDAY.

Not a coward by nature, Annette wouldn't have been bothered by the threat, not even with Gordon slumped in the car seat less than a metre away. Ever since her first baby took his first gulp of air, though, her life wasn't her own anymore.

If she died, who would look after the children? Her mother? Annette shuddered at the prospect. She couldn't let it happen. To live, she had to do what they wanted.

She'd hidden the note in her bra, because her evening dress had no pockets. The paper's hard folds had stabbed her skin as she bade the party guests goodbye and rushed upstairs. The stiff corners kept biting into her flesh, yet she made no move to take it out.

*What files? Where would she find them? How would she prove that she'd destroyed them?*

*Enough.*

She didn't recognise the helpless person she'd become. Whatever happened to the rebellious redhead who used to read banned literature and, on one wine-filled evening, had set fire to her sensible beige bra?

*Get yourself together, silly. Look for the files. Read them. Throw them in the fire.*

She straightened her spine and, on still-shaky calves, walked over to Gordon's nightstand. Yanked open the top drawer.

A memory stabbed her right through the heart. Her old

vitamin pills. What on earth were they doing in Gordon's drawer? She'd started taking them over a decade before, feeling run down after the birth of her second baby. Gordon had brought them back from work, an experimental pill that would make her feel better.

It had made her feel stronger, if a bit dreamy and untroubled by reality. But then the miscarriages started, and she felt weak and depressed no matter how many of those vitamin pills she took. In the end, she'd flushed them down the loo, but in her mind the sparkly blue pills that looked like sapphires would forever remind her of the five babies she'd lost, each of them as small as the tube of blue vitamin pills.

And now the vitamin pills were back, one tube almost empty, two untouched. She slammed the drawer shut. Opened another. Still, the questions gnawed at her like a termite in skirting.

*Had Gordon been taking the blue pills? Why?*

*At least the dead scientist didn't kill his family.*

The thought echoed in Watson's mind as he closed the internal garage door behind him and stared at the portraits of the man's three children in the entrance hall to the mansion.

*At least he didn't kill the family.*

The way these suicides usually worked, the bloody bastard shot his wife and children before turning the gun on himself. The change was refreshing. Still, a small part of Watson's self-interest wished the scientist had waited till morning. That way, he wouldn't have to face Charlene's accusing glare when he got back home.

A domestic servant appeared in the hall.

*This time of the night? Shouldn't she be asleep in her own quarters?*

"Baas," she said instead of *good evening*.

Watson didn't waste time on social graces, either. "Where is the lady of the house?"

The whites of the maid's eyes gleamed under the chocolate-coloured lids. No reply. Didn't she understand?

"Your madam," he rephrased, consulting his hastily scribbled note. "Annette—Annette Pretorius?"

He'd known an Annette once, long ago. Her hair glowed red as though fashioned from all the fires of hell. She'd made him fail three maths tests in a row. Back then, he'd have walked barefoot on melting pavement for Annette LeRoy.

Watson shook his head. Annette LeRoy had long been gone from his life. It was another woman he'd left in the snug bed when the call came to investigate this case. Peeved by the call-out, his lover had probably gone home.

*Damn.*

He wouldn't allow his life to interfere with work. Not now. Not when he'd finally regained his lost rank and status.

He stepped past the still silent woman into the spacious hallway, coated with the smell of stale cigarette smoke. "Call the madam." Harsher than intended. His patience ran in short supply tonight.

The servant averted her gaze. A cultural convention, he knew, not a sign of a guilty conscience.

"The madam is asleep." Her voice carried a gracious, educated quality. "First she tells everybody to please go home and then she goes upstairs."

"She—what?" The cop in him was fully awake now.

*Asleep, hey? Curious.*

You didn't go to bed when your husband killed himself. You fainted. You cried. You pretended to faint or cry. But go to bed? Then his brain caught up with the other titbit of information. "What do you mean, she told *everybody* to go home?"

The maid gestured towards the open door, through which he could glimpse kitchen counters with smudged wine glasses, squashed beer cans and dirty plates. "I'm washing up after the party when she comes up from the garage—"

"Your madam? Madam Annette?"

A nod. "She says to the guests, 'You will have to excuse us. Gordon is not feeling well. I think it's best if we called it a night.' And then she says she's so very, very sorry."

He was glad the maid spoke good English. Thanks to the

government policy of limiting the duration and quality of Bantu education, few black people did. "What's your name?" he asked.

"Hester."

"What happened then, Hester?"

"Madam tells me to call the police, she says the number is on the phone pad, and to tell them the master gassed himself dead in his car."

"And then?"

"Then she is sick all over the kitchen floor." A false note in Hester's voice. Triumph? Glee? "To the master, she pretends she doesn't eat. Coffee for breakfast, a leaf of lettuce for dinner, that's the way he likes it. But tonight she throws up steak and prawns and potato. And chocolates."

"Thank you, Hester, you may go now." A new voice, soft and slightly hoarse, came from the staircase. "You'll finish the dishes tomorrow."

"Yes, missus." The black woman shot him one direct frightened gaze before she withdrew.

His tired brain decided to file it under follow-up-sometime, as he turned his attention to the widow.

Annette Pretorius. Red-rimmed eyes, fever-red cheeks, and red hair fashioned from all the fires of hell.

His Annette. Annette LeRoy.


Hester's feet fell lightly on the floor tiles as she crossed the kitchen floor and locked the back door behind her. The sky was as black as the inkwell she had used at school in an era where white kids used ballpoint pens. This late at night, with most residential lights out, the blackness was studded with the glimmer of many, many stars. As many stars in the sky as there were freedom fighters down here, on this sun-baked soil of Africa.

*Find the files*, the leader of her resistance cell had told her at the last meeting. *Those who aren't with us, are against us.* Hester didn't waste energy philosophising about loyalty and trust. Her action had nothing to do with grudges or her people's struggle against apartheid. The leader had asked and she had promised. It was as simple as that. With Master Gordon dead, the task had become trickier or trivial, depending on the madam's reaction.

The door to her quarters, in the far corner of the garden, stood open for air circulation. Now Hester closed it behind her and surveyed the cement floor for snakes and scorpions. She repeated the procedure with her narrow bed. Columns of bricks under each leg added extra height and guarded against the evil spirit, the Tokoloshe. The leader said that's nonsense, a myth invented by the witch doctors to scare the people into giving them money. Still, Hester reckoned you couldn't be too careful. Master Gordon hadn't slept on a bed raised by bricks, and look where it got him.

*Trevor!*

The air, thick as treacle, stuck in Annette's lungs, threatened to explode in her chest.

Trevor. An old school friend. An ex-boyfriend. The only man who knew her the way she really was, because he himself awakened the very worst inside her.

His presence should have made the situation better. It made it infinitely worse. She'd never been able to keep a secret from him. Now she had to.

Adrenalin propelled her forward, one gluey step after another.

"Annette."

She cleared the rasp from her throat. "Trevor Watson." She made herself walk faster, her bare feet registering the coolness of the terracotta. "I'm so glad it's you." One more lie for the evening—what did it matter?

"Annette," he repeated. His voice was fuller now, his face all grown up. "You haven't changed a bit."

*You have no idea.*

On perfect-hostess autopilot, she took his hand in both of hers and led him into the lounge. Her knees were jelly, and she still couldn't remember how to breathe.

"I'm sorry we meet under these sad circumstances," Trevor

said. "Your husband…"

The remainder of the sentence slid off her earlobes without reaching the eardrum. She couldn't concentrate. They stood in the middle of the room, his hand still in hers, until her upbringing took over. "I'm sorry. I can't seem to concentrate."

Trevor started talking again. She watched his lips, and again couldn't distinguish the sounds, as though he spoke in a foreign language. Shell-shocked.

*Is that what soldiers meant, this inability to use your senses?*

*If only her brain worked properly!*

She wasn't stupid, contrary to what Gordon sometimes said—shouted—during his lapses of temper.

She let go of Trevor's hand, rubbed her forehead.

"I feel so—" she broke off. What did she feel? Wrapped in cellophane? Guilty? Lost? All her life, she had trained hard to suppress her emotions, to please first her parents, later her husband. Tonight was an exception. "Please," the words escaped before she could bite down on them. "I don't know what to do."

"What do you mean?"

BURN ALL THE FILES…

Should she show Trevor the message?

DON'T TELL THE COPS.

Somehow, she didn't think so. She forced her face into a mask of a helpless female. "What's the protocol, Trevor? Do I call the funeral home? Do the police do it? How do I tell people?" The mask immobilised her face. Oh, dear Lord, she had to tell the children.

Trevor's gaze became more focussed. "And your worry, at this point in time," he accentuated the last word, "is *protocol*?"

No, her mind screamed, my worry is the children's reaction, their tears, their future without a father. My worry is money for Monday's dinner, and for the Monday after next. My world has screeched to a halt and derailed, my ears are ringing and all I want right now is to wake up from this nightmare.

BURN…

Her mouth hurt to form words that suddenly grew a hard edge. "Nobody taught me how to be a widow." True enough. Somehow, her voice came out cool, calm and collected. Thank the Lord for small mercies.

The pause stretched forever before Trevor broke the silence. "Did your husband have life insurance?"

*Insurance?*

Annette tried to remember whether Gordon had ever mentioned the subject. She forced her lips to form words again. "I don't know."

Exhausted by the effort of speaking when she wanted to scream, she sank onto the sofa, allowed herself the luxury of leaning into the creamy upholstery. She gestured Trevor to sit, too. "I just don't know anything anymore."

"Did your husband have any enemies?"

*Enemies?*

Her vision tunnelled, then broadened with alarming speed. "What am I going to do?" She stared down at her lap where her trembling fingers kneaded the material of her skirt. They refused to settle.

The sofa hissed under Trevor's muscled body. "You loved your husband that much?"

Annette flinched. The question, in all its absurdity, penetrated through the fog in her head. "I beg your pardon?"

Trevor must have misunderstood her reply. "I'm sorry," he said. "My comment was inappropriate."

*Was it?*

Annette couldn't tell. He was the investigating officer. Surely he had the right to ask personal questions. Still, nobody had the right to hear the truthful answer to this one. "Of course I—loved…" she trailed off.

Even to her ears, it sounded weak and false. She tightened her lips against her teeth, blockading the emotion she kept deep inside. "Without Gordon, I don't know how I'm going to live from day to day. He took care of the finances. Tomorrow is pay-day for the staff and the children need bus money on Monday..."

The arrangement of the husband looking after finances was commonplace, yet Annette felt sick with shame. Why had she allowed herself to become ignorant about her family's money matters?

"Did your husband keep any cash in the safe?"

Annette tried to concentrate, though it was growing harder to do so. Her spine burrowed further into the couch. "Documents, I think. And some gold collector coins. Not money, though."

"Do you have your own bank account? Your own chequebook? Credit card?"

The questions came fast. Annette couldn't keep up. The adrenalin rush died away, leaving her spent. Due to her punishing diet, she never had much energy these days. "I—I ..."

BURN ALL THE FILES, OR YOU DIE, TOO.

The room swooped into a spin. Sounds grew muffled. She would not faint. She would not allow herself that pitiful way out. "Perhaps we could talk—tomorrow? Please. I'm not feeling myself..." She grasped for control. "The children—are with Mother. Safe—Yes. Quite—safe now."

The last three words had come out slurred and soft. Watson had to strain to catch them. Annette's head fell back, and for a moment he thought she was asleep.

Her normally milky skin, though, looked even paler than usual; felt clammy when he touched her wrist to count the beats. Pulse under fifty. Not asleep or faking—she had fainted.

He lifted her legs onto the sofa and lowered her head onto the armrest. He noticed how skinny her limbs were. Must have lost weight since high school, not that she'd had any puppy fat to begin with. Small, more like a child in size. This was not how he usually conducted a suicide investigation, but then, he did not usually meet Annette LeRoy on the job. Should he hand over the case? Absolutely the proper and correct thing to do, and what he liked best in life was to do things properly and correctly. Not because he was saintly—because life was simpler that way.

He needed this case, though. And Annette meant nothing to him—now.

"Captain?" The constable's eyes flickered from the sleeping woman on the sofa to Watson, then back again.

"At ease, Jones. What do you have for me?"

"HQ radioed twice for an update. Are the preliminary interviews completed?" Jones glanced at Annette again, more pointedly this time.

Watson ignored Jones' implied question.

*Interviews?*

The guests had been sent off, the kids had evidently spent the evening with their granny, and the lady of the house had fainted. He needed to think.

"Go touch the car's engine, Jones. And check the level of petrol left in the tank."

"Yessir."

Why would HQ need an update already? Big fish scientist or not, that's not how they did things. Watson rifled the pages of his notebook again. Pretorius, Gordon Pretorius. A common enough Afrikaner surname, a bit at odds with the British first name, but such things happened. Pretorius? It rang a bell. His memory flicked through its neat catalogue of facts until it settled on the list of ministers. No Gordon Pretorius there. Not a political figure then, thank his lucky stars.

Jones rapped on the doorjamb.

"The engine is still warm, sir, and the petrol tank almost full. The boys from the lab will be able to do an exact measurement."

He thought some more. "Was the engine running when you got here?"

"Negative, sir."

Watson stood up from the sofa, careful not to disturb Annette, and took out his radio. He knew Jones had toned down HQ's request. They didn't *want an update*. They demanded his immediate attention, utter deference and brilliant conclusions.

When his superior answered, Watson's gut twisted. The old fox, at HQ, on a Saturday evening? The case must be huge. "Watson here, Brigadier."

He wasn't allowed to say more. For the next ninety seconds, he listened.

Most officers loathed landing high profile cases. The potential glory wasn't worth the hassles with the influential family members who were more than used to throwing their weight about.

Watson was unlike most officers. It'd been six years since he was allowed to lead a case of any substance. Tonight, his luck had changed.

"You can count on me, Brigadier," he said.

When he disconnected, he looked straight at Jones, channelling his bafflement. "I'll be damned," he said. "HQ wants us to treat this as a murder case. Not a suggestion, an order. Have the team dust for prints."

"Yes, sir."

"Photographs?"

"Just the corpse."

"Take snaps of everything. The hose, the exhaust, the petrol gauge, the garage doors, the spiders on the ceiling. Is the medic here?"

"Should be arriving any minute, sir. Said he's not in a state to drive, it being a Saturday night, so we sent a car for him."

Watson forced a laugh. "Let's hope he's not too drunk to give us an initial opinion. The suicide—or the victim, if we're to accept HQ's theory—was one of our top scientists working on something super secret."

"Which was?"

"They won't tell us."

Jones scratched his head. "Did they say why we're treating it as a murder?"

A deep breath to steady the hammering in his chest. This would be his big break. His way up. If he solved it. "Because it's happened before."

"With respect, Captain, we get a fair share of suicides."

Watson knew it only too well. Suicide, often preceded by family murder, was on the rise. Heads of families unable to cope with stress, too proud to seek professional help when depression struck or when things went awry at work—sometimes they chose to end it, no matter what they heard in church every Sunday.

"Suicide happens," he said. "But when it happens to the second top scientist in less than five weeks, HQ sits up and takes notice."

Jones exhaled a whistle.

"Hold the amazement, Constable. You don't know the best bit. The other dead scientist was also called Pretorius. Pieter Pretorius."

"A coincidence?"

"No. His father."

Annette Pretorius woke with a start. Something was wrong. The light. Artificial and hard on the eyes. Also, not her bed. Not a bed at all.

BURN ALL THE FILES, OR YOU DIE, TOO.

Memories flooded back, crushing. She buried her face in the leather of the sofa. No escape.

"Annette."

If she kept very still, perhaps he'd go away. The approach usually worked for bullies: Gordon, her mother—mainly Gordon.

"Annette, listen to me. I need to ask you a few questions, and I need you to answer them. Please. It's important."

*Important?*

Important was a word reserved for things that had to do with Danny, Julie and Beth. Homework. Swimming galas. Protecting the children from Gordon's temper. Those were the important things in life.

"Annette?"

Like a slap. She sat up, shielding her eyes from the harsh light of the chandelier. Fury rose acerbic to her mouth. She was done living by somebody else's priorities. "Don't you use that tone of voice with me again, Trevor Watson. Not ever."

His Adam's apple moved up and down several times. "I apologise, Mrs. Pretorius." Nothing personal in his voice now, a textbook example of a policeman. "Please understand. Your husband," a slight pause, "passed away in unexplained circumstances, and it is my sad duty to investigate it. Should you prefer, I could have you escorted to the police station for official questioning."

It didn't make any sense. "But Gordon—I saw him—the hose." Images blazed in her mind, sharp and absolute. No ambiguity in the horrid garage scene. Gordon had taken the coward's way out.

Anger pooled in her head. She had to ask Trevor to repeat what he'd said.

"Was it you who found the deceased, Mrs. Pretorius?"

The *deceased*. She pushed the word away. "Yes."

"What did you see?"

She cast her mind back. The stairs—the door—*the deceased*. A sharp ringing, like the TV signal once transmission had ended, filled her ears. All she managed was a small shake of her head.

"All right," Trevor's voice softened. "Please tell me about the children. You mentioned they were out of the house? With your mother? Or with your mother-in-law?"

"With my mom. She lives nearby."

"How many children do you have?" The question had a spike at the end.

"Three. Danny's thirteen, Julie almost twelve, and Beth's just a baby." With every word, tranquillity spread through her.

She looked at the family photographs displayed over the mantelpiece. When she rose from the sofa, she thought her legs might cave in before she reached the wall.

One by one, she moved the frames of the photos until they were all askew, hanging at haphazard angles to one another.

She surveyed the end result, waited for its impact.

No use.

"Mrs. Pretorius?"

Unfair. For fourteen years, she would align photo frames on the walls with an aluminium level and place the mugs in the pantry rims down, so dust wouldn't get into them. She would turn the standing fan a precise thirty degrees inwards whenever she switched it on, place the toilet roll the correct way in its holder and always squeeze the toothpaste tube from the bottom.

For fourteen years, her life had been filled with rules, small and big rules, bloody annoying rules, Gordon's rules.

Every day, for fourteen long years, she would rush around the house ten minutes before he came home, straightening photographs, putting away toys and pulling down the blinds for privacy.

"Mrs. Pretorius."

Now that Gordon was dead, she thought it would give her pleasure to turn the mugs over, to squeeze the toothpaste tube where she damned well pleased and to leave the cap unscrewed too. But the experiment with the photo frames had proved futile.

Was Gordon's imprint on her psyche too deep? Had his way become her way now, too?

*The hell it had.*

"Mrs. Pretorius. Please tell me about your movements earlier tonight. You had a party? You asked the guests to go home?"

She wanted to throw Gordon's photograph across the room. But even with Gordon dead, now was not the time to give in to her impulses. She needed to come across—what? Sympathetic. Yes. And weak.

No problem. Fourteen years with Gordon could have made a

wooden dummy an Oscar-winning performer.

The pale blue of Watson's police shirt was getting darker—and decidedly wetter—from Annette's tears. Her head rested on his chest. Watson loathed himself for noticing how close her body was to his. The dead were not the only victims in a house of mourning—their families suffered emotional wreckage, too.

*And yet, if this wasn't a suicide?*

Watson knew how often, how bloody amazingly often, the murderer was the one who reported finding the body. Not very likely if this vic's murder was linked to his father's, but still.

*Shit.*

He heard Jones's embarrassed cough. "Captain? The medic wants a word. It may be nothing, sir—"

Annette's physical closeness held far more appeal than any breakthrough in the garage.

"So why—" He checked his tone. "Sorry, man. Shoot."

"Sir." Jones cut his gaze to Annette. Clearly, the matter was not for civilian ears.

"Go ahead, Jones."

Jones lowered his voice. "The deceased was holding something in his fist."

Watson's hopes skyrocketed, trumping—for the time being—the warmth of Annette's skin. "A suicide note?"

"No, sir. A white unicorn."

Those who knew what his job entailed sometimes asked the The Minister With No Official Portfolio how true the rumours were. About South African security forces participating in exchange training programs, learning interrogation methods in Italy and swapping torture stories in Argentina. The minister always smiled his honest smile and said, "I know of no incident in which my people ever tortured a political prisoner."

It was true. His people mopped up the blood in the prison's dungeons, sluiced away the body fragments, disposed of the mangled corpses. The actual torture he always administered personally. Not because he had a taste for it, quite the contrary, he abhorred pain. Consequently, he had no right to ask anybody else to inflict it. Some things, though, simply had to be done, and so he did them. For the fatherland. To keep South Africa white.

"Daddy? Daddy?" The cry of his three-year old daughter pierced the thick night air of his mansion.

He glanced at the security screen. The guards were alert but not anxious, the alarm circuits not triggered. Monsters under the bed, most likely. "Coming, honey."

His wife stirred, her pregnant belly protruding through the thin summer blanket. He planted a kiss on her cheek, warm and soft with sleep. "Shhh. I'll handle it," he told her.

He'd handle it. His daughter's nightmares and the threat hanging over the country's future. For her, and for his unborn children, he would do wrong things to get the right result.

"Daddy?"

"Just fetching some anti-monster spray. Daddy's going to get rid of all the monsters."

Those under the bed and those threatening their country.

# Chapter 2—Earlier That Saturday, Hours before the Murder

THE MINISTER WITH No Official Portfolio answered his home phone on the third ring. "Yes?"

The voice on the other end uttered a single dry word.

"Problem."

"The paperwork?"

"Some at the Pretorius house. The rest mailed to his lawyer."

The minister milled a curse between his teeth. He had planned to go to Mauritius next week, a family holiday before baby number two made it impossible for his wife to travel. "Arrest the lawyer."

Section 6 of the Terrorism Act allowed indefinite detention without a trial, in solitary confinement, for the purposes of interrogation.

*Interrogation.*

He gritted his teeth until the little muscles in his jaw went into a spasm.

*For his country. For his family.*

"*Bokkie*," he said to his wife, "you go ahead and pack. I'll be a day or two late joining you in Port Louis."

The party had been Gordon's idea. "I've invited a few people for a *braai* this afternoon," he'd said.

Another woman might have panicked at the news of an

impromptu barbecue. Not Annette. Annette's apathy had long ago reached levels of no return. "All right."

The wrong thing to say, she realised at once. Too lethargic. Too indifferent. Gritting her teeth, she pasted a cheerleader smile onto her lips and crinkled her eyes to make it look real. "That's a splendid idea, darling. What with your birthday coming up."

One bright smile, faked. One adoring glance, faked. One silent scream, genuine.

"Mhhm."

Annette checked her watch. Plenty of time. She knew the drill well enough to execute it in her sleep. Perhaps she *did* execute it in her sleep. Perhaps she had spent the last fourteen years asleep, ever since her dreams of going to university had fizzled out.

Anyway. She made a mental list. Make her secret-recipe apricot chutney. Get the eye fillet and sausage from the butcher. Get the vegetables from the Portuguese green grocer. Get the maid to marinade the meat and put together the salads and cook the potatoes. Make sure there's enough charcoal.

Gordon would take care of manly things like the drinks and the fire. At the crucial moment during the party, he would light the fire in the outside brick grill and fry the meat.

*Big wow.*

"Who's coming tonight?" It should have been a safe question. Today, it wasn't. A flash thunderstorm crossed Gordon's face. "Just a few people from the office."

"How lovely," Annette injected fresh enthusiasm into her voice. "I'll drive to the shops straight away."

"No garlic bread," was Gordon's only instruction.

"Of course."

She'd learned long ago not to ask why. She'd also learnt not to ask for money. Not directly. "Will you be going with me?"

"No."

Annette waited, the smile still in place.

"Oh, right," he remembered. Or pretended to remember. They'd gone through this charade every week for the last fourteen years.

He took out his wallet, counted out the banknotes, as green as the grass in her parched garden never was. Green. The colour of hope.

Except, for Annette, there was no hope.

Gordon spent the rest of the afternoon preparing his big announcement. His head pounded. Five hours till the dinner party. Five hours till the biggest gamble of his life.

A fresh shot of adrenalin buzzed through his body. He'd never been Mr. Popular, and tonight would probably cost him the few casual friends he did have.

Still. It felt damned good to be doing the right thing at last. For almost twelve years, he'd been feeling guilty about his research into long-term contraception drugs and the miscarriages Annette had suffered as the result.

Nothing could bring the dead babies back. Nothing could undo the damage his work had already done. Tonight, at least, he was going to prevent another streak of evil from spreading into the land, into this country he loved so much.

*Just a few people from the office*, Gordon had said. Technically correct, and yet something seemed off. The atmosphere had more in common with a concrete block than a helium balloon. It was just a feeling Annette couldn't even put into a thought.

And so she beamed her hostess smile to welcome Gordon's boss. Dr. Monterra had such an unusual surname that everybody resorted to calling him Doc. Funny, warm, wonderful Doc. His charm would soon lift the mood, she was sure. Annette had yet to meet his wife, who was once again visiting her parents in South West Africa.

Annette turned towards the director of BRAVO. "Good evening, Professor Adelbrecht."

Unlike Doc, Professor Adelbrecht was a man nobody dared called Prof, not even out of earshot.

"Are we all here?" he asked.

Sally, Gordon's secretary, had just returned from a stroll around the garden, hand in hand with her current boyfriend. Annette didn't have to be an expert at body language to know her roses hadn't been the main attraction of the secluded garden. Nick's whole demeanour shouted sexual frustration.

The only guest still to arrive was Gordon's research partner. Annette didn't even know her full name. She was always just Lula, and she was always late. More than fashionably late.

Lula was late. Gordon despised himself for noticing and he despised himself for caring.

In his experience, there were two types of women. Those who were wife material, and those who were so sexy they had to be sluts. There were two types of women, and then there was Lula. As sharp as African bristle grass. As smart as a man. And sexier, infinitely sexier than any slut Gordon had ever known.

Lula was—confusing.

He forced himself to concentrate. Less than one hour till the announcement.

Lula had better not miss it.

Annette opened the front door and stifled the overwhelming urge to touch up her lipstick. Lula, glamorous and confident as a celebrity, glided inside.

"Welcome, my dear." Annette tilted forward to kiss the air. "Where's your husband tonight?"

"I forget. Zurich? Madrid?" Lula's smile revealed all her upper teeth and a band of pink gums too. Annette didn't think it particularly pretty, yet she had to admit it looked striking. On Lula. "He'll be back on Monday."

Annette envied Lula her poise and magnetism and—most of all—a husband who spent his life away from home.

If Gordon were a pilot, like Lula's husband, would her own marriage be happier? She had no doubt. Still, conventions had to be observed. "It must be hard for you."

Lula shrugged. "Must it?" A tiny, amused pause, then Lula

slithered past her into the hallway. "Now, where is everybody? I've heard of this great party game where you put all the car keys in a large bowl and…" Her voice trailed off and she raised a lean eyebrow. "Get it?"

Annette kept her face poker-player still. Never in a million years would she let on she was familiar with the game of car keys in a bowl. The South African Censor Board, the same one that had blacklisted "Lady Chatterley's Lover", had no clue what ideas an ordinary housewife could find in ordinary American novels. Swinger parties were among the least outrageous.

"You put all the car keys in a large bowl and then what?" Annette asked serenely. She had tons of experience playing the naïve arm-candy. Worked like magic and saved many an awkward situation.

Lula's laugh was short on merriment. It said, *okay, you have me there, you win.* "You put all the car keys in a large bowl and what happens then, of course, is we'll try to work out whether the key rings can tell us something interesting about their owners. It'll be a blast, you'll see."

Gordon watched his boss's face with grim resolve. Doc had been pretty good at covering up his emotions when Annette was in the room, but the moment she left to answer the door, all the zeal whooshed out of Doc midway through a joke he'd been telling. His intended audience had been Annette and, with Annette gone, he delivered the punch line like an auditioning actor who already knows he's not getting the part.

"Have another whisky, Doc?" Gordon called out.

"*Ja*, why not."

Because you'll be a softer target when I deliver my blow later, that's why not, Gordon reflected as he jingled fresh ice in a tumbler.

No malice in the thought. Only unrelenting logic.

The key ring idea was indeed a blast from the moment Lula sashayed onto the patio with Annette's fruit bowl. A blast for everybody except Annette

"May I have your car keys, ladies and gentlemen?" Lula said instead of a greeting as she proffered the bowl.

The knowing *ahs* and *ohs* made Annette wonder. Surely these people didn't spend their time reading the same American novels?

As the first set of car keys clinked into the hollowed out wood of the bowl, Annette bit into her lower lip. Irrational pain seared through her chest. It was her bowl, the one her son had made for her. Danny's hands had touched it and shaped it and loved it into existence. Now it was being desecrated in a double-entendre party game.

She almost screamed a *no*. But she was a perfect hostess, after all, and perfect hostesses did not snatch objects from their guests' hands.

"Annette? Where are your car keys?"

She bullied herself into a smile. "Upstairs. Never mind about them."

"Nonsense." Lula's lips looked equally strained. "You have to play."

"Do I?"

"I'll get them, darling," Gordon called out. He only ever called her *darling* in public.

Tiredness washed over her, seeped into every cell. She wished the party over. Wanted everybody to go home. Right now. Heck, she wanted to go home herself, except she was home.

Doc touched her shoulder. "Chin up," he whispered. "All bad things come to an end, sooner or later."

*The sooner, the better.*

She leaned into Doc's fingers. "I'm having a wonderful time," she lied.

Doc knew he had to make his move. He wanted Annette in his life, in his bed, at the breakfast table. The way things stood at work, his window of opportunity was now, this weekend, before Gordon did anything silly.

"Say the word," he whispered as his nostrils caught the scent of her spicy perfume, "and I'll stop the game right now."

Annette turned to him, her smile so warm it trapped the breath in his throat. "Very kind of you," she whispered back. "But let them have their fun."

So much for playing her knight in shining armour. Still, the evening was young. Another opportunity was bound to come along.

Lula climbed onto the patio table, a move calculated to put her bare knees and thighs directly at eye-level of those sitting down. A woman in a chauvinist society had to use every advantage.

She held up the first key ring, a rectangular locket engraved with a cross. "Let's see now." She opened the clasp. "The Bible in miniature? I wonder which one of us needs the Holy Book when driving. Gordon? Is it yours?"

Gordon, she sensed immediately, was not amused. The conservative in him didn't consider religion a topic for comic relief. "My own Bible's bigger, Lula," he snapped. "I doubt I'd be able to read anything in this one without a magnifying glass." That scored Gordon a few chuckles. "Probably belongs to one of the young people, either Sally or Nick. I can see a bullet dangling off the chain, too. I'll guess the keys belong to Nick. Sally is wary of guns."

Why were they even a couple, if they disagreed on something so fundamental, Lula wondered?

"Right." It was Nick who spoke. "Deduced like a true scientist."

"Hey." The comment stung. "Are you saying I'm less of a true scientist for guessing wrong? My female brain's not analytic enough?"

"If the shoe fits…"

*The bigoted, chauvinist swine.*

"Oh? And who messed up Project Hydra's report by listing *sodium fluoride* as a water-soluble poison? Which it is—to rats."

Nick's grin dimpled one of his cheeks. "South Africa's enemies are rats, Lula. You simply didn't get the joke."

"Moving right along," prompted Doc, his voice like cotton candy wrapped around a chunk of iron.

The incident didn't bode well for her promotion, Lula realised. The unplanned distraction was worth it, though, because it took people's eyes off her hands.

The remaining key rings rattled reassuringly against the wood as she slid two strips of modelling clay—now imprinted with the professor's strongbox key—deeper into the bowl.

A woman with ambition had to use every advantage.

Annette understood Doc's agitation. Gordon had never mentioned Project Hydra at home. Must have been highly confidential.

*Why had Lula mentioned it? What was her game?*

Lula's game turned out to be Russian roulette. "All right, Doc. No need to get grumpy. We're all one big happy family here. Coming right up we have—a key ring that's an actual pen in a velvet pouch."

"It's no ordinary pen." Sally's mouth formed an infantile pout. "A Montblanc."

Lula bowed a deep curtsey. "Even lesser scientists can draw the obvious conclusion here." Sarcasm dripped off her words like summer rain in the highveld.

Annette's knees trembled. Surely it was a coincidence Sally's pen was similar to the one she herself got from Gordon after his business trip to New York? Hers was also a Montblanc, also in a velvet pouch, but without the key ring attachment, because Gordon knew Annette wouldn't want to replace the key ring she always carried.

So, Sally owned the same pen. What of it? Even if it had come from Gordon, it was perfectly appropriate to bring back a gift for his secretary.

*Without a doubt...*

A gift of the same value as the one he brought back for his wife, whispered a contrary imp behind her ear.

*No.*

Annette gritted her teeth until her jaw muscles ached. She would not be petty.

"Next we have a Swiss army knife. Small but packing punch." Lula opened the blades. "We have a pair of pliers, a mini-saw, even a nail file. A corkscrew and a screwdriver. My-my, what a lot of screwing—"

"It must be Doc's," Annette jumped in hastily. "His real name is Bond. James Bond."

Sally opened her eyes extra wide. "I've never realised how much Doc and I have in common. He *also* files his nails when work is slow."

"The tool is for filing metal." Doc said when the laughter died down. "The knife also has wire crimpers and cigar cutters. But the invisibility shield is on the bigger model at home."

Annette caught his eye and nodded with gratitude. She thought the awkwardness averted. She was wrong.

"Doc," Gordon's face was smug. "Are you like your pocket knife? Small yet packing punch?"

Doc stretched out his long muscular legs. At six foot four, he was anything but small.

"Such information is strictly on a need-to-know basis, Gordon," he said. "And you will never need to know, I promise."

Annette felt a blush spread across her cheeks and throat. A few sniggers, a *tsk*, somebody calling for a bottle of champagne to toast Gordon's birthday.

Two manicured fingers snapped right by her ear. "Earth to Annette," Lula said. "It's dinner time."

To Gordon's annoyance, Doc flirted with Annette all evening. Gordon found it difficult to keep his mind on the objective of the whole stupid dinner gathering. His bombshell couldn't wait till Monday, though. He had to set it off or it would end up ripping him apart.

He drew a deep breath.

*Now.*

No, not now. Now, a soft hand touched his forearm.

"Come sit with me while we eat," Lula said.

Golden Lula, supple Lula, Lula of the thousand-and-one sleepless nights, his daily temptation. The fling with Sally would never have happened, he was sure, if his resolve hadn't been eroded by Lula's unintentional sexuality.

"Of course."

Lula ate like a lady, which he liked, and drank like a man, which he detested. When she finished pushing ice cream around her bowl of fruit salad, she undulated her body in a cat-like stretch that sent shivers of disquiet and guilt down his abdomen.

"Who's keen on a swim?" she asked.

They all were, it seemed, the women delighted to show off what as a rule remained concealed, the men delighted at the prospect of seeing it.

Forbidden images filled his mind and he fought to annihilate them. Lula was somebody else's wife. A no-go area. Better rehearse his speech.

Gordon remained outside while the rest went in to change. Darkness had fallen already—with the briefest of sunsets and its sudden black curtain so typical of places close to the tropics. He had to pull himself together, stop acting like a besotted teenager. For crying out loud, why was he stalling the announcement, sabotaging his own freedom?

Without verbalising it in his mind, he knew. His plan had one flaw: it was a form of escape. Cowards ran away. Men stayed to wage war.

He would wage war instead.

"Gordon? Are you all right?"

His elegant, graceful Annette walked down the stone steps to the glistening kidney of the pool.

"Fine," he lied.

A good wife. A good hostess. A good mother. No, more than just a good mother—he winced as he recalled his stupid incident with Julie's braid—a great mother. When all the tension of the last few weeks was over, he would make it up to her.

The men drank beer, the ladies sipped wine. The African

night enveloped them with a shimmer of stars and the chirping of crickets.

Gordon sat further back, away from the crowd, away from Lula in a skimpy bikini, white and semi-transparent and clinging.

Doc and the professor didn't seem uncomfortable, though. Gordon watched in stunned disbelief as the two men converged on Lula.

"Dunk, dunk, dunk," they chanted.

That's what happened when you suppressed society's natural hunger for sex, he reasoned. Logical, when you think about it. Still, the balance of the world appeared shaky. Doc and the professor should know better than to act like teenagers.

Lula dived to the very bottom of the pool and got away. Sally was less fortunate. Her squeals of "I want to keep my hair dry" only inflamed her pursuers.

"Nick," she begged. "Do something."

With a cheeky grin, Nick joined in the chase, and when he dunked her, his hand tangled in her bikini top along the way.

Gordon moved forward, anger squeezing his chest. "I will not tolerate such behaviour in my house," he said through clenched teeth.

Nick lifted himself out of the pool and started drying his shoulders. "Just a bit of fun."

*Yeah, for you.*

"She loved it." Nick shrugged into his shirt. "Underneath that stiff buttoned-up blouse there's a goldmine of passion waiting for the—"

Gordon hit flat-handed, yet the sheer force of the blow made Nick lose his footing. The younger man slipped on the wet tiles, flailed his long arms and fell, buttocks first, back into the swimming pool.

It had felt good, but not good enough. "Please accept my apologies," Gordon managed, his teeth clamped together. "No, no," he addressed the other guests, "no reason to end the evening early. I'll fetch that birthday bottle of bubbly to put us back in a party mood while you people get dry. I still have an announcement I'd like to make."

It would be a different announcement to the one he had prepared. Fight not flight. In the morning, he'd be able to look himself in the eye when shaving for the first time in weeks.

He marched off, leaving Annette to smooth and soothe. Selecting bottles from the cellar was traditionally a man's job, just as soothing and smoothing were—not.

An announcement, thought one of the visitors. An announcement was bad news. Gordon had to be stopped, no matter the cost.

A good thing the preparations for Gordon's demise were already underway. With luck, it would all play out the right way.

The wine room's only door was an internal one leading off the garage. Gordon unlocked it. As he turned the handle, something sharp stung the side of his palm.

*Spider?*

Gordon winced. A Black Widow's venom was nasty, even if rarely fatal. He scrutinised the door. No, no spiders. Just a spiky nail above the handle, its head filed into a point sharp enough to draw blood.

*What the hell?*

Rage rushed through Gordon's arteries. Bloody Danny and his pranks, he thought. He took a few deep breaths to get a grip. Enough damage had already been done by decking Sally's boyfriend. The memory clammed his jaws together so tight they hurt.

He forced himself to breathe. Slow and steady. Think about the problem at hand. The other side of the door was intact, the nail not long enough to have gone right through.

With no head to offer a grip, he couldn't use a claw hammer to ease the nail out. Pliers wouldn't provide enough leverage.

He had no time for this.

The first tool he found in the toolbox was a hammer, so he knocked the razor-like tip of the nail deeper into the door.

He would tan Danny's hide tomorrow, he promised himself

as he dropped the pliers and hammer back into the toolbox. No, not tomorrow—Sunday was God's day, inappropriate for disciplining teenagers—but on Monday morning, first thing, before work.

If indeed he would be going to work on Monday.

Gordon shook his head. Too late for second thoughts. What had to be done would be done, no question about it.

And what had to be done now, was the sparkling wine. Personally he liked the crispiness of a brut, though most of his guests preferred their bubbles sweeter. His hands were getting numb. He settled on something in-between, cursing himself for the compromise. Compromises, in his experience, seldom satisfied either party.

Time to rejoin the others. He tucked the bottle of Grand Mousseux under his arm, rugby style, and re-entered the garage.

His sixth sense alerted him to somebody else's presence. He spun around and surveyed the room.

It took him three steps to reach the passenger's side of the BMW.

"What are you doing?" he said into the rolled-down window.

Where was Gordon? A good half hour had passed since he'd left to fetch the bubbly. The guests had changed back into their clothes and finished their coffee on the terrace, and still no sign of the host. Annette excused herself and went searching for her husband.

She found his body on the front seat of his car.

"Did you destroy the files?" The Minister With No Official Portfolio asked two hours later.

"All taken care of, sir."

A lie. The bitch had till Monday to make it true.

# Chapter 3—Sunday, One Day after the Murder

IT WAS WELL after midnight by the time Captain Trevor Watson parked his car outside his apartment block, right under the street lamp. He bent down to lock the driver's door. And heard the shot.

Did he only imagine the bullet zoomed inches above his head? He acted on pure instinct. Drop to the ground. Grab his own gun. Scan the area.

He used his eyes, his ears, his nose. Nothing. The circle of light from the street lamp poured onto his car. The rest of the street melted into the darkness.

Crouching behind his front wheel, he waited for his eyes to adjust. Listened again. Still nothing at first, just the usual ringing in the ears following a shot. Then, in the distance, the thud-thud-thud of running. Firm. Heavy. A man's footfall.

No longer caring about the possibility of getting shot, he leapt to his feet. Sprinted after the disappearing silhouette. The perp wasn't as fit. Watson gained on him with every step. Fifty metres. Twenty-five.

The shooter rounded the corner. A trap? Watson, adrenalin propelling him forward, didn't even slow down. A car engine revved. Tyres squealed. He burst into the side street just as a white car melted into the night, the stench of burned rubber still fresh.

*Bloody hell.*

No number plate, but the rear lights looked like a Ford. Fat lot of good that did. Every third car in Pretoria was a Ford. Most cop cars were Fords, too.

He picked up a stone. Hurled it into the empty road. Then another and another. Somebody had shot at him. *At him.* His muscles tensed at the memory, ready to squeeze off a round at the first thing that moved.

*Fuck.*

Didn't make sense. Why kill him? Not as though he was about to get a major breakthrough on the Pretorius case. The mind boggled.

The city air felt dense with exhaust and human presence, not fresh as in the suburbs, but he gulped a greedy lungful anyway as he jogged toward his front door.

Inside his apartment, the peeved woman no longer waited, yet her presence lingered. Her glass was on the bedside table, a half-empty tube of lipstick sat in his bathroom like a territory marker. Her musky perfume clung to his bed linen together with the sour smell of stolen sex.

He reached for the corner of the sheet. Stopped. Too damned tired to do laundry. Too damned tired to phone in the shooting incident. Still, after the latest warning from the brigadier, he had to do everything by the book.

Mincing a swearword, he picked up the phone.

"Just some teenagers messing around with their father's gun," the officer on duty told him. "We'll put out an alert for a white car with no plates."

"White or yellow," Watson said. "Likely a hatchback Ford."

"Okay. Do you need a babysitter?"

Watson considered it. A uniform stationed outside his apartment, following his every move. He thought about Charlene. A witness was the last thing he needed.

"Negative," he replied. "No babysitters." Couldn't resist quipping, "Unless one of the female sergeants…"

"In your dreams, Captain."

His sweaty clothes stuck to him like cling wrap. He peeled them off and collapsed onto the bed, his head sinking into the pillow that only a few hours earlier had cradled Charlene's milky neck. The memory made his tongue taste like termite poison.

This investigation was going to hell in a hand basket and now somebody had taken a pot shot at him.

*Why? Why, why, why?*

If he could just get a few minutes of rest, he knew he could catch the loose ends and beat them into some kind of plausible theory.

His thoughts hovered around Annette. As the victim's wife, she was a potential suspect.

*Damn it.*

He dozed off, his dream a kaleidoscope of images of a red haired woman riding a white unicorn inside a fume-filled garage. The unicorn was making a regular, buzzing noise.

Trrrrrrrrrrrrrrr. He jerked awake and fumbled for the receiver, surprised it was morning.

"Watson speaking." The inside of his brain felt worse than elephant dung.

The brigadier's hardened, commanding voice cut through the last vestiges of Watson's sleepiness. "Get back to the Pretorius house. Serial killer alert."

*Annette's in danger!*

Watson jumped out of bed and made for the front door. Stretched to the limit, the cord of the phone leashed him back in.

He scanned the room for his boots. "Any clues?" he said into the phone.

The brigadier emitted something that could have been a whooping cough bark or a tense snigger. "Look for white unicorns."

"Sorry sir?" Watson didn't catch the joke. He rammed his bare feet into police boots.

"Your report says Gordon Pretorius was holding a white unicorn."

"Correct."

"So was his dead father."

The implication chilled Watson's guts. He slammed down the phone. Grabbed his holster. Halfway down the corridor, he realised he was still naked.

Eight o'clock. Annette knew she should be going to church. It's what everybody did on a Sunday morning, if only to show off their new hats or their latest Mercedes.

Today, however, held other priorities. Today, she had to tell her children their father was dead, and burn a bunch of mysterious files.

Gordon was dead.

The words echoed in Annette's ears, dull and meaningless. Here was his side of the bed, unslept in, though that in itself hadn't been unusual lately. Here was his towel, pepper-dry. Here was his shaving gel and razor and toothbrush...

She hadn't liked her husband very much. She hadn't liked his sudden flares of temper, his controlling personality, the words like bullets. She hadn't liked him, yet she'd always assumed she loved him.

With Gordon dead, her only concern was for her children. No sorrow for the man who'd been her husband. No mourning for a life companion. No sense of loss.

*A bad wife.*

The kitchen door creaked. "Good morning, missus."

"Morning, Hester."

The maid didn't move to her usual station by the sink. "Sorry about master Gordon," she said.

Annette's eyes prickled. Her eyelids felt like sandpaper. If only she could cry. "Thank you."

She had to tell the children. Normally, she would drive the quarter mile round the block to her mother's house, because white madams never walked. Today was different. Even though there were no policemen about to prevent her from using the car, Annette couldn't force herself to enter the garage in which she'd found Gordon's body. The mere notion made her feel dizzy, so in the end she opted to climb over the back wall into her mother's garden, the way Julie and Danny usually did when they went to visit Grandma.

Despite the morning hour, the sun baked down on her back as, dressed in her customary high heels and a fashionable summer frock with frills that reached the ankles, she walked over the hardy kikuyu grass of her back yard. All around her, the lawn was still straw-coloured from the dry season. Water restrictions prohibited residents from watering their gardens unless they had access to a borehole...

*What on earth?*

A faint mist of water from the sprinkler, aimed at the rosebushes around the gazebo, hit her skin.

"Johannes," she called out.

The gardener appeared out of nowhere. "*Hau*, madam." Even in his blue overalls, he had the ability to blend into the lion-brown background. "It's a terrible thing. Terrible, terrible thing." His eyes never once lifted to hers.

"Yes, indeed Johannes, thank you." Annette's stomach fluttered as she remembered the staff would have to be paid today. Gordon always waited till the end of Sunday with the servants' money, so they wouldn't spend it on alcohol in the local shebeen. 'Protecting the people put under our stewardship', he used to call it. In his view, the blacks were as irresponsible as teenagers and even more incapable of looking after themselves.

"Don't worry about the pay. Please come to the house after dinner today, as usual." Oh Lord, what was she going to do about his wages? "And Johannes?"

"Missus?"

"Is it borehole water you're using?"

Johannes gave the grass a sullen stare. "The master says as long as we have a borehole, it's okay to use water from the mains."

Of course he would. Gordon was a stickler for rules, and he would never break one. But the law did say people with boreholes were allowed to water their gardens, with no explicit stipulation as to the source of the water. Stick to the letter of the law, not to the spirit in which it had been intended. Gordon's recipe for life.

And now he was dead.

"The master is no longer here," Annette said. The firmness in her own voice surprised her.

Another sullen stare. Honestly, what was it with these people? Annette knew in African culture a woman was inferior to a man, both in the black and in the white echelons, but Johannes would just have to learn to take orders from a female. "We will do things my way from now on. Are we clear?"

"Yes, missus."

"Good. And don't let the rose leaves get wet. It'll make them spotty."

Her chin held high, Annette marched off towards the brick wall. Conscious both of the gardener's eyes and of the sun on her pale skin, she lifted the hem of her dress and hoisted herself up and over the rough brick wall, flinching as one of the bricks loosened and almost came away in her grip.

Johannes didn't switch off the water. The garden was his domain. Without interest, he observed as the madam climbed the garden wall. He had long ago given up trying to understand white people. Like on the night of the party, the things the guests got up to. The couple in the rose garden. The guest who entered the garage. The commotion by the swimming pool. He could have told the police, if only the police had asked him.

Nobody noticed the black people in this country, so nobody noticed how much the black people noticed.

Watson ran a red light, his left fender whistling past the taillights of a white Ford with the width of a matchbox between them. His forearms tensed as he jerked the steering wheel to the right and screeched past a beat-up mini-bus filled to the brim by blacks on their way to church. In his haste, he hadn't put on underwear, and now the uncomfortable seam of his pants dug into his skin.

At the Pretorius mansion, he stepped on the brakes, heard

them moan. Breathed out the long held breath when he spotted the uniforms.

"Both cars are in the garage with the tape intact, Captain," the leader of the protection team reported. "No sign of the family, though."

The fear returned, solidified in his lungs like a chunk of ice. "She can't have gone far, man. Spread out and search the grounds. I'll talk to the maid."

Hester had seen Annette earlier, which was a relief, yet she had no clue where the madam could have got to now. He needed to question the maid again, but it could wait. Everything could wait. Finding Annette took priority.

"The garden boy," Watson asked Hester. "Where is he?"

"I'll go look for him, *Baas*."

The white unicorn at the death scene of both Gordon and Pieter Pretorius could mean both men committed suicide, the white unicorn a symbol of their pact. Or, it could mean a serial killer was on the loose.

*Targeting the Pretorius family? Targeting scientists?*

He didn't know, and he wasn't taking a single chance.

"Annette," he called out, knowing only too well how ridiculous he sounded. His mouth felt dry. "Annette."

The kids might still be at their grandmother's, Watson recalled the scant information he had managed to solicit the previous evening. What was her address? Bloody idiot, why had he not followed standard procedure last night? Curse Annette LeRoy and her flaming red hair.

He had to look old Mrs. LeRoy up in the phone directory.

Engaged signal. Watson stared at the address printed in the directory. Where the hell was Edward St?

Hester's voice crunched through his panic. "Johannes says the madam climbed over the back wall."

"She—what?"

"To the old madam's garden."

Watson yelled for his men to stay put. Broke into a run.

\* \* \*

"Mom," shouted Julie as soon as Annette walked through the front door, which always stood wide open during the day. The radio station, most likely 702 if Julie had any say in the matter, blared out the words *'tainted love'* in various intonations. "Mom, you gave me a fright. I didn't hear your car. Listen, I've just been talking to Rachel on the phone and she says after church we can come back to her place and—"

"Julie, darling." Annette tried to say it calmly, but something like a sob tore out of her throat.

Julie's eyes turned into green-grey circles. "Mommy?"

Annette hugged her daughter, breathing in the scent of chlorinated swimming pool and chicory coffee. She kissed the short damp feathers of Julie's new hairstyle. It still hurt to remember her daughter's braids.

"Let's go get the others," she said. Was it wisdom or cowardice making her delay the moment? She wasn't sure and she didn't care. All she cared about was the damage to the children.

"Annette? What is it?"

*Drat.*

Her mother knew her too well, an instant sensor and interpreter of all Annette's moods.

Annette shook her head. She followed Julie, high heels clicking on the creamy tiles in unison with the soft *plsk-plsk* of Julie's bare feet.

Danny was still asleep. As soon as Annette touched his cheek, though, he rubbed his eyelids and grinned a hopeful thirteen-year old grin.

"Hi, Mom. Am I too late for church?"

Annette felt the warmth of his arms as he squeezed her good-morning, his hard ribs too close to the surface. He smelled of soap, sleep and boy sweat. "Sit up, Danny. We need to talk."

She insisted on lifting Beth out of her cot, too, and when the movement failed to wake the baby from her morning nap, she kept dropping light kisses onto the smooth cheek until her milk started flowing again and Beth's eyelashes fluttered open.

How much Beth would understand was another matter, but she needed them to be together. All of them. As a family.

Her perfect family.

It was indeed quite perfect now, without Gordon.


Watson leapt over the back wall of the garden, sprinted around the house and burst through Mrs. LeRoy's front door.

This was a much smaller house than the Pretorius mansion, though still too big for a single occupant. The entrance hall had several doors. They led, Watson deduced, to the guest toilet, to a coatroom—a redundant luxury in the African climate—and to the kitchen. A two-winged door opened into a trio of family room, formal lounge and dining room. Watson followed the trail of muffled voices through the family room into a corridor to the private wing.

For a split second, he hesitated before crossing the boundary. The last time he'd seen Mrs. LeRoy was tattooed on his heart in gall.

Annette's voice yanked him forward.

In what he assumed to be a spare bedroom used by the children, Watson witnessed three things.

One, raw panic in the eyes of an adolescent boy.

Two, Mrs. LeRoy's expression, fifteen years older than when he'd last seen her, and showing every day of it. She wore a determined look of sympathy and concern, yet Watson saw it slide off like a faulty blind, revealing a momentary look of—what? Relief? Satisfaction? He couldn't tell.

The third thing Watson witnessed was a sudden howl from a red-haired girl who wrestled out of Annette's grip, yelling into her face: "I hate you. I hate you. It's all your fault. You killed my Pappa. You've always hated him…" her voice broke, "and now he's—d-d-dead."


Even though Trevor conducted the interview in her lounge, Annette realised he had gone to great lengths to show her the formality of the occasion, complete with a tape recorder, a notebook and a pencil. Mental shrug. Didn't cops know about Bics? Annette wondered what they did when the pencil needed sharpening. Used a pocket knife?

*Pocket knife—Doc's pocket knife—the key ring game...*

She tried to focus. The sooner the police left, the sooner she'd be able to pick up the pieces. Create a stable home for the children. Move on.

"I don't see the connection," she repeated to Trevor. "What does my father-in-law's death have to do with anything? He committed suicide, even though you people called it *a tragic accident with a firearm.* What of it?"

"How did your husband take his father's death?"

She remembered the day of the funeral. Gordon's face, when he came home from his father's house, half-crazed like a zombie's. Aloud she said, "Gordon coped well. Shocked and sad naturally, but that's the sequence of life. You bury your parents and go on living."

"Was your husband distraught enough over his father's death to kill himself?"

"Definitely not."

Trevor's expression was one big blank. Must have learnt that trick since high school. He asked in his policeman's voice, "So what do you suppose brought on your husband's suicide, Mrs. Pretorius?"

Annette battled with the enormous headache she'd had ever since Julie accused her of killing Gordon. She just wanted the whole nightmare to end. "I don't know."

"Did he act peculiar lately? Out of character?"

*The incident with Julie's braid. The dinner party. The fingers cutting bruises into her arm...*

BURN ALL THE FILES, OR YOU DIE, TOO.

She injected extra firmness into her voice. "Not unusually so, given his fresh grief."

From the terrace came the sound of a rattle, then silence. Beth must have flung out her tiny arm in her sleep. Annette checked her watch. Almost feeding time. "Sorry," she said. "Where were we?"

"Talking about your husband's state of mind. How about his work? Was it a source of stress?"

*Yes. No. Yes!*

"He liked his job. Most of it was classified, so he never told me much."

Trevor's face was still professionally blank, but his spine suddenly seemed straighter. "What did he do, exactly?"

So many questions. Fatigue seeped into every pore of Annette's skin, mingled with the headache in a vile concoction. "Scientific research at BRAVO. It's a government laboratory."

"What did he research?"

"Chemicals," she said. "Medicine. Gas masks. I'm not sure. Look, why don't you ask his colleagues? Why is it even important?"

Her head was killing her. All she wanted was a glass of water and two Disprins. And for Trevor to stop talking.

It wasn't important. Watson simply liked to observe his interviewee talk about neutral topics. That way, he saw the person's base behaviour when they were relaxed and telling the truth. A useful policing technique, yet he hated himself for following the same procedure with Annette.

He ignored her question. "Do you happen to know when your husband last refilled the BMW's tank?"

"Friday night." Instant, without a moment's deliberation.

"What makes you so sure?"

"You must understand," she replied, her voice slow. She looked worn out. "Gordon was an unusual man. A brilliant mind, with a few—peculiarities. Having enough petrol in the car was one of those peculiarities. He didn't like having to stop for fuel when he was on his way somewhere. It—it disrupted the pursuit of his goal. He always filled up the car on Friday evening after dinner, so he had a full tank for the weekend."

It made sense. Most petrol stations were closed on Sundays, together with the rest of the country, and those few open charged five Rand on top of the bill. You could get two paperbacks at the local bookstore for five Rand and still have change left over. Not that five Rand would have made a man like Gordon poorer, but Watson could relate to the principle. Waste not, want not. Penny-wise did not necessarily make you pound-foolish.

Annette gave him the particulars of the petrol station Gordon had always used and Watson jotted them down to verify later.

"Sorry to interrupt, Captain," he heard the constable's voice. "Please won't you take a look? In the garage."

As soon as Trevor was out of the room, Annette checked on the still sleeping Beth, swallowed two white bitter-sour powdery tablets, and coerced her weary legs to climb the stairs.

Julie's door was shut. Usually, the girl left it wide open. To feel part of the family, she said. Clearly, she didn't want to be part of the family right now.

Annette understood, yet she couldn't help knocking. "Julie?"

"Go away."

"Julie, I'm going to count to three, then I'm coming in. Like it or not."

Triumph in Julie's voice. "It's locked."

Annette pressed the handle down. The door didn't budge. "We don't lock doors in this house, honey."

"We do now."

If Gordon were alive, he would never tolerate this kind of behaviour. Annette knew better than to say it, though. What she wanted to tell Julie was how much she loved her.

Grief, Annette realised, was a selfish, self-absorbed, self-centred emotion. Unable to empathise, she should let her daughter mourn alone.

Eventually, she persuaded herself to walk away. Her shuffling feet sank into the thick creaminess of the carpet, the wool immaculate thanks to Hester's ministering. The sensation of luxury failed to make a difference. When it came to happiness, the power of money could only stretch so far.

The files, she thought. Her head still throbbed. She wanted to lie down on the soft rug and never get up again. From downstairs, she heard Beth's squeal.

"Coming," she called out.


I'm going to run away, Julie repeated to herself as she rummaged in her closet, sorting her T-shirts and shorts into to-take and to-leave piles.

*She doesn't love me. If she loved me, she would have stayed. Knocked her knuckles raw on the wood. Battered the door down.*

The ache in Julie's chest sharpened. Gritting her teeth, she added a handful of hair ties to the to-take pile before she remembered her short hair and forced her mouth into a defiant smile.

*Good.*

She didn't need stupid braids. Pappa had been right to cut them—no, she wouldn't go there.

Danny didn't love her either. With Pappa gone, there was nothing for her here. She would go to Nick. Images of last Thursday afternoon flooded her mind, cushioned the pain in a foam of numb. Nick's fingers on her bare skin. The wink he'd sent her way. At least Nick liked her. The only person on earth who cared.

Another image, more disturbing, threatened to surface, and Julie squashed it into the very back of her mind. She would run away to Nick no matter what. Let her mom worry herself sick.

*Swimming costume? Did Nick have a swimming pool?*

She hesitated, her fingers plucking at the smooth fabric the colour of her school uniform. A schoolgirl's bathing suit. Not the image she wanted to project. The cozzie would stay at home together with her childhood.


Watson followed Jones to the garage. The nail hammered into the wooden door of the wine cellar was only visible if you bent your spine ninety degrees and twisted your head to look up.

"Well done, Jones." Watson straightened, massaged his neck, then sat on his haunches, his nose almost touching the nail. No structural reason for the nail to be there. "The wood chippings seem pretty fresh, wouldn't you say?"

"Yessir."

"Don't *yessir* me. Tell me what you think."

"Yessir."

Watson raised his eyebrows.

The constable said quickly, "The nail must have gone in recently, two days tops. And the tip looks like it may be stained with brown. Dried blood if we're lucky."

Or unlucky, thought Watson. A suicide would be so much simpler.

"If it's not connected to the case," he said aloud, "let's not waste our time. The nail looks like a bitch to pull out. I'll ask Mrs. Pretorius."

"To pull the nail out, sir?"

Watson searched the constable's face for a smirk. Found none. "Ask whether she knows about the nail."

"Right away, sir."

The youngster was screwing with him, no two ways about it.

All four hidden security cameras in the Pretorius mansion were still showing one big fuck-all. The police meandering to and fro. The maid going about her chores. The empty barbecue grill.

The bloody bitch still hadn't found the files.

As a rule Annette breastfed Beth in the nursery upstairs. Right now, however, the thought of climbing the stairs yet again made her want to curl up in the corner and howl. She was tired, so very, very tired. The sleepless night, the constant police presence, the worry.

She had just enough energy left to carry the baby to the breakfast nook and close the door. It was not a private area the way a bedroom would have been, but it had comfortable chairs and lace curtains that prevented the garden boy from seeing inside.

It would have to do. On semi-automatic pilot, Annette undid her blouse and used the corner of the tablecloth as a feeding blanket.

BURN THE FILES.

*How?*

With Trevor striding through the house as though he owned it, and that young constable watching her every gesture, she'd had no opportunity to look through Gordon's things.

She closed her eyes. After, she promised herself. *I'll look for the files when Beth's done.*

The lounge was empty except for the scent of potpourri. Annoyed, Watson checked the dining room and the kitchen. No Annette.

Damn that woman. How was he supposed to protect her if she kept vanishing?

Jones, who'd followed his every step like a lost puppy, pointed to a closed door leading off the kitchen. Probably a pantry. She wouldn't be hiding in the pantry, would she?

Without knocking, Watson jerked the door open. One didn't knock on pantry doors.

Except—it wasn't a pantry.

"Ah," Watson said, his attention glued to the tableau before him. "Please, er, excuse us."

He aimed for professional, but his mind was playing tricks, delivering images of Annette's boobs underneath the damned feeding blanket.

His heels squeaked on the kitchen floor as he spun around and walked smack bang into Jones. The constable reeled backwards, yet his eyes remained glued to Annette. You couldn't see a lot, as Watson was well aware, which only made the bits you could see all the more tantalising.

"Right behind you, Jones."

When Jones didn't move, Watson dug his fingernails into the constable's shoulder and forced him to execute a parade-perfect about-turn.

*Damn it.*

He hadn't even asked about the stupid nail.

YOU HAVE TILL MONDAY.

Annette didn't feel like talking to the police. Whatever they wanted could wait. She finished breastfeeding and changed the nappy right there on the breakfast table, marvelling at the delicate skin and the tiny folds on the baby's legs.

Beth screwed up her face and emitted an experimental sound, half-drone, half-shriek.

"Exactly. What we will do now is look for some money to pay Hester and Johannes. Perhaps we'll find some files to burn, too. Let's go to the study and do a treasure hunt. When you're older, your brother will organise a real treasure hunt for your birthday. How does that sound?"

"Ehhhh."

*Ehhhh* was about right. What kind of woman relied on her husband to dish out the cash every time she went shopping? What kind of woman didn't know about insurance or how much the latest telephone bill was? A typical South African wife, that's who.

Now that she was a widow, it was time to grow up.

She entered Gordon's study without any sense she was snooping. The room was oddly impersonal, even though—or perhaps because—Gordon had furnished it himself. There was no theme, no paintings or diplomas on the wall, no indication whatsoever of who Gordon was as a person. Just a desk and a chair and a bookcase full of technical books. Three stuffed leather armchairs huddled in one corner like an afterthought, as though Gordon had never expected, nor welcomed, visitors.

Where was Gordon the husband, the father, the human being?

Annette shooed the thought away. Find cash for Hester and Johannes. How difficult could it be in a room so devoid of hiding places?

Not difficult at all, as it turned out. The desk was a massive roll-top, made of honey-veined teak. A column of big drawers adorned either side of the chair. A vertical wall of pigeonholes and toy-like drawers served as a backdrop.

The smaller drawers were full of pens, postage stamps, paperclips and writing pads. The pigeonholes were mostly empty, because Gordon hated clutter. One of them held a studio portrait of their three children. Another—an ivory carving of a unicorn.

A sudden memory exploded. Red spots. Wherever she looked, Annette saw red spots. Floating. Pulsating. Screaming. Her fingers coiled around the unicorn, then unfurled as she flung it into the far corner of the room.

The clang brought her to her senses.

"Sorry, Beth," she murmured.

Beth didn't care. She looked a little amused, a little puzzled, but most of all—lost in her own baby world.

The larger drawers were segregators for folder and files. Files. While Beth kicked her legs on the carpet, Annette went through the papers. Gordon had kept all his paperwork in neatly labelled folders. Electricity. Municipal rates. Telephone. Staff.

Were these the files she was supposed to burn?

Somehow, she didn't think so.

Inside the folder labelled Staff, Annette found a handful of crispy blue-grey two-Rand notes, straight from the bank. The notes were already paper-clipped: forty Rand for Hester and forty-four for Johannes. They worked the same hours, but Johannes was a man. Annette made a mental note to rectify the injustice.

She kept looking. House insurance. Life insurance—Annette opened the folder and scanned the legalese until she found the Sum Assured.

That couldn't be right. She blinked. The amount didn't change. Gordon's life insured for three times the value of the mansion? She counted the zeros one by one.

One million Rand.

Beth's opening "Whaaa," sliced the room, a prelude to a full-blown concert should her initial communication be ignored. Annette picked her up and held her close, rocking on her feet until Beth settled. Now she needed five minutes of cuddles before she could be safely deposited in the cot for her nap. Baby life was simple: eat, play, sleep.

Annette's life, on the other hand…

*One million Rand?*

Annette sat in Gordon's plush office chair, Beth in the crook of her arm. Waiting for the baby to fall asleep, she nudged the bottom drawer with her foot.

"Take photos. Dig out the nail. Process it." Watson spoke only when back in the relative safety of the garage.

The constable avoided his gaze. "Yessir."

Watson took in the stooped shoulders. "Look, Jones, there's no need to act so bloody guilty about it. We've all seen a bit of boob before, hey?"

Jones blushed a deep shade of pink, as if a red globe ignited right behind his ears. The constable was seventeen, a high school graduate who chose four years of police service over two years of being shot at by the commies on the Angolan border.

"Come on, man, don't you buy *Scope*? Or *Bunny Girl*?"

"They all have stars covering the—ahem." Jones coughed, then added quickly, too quickly, "Also, those magazines are for the over-eighteens. Sir."

Watson shook his head. Only in South Africa were seventeen-year old boys deemed old enough to die soldiers in a real war, yet too young to see a female nipple. Correction, too young to see a star-covered female nipple.

Aloud he said, "Well, in this case, the baby's mouth was acting like a star too, covering Mrs. Pretorius' *ahem*."

"Not from where I was standing, sir."

*Bugger.*

Watson tried to get a grip. His whole body screamed with frustration. He wasn't going to get jealous over an old girlfriend's nipple, now was he?

He was.

Annette spotted the sticker straight away. "Project Hydra". The name Lula had dropped at the party on Saturday. The party—it seemed a lifetime away.

BURN ALL THE FILES...

To hell with that. She needed to know what she was burning.

The first pages disappointed her. Diagrams—she'd always been rubbish with diagrams—most of them a cross between a map and those blueprints for their mansion's plumbing layout Gordon had tried to show her when the house was being built. Totally incomprehensible, except for the labels: pipe layout, drainage, mains.

At the bottom of the pile nestled three typed sheets. The heading read: "Hekate—Introduction."

> *Hekate is a mythological Greek goddess. Her power can poison as well as heal, and it is appropriate to name the newly developed substance after her, as it is meant to heal South Africa's political problem. Poisoning the drinking water of those who stand in the way of our country's greater good...*

Annette looked up from the text.

*Oh, Lord.*

She turned the page. The next heading leaped out at her. "Hekate—The Making of".

> *Bushmen's poison is readily obtained from the...*

She scanned the details without taking them in.

> *Advantage: death occurs through cardiac arrest.*
> *Disadvantage: Bushmen's poison takes at least 24 hours*
> *to work from the time it enters the bloodstream.*

> **Aconitine**—$C_{34}H_{47}NO_{11}$—*a*     *highly*     *poisonous*
> *alkaloid…*

Next followed a medical bit with more chemical symbols. This is not happening, Annette repeated over and over, as though her denial held the power to make the text disappear.

> *…quickly absorbed through mucous membranes, skin*
> *and blood.*

The words slid off her mind. Respiratory paralysis. Cardiac arrest. Numbness. Sweating. Nausea. No known antidote.

The text wobbled. Her body felt as though somebody had administered a dose of aconitine. Queasiness radiated from the core of her heart, spreading into her stomach and her limbs.

Her husband. *This* was his research?

Careful to knock on every door this time, Watson located Annette in Gordon Pretorius' study. She was so pale, her translucent skin had an almost greenish tinge to it. The baby was tucked up in a deep leather armchair, snoring with gurgles and grunts.

"Sorry about barging in earlier," he said, his face burning with the memory. "We found a nail in the door leading to your husband's wine cellar. Did you ever hang an ornament there? A Christmas wreath maybe? A child's painting?" A silly place for a decoration, but he had to ask.

Silence.

"What's wrong?" He despised the gentleness in his voice. "Annette?"

"Nothing."

She sounded broken, passive. The image Watson had of her was anything but. Fifteen years ago she'd been the one who ended their relationship.

He coughed. "Right, ma'am. Now, when my constable called me away earlier, we were talking about your husband's work at BRAVO——"

Annette surprised him yet again. She jumped to her feet, pressed her palm to her mouth and rushed out of the study.

Watson cursed. What he ought to do was treat her the way he would any suspect in a murder investigation. Run after her. Make her talk. Take her to the station. They usually said more than they intended when they were in a vulnerable state of mind. What he ought to do…

Crack.

The baby shifted in its sleep. Watson didn't know much about babies, but he did know about gravity. He assessed the armchair. Yes, the extra cushion prevented the baby from rolling off, if it was old enough to roll over.

"Jones," he called out.

The constable slid into the room. "Sir."

"Any reports yet? Fingerprints, post mortem, anything?"

"It's Sunday today, sir."

Sunday. A lifeless, boring, mind-numbing day, on which all the shops and cinemas stayed closed. Sunday, the day of the Lord, reserved for your religion and your family. It was a sin to work on a Sunday. Judging by his typical workload, Watson was going straight to hell. Except he didn't fear the hell after death ever since the hell he'd lived through in Soweto.

*Don't go there.*

"Sunday. Right." Watson exhaled a long breath. So tired he could feel his knuckles drag on the carpet. "Let's wrap it up for today."

"Yes sir. But sir, we need somebody to look after the family."

As if it had a mind of its own, Watson's glance travelled to the baby. Beth, he remembered her name. Beth was awake now and eyeing him with intense concentration in her tiny face. He shrugged as though the issue didn't matter one way or another. "I'll take the first shift."

It seemed the most natural thing in the world.

It should have been the most natural thing in the world, Trevor staying at the house to protect her and the children, even if Annette was not a hundred percent convinced the danger really existed. It should have been the most natural thing in the world, because he was an old friend as well as a police officer assigned to the case. It should have been the most natural thing in the world. It wasn't.

This was the house her husband had built for her. Her husband, the mad scientist bent on poisoning the black people's water supply.

The dry retch took hold of her throat again. Annette knew she wasn't grieving the way a widow should. Now that the initial shock was wearing off, however, she did grieve the pointlessness of premature death. She grieved the passing of her children's father and the absence of the person with whom she'd spent the last fourteen years. Most of all, she grieved the loss of the image she'd had of Gordon. She had known his work involved chemical and biological weapons, still, the theory was one thing, and seeing the proposed application was quite another. Millions of lives at stake, millions of lives endangered by Gordon's work. Was it less of a sin because the people in jeopardy were black?

The secret smouldered inside her. Go to the newspapers? No, the government would never let them print any of it. A radio or TV show, live to prevent censorship? She searched her soul. Was she brave enough to go through with it?

She could tell Trevor. Ask his advice.

DON'T TELL THE COPS.

Trevor. Her stomach flooded with acid. The last thing she needed was her ex-boyfriend overnighting in her dead husband's house.

If there ever was an etiquette book for widows, staying the night under the same roof as an ex beau would surely be on the "no-no" list.

What would the book say, she wondered, about the etiquette of finding a dark secret that could poison the history of her country?

That reminded her. She still had to read the other documents. Project Hydra was not the only one. On tiptoe in her own house, she slipped into Gordon's study again.

Watson found the maid in the kitchen, scrubbing the floor on her knees. To his eye the bits that hadn't yet been scrubbed looked spotless enough.

"Hester."

The bucket of soapsuds crashed onto the floor.

"*Hau, baas.* You gave me a fright."

"Why? White people don't know how to walk quietly?" He laughed to put her at ease.

"Not in this household they don't." Hester heaved her broad body onto her feet. "In this household, I am the one who creeps up on them unnoticed."

Watson believed her. Despite her weight, Hester did not make a sound as she moved on bare feet across the room to fetch a cloth for the spilled water. Add to it the natural inclination of the master to take no notice of the servants, nothing to do with colour and everything to do with class segregation. Hester could prove very useful indeed.

"Here, *baas*, let me take the baby," Hester said. "Coffee?"

"Please."

He watched as she got two mugs ready. A porcelain one for him, a tin one for herself, as was the custom.

Watson wasn't sure how to proceed. He rarely spoke to domestic servants because: A, he didn't have any, and B, thanks to the language barrier. If he needed a maid interviewed, he sent one of the black policemen to do the job. Hester's good English was an exception in a country that provided inferior education for its black populace.

The kitchen had nothing to sit on apart from the chairs around the breakfast counter. Watson was sure sitting there would be inappropriate in a house that had a separate set of crockery for the servants. Not that the Pretoriuses were an exception: every household he knew had tin plates and mugs "for the blacks", a cheaper jar of jam, a different loaf of bread. He'd been told black people preferred the highly processed fluffy white loaves. Still, the principle...

"Shall we take the coffee outside?" he asked.

Hester looked at the scrubbing brush. "Just for a minute," she warned.

The summer sun, white with the heat, beat relentlessly on his head as he sat down on the kitchen stairs. Hester chose a patch of thirsty grass under a bougainvillea shrub for herself and the baby.

He began without a preamble. "Did you see anything suspicious at the party?"

"No."

*Too much too fast. Back off.*

"Tell me about your dead master. Was he a good man?"

"There's worse."

"Did he treat you well?"

"I don't have much to do with him."

Watson could tell he wasn't asking the right questions. He sipped the sweet chicory mix. Waited.

"The odd thing," Hester broke the silence, "he becomes more friendly in the last few weeks."

A wave of revulsion washed over Watson. He'd heard of white men who took advantage of their black servants in *that* way. It was rare, it was a criminal offence, and usually it was swept under the carpet as something that never happened, couldn't possibly have happened.

"I see." It came out as a croak, his throat dry despite the coffee.

Hester looked at him, laughed a hearty guffaw. "Not what

you think."

*Oh, thank heavens.*

Investigations into trans-racial sex crimes were not his forte.

"What did you mean, then?"

"I work in this house for a year and Master Gordon never notices me. Never a *thank you* or *good morning*. If he wants me to do something, he asks his wife. *Make sure the blue shirt is washed for tomorrow*, he says, or, *there's dust on the piano*. It's like I'm too small to be seen. Or too black to be seen." Hester drank a long sip from her tin mug, jiggled the baby on her knee. "Then, about a month ago, he asks me how old I am. And where I come from. And my surname. Madam Annette knows all that, from my ID book, but what's it to him?"

"Did you ask him?"

Hester shot him a look of disdain, though her words were proper enough. "No, *Baas*, I do not ask."

Of course not, what was he thinking? She could have been sacked for impudence.

"Sorry, go on."

"Then Master Gordon says do I know a family called Sibisi. I say it's a common enough Zulu surname, though maybe not as much as Mkhize."

"All right."

"Then he asks me how to find a Sibisi woman in her mid-thirties. I tell him he needs a photo or her parents' names or her first name. He says the woman is called Lesley, and the mother Rosina. I tell him he needs their real names, Zulu names, not the names they use so the white people remember easily. And he just shrugs and walks off."

Watson processed the information in silence. What would motivate a conservative white male to track down a black woman?

"Hester," Annette's fiery head and shapely boobs appeared in the upper half of the kitchen door, left open for ventilation. "When you're done answering the policeman's questions, please make up the spare bedroom for him. Afterwards, you can take the rest of the Sunday off."

"Yes, Missus. Thank you, Missus."
*How long had Annette been standing in the kitchen, listening in?*
"About the party, Hester," he tried again.
"I see nothing, *Baas*."
Again, too quickly.

Hester hoped she had muddied the waters enough. Let the police draw inferences, let them hunt for the mysterious Lesley the master was so interested in.

Anything to keep their noses away from her political cell and from the leader. Hester had never understood patriotism, it seemed silly to love a piece of land so much you're willing to die defending it, but the leader's eyes and mouth were something definitely worth fighting for.

Find the files, he had said. As easy as finding a lizard on a sunny wall. This morning, while the madam was visiting her mother, Hester had gone through the master's desk and read all the work-related documents. She hadn't dared remove any of them for the fear of the police searching her quarters, but their contents were now safe inside her memory. One good thing of Bantu education was the way the shortage of textbooks trained you to remember things you'd only read once.

Anger burned inside her every time she remembered a bit she'd read in those files. She was glad master Gordon was dead. Else she would have been tempted to kill him herself.

Although he had nothing to report, Watson phoned his brigadier with an update. His job was still on the line, and the least he could do, was to give his superior officer as little to complain about as possible.

The brigadier, however, wasn't interested in the preliminary findings.

"Look after yourself, Captain," he said. It came across like an order.

"Sir?"

"I've had a report of a shooting incident outside your

address, man."

*Oh, shit.*

He'd forgotten.

"The report," the boss's voice stung him like a hornet, "didn't come from you."

*Double shit.*

He'd decided not to disturb the brigadier last night, meant to send a memo first thing today, only today he had sprung out of bed to protect Annette from a serial killer with a white unicorn.

"Bloody hell, Watson. You trying to make me fire you?"

Watson promised to do everything by the book from now on. He only hoped the brigadier believed him.


Rosina, mused Annette. Her father-in-law's maid, who had helped raise Gordon and his brother, the way Hester was now helping with Beth. Why would Gordon want to find her after all these years? And not Rosina herself, but Rosina's daughter, Lesley.

*Lesley.*

Annette paused. Where had she heard the name before? A black woman called Lesley. She'd noticed because it was such an atypical name, especially for a person of colour.

*Lesley.*

So recent. So familiar.

*No matter. Forget the elusive Lesley.*

Annette had a bigger problem to solve.

There was more horror in Gordon's files. The sex virus the scientists were proposing to develop had the potential to kill not only one township, the way Project Hydra proposed, but the entire country.

What should a good white citizen do upon discovering a government plot to kill South Africa's black population?

BURN…


Annette didn't want to be a hero. She was happy to burn the files and get on with her life, with patching up her family. Still. How would they know whether she'd complied with the instruction?

Easy. If one word of what's in the files leaked out, he'd know that she *hadn't*.

And an even more frightening thought: what would the government do to someone who tried to expose their plans for genocide?

The camera hidden inside the barbecue enclosure at the Pretorius mansion hit the jackpot. The image of a female figure burning a stack of folders was unmistakable.

The footage from the other hidden cameras provided nothing of use. For now.

Perhaps tomorrow...

# Chapter 4—Friday, One Day before the Murder

BEFORE HER WEDDING night, Annette would never walk around the house underdressed. Gordon, however, enjoyed the sight of his wife in a nightie as he took his breakfast, her breasts unrestrained by a bra, free and visible through the flimsy fabric.

After the week they'd just had, Annette had to make an extra effort to keep Gordon happy. A happy Gordon equalled a happy household. As simple as that.

She leaned over his sleeping body, pressed her fingertips into his shoulder. "Time to get up."

"Mhm."

Since Tuesday night, there were limits to how happy she was prepared to make her husband. She didn't want to be in the bedroom when he woke up properly, didn't want him to see her, even though a long-sleeved dressing gown went some way to cover her this morning. It covered the transparent fabric, but also the bruise above her right elbow.

"I'll get your coffee ready," she said, already in the doorway.

When she opened the front door to collect the milk, the faint breeze wormed under the nightie between her breasts, every bit as longed-for and as deliciously improper as a lover. A gasp caught in her throat and she forced it back into darkness. No room in her life for nonsense.

"Mom, we're off."

Her attention snapped to the children, dressed in identical battle blue and bland beige school uniforms.

"Bye, Julie. Don't forget your swimming practice this afternoon, darling. I'll pick you up at three." She bent down to kiss the neat strip of pink skin between the two ginger braids. "Love you, Copperlocks."

Julie raised her eyes to the cloudless sky. "Love you too, Mommy," she recited, her bored expression exaggerated in an onstage-performance style.

Annette suppressed a smile. "Bye, Danny. Ace that maths test."

"Thanks for remembering, Mom."

As though she could forget. The children's schedule was engraved on her soul. Probably a bad thing. Probably, she should get a life. "Have fun at the movies this afternoon," she added.

"Will do, Mom. Bye." Danny stood on tiptoe to kiss her cheek.

Annette ruffled his dark blond hair, and he allowed the caress. How long still before he found it unmanly? Un-grownup? Uncool?

She watched the children race down the garden path, chased by their bouncing backpacks across the quiet suburban street and down the gentle incline, until they disappeared around the corner.

Her children. Her meaning of life. The desire to follow them—through the safe streets of the safest suburb and watch the school bus encase them like protective armour—was overwhelming.

In that instant she realised there was nothing she would shirk from doing to guarantee their safety.

Johannes, the garden boy, was in his mid-thirties, yet his employers still called him a garden *boy*, a colonial word in a rapidly vanishing colonial world.

He spat into the rose bushes. Changes were coming. Perhaps not today, perhaps not tomorrow, but come they would. It was a simple matter of demographics. Amazing that the whites, with all their fancy white education, couldn't do the simple sum: out of every ten people in South Africa, eight had black skin.

He watched the madam as she stood in the doorway to her grand mansion. Waving goodbye to her children, she resembled a slim flame of fire, with the red hair all the way to her bum and her yellow dress not much longer than that. The large nipples poked into the fabric. From his spot, not five steps away, Johannes imagined he could see where her thighs met.

The madam didn't pay him any heed. He may as well have been a garden gnome, or part of the outdoor furniture. If he called out to her, she probably wouldn't bother to cover herself up. To her, he was not a sexual being.

Neither was Madam Annette to him, all skinny with no buttocks. He preferred his Lesley back home.

The glass milk bottles clanged against each other when Annette picked them up. Gordon claimed he could taste the difference between fresh milk and milk left in the fridge for a day. Annette had never called him on it, opting to unseal a new bottle every morning. Anything to avoid a fight.

Back in the kitchen, she started the coffee machine and took out the iron. Hester did all the washing and ironing, but shirts tended to crease in the wardrobe, so every morning Annette made a point of giving the day's shirt a quick lick of hot iron before Gordon dressed.

On Saturdays and Sundays, she also ironed his newspaper, to set the ink and prevent it from smudging. It's what her mom used to do for her dad when he was still alive, and their marriage seemed to have worked. So Annette clenched her jaw and ironed, yet her own marriage didn't work.

The percolator hissed and the aroma of exotic lands filled the kitchen, exotic even though the beans came from the same continent. Sometimes, though, South Africa felt as un-African as you can get. Annette selected two newly ripened bananas and placed them on the breakfast counter. When she heard the shower in the main bedroom stop, she poured the coffee into a porcelain cup, added fresh milk and stirred.

Gordon emerged a minute later, bare-chested, his hair still damp.

She placed a smile on her lips. "Good morning." After fourteen years, the fake cheerfulness came automatically.

Gordon didn't reply. He gulped his coffee, threw the bananas into his briefcase and stroked a proprietary hand over her buttocks. His fingers did not feel as longed-for or as deliciously improper as a lover's.

Teaching her a lesson. Showing who was boss.

Annette's smile failed to reach the skin around her eyes as she buttoned up Gordon's re-ironed shirt and knotted his tie. "All done."

"That's my girl." The playful pinch, when it came, was harder than usual.

"Oh, Gordon, you naughty man."

A perfect picture of a perfect couple.

"Mmmm, nice." He fondled her bottom again. "I'll have more of that tonight."

Annette hoped the sigh that escaped her sounded more like anticipation than whatever it was she felt. Resignation? Reluctance? How long since they'd last made love? Weeks. Not since Gordon's father passed away.

"Bye, Gordon. Have a good day at work."

The purr of the gold BMW leaving the garage mingled with the baby's first cry of the day.

"You want me to get her, Missus?" Hester asked.

Annette's heart leapt into her mouth. "Gosh, Hester, you gave me a fright. I didn't notice you come in. Good morning. No, it's all right, I'll fetch Beth. You get the nappy ready."

Her day was suddenly very, very good again. Without Gordon.


Normally, Gordon savoured his daily commute. Today his mind was far from the pleasure of driving a flawlessly designed, flawlessly manufactured machine. His life lay in shambles. Time he took control, no matter the outcome.

A quote came to him. Something about courage not being a gun in your hand, but knowing you're licked before you begin and beginning anyway.

He would begin today. In his mind, he composed a line of attack.

One: Get out of the mess at work. Quit. Abscond before it's too late.

Two: Mend his marriage. He had never loved Annette the way a husband should, but she was a good wife, a great mother. The children were better off with two parents, he knew that much from experience.

Three: Forgive his father.

Sounded easy when you put it like that. Gordon wasn't sure, though, that he could accomplish any of the three goals.

Another bloody press conference. Although Watson photographed well, he knew he came across like a moron whenever he opened his mouth in front of a reporter. This time, he vowed to play a mysterious cop, silent and sage and sexy. He knew he could pull off the silent and sexy, at any rate.

The brigadier shook his hand for the cameras, grinned what was supposed to be a warm congratulatory smile. To Watson, it looked more like his superior was giving birth to a pineapple.

*Click*, went the flash. *Click*.

"Another few years, Captain, and I'll be proud to recommend you for my job," the brigadier said as though last week's final warning hadn't happened.

*Liar*.

Watson returned the full-of-shit grin. He wanted his boss's job more than anything in the world. His list of incessant successes in solving cases was crowned by this latest feat, and he knew the only thing that stood between him and promotion was his history.

"Captain," the journalist said, "it was a devil of a case. The whole city is proud of you."

"Except for the culprit," Watson quipped. All right, that one wasn't too bad. Perhaps a bit too smart. Silent and sexy, he reminded himself.

Had indeed been a devil of a case.

"As a man," the journalist pressed, "do you think the husband was justified in murdering his wife's lover?"

Watson smiled, shrugged, smiled again.

*Silent and sexy and sage.*

"Captain?"

"Wouldn't know. Never married."

*Sexy?*

He hoped so.

*Sage?*

*You bet. Marriage was for fools and incurable dreamers.*

"What about as a policeman," the journo persisted. "Didn't you feel male solidarity with the killer? Didn't you think he was justified?"

"All I can say is, the law is the law. I'm here to uphold it. Nothing justifies premeditated murder."

The photographer clicked away, trigger-happy. When he left, the brigadier put away his constipated grin.

"Don't let it go to your head," he told Watson. "Your warning still stands."

The day was still very, very good when Annette finished breastfeeding Beth and handed her over to Hester for a nappy change and a play. She selected Beth's outfit, a tiny pale green dress with delicately embroidered white daisies, and went back to bed, her bones liquid with physical exhaustion, her emotions in turmoil.

Gordon expected to make love tonight.

She'd rather eat a plateful of maggots.

Toss, turn, toss, turn. It wasn't the lack of physical desire. Daydreams of wild sex flashed behind her closed eyelids, loud and hard and—different. Under the table. On top of the desk. In the swimming pool.

Her breath escaped fast and shallow, her face felt hot.

Annette bit back the longing. Idleness led to idle thought. Time to get up. Gosh, she was tired. Never mind. Time to get busy.

*Busy with what?*

TV did not start till late afternoon, there was nothing of interest on Springbok Radio, and when Annette flicked from FM to AM, she heard the slogan "In touch, in tune and independent", which sounded too much like communist propaganda, so she switched the radio off.

The open window let in the fragrance of freshly cut grass and sun-soaked dust. Somewhere in the house, Beth made happy gurgling noises and Hester replied in Xhosa. The baby's first word, when it eventually came, may not even be English.

Annette crawled out of bed.

*Beth.*

It was time to break with tradition. Other women may be happy letting the servants do all the mothering. Annette was not going to turn into one of them.


Gordon had spent the morning going through his documents, all twenty years' worth of pulped trees, and now he stepped back to inspect the result.

The leftmost pile was heading for the shredder: all his research into toxins and chemicals and viruses, every one of them a threat to South Africa's future.

The middle pile, the smallest of the three, he'd take home to work on. Should the talks with Doc and Professor Adelbrecht not go the way he planned, he'd start working on an antidote, fast.

The pile on the right—he pressed the buzzer. A few seconds later, Sally came in.

"You wanted me?" She emphasised the double entendre with the tilt of her head.

"Bring me a roll of brown paper, scissors and some Sellotape. Also, put me through to Vermeulen."

"That's Hendrik Vermeulen, Gordy?" Sally broke into a smile. "As in, the lawyer? Are you finally getting a divorce?"

The familiar wave of irritation engulfed him. "Sally—"

"Sorry, bad joke. But is it my fault if I sometimes dream you'll make a decent woman of me?"

"Sally."

"No strings, I remember. Speaking of which, if you're sending a package, how about I bring you a ball of string too?"

An idea, that, Gordon thought. It'll make the charade all the more credible.

"Yes, please."

As soon as the door clicked shut behind Sally, he quickly extracted eighteen typewritten sheets from under a pile of blank pages. The decoys he'd wrap in brown paper and string, to post to Vermeulen. The real documents he'd deliver to the lawyer's house in person. A real godsend Vermeulen was on holiday. By the time the lawyer returned to read the country's top secrets, the matter would be resolved.

One way or another.

Watson's phone rang just as he was tiding away the case files. The murdered lover's story would be buried in the police archives. His killer would serve time, but a good lawyer could spin the whole tale into an accident. And the wife? The wife would cry and forget. Women did that. They all forgot.

"Watson speaking."

"Hi, Tiger." Charlene's voice promised sweet sin wrapped in the adventure of sneaking behind her husband's back. "I'm free tomorrow night."

Watson thought he'd misheard. "Tomorrow is Saturday."

Married women were rarely free on weekends.

"He's going to a game farm with his cousins. Family tradition. He'll overnight there. What do you say?"

RRROW would have been silly, so Watson settled for, "Sure."

In this scenario, he was the lover. Would he also end up dead before his time, murdered by the jealous husband?

He didn't care. Charlene would have been thrilled to realise he was willing to risk his life to fuck her. She would have been wrong. He was willing to risk his life because his life was worth shit.

Lula stared at the proposal in stunned disbelief. Project Aphrodite. Its name was innocent, hinting at love and beauty. Its intention was deadly.

On an intellectual level, modifying an existing immunodeficiency virus so that it could spread only through sexual intercourse presented a challenge. On the practical side, she was all too well aware of ramifications should the virus mutate.

Then there was her career to consider. Refusal would mean the demise of her ambition. Gordon would automatically be promoted to senior scientist, a post recently vacated by James Campbell who'd left to start a computer company. A stupid move. There wasn't going to be much more advancement or business opportunity in computers. Though, thinking about it now, was Project Aphrodite the real reason James had left?

"Lula?"

*Bother.*

Not now. Why was he here? Gordon seldom left his office. Lula flipped through a list of options and chose the most palatable one. "Did you want to comment on my brainwave?"

Gordon's eyebrows drew together quizzically, his eyes searching her forehead for clues. Sometimes he could take things too literally.

"My brainwave, the crowd-control hose," she explained.

Lula was proud of the crowd-control hose. It was a far more humanitarian way of dealing with panicked school children than the indiscriminate gunfire in the Soweto fiasco of 1976.

"Ah, the crowd-control hose. No, not yet. I'm here to ask if you're free to join me for a barbecue tomorrow night. My place."

A dinner invitation, yet Gordon's voice came out all wrong. Anxious? Anguished?

"Sounds lovely," she replied, though she was not at all certain the idea appealed. "I'll be there. A special occasion?"

Her question threw Gordon off balance. "It's my birthday next week," he said at last. "But please, no presents."

"No presents," she agreed. "The only thing you'll get for your birthday will be a year older."

When Gordon didn't laugh, Lula noticed his absent stare and the thin line of his mouth. Even his shoulders looked troubled. Was Project Aphrodite eating him as much as it was eating her? "Gordon, is anything the matter?"

"No." He hesitated before adding, "Nothing that can't be fixed."

There were no monsters here at BRAVO, of that Lula was convinced. Just a group of ordinary people in charge of their country's destiny. Their choices were not between good and evil. Their choices were between two kinds of bad.

What choice was Gordon going to make when it came to creating a sexually transmitted illness?

Lula was sure she knew the answer to that. What she didn't know was the choice she herself was about to make.

By lunchtime, Gordon had invited everybody to the dinner party. The rightmost pile of documents he dispatched to his lawyer, together with a set of instructions and a letter to Annette.

Satisfaction swelled inside him at the sight of the empty desk. Almost one o'clock. Three hours to kill.

"Gordon?" The door opened and the professor walked in. "No, no need to get up. How are you?"

"Fine." The untruth formed a double-bladed razor in Gordon's mouth. Falsehoods did not rest easy with him. He prayed Adelbrecht wouldn't notice how free of paperwork the office was.

The professor's gaze combed his face. Probing. Kind. "Your father's death was a great loss to this country. The last four weeks placed a tough toll on all of us. On you especially. Losing a parent upsets the balance, no matter how old you are."

It had upset him, though not for the reason Adelbrecht imagined.

"When Piet passed away," Adelbrecht paused, "I assumed you'd become more involved in the Order. We missed you at last night's meeting."

Gordon didn't know what to say. The secrets he'd dug up after his father's funeral had pushed the Order of Unicorns out of his mind. He rubbed his cheek, felt the first grains of a stubble. What was he going to do about the Order? Expose it? Dismiss it as a bunch of harmless members of the old guard?

Adelbrecht misinterpreted Gordon's reaction.

"Treasure the things that remind you of your father, Gordon, even if remembering him causes sorrow. He lives on in your memory."

God, he hoped not.

He broke off the thought. Point number three from this morning's resolution: forgive his father, misguided as the old man had been.

Adelbrecht's words broke through his deliberation. "At BRAVO, we've decided to honour your father's memory by dedicating our efforts to Project Aphrodite."

Poison. Mass sterilisation. And now, lethal pathogens.

*Would BRAVO really stop at nothing to implement the government's agenda?*

The professor took off his glasses and leaned forward, his face centimetres from Gordon's. "Your main argument against Project Hydra in its original form was the *slaughter of the innocents*, as you so eloquently expressed it. We've taken it on board when designing Project Aphrodite, and I can personally assure you no child or virtuous person will ever be harmed by the virus we're creating." Adelbrecht made the pause meaningful. "I look forward to your feedback."

Look forward to tomorrow night instead, Gordon thought.

Disappointment seeped through the professor's body. He had watched Gordon grow up, raised by one of the most principled men Adelbrecht had known. He had witnessed Gordon's blessing by the Order. A crying shame how Gordon had turned out.

Back in his office, Adelbrecht removed the portrait-sized photo of his grandchildren from the wall and pressed a tiny button concealed in the metalwork. A television screen showed him the inside of Gordon's office.

It was a funny old world. They all worked for a secret service agency, yet his employees never imagined somebody might use all that spying technology on them.

Adelbrecht took one look at the screen and picked up the phone. "Nick. I need you to go talk to Gordon about Project Aphrodite. He hasn't fully come on board on this one."

"I'll call him straight away, sir."

"No, Nick. Go in person. Show him your findings. It's crucial we get the project off the ground as soon as possible."

The crunch of the key turning in the lock made Gordon look up.

Sally locked his office door from the inside. Her top was unbuttoned. No bra.

"The professor suggested I take you out to lunch," she said. "But I made us a few sandwiches at home this morning, in case you wanted to—*stay in*." Her voice was intense. "What do you think? Do you want to stay in?"

"No."

"What is it, honey?" Sally took three steps towards him, hesitated when she saw his expression.

Gordon turned to the window. "Please go."

"Come on, Gordy. You know you want me." She closed the gap between them and straddled him, her naked breasts almost in his face.

"Go away," he managed.

"Gordy." She touched his chest. A mistake.

Gordon pushed her off. Jumped to his feet. Something exploded in his head and when the blaze faded he saw Sally press her hand to her reddening cheek. The memory of the previous two seconds came flooding.

"Oh, God. Oh, dear God," he kept repeating, a prayer, not a breach of the second commandment.

Sally shot him a glare full of venom. "You will pay for this." She sounded so young, so pathetic.

And he had slapped her.

"Sally. I'm sorry. I'm so very sorry."

"Not as much as you will be."

He believed her.

Her cheek smarting, Sally opened her desk drawer. The banned book with its steamy cover lay where she had dropped it the afternoon before. The negatives, however, which she used as a bookmark, were missing.

Methodically, Sally searched her desk, the filing cabinets, her handbag. When she was finished, she started all over again.

No negatives.

*Damn.*

She would still make Gordon sorry. Just had to find another way.

When the blood in his ears stopped pounding, Nick knocked on the door to the professor's lair.

"Sir, just wanted to let you know I couldn't get hold of Gordon. Must have stepped out for lunch."

The professor took off his glasses. Without them, he looked even more menacing, like a mad prophet. From his pocket, he extracted a small white handkerchief. The similarity to a prophet dissipated. Now he looked like Nick's grandfather, the one who'd died in battle.

"Thanks." The professor began the laborious action of cleaning the lenses. "Try again later. We need Gordon on board."

Nick nodded.

"Nick. About that new poison. It's time to test it."

"With all due respect, professor, I see no reason to subject more fluffy bunnies to the poison."

Something glinted in the professor's eye. "Is a human subject more acceptable than a rabbit?"

"It would be more scientific."

The professor coughed. "Hope you're not having second thoughts, Nick. The tools we devise here are all for the safety of our country. Too many black buggers around, every one of them dumber than the last."

Nick didn't hesitate. "No second thoughts."

The day marched on, every hour pushing Annette closer towards the evening and the marital coupling it would bring. Driving to pick up Julie after swimming practice, Annette considered her options.

Pretend her period was early.

Fake a sudden onset of thrush.

Slip a handful of sleeping pills into his whisky.

*Hmmmm.*

As it was his privilege on Friday afternoons, Danny had gone into the city with his friends to see a movie or ice-skate at the artificial rink. At thirteen, he revelled in his newly found self-sufficiency. In three years' time, he'd be old enough to go to the army, get sent to the border to fight for his country. Dread gripped Annette's throat, squeezed the air out of her.

"Are you all right?" another mom asked.

Her nod was automatic. "Too much sun, I suppose."

Too much war, she added to herself.

She watched Julie swim the last lap of freestyle, towel-dry her long hair and pull the school dress directly over the wet swimming costume. The day was so hot, Annette didn't object.

"Hi, Mom," Julie started talking as soon as she left the pool area. "Guess what? I got another star for my spelling today, that made ten in total, so I went to Mr. West's office and he gave me a certificate."

"Well done, Copperlocks."

Julie prattled on about Rachel and Natasha and the mean boy Robin who pulled her braids in class and the new school project about South Africa's homelands.

Then it came: "What exactly are homelands, Mommy?"

"Bits of our country set aside for the black people."

"You mean we gave them bits of our country? To keep?"

Annette hesitated a fraction. "Sort of. Not exactly gave. Rather, we let them rule those territories so that one day they may become countries separate from South Africa."

"Why?"

"So the black people can vote there. In their ancestral lands."

Julie fell silent, but not for long. "Mommy?"

"Yes?"

"Wouldn't it be easier if they simply voted here?"

Annette slammed on the brakes.

*Phew.*

Nearly smashed into the Audi in front. "Blacks voting in South Africa? Choosing a black Prime Minister to rule over us?"

Julie giggled. "I guess not. That would be silly. No, more than silly. It would be—impossible."

"Impossible," agreed Annette. What else was there to say? That the blacks were too poorly educated to run the country? That the rest of Africa suffered more under black dictators than they ever had under colonial rule? "Now, Copperlocks, when we get home and you've had a bite to eat, will you remember to shampoo and condition your hair? Chlorine is ever so damaging, you wouldn't want it to discolour your pretty braids."

"They are pretty, aren't they, Mom? Even prettier than your hair?"

"Definitely."

Prettiness was overrated. Annette would gladly sacrifice her own hair, shave it all off, if it meant not having to perform her marital duties tonight.


Gordon looked at the Montblanc key ring he'd found clearing his office earlier that morning. He had bought it for Annette before he remembered she would never part with the key ring photo of the children, so he'd selected another present and dropped the key ring into a drawer upon his return.

"Sally," he said into the phone. "Could you please come in?"

He wasn't sure she would, not after what had happened.

She did. Her cheek looked better, though it didn't make him feel any less of a cad.

"I have no excuse," he said, "but I have this." He placed the key ring in her unresisting hand.

Sally said nothing.

"It's a real Montblanc."

No response.

"It's a status symbol. Worth quite a lot of money." As much as a gold bracelet, at any rate, with the price of gold so low in the gold-glutted South Africa.

That got him a smile.

"Friends again?" he asked.

"Sure," she replied. "I wouldn't miss your party for anything in the world."

*Damn it.*

He had forgotten about that. Sally at his house, talking to his wife—he should have let the girl pout a few days longer.

Dinnertime was always a test of Annette's skills as a wife and mother, and it had nothing to do with a three-month old baby whose schedule differed from the rest of the family's.

"For what we're about to receive may the Lord make us truly grateful, amen," said Gordon.

Annette was truly grateful for many things in her life: for her wonderful children and for abundant food on the table and for her lovely house.

She was not grateful for the atmosphere in the dining room.

"Mom? Do I have to eat the peas?"

"Yes, Copperlocks, I'm afraid so."

"I hate vegetables."

"Julie," said Gordon, his voice already on edge.

Adrenaline surged in Annette's chest. She had to stop the conflict before it cascaded out of control.

"Vegetables are good for you, Copperlocks. They will make you pretty and clever."

"I'm already pretty and boys don't like girls who are too

clever."

Gordon's fork clanked dangerously against his dinner plate. "Julie, that's enough."

Something was wrong. Normally, Julie's comment would have made Gordon laugh. He seldom tolerated backchat, though Julie had a way of sounding charming when cheeky. And she was spot-on about men appreciating skin-deep beauty while being threatened by brains. Annette had learnt that lesson many years ago.

Danny cleared his throat. "Mom. Pa. Today's maths test was a breeze."

"Well done, Danny." Annette understood her son's attempt to defuse the tension. "That's the one on ratios, right?"

As though she hadn't spent the last three days thinking up new ratio problems for him to solve.

"Bull's eye, Mom. Well guessed." As though Danny too had forgotten.

Like mother, like son.

"Julie, sit up straight and watch your spoon," Gordon said. "You've spilled bits of your dinner all over the floor, like a pig."

Pain spiked right through Annette's heart on Julie's behalf. What *was* it with Gordon lately?

Julie ignored the insult. "What are ratios?" she mumbled through a mouthful of ginger hair.

Evidently, Gordon did not want to discuss ratios. "Take your braid out of your mouth, Julie, eat your peas, and be quiet."

Annette blinked back the tears and allowed twenty seconds of silence to elapse before she asked, "How was your day at work today, honey?"

Gordon's expression told her to eat her peas and be quiet.

The lab door opened with a tinny scrape. "Working late, Nick?"

How dare she, whispered a voice in his head. He didn't look up, didn't want to see her. It took all his willpower to control his voice. "Sally. What are you doing here? You don't have clearance…"

"Might not have clearance, but I do have a hotshot scientist of a boyfriend who happens to work here." Sally's voice was half-teasing, half-promising, all female.

Don't be so sure, the voices sniggered. The boyfriend part is history.

She walked around his chair. Sat in his lap. "Will my hotshot scientist boyfriend escort me to a party tomorrow night?"

Gordon's party. Nick's blood spiked to the temperature of barbecue coals.

"I'll be delighted." He spiced the lie with his most charming grin.

Gordon willed the family dinner to end. The screech of knives on china drilled into his brain. The words of the conversation, their meaning too slippery to penetrate, fell into his mind like sharp pebbles.

"Quiet, please." The urge to cover his ears intensified.

Tomorrow this time he would be talking to his superiors, presenting his case, waiting for the decision. By tomorrow this time, his career could—probably would—be over.

He should tell Annette, about the barbecue at the very least. Didn't want to. BRAVO would invade his house tomorrow. Today was for the family.

The forced silence at the table weighed him down. Gordon combed his brain for something to say. "What movie did you end up watching this afternoon, Danny?"

Danny's shoulders stiffened. "*E.T.*, Pa."

"How was it?"

"Not bad."

"What's it about?" Gordon felt like an interrogator, even though all he wanted was conversation.

"This alien who's nice, but people are scared of him because he looks weird and they don't know what to expect."

Just like real life. Whites were scared of blacks because they looked different, and of communists because they didn't know what to expect.

"We wanted to catch *For Your Eyes Only*," Danny's posture looked more relaxed now, "but it's not showing anymore. And the new one is not out till next year."

Gordon recalled the office rumour that the next James Bond was to be titled *Octopussy*. Nick had laughed then, "As in Octo-Pussy, get it?" Gordon still didn't find it amusing.

Meanwhile, *For Your Eyes Only* had that scene at the end, with the leading girl's perilously long legs, long naked legs. And the dialogue about not being a virgin.

"Danny, I'm not sure James Bond movies are appropriate for you."

"Aw, they are rated 'no 2-12'. I'm thirteen, it's okay."

"Still. Movies are supposed to be about something. They are meant to make you think and feel. James Bond is all about bang-bang-you're-dead. Hardly an enriching experience."

Danny's expression was pure teenager, his tone though, was polite enough. "Pa, we didn't go to see a Bond movie. We went to see *E.T.* But, for the record, I don't want to be enriched. When I go to the movies, I want to be entertained."

Defeat bitter in his stomach, Gordon looked away, straight at Julie. His daughter watched in mute fascination, the tip of her orange braid between her teeth.

It looked obscene. Nice girls didn't put things in their mouths. So—so suggestive. The anger rose swiftly, muffled his senses. Gordon was barely aware of his chair that had thudded onto the carpet. "Julie, how many times do I have to tell you? Don't chew your hair." He walked toward her, still clutching his steak knife.

Julie shrank back. He didn't stop.

Annette cried out, "Gordon."

He didn't stop.

It was a sharp knife. Gordon yanked the offending hair in his left hand and sawed at it with the knife. The braid fell off and rested in the palm of his hand, orange and beautiful, like the rare Aurora house snake Gordon had once hunted and killed in their garden.

\* \* \*

Lula returned to a dark, empty house. As she unlocked the door, her hand encountered the rough edges of the elaborate gold-and-diamond key ring, a present from her forever-absent husband.

Another lonely Friday night. The person who said diamonds were a girl's best friend had no clue.

Ten deep breaths, in and out. Her loneliness didn't matter. Her marriage didn't matter—much. What mattered was her dream. Her passion. Over the years, she'd worked so hard, harder than any man she'd known, sixty to eighty hours a week. Gordon, for instance, only worked the prescribed forty and never took work home with him, yet the other men at BRAVO valued him more than they valued Lula.

The unfairness weighed heavy.

Tomorrow, at Gordon's party, she would find a way to get hold of the professor's keys. He kept all sorts of secrets in that strongbox of his. Bound to be useful.

She curled up on the empty king-size bed and opened her briefcase. The irony of taking work instead of a lover to bed didn't escape her.

The risk analysis of project Aphrodite came out better than anticipated. If the virus spread only through sexual intercourse, as the anecdotal evidence in the USA suggested, then children and people who didn't sleep around would be safe from it. Morally, it was sound.

*Wasn't it?*

Blood became ice in Annette's heart. The world lost all colour. This time, things had gone too far.

Gordon would fly into a rage from time to time, he'd yell and say words he didn't mean, but he had never before resorted to bodily damage. Even the children's corporal punishment he would only deal out once calmed down.

Chilled to the bone despite the summer temperature, she

caught sight of Danny's clenched fists and lay a warning hand on his, pressing it into the table. They were alike, she and her son, they didn't need words.

Her daughter surprised her. Annette expected a tantrum and tears. Julie didn't even bother to touch the stump where the braid had been. She straightened her narrow frame, lifted her chin and turned her stare into spikes.

"My hair," she said it in a quiet voice. Her calm was eerie. "How dare you do this to me, Pappa? How dare you?"

Gordon's face crumbled under Julie's eyes. He fled from the room, clutching the braid to his chest.

Annette gathered the children into a silent embrace. Her heart raced as though in a marathon. She didn't know the stranger in Gordon's body, and she didn't trust him. It was time to leave.

*Leave—and go where?*

One: she had no money of her own.

Two: the jewellery in her dressing table was enough to purchase a native village, but she didn't know a single pawnshop or moneylender who would exchange her diamonds for cash.

Three: as a married unemployed woman, she would not be able to get a bank loan without her husband's signature.

Four: her own mother lived on whatever Gordon gave her for the daily expenses and had no cash.

These points were as valid when it came to leaving Gordon as they were for getting Julie to a hairdresser. Annette didn't want to add to the trauma by letting her daughter see a mirror before she was safely in the hands of a professional stylist. So, hair first. Divorce could wait.

The dining room clock chimed the half hour as though the world hadn't collapsed. Half past five. Their local hairdresser would be closing up already, and he was the only one who'd consider cutting Julie's hair on credit.

Right. Deep breath. Normal tone.

"Honey," Annette said to her daughter. Just in time, she remembered not to call Julie *Copperlocks*. "Can you put on your sandals quickly?" Thankfully, no mirror in Julie's bedroom.

Gordon's rules.

As soon as Julie turned to go, Annette dialled the hairdresser's number and listened to the ringing on the other end.

*Drat.*

He must have closed shop early.

*Think, think, think.*

Friday night. Women would want to doll up for the weekend. Annette opened the yellow pages directory for Johannesburg. Pretoria might be the capital of South Africa, but the nearby Johannesburg was where the city life happened. And the Carlton Centre was where the richest of the rich went to spend their money. She found the number of a hairdressing salon.

"I have a hair emergency," she said in her most sophisticated tone. "What time are you closing tonight? I see. Could you possibly extend that by an hour? Very happy to make it worth your while."

Another number. "Mother. No time to explain. I need you to come over. Please."

*Come over and what? Watch Gordon to make sure he doesn't harm the children?*

She put down the phone. "Danny, love. When Beth wakes, please give her the bottle." Her breasts were beginning to swell with milk, but she would just have to put up with it. Beth took formula whenever her granny babysat. "Hester's gone already, but Granny will be here soon."

Danny gave her a quick hug. "Don't worry, Mom, I can look after Beth. I even know how to change a nappy."

"My boy."

Baby care was indeed easier nowadays with the latest wonder of civilisation: disposable nappies, imported from overseas. When Danny was a baby, Annette had learnt to fold cloth nappies into bulky origami, leaky no matter what. Thirteen years later, Danny was able to change his baby sister with one flick of his wrist.

Knowledge beyond his age reflected in Danny's face. "I won't let Granny leave before you get back."

He was growing up too fast.

*SLAM*! Like a gunshot. Annette's stomach lurched to her throat. Only a bedroom door. Julie was back with her newest flashiest pair of sandals and a wrist full of plastic bangles.

"Come," Annette put her arm around Julie's shoulders. "We're going for a girlie outing, just you and I."

"Where to, Mom? All the shops are closed."

"Carlton Centre."

"Yippee. The coolest of all cool, Mom."


Gordon hid in his study, his daughter's braid still in his hand. His wonderful, brave, innocent daughter. His little girl. How could he?

It has to end, he thought. It's destroying my family, and it has to end.

Rocking to and fro in his chair brought no comfort. He wished he remembered how to cry.

What he needed now, was to get out of the house. Away from the family he had hurt. The BMW drove him out of the garage, heading for nowhere.


Professor Adelbrecht watched Nick and Sally leave the lab together, then turned off the monitor and replaced the photograph that concealed the screen.

BRAVO did good work, important work, but sometimes BRAVO was not enough.

His gaze fell on the ivory unicorn. Carved from the tooth of a beast that trampled and tore precious South African farmland. It was fitting to fight South Africa's enemies with a symbol fashioned out of another pest's bone. He'd be sure to mention it at the upcoming meeting of the Order.


Only familiar with the malls in the Sleepy Hollow of Pretoria, Annette had to admit the Carlton centre was indeed the coolest of all cool. The overabundance of shops and light made her spirits rise. If Julie's hair could be salvaged anywhere, it would be in this magic place that resembled Santa's workshop.

"Mom, look." Julie halted in front of a boutique, totally transfixed by the spectacle of colours.

A metallic dress, essentially black yet shimmering with the entire rainbow, beckoned from a deliberate heap on a backdrop of white silk and slowly disappeared behind a lowering shutter. But Annette didn't see a pretty dress. She saw a tool with which to stab back at Gordon.

"First the hair."

"But, Mom. They're closing."

The saleswoman wrenched the shutter back up. "I can wait a few minutes. No problem at all."

"Mom. Please."

The desire to compensate for Gordon's behaviour overruled the conventional wisdom of not giving in to your children's demands. Mixed with the need for revenge. Imploded.

"If you can open a credit account for me," Annette addressed the shop assistant, "I'll take that dress in size six as well as in size eight. You can find us at the hairdresser's next door."

"We're buying clothes in the same shop, Mom. How cool is that?"

Annette gathered her close. "You're growing up so fast, we'll soon be able to swap dresses. We'll be like twins, mommy and her little girl."

Julie stiffened and Annette regretted her words. Julie was Gordon's little girl, nobody else's, even when he'd just behaved like a brute.

"Come, honey." She pulled Julie towards the sign *A Cut Of Class Hair Spa*.

It turned out to be a hair spa, all right, with the heavy glass door and marble surfaces, an orgy of mirrors and a hairdresser who looked like a royal lady-in-waiting.

"Thank you for seeing us at such short notice," said Annette. "My daughter's had a bit of a mishap with her hair, and we need to fix it."

The hairdresser took in the single braid and the brush of uneven hair ends where the symmetrical braid should have been.

"We'll have to go quite short," she said.

Annette winced. The verdict hadn't been unexpected, but having it put into words like that made her throat clog up.

"That will be fine," she heard Julie's defiant voice. "All the better for my swimming. It'll dry faster and won't get in the way."

"Great. I'll find a cut to suit this dazzling face of yours, something that won't need mousse to keep its shape. Just one thing…" she hesitated. "We're not actually allowed to stay open this late. It's the law, you see. Would you mind terribly if we worked in the back room? So sorry."

The law. Always the darned law dictating who should live where, who shouldn't marry and how late shops may offer services to people willing to part with money. The Sunday shutdowns of cinemas and shopping centres she understood. Sundays were for going to church, reading the Bible and having the family over for a big lunch. But Friday nights? Please.

"Ma'am?" The boutique assistant stood in the doorway with the two dresses and some paperwork. "Is this a good time?"

Annette filled in the forms to open a clothing account. Predictably, many questions related to her husband, the one footing the bill. She was glad not to witness Julie's second braid coming off. The first one was harrowing enough.

"And if you could just sign here, and here, and here."

Annette signed the docket. A thrill of satisfaction pulsed through her body as she imagined Gordon's expression when he opened the bill and saw the price two simple dresses could reach.

"You don't want to try them on?"

"No, thank you."

Gordon was rich enough to afford it, yet the sheer wastefulness of the purchase would vex his puritan soul—more so if the dresses didn't fit.

Would he understand why she had done it? She wasn't sure. Didn't care. By then, she and the children would be gone.

"Mom, come have a look."

Annette entered the back room. A dark-skinned cleaner was

sweeping away Julie's hair, her long strands of orange-red. Tears prickled Annette's eyes and she rubbed her eyelids to stop them.

She looked at her daughter. Julie's new hairstyle hugged her head in a glory of moist brown curls. Julie held a small mirror in her hand, twisting her neck this way and that.

"Honey. That's so lovely. The fringe brings out your eyes." A large boulder lifted off her heart. The cut was sophisticated, short yet feminine. "I like the new tint, too."

"It'll fade to ginger with time," said the hairdresser. "Auburn's her natural colour, you see, it only goes red in the sun. The curls are natural too, but they straighten out under the weight of long hair."

Another child entered the room via the back door and sidled towards the cleaner. She was about Julie's size, with caramel-brown skin and dark brown curls, not African-tight, more like Julie's new ringlets. Coloured people, a mixture of white and black races, were not widespread in her part of the country, and Annette couldn't help staring. Their faces looked more European in ancestry than African, and their colour ranged from chocolate to tanned.

"That's all, Lesley, you can go now," the hairdresser said to the sweeper.

"Thank you, ma'am. Good bye."

The cleaner left with her daughter, but as she was closing the door, the coloured child laughed. It sounded so much like Julie that Annette lifted her head and listened, like a mother gazelle, startled and confused. Had Julie gone with them? No, she was still in the shop, admiring her reflection.

"Now, about the payment," began Annette, heat building up in her cheeks. She took off her brooch and handed it to the hairdresser. "Please keep it. The diamond is a quarter of a carat. No, I insist. You've earned it."

"Mom," Julie called out across the shop. "The way that girl laughed...Pappa laughs like that too, you know, that little choke at the end followed by a snort?"

"Oh, Julie." A fresh wave of embarrassment swept over

Annette. What a faux pas. She should pay more attention to teaching Julie what's appropriate. Comparing her father's laughter to that of a Coloured was definitely not.

"And did you check out her hair," continued Julie. "Looks just like mine. Brown and curly. Cool, hey?"

Danny's body language conveyed how much he didn't want to talk about it, but her grandson was too polite to leave a question unanswered. Little by little, Ella LeRoy cajoled the course of earlier events out of him. Every detail pierced directly into her soul.

It was all her fault, and she was not used to carrying guilt. Regrets were for the weak and the spineless. Ella LeRoy was neither.

"It'll all work out, Danny," she said at last. "Granny will fix it."

Danny laughed. Actually laughed at the idea. Affection gripped her as she looked into those innocent eyes of his. He had no clue. He'd only ever seen the gentle side of her.

"Trust me, Danny. Deal?"

Before Danny could answer, Beth woke up, demanding food. Danny sorted out the bottle while Ella cuddled her, breathing in the scent of the fluffy baby hair.

If Gordon ever took as much as a lock off Beth's head, Ella LeRoy would kill him, a slow painful death.

Her stomach contracting with dread, Annette made her way back home. She had nowhere else to go, nowhere else to take the children. Her friends were mere acquaintances, her sisters lived far away, hotels cost money, Gordon owned Mom's house.

*Pathetic.*

She couldn't even protect her children from her husband. Her one ambition in life, to be a good wife and mother, had crumbled to dust.

She parked in the garage and turned to Julie. "Would you and Danny like to go sleep at Grandma's tonight?"

"No." Loud and decisive. "Where's Pappa?"

No fear in Julie's voice, no resentment for the cut-off braid. Was Annette the only one who regarded Gordon's deed unacceptable?

"I don't know, honey. Maybe his study. Let's not disturb him."

A tune insinuated itself into her mind. *In the jungle, the mighty jungle, the lion sleeps tonight.*

"I want Pappa."

Annette scrutinised Julie's face. So much unconstrained, uncomplicated love. No forgiveness, because—evidently—there was no need for forgiveness between father and daughter.

"Tomorrow, honey."

"Promise?" Julie's voice was hard enough to slash through diamonds.

Had her daughter sensed how close her parents had come to a divorce? Annette swallowed. She only ever wanted the best for her children. Who was she to judge what *the best* was?

"Promise."

Gordon drove aimlessly for an hour before he decided to call it a day. A lousy day. Tomorrow would be better, though. The thought gave him hope. He had many, many days in which to get his life right.

He refuelled the BMW and headed home.

Annette's car was gone. For a split second, his heart stopped. If she'd taken the children and moved out...They were always too loud, too disrespectful compared to the way he'd been brought up, too irritating, and yet the prospect of not having them in his life brought physical pain to his gut.

When he stepped into the hallway, he heard Danny's voice and his lungs allowed him a much-needed gulp of air. His mother-in-law answered Danny's question, and her presence sent Gordon straight into his study.

A single sheet of paper on his desk caught his attention.

*If you ever touch the children or Annette again, you won't live to regret it.*

Gordon tore the paper into little pieces, dropped them into the toilet, flushed and watched them spiral out of sight.

"Thank you for babysitting, Mother. Let me drive you home."

No explanation of what had happened, no mention of Julie-Ann's new hairstyle. Ella LeRoy understood. If her daughter had made up her mind to leave Gordon, she would have put the kettle on, sat down and started talking. The dismissal meant Annette was going to sweep the day's events under the wall-to-wall rug and glue the carpeting back onto the floor. How long before the bumps started to show?

Never, if Ella LeRoy could help it.

Annette fed Beth and watched TV until the transmission ended for the night, finishing, as always, with a list of South African soldiers killed fighting communism in Angola.

Andries van Niekerk, age 17.

Jaco Theron, age 19.

Michael Roberts, age 21.

So many boys. So many young lives lost. The price white South Africans were paying for their privileged lifestyle was proving to be way, way too high.

With a mixture of heartache and shamefaced relief that she wasn't among them, Annette thought of the mothers of the slain boys. Did a single one of them feel national pride as she heard the anthem played in memory of her child? Could any mother put her hand on the Bible and claim she loved South Africa more than she loved her son? Did they think—for a moment—the sacrifice necessary or the cause worthy?

What about the fathers? Did some of them belong to the Order of Unicorns and deem the sacrifice meaningful? Is that how Annette's father-in-law had felt when Gordon's brother died in the bush war? Would Gordon feel that way if Danny—she refused to finish the thought.

On the screen, the orange-white-and-blue of the flag glistened in the sun before giving way to the psychedelic test pattern. Annette switched off the TV and sat in the dark until she was sure Gordon was asleep.

*Hush my darling, don't cry my darling, the lion sleeps tonight.*

She made up one of the spare bedrooms for herself, the one closest to the children's bedrooms, but she couldn't switch off her mind.

Tomorrow—both Danny and Julie had athletics on Saturday mornings and plans to visit friends afterwards. With luck, she could keep them out of Gordon's way most of the day. Sunday, though, loomed like an ogre, with its endless hours of sheltering her children from Gordon's moods.

*There had to be another way.*

# Chapter 5—Monday, Two Days after the Murder

FOUR O'CLOCK IN the morning. One of the hidden security cameras at the Pretorius mansion flickered. A silhouette holding something white and flat moved into view. It slipped the object under the front door before melting into the pre-dawn murk.

Four-oh-one.

The envelope's corner was a triangle of ominous white under her front door. Inside—a list of names in uneven script, as though formed by a child or someone unused to writing.

    *1.  Pieter Pretorius.*
    *2.  Gordon Pretorius.*
    *3.  Annette Pretorius.*

Annette read the anonymous letter twice. Unlike the BURN ALL THE FILES message that sank a claw of dread into her heart every time she thought about it, this one felt harmless by comparison. Bizarre. Hackneyed. Unreal.

Last night, after much deliberation, she had burned Gordon's files in the same barbecue that had cooked the meat for the dinner party only a day earlier. A coward's act, undoubtedly, but that was not the only reason the deed had left a taste of bile in her mouth.

Like a marionette, she always let somebody else run her life. The baton of control had passed from Mother to Gordon on the day of the wedding, and with Gordon dead, Annette bent to the will of a note left on the windscreen of his BMW.

Annette felt her temper rise like a mixture of vinegar and baking soda. This new letter was a fresh attempt at manipulating her.

*Bugger that for a box of soldiers.*

Because of printing press deadlines, the Sunday papers had missed the story of Gordon's death. Monday's *Pretoria News* made up for it with its sensationalist headlines.

## PROMINENT SCIENTIST DEAD

### Foul Play Suspected, the Police Will Not Rest…

At least they got that straight, thought Watson as he stirred extra sugar into his morning cup of coffee. Weariness weighed down his limbs and he resisted the urge to plant his nose in the hot liquid.

*The police will not rest. Not this policeman, at any rate.*

He stifled a yawn.

The night had been anything but restful. He'd spent it in the spare bedroom of the Pretorius mansion. The gesture was window-dressing. In an emergency his presence would have been useless. For body-guarding duties, he needed to be much closer.

*Like in her bed.*

*Yeah, right.*

The dark hours had engulfed him as he tossed and turned in the spare bedroom's bed, feeling very much the spare wheel. Memories flooded back. Annette LeRoy, seventeen years old, holding his hand at the bioscope, a barrier of popcorn crumbs and salt grating between their fingers. Annette LeRoy stunning in her ball gown at the school dance, her body pressed to his in a tango. He had been patient, waiting for a signal from her, a signal, he now knew she'd been too innocent to give. Annette LeRoy's mother shouting that he, Trevor Watson, was not good enough for her daughter.

*The police will not rest.*

When he'd joined the police force fifteen years ago, it was with the ambition of solving convoluted crime puzzles, like his childhood heroes Hercule Poirot and Sherlock Holmes. He didn't want to live down to his sidekick surname, didn't want to be a passive observer, didn't want to chase speeding cars or petty thieves. His dream was to be the finest investigator ever.

Reality had caught up with him with a sobering crash. Crimes in South Africa were seldom sophisticated or puzzling. Worse still, policemen were expected to squash political disturbances. Six years ago, when ordered to ride an armoured personnel carrier into Soweto in full combat armour and to shoot at the rioting students, he'd had to ask himself who the real criminals were.

*The police will not rest.*

Heroism comes in different flavours, like Beechies chewing gum. After the Soweto disaster, many of his colleagues had quit the police force altogether, or turned to the bottle, or started taking bribes to justify the rotten image they held of themselves. Anything to deal with the nightmares.

Not Watson. Watson became the most conscientious investigating officer and the cleanest cop between the Limpopo and the Orange River. Satisfied his ambition. Helped fuck-all with the nightmares.

The knock on his door was a welcome disruption.

"May I come in?"

Annette, dressed in a nightgown, *only a nightgown*, entered the guest bedroom. Watson clamped his jaws together, all too aware of her breasts and hips and legs.

"Good morning, Trevor. Sleep well?"

Why was she here, in his bedroom, two metres from his bed, practically naked, worse—titillatingly worse—than naked? Why? What was her game plan? Did she imagine he'd wipe out the past fifteen years, take her back without a word of explanation or apology? Had she killed her husband and wanted him to cover it up in exchange for what lay under the nightgown?

"Sorry to bother you so early," Annette said and Watson forced himself to pay attention, "but I found this."

She thrust something at him. Watson took it automatically. A bolt of heat burst up his arm as their fingers touched for the briefest of moments.

"Aren't you going to read it?"

When her folded arms covered her chest, he managed to look away. The object in his hand was an ordinary white envelope, one you would use for a birthday card. The paper inside came from a smallish spiral-bound notebook. Watson read the words. Felt a clammy hand reach into his gut and squeeze. The words were ridiculous, the idea of an anonymous death threat even more so. Killers seldom warned their victim in advance. And yet...

Annette asked, "Is someone trying to kill me?"

When office hours began, Annette pulled herself together enough to contact the school. The phone call was torture. The school secretary hadn't seen the paper yet and Annette was forced to listen to gasps of shock and broken up words of sympathy.

"I'll inform the headmaster immediately," the secretary said. "Of course, the children are excused for as long as...If there is anything we can do for you as a school...Such a loss, such a terrible loss."

"Thank you," said Annette. "The children are taking it hard."

She put down the phone. The children were taking it very hard. She didn't know how to help.

The ringing by her elbow startled her.

"I've just heard the news on the radio," Doc said. "How are you holding up, my dear?"

"So-so. I'll feel better once I have a good cry." Opening up to Doc was easy. His tone carried no starched formality, which in turn relieved Annette of the social pressure to say the right thing. "Worst of all, the children are not talking to me. Well, that's not quite true. Julie keeps yelling she hates me, and Danny gives me sweet hugs, but neither is really talking to me about—what happened."

"Give them time, Annette. They need to grieve in their own way."

"I respect that." She tasted a salty drop of blood on her lower lip. "I just want them to know I'm here if they need me. I don't want to fail them, Doc."

"Would you like me to come over? Talk to them?"

Annette wrestled with the sudden temptation. The problem was, Doc had never visited their house without Gordon present. What was the correct protocol for new widows' visitation rights?

"Sure, why not," she said at last, aware of the stretching silence. "Come for lunch and bring your wife."

"She's still with her folks in South West."

That seemed an odd time of year for such a lengthy vacation. A weekend, maybe, but longer than that? Most people visited their parents at Christmas, and they usually took their spouses along.

Still, what did it matter now? Trevor had stayed the night, so Doc might as well have lunch with her. All her life she had paid heed to propriety. It hadn't worked out.

An unmarked police car drew to a halt outside the mansion. Jones slammed the driver's door, a skinny folder in hand. Watson checked his watch. Nine o'clock. Hadn't expected the forensics team to finish this fast.

He met Jones in the driveway.

"Preliminary reports, sir."

The technicians must have worked on a Sunday, after all. That could mean only one thing: the case was huge.

Watson opened the folder. Fingerprints from the BMW: only the victim's and his family's. The children's at the back, Gordon's on the driver's side, Annette's on both the driver's and the passenger's side. Also on the car keys...

*Bloody hell.*

If HQ wanted to make a case against Annette, they wouldn't have to search far.

*And he? What did he think?*

He didn't want to think. Went on reading. Chlorine stains on the passenger's seat and ice cream residue mixed with leather cleaner at the back. Petrol level in the BMW—

"Where is the death threat you wanted analysed, sir?"

Watson handed him the white envelope, belatedly protected by a plastic bag. "Has my prints on it, and those of Mrs. Pretorius," he said. "See if you get anything else."

"Yes sir."

If Jones had wondered about Watson's lapse of professionalism, he knew better than to show it. He handed Watson another document.

"The search warrant for the house, sir. Team's on standby."

"Bring them in."

With luck, they wouldn't find anything incriminating. If they did, how far would Trevor Watson transgress to protect a girl who'd dumped him, against Captain Watson who couldn't afford to screw up another case?

Whatever the answer, he hated what it would say about him.

Over the soft hum of the radio, Danny heard his mother's footsteps in the corridor of the children's wing.

"Julie?" There was a muffled knock next door. "Julie."

"She's all right, Mom," he called out. "Don't worry."

Got a shock when he stuck his head into the corridor.

*Shit.*

Mom looked like hell, her eyes framed by dark shadows. "Honestly, Mom. Julie raided the kitchen at night and brought back enough food to supply an army. She'll come out when she's ready."

His mom put her arms around him and clutched him tight. Too tight. He stifled a groan of pain.

Beth's sudden wail rang out, reaching every corner of the house, followed by Hester's soothing coo. His mother seemed oblivious to the baby. "How are you, Danny? Coping?"

"Fine. Terribly sad, of course…" Was he sad? He couldn't tell.

The baby, used to having her ultimatums met straight away, yelled even louder.

"You'd better go downstairs, Mom."

"My golden boy."

Danny went back to his room, flung himself onto the bed. He wasn't a golden boy. Far from it. He'd just lied to his mom, and—and that was the least of his sins. He punched his open palm with his fist.

*Shit, shit, shit.*

At least all the compromising stuff was safe. He should get rid of it, as soon as that cop left them alone for two seconds. Fortunately, there was no way the police would ever find the hiding place. If his mom ever saw it…

Mom. Wonderful, loving Mom. So broken over Julie.

He punched his palm again. Jumped up. Within seconds, he was knocking on his sister's door.

"Open up, you little fool, or I'll tell Mom about the book you found in Sally's desk on Thursday."

Hester observed Madam Annette move from room to room, aimless and restless and lost, clutching the baby like a rubber float in a flood-swollen river.

"A cup of tea, Missus?"

"Yes, please, Hester."

Always polite, this one. Some madams treated their maids like slaves or half-wits, but not madam Annette.

The madam had barely enough time to sit down with her tea when the policeman, the same one who had spent the night in the guest room—alone, judging by the state of the bed sheets—knocked on the open door of the room.

"Mrs. Pretorius? We'd like to ask you a few more questions."

*We?*

Hester looked again. Another white guy, this one too young

to be a policeman, hovered in the background.

"Of course. I was just about to have a cup of tea. Will you join me, gentlemen?"

The two policemen nodded.

"Or would you prefer coffee, Trevor? You used to—"

"Tea will be fine, Mrs. Pretorius."

Looking only with the corner of her eye, so as not to appear disrespectful, Hester tried to read his face. Pleased and annoyed at the same time. Odd. Just as odd as the madam calling him by his first name.

"Hester…"

"Yes, missus."

The policemen avoided looking at Madam Annette. Do they think she killed her husband, Hester wondered as she filled the kettle. She distrusted policemen, black or white. Unnoticed by the three white people, she walked through the lounge to the adjoining dining room, where she took her time preparing a tray of the better china.

She listened. The madam was talking about the guests at the fateful party on Saturday, just the bare facts and no emotion. No comments like 'he's a nice man' or 'she's a good friend of mine', just the names and job titles.

No mention of the silly key ring game, the one Hester had spied on when serving the pre-dinner snacks. No mention of the incident by the swimming pool, when the master had hit one of the guests—Hester had seen it through the kitchen window while washing the dishes.

She brewed the tea, filled the milk jug and the sugar bowl, laid out five biscuits on a plate and carried the tray to the lounge.

"So the last time you saw your husband was by the swimming pool, on his way to get a bottle of sparkling wine?"

"Yes."

"What time was that?"

Hester kept her eyes on the tray, so she couldn't see the madam's expression. The voice, however, came across strained.

"No idea," madam Annette said. "Sometime after dark."

"Five minutes after dark? Half an hour?"

"More like half an hour."

"That would be around nineteen-thirty?"

The madam kept ignoring the tea tray. Hester started pouring, the way she had seen the madam do: the milk in first, then the tea, then deliver the cup—Hester used both her hands for that—and open the sugar bowl with an inviting gesture.

"And then you all changed back into your clothes and went inside, and had dessert, and that's when you went looking for your husband?"

"Yes."

"How long—"

"I don't know, *Captain* Watson. Five minutes? Half an hour? I didn't check my watch. A hostess never does, it would be—bad manners."

Hester offered the plate of biscuits. The madam's eyes were bright, her cheeks red under the makeup.

"All right, Mrs. Pretorius. I'm sorry to bring up memories that may be—will be—painful, but I need you to tell us exactly what happened when you found your husband."

Madam Annette rubbed her temples.

"I went straight down to the garage where the wine room is," she said. Her voice was hollow. "I thought he had lost track of time, selecting the champagne. He was a bit of a connoisseur, you see. Collecting wine was his hobby."

"I understand. So you went to the garage. Was the door connecting it to the rest of the house open?"

Silly man, thought Hester. It stood to reason that the door would have to be shut, else the petrol fumes would have escaped through it.

"I—I can't remember."

"Was it locked?"

Nobody was paying Hester any attention. She watched more boldly now.

The madam shook her head, remembering. "I didn't have my keys with me, they were..." she trailed off, probably recalling the key ring game. "It must have been unlocked."

No, the madam didn't have her keys with her. They would have still been in that wooden bowl on the patio, together with everybody else's. Except the master's keys, that is. The master would have taken his keys on the way to the wine cellar.

"So you went into the garage," the policeman prompted.

The madam curled her shoulders and hugged herself. "I saw Gordon straight away," she said. "He was sitting in the driver seat of his car. I could hear the engine and smell the exhaust fumes and at first I thought he must have gone for a drive and was now coming back. But he didn't move. I went to his side of the car and I saw the hosepipe..."

"Then what?"

"I can't remember."

Even though the madam was looking directly at the policeman, Hester knew it was a lie. Danny had the same wide-eyed innocent stare whenever his mouth overran with fibs.

"Did you try to help your husband? Did you check whether he was still breathing?"

"Can't remember."

"Your fingerprints were found on the car keys and on the door handles, Mrs. Pretorius. The engine was off by the time we inspected it. Did you open the car's door and switch off the engine?"

A helpless shrug.

"All right. Let's go back to before you started to look for your husband. You're on the patio having dessert. During all the time you were drinking coffee and eating sweets, did anybody leave the room?"

"No."

*Leave the room?*

That wasn't the right question. If it were up to Hester, she would have asked who'd turned up late for coffee, or who hadn't turned up at all.

Hester did a mental playback of all the guests to whom she'd served coffee.

\* \* \*

Contrary to Watson's hopes, interviewing Annette hadn't brought anything new into the investigation.

"Jones?" he said as soon they left the lounge.

"Yes, sir."

"Set up interview times with those who were here Saturday night. BRAVO offices are the easiest. We'll fingerprint them there."

"With respect, sir, it seems a bit pointless. Given that the only prints found in the car and the garage belong to the family members?"

Privately, Watson agreed. "Do it by the book. Can't afford HQ faulting us on this." Can't afford to lose his job. "House search results?"

"A life policy, sir."

Watson skim-read the document, found the Sum Assured.

*Hell.*

The murder case looked as clear-cut as any textbook example. As though somebody had gone to the trouble of ticking every box to make sure Annette would go down for the crime.

He grit his teeth, felt the muscles in his jaw clench. "Anything else?"

"Some pills found in the victim's nightstand, sir. No pharmacy label. No writing on the pills themselves. And," Jones lowered his voice, "three boxes of chocolate pralines in Mrs. Pretorius' bathroom cupboard, tucked away behind, er, female sanitary products."

What was it that Hester had said? *To the master, she pretends she doesn't eat...*

"Thank you, Jones. Send the pills to the lab. And keep an eye on Mrs. Pretorius while I'm away."

"You think she's guilty, sir? Because of the chocolates? You think they're poisoned?"

So young. So eager.

"She's a potential victim, Jones. The death threat?"

The look on Jones' face spoke volumes, if only Watson could read the constable's particular language. He had no time for puzzles. "Spit it out, Jones."

"With respect. We only have her word, sir. We didn't see the letter under the door. For all we know, she may have written it herself."

Watson felt old. Old and jaded. "Jones?"

"Sir?"

"You think too much. Don't."

"Yessir."

Annette tried to pretend the search was not happening. Strangers trampling her pristine bedroom carpet were a desecration, hands among the children's toys, eyes on the underwear in her closet.

Trevor joined her on the patio, where they were shaded from the relentless sun by a gigantic thatched umbrella and cooled down by a spray misting from a mini-waterfall.

"Refreshing," he said, pointing to the wall of cascading water.

Something metallic glittered in the palm of his hand. He opened his fingers.

"This key fits the large safe in the study. Found it in the false-bottomed drawer in your husband's desk."

"A—a false-bottomed drawer?" Annette thought she'd misheard.

Trevor's eyes narrowed in intense concentration. "Didn't you know?"

She didn't. Her world wobbled again. How many other secrets had Gordon kept from her? "He never told me where the key was."

"Did you ask?"

"Wasn't curious."

She took the key and rolled its long cool stem between her fingers. When she'd rummaged in the desk herself the day before, it had never occurred to her to look for hidden compartments.

Not that it mattered. She'd found what she'd been looking for, and then some.

Trevor shot her an incredulous look. "You weren't curious," he repeated.

Annette said nothing. How would she even begin to explain the veil of indifference shrouding her for the past fourteen years?

"Naturally, we've looked in the safe," Trevor continued.

Naturally. Ever since Gordon's death, her house, her time and her life had become fair game for the police, to be scrutinised and encroached on as they saw fit.

"How much money did you say your husband kept there?"

Annette gathered her thoughts, slippery like strands of silk. "Nothing, apart from his collection of gold Kruger Rand coins. All his savings are in the bank. Money for the staff he left in the study desk, and he kept ready cash in his wallet."

Trevor watched her the way most men watched a rugby final. "So would it surprise you to learn there's money in your safe? Five thousand Rand, to be exact?"

Five thousand Rand was what an office clerk took home in a year.

*What would Gordon want with that kind of money?*

"Mrs. Pretorius?"

Always so official, even when it was just the two of them alone.

"Yes?"

"I asked whether it was a surprise to you."

The strain of the past few days exploded in Annette's head. "You know me well enough, Trevor Watson, to see for yourself it was a surprise," she snapped. "I don't understand why you're asking me about safe keys and money. Why don't you ask," the words of the anonymous letter swam before her eyes, "who hated my husband enough to kill him? Gordon was a religious man. He would never commit suicide."

Watson opened his mouth, but closed it when Hester appeared in the doorway with a guest. He was in his forties, tall, suave and—

Watson had to admit—the type of smarmy good-looking that invariably appealed to women.

As far as the timing of the visit went, this scored about minus five out of one hundred.

"From everybody at the office." The man handed over a basket arrangement of white flowers.

The roses Watson recognised, but there were others whose names he didn't know. Blood rushed fury-hot in his veins.

The smarmy bloke continued, "We are all deeply shocked and deeply sorry for your loss."

Watson looked away as Annette kissed the newcomer's cheek.

"These are lovely, Doc. Thank you," she said. "Doctor Monterra, Captain Trevor Watson."

Doctor Monterra. One of the people who were here Saturday night.

The guest offered his hand. "Watson? Really? Do people ever comment on your surname in the context of your detective work?"

Watson crushed Monterra's fingers with his own. Several more or less suitable ripostes buzzed about in his brain: Doctor Who, Doctor No, Doctor Death. All beneath him.

He settled for, "As in Watson and Holmes? Why, no, Doctor. How original."

*Take that.*

"Hester," said Annette quickly. "We're ready for lunch now, I think."

Watson wanted to get out. There was something about Monterra that rubbed him the wrong way. He shook his head. "Nothing for me, thank you."

"Nonsense. Please sit down, gentlemen. The children are coming."

"Danny, Julie," Monterra's joviality was as convincing as a politician's. "Hello, you beautiful creatures."

The beautiful creatures mumbled their greetings just a hair's width away from rudeness. Watson's regard for them escalated a thousand-fold.

Julie, squirming under her brother's stare, walked towards Annette and gave her a hug. Even from where he sat, Watson noticed the girl's inflexible spine.

The boy, Danny, kissed the top of Annette's head, as though he were the parent and she the child.

"Mom?" he said. "Is it all right if Julie and I take our lunch by the pool? It's too hot to do anything except swim."

"Of course."

Watson could have sworn Annette wanted to hold on to her daughter a moment longer, but Julie slid out of her embrace with a *so-there* look towards her brother and ran off.

Danny brought his mother's hand to his cheek. "I'll make sure she eats." He sounded very grown-up.

The maid brought in a platter of finger food and an icy jug of lemonade.

"Please help yourselves," Annette pointed to the savoury pastries and grilled prawns on kebab sticks. "Would you two like a beer?"

Perhaps they would have, but they both declined. It was all highly irregular, having lunch with potential witnesses in a hypothetical murder. What next? Sex with the prime suspect?

Watson stole a glance at Annette. She played with her kebab stick, her thoughts clearly elsewhere. So far, she had not taken a single bite.

Monterra. Confident, charming, utterly untrustworthy. No woman would choose a police captain over a flashy doctor. Not that Watson gave a damn.

Monterra's large hand slithered across the table and settled on Annette's small one. "Chin up, that's the spirit. Tell yourself you're fine, and fine you will be."

It was like watching a snake. Monterra's eyes glinted in Annette's direction, a signal Watson couldn't make sense of. Annette couldn't make sense of it either, or at least that's what Watson was hoping, for she removed her hand with an absent-minded smile.

Watson's lungs screamed for oxygen. He breathed.

"If you tell a lie often enough, it will become the truth," Annette said in that carefully neutral voice he remembered so well. "I sometimes wonder whether that's how the world works, all the propaganda in the newspapers and on TV."

Monterra's cobra-like grin showed a suit of healthy teeth. Watson longed to kick them in, for no other reason than that they looked too good. Everything looked too good on the bloody Monterra, who now said, "That's exactly how the communists operate, my dear. They say there's no God and no class distinction. Unfortunately, the longer they spread their commie lies, the more people they brainwash."

Propaganda and brainwashing, in Watson's experience, went both ways.

"Is this why we have to be vigilant? Inform the government if any of our friends show communist tendencies?" Annette's tone bore an impish sparkle he had once known so well.

"Exactly so, my dear."

Watson would give a month's supply of coffee to wipe the smirk off the other man's face. He cleared his throat. "Doesn't follow why our soldiers have to fight the communists all the way up in Angola."

The smirk remained. "To stop them from coming into our country to broadcast their nonsense, of course."

*If you tell a lie often enough, it will become the truth,* was equally applicable to the commie propaganda and to the party line touted by the South African government. Whoever said the first casualty of war was truth, had it exactly right. Watson got up, scraping his chair on the patio floor.

Monterra jerked his head in a dismissive bow. "It was a pleasure meeting you, Captain."

"*Ja*, same here. We will resume the pleasure later this afternoon." He watched with satisfaction. For a blink of an eye, Doctor Monterra looked uneasy.

In the game between cop and suspect, the score was now one-zero. In the match between one red-blooded male and another…Watson didn't want to go there.

"Enjoy your lunch," he said, wishing he could think up a wittier parting shot.

"Doesn't follow why our soldiers have to fight the communists in Angola," Trevor said.

Annette didn't hear Doc's reply. Her chest was tight, and for a moment she believed she'd choke on her un-exhaled breath. We raise our sons to die on our country's border defending our way of life, she thought. We raise our daughters as sacrificial virgins. Something was very wrong with the arrangement.

At school she'd learned dying for your country was romantic and right and righteous. Now she was a mom, dying for South Africa was stupid. Having her son die for his country heart-wrenchingly, fist-curlingly impossible to imagine.

Annette swallowed the marble of dread, smiled her Stepford Wife smile and longed for the lunch to end.

When Doc excused himself to go and speak to the children, the pincers around her heart began to slacken. Perhaps Doc would perform a small miracle with Julie. Although the girl had been sweetness itself when she came to apologise, Annette knew her daughter was acting under duress. She briefly wondered how Danny had managed to bully his sister into the apology, before her mind turned to the false-bottomed drawer in Gordon's study.

Fancy living with a man for fourteen years and knowing so little about him.

She was curious. What did a false-bottomed drawer look like? Would she be able to find it now that she knew it was there? Would she find another one, perhaps overlooked by the police?

The police. Trevor. *Captain* Trevor Watson. Another issue Annette was not prepared to deal with. She fed Beth, kissed the silky down on the top of the baby's head and left her in Hester's care.

When she opened the door to Gordon's study, she spotted Doc by the roll-top desk.

"Oh, I'm sorry," she exclaimed. Acute embarrassment

gushed over her, as though this were Doc's house and she the one caught snooping. Not that Doc was snooping, Annette admonished herself. As Gordon's boss, he had every right to be in the study, taking care of the classified paperwork.

"There you are," he said, his hand extended in invitation. "I've spoken to the children. They are naturally disturbed and confused by what's happened. The constant police presence in the house isn't helping." He paused, the question implied.

Implied and unanswered. Annette didn't want to discuss Trevor's toothbrush drying in the guest bathroom.

Doc touched her shoulder. "They're doing fine. As fine as can be expected. The funeral should provide closure." Another pause. Doc's fingers stroked her bare skin in long comforting strokes. She froze. Didn't he realise he was touching her?

Evidently not. His face was all business. "Would you like me to take care of the arrangements?"

Tempting.

Every time Annette thought of what needed to be done, she felt a cloud of lethargy descend on her. What were the arrangements, anyway? Phoning relatives and friends? Organising a funeral parlour? Choosing a coffin? What?

"No, thank you," she said with a sigh. "Sweet of you to offer, but it's only right that I take care of it all."

His hand was still on her shoulder, firm and reassuring. "Nonsense, my dear. You're grieving. Your children are grieving. Concentrate on being a mother. Allow me to deal with the administrative details."

"If you're certain..."

"I'm certain." Doc gave her shoulder another pat. "Do you know whether Gordon had a funeral benefit in his life insurance policy?"

Life insurance. Annette had quite forgotten about that. Fancy forgetting about being a millionaire.

"I—I'll check and let you know."

"Would you like me to do it?" Doc extended his hand towards the drawers of the roll-top.

"No-no, that's quite all right. But thank you."

Like a true gentleman, Doc shifted his hand in one smooth gesture away from the drawers and towards the ivory figurine in its pigeonhole, where Hester must have replaced it at cleaning time.

"The unicorn's horn has broken off," he said. "I wonder how. Ivory is a strong substance, it doesn't fracture easily."

Annette's mind flashed back to her fit of temper. Had the carving already been damaged when she'd flung it across the room? She couldn't remember. Could the force of the pitch amputate the horn? And if her strength wasn't enough, what about Gordon's? Had he ever flung the figurine in a rage?

Click. That was it. Gordon. Gordon in the fume-filled garage, holding his unicorn in his hand…

*His unicorn? His unicorn was right here, in his study. So whose unicorn…*

She swallowed a gulp, closed the desktop. "Every time I see something made of ivory," she was proud of how steady her voice sounded, "I can't help feeling sorry for the elephant."

"I'm sure they wait for the elephant to die a natural death before they utilize the remains." Doc touched her arm again. "The government wouldn't have it any other way."

Annette doubted the government had the time. What with the bush war in Angola, movies to censor for profanities and sex, and of course the blacks to keep in check.

She smiled her prettiest smile, the one she knew made men forget their first names. "The government does so many important things. Thank goodness BRAVO's there to help them."

Doc kissed her hand. "We are here to protect you, Annette. Never forget that. We only have your best interest in mind."

*Project Hydra. How was that the best?*

When Doc left, a more pressing question returned. Whose unicorn had Gordon clutched in his dying fist?

Professor Adelbrecht's giant desk was bare except for a small South African flag and an ivory statue of a unicorn.

*Another frigging white unicorn.*

Watson hoped his eyes had given away nothing.

A tie-less, jacket-less young man stood at a portable blackboard that went blank at the press of a button. Watson stifled a whistle. The gadgets *some* government agencies got to play with! Straight out of a Bond movie. The police force had never seen such magical blackboards. His own office didn't even have a fan. Air-conditioned BRAVO, however, was on a budget of a different magnitude.

Professor Adelbrecht looked mid-sixties and close to retirement, a full mane of straight white hair, a salt-and-pepper beard, wire-rimmed spectacles, and the obligatory business suit. He said, "Thank you, Nick. Please discuss your latest improvement with Lula."

So that was Nick Haddow. Watson took a liking to him on the spot. The only man at BRAVO who dressed for the weather in this subtropical climate, giving etiquette the symbolic finger.

"We'll try to take up as little of your time as possible, Professor," he said when the introductions were out of the way. "Gordon Pretorius worked for BRAVO. What exactly does your agency do and what was Pretorius's specific role here?"

Adelbrecht leaned back in his chair, his posture presidential, full of self-importance. "Our agency is best explained by telling you what it's not. We are not like the Council for Scientific and Industrial Research, whose focus is often more academic than practical. We are not part of the military and we don't report to the Ministry of Defence. Nor are we," he hesitated, "associated with the Security Police."

The branch of the South African Police whose inconvenient prisoners sometimes suffered a fatal slip in the shower. Watson ignored the dig. "All right. I understand what you aren't. So what *do* you do?"

"We help the government implement its agenda."

Very glib and equally vacuous. "So do the army and the police."

And so did all the civilian informers who'd spy on their

neighbours to make sure they didn't disseminate communist opinions, and so did the newspapers reporting only the glorious bits of the regime. Watson remembered what the South African media had done with the truth of the Soweto Riots in 1976. His spine felt like a shongololo had just slid down it with its thousand legs.

"BRAVO helps the government by using science and technology instead of brute force."

Soweto 1976. To say the police used 'brute force' there, was an understatement. Adelbrecht was playing dirty.

"Is that as in *bravo, you've done a good job*, Professor, or is it an acronym?" *Like Brute Ruthless Atrocious Villains Organisation.*

"BRAVO describes our work quite well, as a matter of fact." The professor beamed a self-satisfied smirk. "The acronym stands for Biotech Research Agency for Vital Operations."

"Vital operations. So you have nothing to do with the Censor Board, either?"

"That's not funny, young man. The Censor Board is an important instrument in maintaining peace and racial harmony in our country."

Watson felt rapped over the knuckles. "It would probably help if you could give me a few examples of the types of projects you do run here."

"I'm afraid that's all classified information, Captain."

Watson had come prepared. He took the necessary permits out of the murder-case folder and slid them across the desert-size desk. He'd speculated how far he would get without them: surely BRAVO had a legitimate-sounding cover that could be peddled to the public and the media?

"Very well," the older man said. "I presume you're interested in projects Gordon Pretorius worked on? I'm afraid that'll be tricky. We found no paperwork in his office."

"No paperwork?"

"None. At first we suspected burglary, but Sally—that's Gordon's secretary—saw him sort through all his papers on Friday morning."

Why would Gordon Pretorius sort his files the day before he died? Seemed to point to suicide. Unless Pretorius suspected somebody was planning to get rid of him.

"What happened to the sorted papers?"

Adelbrecht rubbed his beard. "Frankly, we hope he shredded the lot."

"Why?"

"Captain, let's not play cat and mouse. You surely understand some of our work is not for public knowledge. If word got out to the media..."

If word got out to the media, it would probably be quashed by the government before it had the chance to go public. What was the old man worried about?

"So what did Pretorius work on?"

The professor stroked his beard. "One project involved slowing down the growth of the black population of this country."

Watson wondered whether that was a euphemism for killing off half of them.

"How?"

"Forced contraception," Adelbrecht sighed. "Look, I'm not claiming it's an ideal solution. But face the facts. Blacks won't use prophylactics. They multiply like rabbits. If we don't do something, they're going to take over the country."

Watson waited.

"So. We've devised an oral contraceptive that can be distributed via the water system into the townships. Totally harmless. No side effects. The only result is a decrease in the pregnancy rate."

It sounded too good to be true. It was. Blacks took pride in large families, they wanted to have children. Who didn't?

"Did the Prime Minister approve your proposal?" Watson could hear his own voice, croaky and faint.

"We do not answer to the Prime Minister."

"Do you answer to anybody?"

"To God."

If you repeat a lie often enough, it will become the truth.

"And God told you it's all right to remove people's right to procreate?"

"God speaks but in a whisper and a riddle, Captain. Look at the black population. Most women have at least six, and often as many as twelve children, during their lifetime. And not a brain cell to share among them. Is that the kind of future we want for our country?"

Watson said nothing.

"Non-whites already outnumber us eight to two. It'll be the death of us if we don't do something about it. It's us or them." The professor removed his spectacles and rubbed the lenses with a beige cloth. "In Greek mythology Hydra was a nine-headed serpent whose blood was poisonous, so poisonous it tainted the waters of the river. We liked the allegory and we found a divine meaning in the project's name."

Watson still said nothing. His nothing spoke volumes.

"What else can I help you with, Captain?"

*Oh, right, the murder case.*

The one that could make or break his career. He'd almost forgotten. "What else can you tell me about Gordon Pretorius, Professor?"

"I knew Gordon's father, Piet Pretorius, all my life. A good man, Piet. A rare example of an Afrikaner the way God intended our nation to be: God-loving, God-fearing and with the right mindset."

"By the *right mindset*, do you mean *conservative*, Professor?"

"I mean, *right*."

"Right," said Watson. He thought, *riiiiight*. "What about *Gordon* Pretorius? Was he a good man like his father?"

The old man arranged his fingers into a steeple. "He was."

Watson didn't believe him. "Pieter Pretorius, Piet, as you call him, was also a scientist. Did he work here, at BRAVO?"

"Not anymore. He took early retirement several years ago, though he still consulted for BRAVO from time to time."

Gordon's father had been connected with BRAVO. Implication: the killer may be after the Pretorius family or after the scientists from BRAVO.

*Except it was Annette who'd received a death threat.*

"Genetics was Piet's passion," continued the professor. "He developed a new way of testing to which race an individual belongs. As you're aware, Captain, the pencil test is not always reliable."

Watson knew about the pencil test. Stick it into someone's hair, and if the pencil falls through, you're considered white, but if it stays in the hair's tight curl, you're classified as black.

"Piet's research in the 1970s led to tissue typing instead of blood typing as a valid proof of paternity. But he wanted to take it further, to achieve a hundred percent certainty. I used to joke he couldn't disown his children, it was enough to take one look at his boys to have a hundred percent certainty as to who the father was, but to no avail. When Piet retired, he still used BRAVO's lab for his research. About a month before he died, he told me DNA was the way to go. Claimed he'd found a workable procedure that only required a small amount of genetic material scraped from a person's mouth. After his death, however, we never found any of his documents."

Watson backed up. "You said, *his boys?*"

"Piet had two sons, Captain. Stuart, Gordon's brother, was killed two years ago in Angola. An unlucky family. God's will manifests in mysterious ways."

About the murder being God's will, Watson couldn't agree less. "We're doing everything we can to ensure the perpetrator does not escape punishment."

"Even if he is only God's tool on earth, Captain?"

"Indeed." Time to wrap up. He kept his voice casual. "An interesting sculpture you have there, Professor."

"Ah, the unicorn." Adelbrecht took the statue in his fingers, and his wrinkled face softened.

"It's an odd thing to carve out of ivory. I would have expected an elephant or a lion."

Adelbrecht's beard lifted in a grin. "Or a springbuck?"

"*Ja.*" In fact, the unicorn in the professor's hands did look more like a springbuck than a horse. "Something South African anyway. Aren't unicorns make-believe?"

"A unicorn is a creature found in legends and myths, but that doesn't mean it's make-believe. Legends are full of heroes and beautiful maidens, too, and those certainly are alive and well in South Africa today."

"What about unicorns, Professor? Are they alive and well?"

The old man shepherded Watson to the door. Standing upright, he looked shorter than when sitting. A web of broken capillaries criss-crossed his nostrils. An old man.

"Perhaps," the professor said. "Perhaps they camouflage themselves among the paler springbucks. In the end, we all are responsible for our own make-beliefs. Good day, Captain."

Paler springbucks, thought Watson, but with only one horn. If he were to carry the metaphor further, he would ask whether the single horn was an aberration of birth.

Annette went back to Gordon's desk.

The police had removed nothing. The life insurance policy with its funeral benefit, a document confirming Gordon's ownership of a family tomb, his last will and testament—no, it was not his last will and testament. In a folder marked "Testament" she discovered a hand-written note, confirming that a signed copy was deposited with Gordon's lawyer, a Mr. Vermeulen. The law firm's business card was attached.

She dialled the number.

"I'm sorry," she heard. "Mr. Vermeulen is away this week. Would you like to leave a message?"

Annette recited her name and number. A feeling of unease inched between her shoulder blades.

*Why wasn't the testament here? Or a copy of it at the very least? What had Gordon wanted to hide?*

The Minister With No Official Portfolio waited in his office. Years of training had taught him patience, yet he couldn't help thinking about his wife and daughter getting into a small luxury aeroplane reserved for the country's elite. Soon they'd be flying over the Indian Ocean on their way to a tiny African island where the sand is always white and the water always blue. While he, he'd be imprisoned in an underground room reeking of old sweat and new blood. Performing his patriotic duty, in the name of God and the Fatherland.

The personal assistant, chosen by his wife because of her years of experience (and, he suspected, the sagging boobs), opened his door to announce his visitor.

"Sir," the visitor said as soon as she'd left. "The lawyer's on holiday. Nobody in his office knows exactly where. Every summer, he just takes off in his Land Rover. No plans, no bookings. Last year he was in Namibia. The year before, St Lucia."

On holiday. The irony wasn't lost on the minister. "Has the parcel arrived at his law practice?"

"Negative, sir. Our people are searching the postal system."

Like searching for a flea on a giraffe's neck. The post office was a slow, paper-laden mechanism. Even if they didn't lose the parcel, which sometimes happened when the black postmen stole, there was no way of telling when it would reach the recipient. The joke ran that to dispose of a corpse, all you had to do was send it by mail and it would never be seen again. He and his people knew more efficient ways, but there was a grain of truth to the joke.

"The lawyer's secretary?"

"Claims client privilege, sir."

He calculated. If the parcel had been sent as priority mail on Friday, it could have arrived Monday morning.

"Where is she now?"

"Interrogation room."

So it had come to that again. This time, it wouldn't be a terrorist or a known political militant. This time, it would be an innocent whose only misfortune was to have information. Or—to be suspected of having information.

The minister gritted his teeth. His mind switched tack. "The wife."

"The lawyer's a bachelor, sir."

"Gordon Pretorius's wife."

"Reporters are guarding her. Ours are not a problem. But there's this American…"

Enough said. They could control only South African media. Arrest the wife and word would spread internationally. Not a showstopper. Still, after the latest series of exposures in the international media, South Africa could do with a low profile. No need to draw attention to the way this country dealt with internal affairs. Let Poland's martial law occupy American newspapers for a while longer.

So. Let Mrs. Pretorius be for now.

*Kak.*

He hated waiting.

"The security tapes from the Pretorius house."

"Sir, our team's reviewed them and they confirm Mrs. Pretorius destroyed the files."

The minister gave his visitor a look.

"Right away, sir."

When alone again, he placed a radio call to the government aeroplane. "*Bokkie,*" he said, "I may be more than a couple of days."


There was no white unicorn in Monterra's office. None Watson could see, at any rate. As soon as he'd seen the one in Gordon's desk at the Pretorius mansion, he'd realised the one clutched in the victim's fingers had to have come from the murderer.

*Unless that one was Gordon's and the murderer placed his own figurine in Gordon's desk?*

*No.*

More likely, the murderer would have taken Gordon's to replace his own. Keep it simple. Real life seldom worked the way convoluted story lines did on TV.

"Call me Doc," Monterra said. "What can I get you? We have good coffee here, none of that instant nonsense." The good doctor was oozing charm like a cracked crystal ball. "A terrible business,

Gordon's death, terrible. I feel so awful for Annette and the children."

Jealousy knotted Watson's abdomen. "Quite," he said. "You can help by shedding some light on what happened Saturday. How well did you know Gordon Pretorius? What kind of person was he?"

"Hmm." Monterra creased his forehead and drummed his fingers on a small wooden box. "Gordon was—not a complicated man. No shades of grey where he was concerned: everything was either black or white with him, no space to manoeuvre between right and wrong." His fingers played with the box's clasp. "A good bloke. Well-liked. A family man, a religious man, a conscientious scientist."

In his little notebook, Watson wrote down the keyword *good*. "The party on Saturday—was it a regular thing? Did you often get together as a group outside of working hours?"

"Not very often. Christmas celebrations and team building events, but they usually took place at a restaurant or a wildlife lodge."

"So what was the occasion?"

"Gordon's birthday." The clasp on the box clicked open and shut. Open, shut. Open, shut. "I did wonder. He had never thrown a birthday bash before. Late notice too."

"Notice anything unusual?"

*Click.* Monterra opened the wooden box and extended it to Watson. "Cigar?"

"Thank you, no. You go ahead."

Monterra shook his head and busied his hands with a cigar guillotine, wide enough to take off a finger.

Watson leaned forward. "I didn't realise you could get Cuban cigars here. Not with all the trade sanctions against Cuba."

"Trade sanctions?" Monterra shrugged. "That's just for show, to make the world feel good. Everybody's shouting for sanctions against South Africa, but you don't see any big clever companies listening. Coca-Cola knows if they withdraw their business, they will lose a lot of money for no good reason. The South African government is not going to give in to the demands for one-man-one-vote just because they can't drink Coke with their dinner."

"As an employee of an agency actively fighting communism, though, how can you justify paying for communist products?"

Monterra inhaled the fragrant cigar smoke, held it in his mouth the way a wine connoisseur holds a swig of Pinotage. "That's exactly what Gordon would have said. Black or white, right or wrong, no compromises," he said on the exhalation.

"What are the things he would not compromise on?"

A self-deprecating smile. "Oh, Captain, you're putting words in my mouth now. I didn't say he wouldn't ever accept a compromise. He was a good scientist and good scientists always keep an open mind."

Watson was getting fed up, fast. "How open is your own mind when it comes to Project Hydra?"

"Wide open. Project Hydra is still in its proposal stages. At present, the most viable scenario involves distributing permanent birth control throughout the water system of a test-case township."

*Permanent?*

Adelbrecht hadn't mentioned that. "You mean it would render the residents of the *test-case township* sterile?"

"Possibly. We don't have enough data to know for sure until we try it."

*Until we try it.*

Dread slithered down Watson's throat. "Just out of interest, which township is singled out for the Project Hydra test-case?"

"Does it really matter, Captain?" Monterra sucked on his cigar and blew three concentric smoke rings. Through the haze, his eyes met Watson's. "It's Soweto."

As though Soweto hadn't suffered enough.

The Minister With No Official Portfolio reviewed the security tapes. The wife had burned some files, all right. Problem was, those were the wrong files. The camera's resolution wasn't high enough to read the typewritten text, but the small number of pages meant these were summaries.

He needed to destroy the original research documents, everything and anything that could be leaked to the media overseas. Internationally, South Africa was in enough *kak* already. If word got out...

It would start small, the United States condemning this country. Withdrawing their unofficial support of South Africa in the bush war. And with the Angolan commies on the brink of victory, would the South African government hesitate to deploy the secret nuclear weapons?

The Minister With No Official Portfolio knew the answer. He shivered.

It was easy to find the drawer with the false bottom once you knew it was there. Annette pressed on handles and knobs without success, until she lost her patience and simply inserted her long painted nail between the sides and the bottom of every drawer.

The base of one of the small drawers peeled upwards under the pressure, revealing another base, with enough space in-between the double layer to hide documents or keys or jewels.

It was empty now, the key to the safe stashed in her handbag as a temporary measure. One by one, she pulled out the other drawers, checking the backs for a secret glued or taped there. She didn't know what compelled her, apart from a gnawing feeling that she had forgotten something. Something to do with hidey-holes.

The phone rang. Irritated by the distraction, she took a few seconds to register how robotic the voice on the other end sounded. No way to tell whether it was a man or a woman, or how old.

"Find more files," the voice said without a preamble. "Documents. Any papers with *classified*, *restricted*, *confidential* or *secret*. Bring them to House of Coffees tomorrow noon. We know where Danny and Julie go to school. We can see Beth's pram outside. Noon, sharp. No second chances."

Click.

\* \* \*

BRAVO's lobby was bright and austere, all the secretarial desks in full view. Watson didn't fancy conducting the interview in public. Still, this offered the opportunity to size up Gordon's secretary in her own environment.

So far, the secretary was a French poodle. Over-groomed. Over-sensitive.

"Name?"

"Sally Martins."

"Age?"

"Almost twenty."

For a teenager, her eyes were too made-up and too all-knowing. Nineteen going on depraved forty, Watson thought with sadness.

He asked more gently, "You're Gordon Pretorius's secretary?"

She sucked in her lower lip and looked at him, her expression a perfect mirror of a child in distress. She was good with mimicry and Watson hoped like hell he'd remember it in all his future dealings with Miss Martins. "Yes, until—you know. Lula—Doctor Lula Nortje—has taken over all Gordon's responsibilities, and I've been assisting her, so I'm guessing I'll be her secretary now."

"How do you feel about it?"

"I like Lula."

"Did you like Gordon, too?"

She winced. "Sure. He was a good boss."

"How well did you know him?"

Sally looked so casual, alarm bells went on in Watson's head as soon as she replied, "Not very."

His nod belied his thoughts. "How long was he your boss?"

"Two years." Sally shifted in her chair, leaned closer, allowing Watson a more generous view of her chest. Her teenage chest, he reminded himself and looked away.

Sally continued, "You have to understand. Gordon sat in his office, over there," she pointed, "behind that closed door. From time to time, he'd press the buzzer and ask for coffee or a file from the storeroom or to set up an appointment with somebody. He was a busy man, you know, not very chatty. Every morning I'd ask how he was, and he would go, 'Well, thank you, and how are you?' and sometimes that would be the sum total of our conversations for the day. I always had his coffee hot and ready on his desk by one minute to eight, because he walked in the door at eight o'clock sharp. So, if he didn't want another cup, or a file from downstairs, or—"

"I get the picture. So what did you do with yourself all day at work when your boss didn't call for you?"

Sally showed him her dimples. "I did my nails. I experimented with eye shadow. I wrote letters to my mom back home. I read books and drank too many cups of tea."

"What books do you like?" A person's taste in books was often more telling than an hour's worth of interrogation.

A blush. "You know. Books about relationships. Love."

"Romance books? Mills and Boon?"

"There's nothing wrong with that."

"Of course not."

*Provided you didn't mind getting brainwashed into an unrealistic view of eternal love.*

"Now, Miss Martins, you have a boyfriend in this agency, don't you? Nick Haddow?"

Sally nodded.

"Didn't you go chat to him when you had time on your hands?"

"No. He's in the lab most of the time, two floors down. I'm not allowed in there and he's usually busy anyway."

"How long have you been going out?"

"Three months and three days."

*Typical woman.*

"Your boss shredded some documents last Friday?"

"Yes."

"You saw Gordon Pretorius during his working day last Friday, then?"

Another nod. "He asked for some brown paper and sticky-tape, and I brought it all into his office."

Watson watched the girl as she braided her fingers together, then forced them to relax. Something worried her.

"Wouldn't it have been more natural for you to wrap whatever it was yourself?"

"Yes, I did wonder about that. But I didn't ask."

"Right. What happened then?"

"He dispatched the parcel."

"Was that before or after lunch?"

"Um, before."

She sounded defensive, suddenly, and very, very young.

"Did he go out to lunch?"

"No."

"Did you?"

"No! Why are you asking me all that?"

"It's just routine, Miss." Watson raised a conciliatory hand. Sally Martins sure had her hackles up and it had to do with Friday lunchtime. He backed off. "Please tell me, in your own words, what happened on Saturday."

Annette still clutched the phone in her hand, its smooth edges biting into her flesh. After the short ominous silence of a disconnected call, she heard the dial tone. Her first instinct was to call Gordon, get him to deal with the situation. How sad was that?

Her lungs, starved of oxygen, took over. She gasped, took large, greedy gulps. Don't you dare cry, she told herself.

Documents. Though she knew it was hopeless, Annette went through the desk three more times, large drawers, small drawers, the hidden compartment. Where the hell did Gordon hide them?

The action of taking out and replacing the pigeonhole drawers, each as small as a building brick, made Annette remember something. Of course: the loose brick in the wall that separated her garden from her mother's.

It could have just been a loose brick. Still, she had to check.

Please, God, she prayed. Please let it be Gordon's stash.

Watson knocked on the door of yet another office. There were no floral curtains, no pink rugs, no potted plants, and yet the whole space exuded femininity.

The magical blackboard stood in the middle of the room, facing away from him.

"Name?" Watson asked, bending over his notebook. He aimed for bored and unapproachably official.

"Lula."

Watson paused over his notebook. "Yes? Lula what?"

"Just Lula. That's what everybody calls me."

Watson slowly counted to ten under his breath. "We need your given names, as they appear in your ID document, please."

"Loraine Ursula Nortje, formerly Larsen."

"Position?"

"Oh, my. Are you asking me what I think you're asking, Captain?"

Watson suppressed a chuckle, put on a baffled expression. "Hey?"

"Never mind," she sighed. "How can I help you?"

As it turned out, she couldn't. Her account of events didn't add anything to his picture of Gordon during the last days of his life.

The investigation was going nowhere, fast. Watson throttled his disappointment. "What are you working on at present?"

"Tying up what can be salvaged of Gordon's projects."

That sounded evasive. Watson got up as though to leave, and walked around the desk, his hand outstretched in a goodbye, then, with a rapid motion, he swivelled the blackboard to him.

*What the——?*

It was a crude drawing of couples having sex, the tableau arranged into a pyramid shape. Below was a row of numbers and ratios. Professor Adelbrecht had mentioned nothing like that.

"Project Aphrodite," Lula said. "Nick Haddow's latest bright idea."

The resentment in her voice made Watson pay attention. "Tell me."

It wasn't just a loose brick in the wall separating their garden from her mom's. Nor was it the place where Gordon had hidden the secret documents.

Behind it, Annette discovered five pages torn out of *Bunny Girl*, three strips of developed film, and a pencil drawing of a nude female torso: faceless except for a full-lipped mouth, with arms ending before the elbows, with thighs not reaching the knees. The anatomically detailed drawing was brilliantly executed for a thirteen-year old, and a sliver of pride pierced though Annette's acute embarrassment.

Danny didn't do art at school anymore, yet Annette recognised his style instantly. The familiar pencil strokes, the minimalist outlines, the crosshatch shading for three-dimensional depth.

He was growing up so fast.

Annette didn't realise quite how fast, until she picked up the long narrow plastic-coated rectangle of the developed negative and held it up to the afternoon sun.

Images of Gordon having sex on his office desk scorched into her retinas. Annette couldn't see the woman's face, bent away from the camera in every shot. Only the neck and mouth showed above the dark pubis and the young breasts.

Behind the curtain in his upstairs bedroom, Danny watched his mother remove the brick. He wanted to call out to her, to distract her, but it was already too late.

*Double, triple shit. What now?*

Formality was not Nick Haddow's style. He reminded Watson of a cowboy: young yet rugged, wild yet smooth talking, somebody with a lot of work to do and all the time in the world to do it in.

He answered the questions wordily but to the point. No, he

hadn't known Gordon very well, they'd worked separately, even though they were both involved in Project Hydra. No, he had not noticed anything unusual on the fateful Saturday night.

Watson's arm itched to fling something at the wall to ease his frustration. "What about a day earlier? The Friday?"

Nick did his cowboy grin. "How do you mean?"

"Did you see Gordon at all last Friday?"

"No. I worked in my lab all day."

Watson remembered Sally's unease when questioned on this topic. He focused his attention on Nick's hands, always more telling than the face. "Didn't you go out for lunch?"

The hands remained steady. "No."

Was there a brief hesitation in Nick Haddow's voice? Watson looked for the telltale signs in the scientist's base behaviour and found naught. Nick kept his limbs still and his eyes on Watson's. Nothing to go on.

"Why didn't you?" In the back of his mind, Watson compared these humdrum questions to what he, long ago, had thought detective work would be about. In reality, all he got to ask was things like, "Weren't you hungry?"

"Can't remember. I must have got engrossed in my work, forgotten it was lunchtime."

Watson could relate to that. His stomach kept reminding him how he'd wasted his opportunity to fill it during the meal with Monterra earlier in the day. "What was the problem that kept you so busy?"

Nick's eyes brightened. "It was a pathogen BRAVO's developing. As with any new virus, children would be hit the hardest, because their immune systems aren't fully developed."

Watson lost his appetite.

"On Friday, I was looking for ways of minimising the risk. Captain, sorry I can't tell you more. I know you have clearance, only we're playing with the hypothetical at this stage. Nothing's decided."

"And it doesn't bother you," Watson needed to know for his own personal peace of mind, "that you're developing a biological weapon? A tool for mass—murder? Don't you feel responsible for how your work's end result is going to be used?"

"Mass murder? That's a bit melodramatic," Nick's drawl was so laid-back and confident, Watson found it hard not to fall for his reasoning. "We develop vaccines and cures alongside the viruses. Besides, I'm a scientist. Responsibility is not my department. I don't decide on the strategy or the wisdom of deploying my projects. I just follow orders, like in the army. If I may draw a parallel, you, Captain, surely won't feel remorse when you arrest the perpetrator and send him to the gallows for murdering poor old Gordon?"

The non-policeman part of Watson couldn't help liking Nick. Lula's comments painted Nick as a genius in his field. Nick, however, put on none of the airs that you'd expect of an over-praised wunderkind.

"How do you know it was murder?"

"Give me some credit. You guys have better things to do than interview every friend and colleague of every guy who commits suicide. Mind you," Nick's eyebrows came together, "if it was indeed suicide, I shan't be surprised. Gordon strikes—struck—me exactly as the type to run away from his problems. He'd never been to the army, you see. He didn't know how to fight."

"I take it you're an army man?"

"Yes, and proud of it. Two years of serving his country is what every schoolboy needs to become a man. They straighten you out in there. Break you down and build you up again, without all your old bull and twaddle. The army's the best thing that's ever happened to me."

"Did you serve at the border?"

A nod.

"And? Was that also the best thing that's ever happened to you?"

Nick looked him straight in the eye. "Yes. It was hell on earth, but it was a necessary hell on earth. The government created it in Angola, far away, in order to protect our slice of heaven here."

"Huh?"

"South Africa is the paradise we're protecting, Captain. It's better to fight a war far away from your country. Trust me, I know."

Watson knew, too. His mind filled with unwanted images of the Soweto Riots, he headed back to Annette's house.

After Gordon's death, Johannes carried on with his duties as usual, so the barbecue grill was clean of the ashes created by the BRAVO files. Acutely aware of the sense of déjà vu, reeling with disappointment that the hiding place in the wall contained no more files, Annette reached for the matches.

Gordon always kept them tucked high up into the thatch of the roof overhanging the barbecue area, away from the children's curious hands. Annette savoured the irony. Danny could reach into the thatch without standing on tiptoe now, and in any case he had been exposed to something far more damaging than fire.

The sturdy wooden match burned brightly, but the negatives didn't want to catch alight. Without kindling, the flame wouldn't last. Despite the discomfiting subject matter, Danny's drawing was precious; the crumpled *Bunny Girl* pages, however, Annette sacrificed without a moment's thought. She hoped they'd burn long enough.

The first strip of negatives was already melting into brown curls on the barbecue tray, when a hand shot out of nowhere and flicked them away from the fire.

"Jeez, woman, what do you think you're doing?" she heard Trevor's voice.

The garden started spinning, the sun darkened and the ground rose up to meet Annette's cheek. She was surprised how soft it felt.

Watson caught Annette before she hit the ground. Her collarbones poked through the thin material of her dress.

*Hell, did the woman live on air? No wonder she'd fainted.*

The scene before his eyes, the negatives and the matches, spoke for themselves. It didn't take a genius to figure out, particularly once he inspected the photo images. His chest was tight, full of thorns that bit deeper into him every time he took a breath. "Jones."

"Sir."

"When the ambulance arrives, go along and stay with Mrs. Pretorius at the hospital."

"Yessir. Do I arrest her for the murder of her husband?"

Loyalty. After Soweto, Watson had become obsessed with it. Now he faced a problem: loyalty to Annette or to his job?

The negatives didn't prove Annette knew about Gordon's affair prior to the murder. If anything, the fact that she was burning them only now, suggested she might have only just stumbled across them.

Even so, he couldn't ignore the incident, nor its implications. Jealousy was a damned good motive for murder. Another damned good one was preventing a divorce and the division of assets, from which the South African wife always emerged with next to nothing.

"Mrs. Pretorius is our prime suspect, Jones. Let's concentrate on finding hard evidence to prove it."

Loyalty to the job first. Annette was nothing but a shadow from the past.

When a large black Mercedes with government insignia stopped directly in front of BRAVO's door, Lula knew her chance had come. She watched Professor Adelbrecht hurry across the lobby to the lift and get into the back seat of the car, which pulled away before the door had banged shut.

Clasping a random folder as justification, she slipped into Adelbrecht's office. With the duplicate key she'd had made after Saturday's party, she unlocked the professor's strongbox. Made of steel, it was as big as a filing cabinet and impossible to lift, not only because of its weight, but also thanks to four gigantic screws pinning it to the floor.

* * *

*Mrs. Pretorius is our prime suspect.*

Danny threw himself onto the bed and pummelled the pillows. The act didn't make him feel any better. Everything was his fault, and now his mom would be arrested for his wrongdoing.

*No!*

He stood up, smoothed his clothes.

Not if he could help it.

"The documents, Professor," The Minister With No Official Portfolio said. "Gordon Pretorius took some of them home, and those are destroyed. He also sent a parcel to his lawyer, and we've recovered that from the main post office."

Adelbrecht dared to breathe out. "Excellent."

"Quite the contrary. The parcel contained only a ream of blank typewriter pages."

"A ruse."

"Correct."

The professor thought fast. "You want me to guess where he hid the real documents."

The minister said nothing.

"There are several possibilities," Adelbrecht extended his fingers one by one. "A bank vault. His father's house—it's not sold yet. His mother-in-law's house, which he owns outright. Let me mull it over and get back to you."

"You do that." The minister cracked his knuckles. Got up. "One more thing."

"Yes?"

"I'd like you to see something motivational."

When they stepped into the cellar, the hairs at the back of the professor's neck bristled.

The minister pointed to a one-way window in the wall. "This is the lawyer's secretary," he said. "We had to make absolutely sure she didn't have the documents. You understand."

Adelbrecht forced himself to look. Inside a dark room lay what was left of a young woman. Streaks of brown blood covered her face and arms and breasts.

The minister pulled down the blind. "Your granddaughter's the same age. Helena. It would be—unfortunate—if her medical studies were to be suddenly—interrupted."

# Chapter 6—Thursday, Two Days before the Murder

THE EARLY MORNING was sunny and fresh, filled with the "whee-whee-whee" of the mousebird. As soon as she opened the front door, however, Ella LeRoy knew all was not well.

Despite her meticulously applied makeup, Annette's complexion carried a sickly grey hue. Her lips were taut, her eyes full of shadows.

"Hello, Mother." Annette's voice belied her appearance. "How's Beth this morning? Slept through the night?"

Ella saw her daughter's hand travel to her breast, likely full after so many hours away from the baby. Annette should really wean Beth, put her on bottle food permanently, introduce solids.

"Beth is fine," she replied. "Really loves her formula. She had a full bottle last night and again this morning. How about you? Did you have a nice evening out last night?" As though she'd noticed nothing.

"Yes, mother, thank you. Lovely." Propriety observed by both sides.

Ella opened her mouth to ask about Danny and Julie-Ann, but her daughter got there first. "Sorry I can't chat, Mother. Just nipped out to get Beth. I need to get back to make Gordon's coffee." Annette curved her mouth into a perfect-wife smile, one that lasted as long as a flash of African lightning, and hurried to get Beth.

Ella LeRoy found the performance painful to watch. Had she been wrong all those years ago when she insisted Annette marry Gordon, the well-known, well-to-do scientist who belonged to the correct church and the correct political party? Certainly, he treated Annette like his own personal piece of equipment, dedicated to anticipate his every whim, without feelings or needs of its own—but that was men for you, plain and simple. In return, Annette had servants and an exquisite home and time to take tennis lessons. That's the way the world worked.

Annette emerged from the house, her arms wrapped tight around the baby.

"Nnnn," said Beth, a tiny fold of skin forming between her eyes.

Ella LeRoy's heart turned to marshmallow, her thoughts equally pink and gooey. Baby Beth, the last love of her life. With Annette and her sisters, she'd been too busy raising the brood to indulge in tenderness. Thank the good Lord for grandchildren. She tickled the baby's chin. "Toodle-oo to you, too, Beth."

Her daughter drew back, baby Beth with her. "Goodbye, Mother. And thank you."

Annette raised her arm in a farewell and her sleeve dropped back. A bracelet of dark marks stood out against the pale white skin above her elbow.

Rage choked Ella's chest, hot, fast, hard. She breathed out, breathed in, then bit her tongue and played blind. If you didn't talk about it, it wasn't real.

Annette was an adult now. It was up to her to speak if she wanted to. The last thing Ella wanted was to trample into her daughter's soul in snake-proof boots.

*Yes, Annette was an adult. Should Gordon ever leave a mark on Beth's beautiful dimpled arm, however...*

She tightened her mouth on the thought.

The morning passed quickly, too quickly. Annette took a deep breath, then another, as the car neared Gordon's office. Gordon hadn't wanted them to come, and yet there they were. She would have to pay the price later, of that she was sure.

The BRAVO building loomed over her despite its unimposing five-floors. Even here, in the very centre of Pretoria, not many buildings were taller than ten floors, with a nearby Volkskas Bank towering over its neighbours in its thirty-level glory, and the Reserve Bank only just emerging from its foundations.

A wrought-iron security gate barred Annette's way to BRAVO's underground parking. Sick with worry, her knuckles aching from clutching the steering wheel, she spoke to the intercom and identified herself to Sally with a password. Sally was expecting them, but rules were rules.

An elevator carried them up to the reception area. Although BRAVO did not have any clients—no official clients at any rate— the entrance lobby included opulent seats arranged into groups of two and three. The secretarial desks hid from view behind mirrored partitions.

Danny put down the video camera he had borrowed from Gordon for his school project and began fiddling with it.

*Boys.*

Julie ran straight to Sally. "Hi," she called out. "Excuse me, but your blouse is not tucked in properly on the side. Here, let me help. What are you reading?"

*Girls.*

"It's just a book about, oh, politics and stuff," replied Sally. A squeal of wood on wood as a drawer slid shut. "I have to keep up to date with what's going on in the world. It's part of my job."

Julie's voice lost all curiosity. "Ah, politics. Boring. Don't you ever read, you know, fun books, to decide whether they should be censored or not?"

"Julie!" Scandalised, Annette rose to her feet. "Please come join me, young lady."

"Right-o, Mom."

Julie ran past her and jumped onto a leather-covered armchair. "I'm a big important client," she intoned in a deep voice. "Bring me a coffee with two sugars and real cream, none of that powder stuff. I want what's inside the fridge, not what's on top." Her giggle referred to a current TV advert for a coffee creamer that didn't need refrigerating.

Guilt stabbed at Annette's conscience.

*The children watched too much TV.*

Perhaps the government had been right to ban television for all those years, claiming it was a devil's tool for spreading communist propaganda and immorality? Was it really a coincidence that the Soweto riots took place six months after the first television broadcast in South Africa?

Sally drew near, the blouse now immaculately tucked in. "Sorry to keep you waiting. You're a bit early, I think."

Just like Gordon to play power games.

"Yes, a little early."

"No problem. Gordy will be ready for you in a moment."

*Gordy?*

An unusual way of speaking about your boss, but then what did she know? She had never held a job. When she'd agreed to marry Gordon, it was on the condition she be allowed to go to university. Gordon had been all for it, but she fell pregnant with Danny almost straight away. Not that she was sorry now, not at all. It's just that…

She studied her own reflection in the partitions. Approaching thirty-three, she looked her age. In contrast, Sally's skin was smooth like fresh cream, untouched by freckles, kissed golden by the sun. So young. So pretty in that sunny girl-next-door way and smelling like garden flowers.

Even Danny looked up from the camera. His face changed. "May I shoot a test video of you, please, Miss Martins?"

When Sally smiled, she smiled with her whole face. She was smiling now. "But of course. Go." With the camera rolling, she swanned up and down the lobby.

Annette watched the performance with growing unease. Although Danny's expression was obscured by the video camera, his body language spoke only too clearly.

"Don't worry," Sally's stage whisper hit her full in the face.

"Your precious boy is safe with me. I only like older men."

The sight of Annette made Doc's breath shallow. He willed his blood to flow back into his brain. "Always a pleasure, my dear. You look stunning."

Her face glowed with pleasure. Doc took her cool fingers in his, cursing Gordon to an eternity in hell.

*Did the stupid sod never pay his wife a simple compliment?*

Annette tucked a loose strand behind her ear. "The pleasure's all mine. Thank you for inviting us. How's your lovely wife?"

Not a single flirty note.

*Christ.*

The most beautiful woman he'd ever met, and she acted like a nun.

"My lovely wife is lovely, as always," he replied with heartfelt indifference. "I see Sally's been keeping you company. And the children are in Gordon's office already. Splendid."

He wanted to take Annette out—the only real coffee shop in Pretoria was a block away—yet he sensed she would think it inappropriate. Damn it, it would indeed be highly inappropriate, the way he felt about her.

"Sally, would you like to take the rest of the afternoon off? Gordon won't need you. I've told him to make his family visit a priority."

"Thank you." Sally zipped up her miniature handbag, hesitated, opened and shut one of the desk drawers, then pushed her chair in with a decisive shove. "That's very kind. See you tomorrow."

"I've asked Nick to show the children around his lab," Doc called after her, "so don't tempt him into going home early with you."

"No, Doc, of course not."

*No, of course not.*

Sally didn't care one bit about Nick. Sally had her eye firmly and steadfastly on Gordon.

And perhaps, perhaps, if he played his cards right, everybody would get their wish. He himself would get Annette, and Sally would get Gordon.

Come to think of it, who cared about Sally and Gordon? As long as he got Annette, he'd be a happy man.

A very happy man.


Gordon couldn't wait for the ordeal to end. Sure, he loved his children as much as the next family guy, but they had no right to be here, in his place of work, talking to Sally, encroaching on his professional time.

Although Doc considered this an important exercise in BRAVO's public relations and an excellent opportunity to invest in the future of the country by promoting science and political principles to young South Africans, Gordon's mind was elsewhere. Peace and quiet as he made the most important moral decision of his life—was that too much to ask?

Danny was anything but quiet. "Julie, open the door again, walk through it, look directly at the camera and say: We're here to look at some cool science."

Julie disappeared through the door leading back to the lobby, only to burst into the office again.

"We're here to look at—Pappa, you need to straighten your tie. And why is your shirt buttoned up skew?"

Gordon adjusted his shirt hastily, his conscience burning. "No, it's fine, honey, just untidy. Let's try again."

"We're here to look at some really cool science!"

"Super. Pa, could you please tell us what you do here?"

The gigantic eye of the camera on his son's shoulder made Gordon uneasy. He was aware that his every gesture was being faithfully duplicated onto the VHS cassette inside, the ill-buttoned shirt the evidence of his indiscretion.

"Um, it's nothing special, really. I think up new projects, analyse the results of experiments and write reports about my findings."

"Julie, say: You see, sometimes there is more to science than mixing *colourful liquids and watching them explode. Science is also about meticulous observation, comparing figures and typing hefty reports."*

Julie pulled a face. "But we haven't seen any colourful liquids explode!"

"We will. Doctor Monterra promised to take us to the lab. Now say: *You see, sometimes there is more to science—*"

Gordon relaxed as he took in the animated face of his daughter. A born actress. The moment her brother aimed the camera at her, Julie became a different person: grownup, confident, radiating that intangible something that could only be described as audience magnetism.

"Pa. May I please have a shot of you typing in your report?"

"I don't type, Danny. Sally does all the admin work for me."

Julie crinkled her nose. "You don't do experiments, Pappa, and you don't type. What do you do at work, then?"

What indeed, he thought. What did he do all day?

I think up different ways in which the government can control the masses, darling, he could say, or rather, could never say to her. I'm responsible for choosing the substance going into the drinking water of the biggest township in the country, he couldn't say that to her either, the same township where school children got shot at by our police only six years ago. In my free time, I cheat on your mother in this very office.

No, he couldn't say any of that. He couldn't tell his daughter what he did all day at work.

"Pappa?"

He put his arm around Julie and kissed the top of her head, right in the middle of the loose orange tangles. She was still in her uniform, but she must have pulled off the compulsory hair ties as soon as she got into Annette's car after school.

"You have a point, darling," he said. "You know what, though? I keep a few neat toys in the lab. This here," the circle he drew with his arm encompassed his desk, three shelves of technical textbooks, a tower of filing cabinets, "is just backstage. The real show is downstairs."

\* \* \*

Nick waited for them with a large block of peppermint Aero, already broken into sharp-edged sections of brown and emerald-green.

"Eat it before it freezes," he joked.

Indeed, the temperature in the lab was well below the norm. Annette felt delicious goose bumps form all along her bare neck. Because of the long sleeves she wore to cover the bruises on her arm, the heat got to her more than usual.

"No, thank you," she said when Nick extended the chocolate her way. The refusal was totally automatic, perfected during the years of her marriage. She never, ever allowed herself to eat anything sugary in front of her husband. Gordon liked having control over her, and it was easier to give in—to pretend to give in. Confrontation always made her throat hurt and her stomach knot. She didn't pick her battles—she simply avoided them.

"I'll eat mummy's piece," offered Julie.

Nick beamed at her. "Good girl. Say, would you like me to show you my spectrometer? All the ladies I meet want to come here to play with it."

An uneasy feeling clouded over Annette, though she couldn't pinpoint why.

Nick talked to the camera. "A mass spectrometer tells you what chemical elements can be found in the sample you're analyzing."

Julie raised her hand. "What sample?"

"For example, you can use it when you want to test for the presence of a chemical in a person's blood."

"Why?" Julie was doing the talking, Danny the filming.

"Let's say you want to see whether they've eaten something they shouldn't have."

"Like?"

Chocolate, thought Annette guiltily, her mind on the hidden stash of pralines in her bathroom.

"Like a certain type of poison. Not all poisons show up in

your blood, but many will, especially if you know what you're looking for."

"Fan-tastic! Do you make poisons in this lab, too?"

"Julie," said Gordon, "I don't think—"

Doc raised a placatory hand. "That's all right. We can talk about poisons in general. Chemistry is fun. Did you know the most dangerous chemicals appear quite harmless? Let's take Dihydrogen Monoxide as an example…"

"Di-hydro-?" Scepticism came through loud and clear in Julie's tone.

"It's a dangerous substance. You die if you inhale it, and yet it's so addictive you die without it."

"Di-hydrogen mono-oxide," repeated Danny thoughtfully from behind the camera. It was the first time he'd spoken since they'd entered the lab. "Di-hydrogen, two hydrogen parts, or H-2. Mono-oxide, or single O. H-2-O. Water."

Pride bubbled over in Annette's heart.

"That's really funny." Julie inclined her head in endorsement. "Will you use it in your project, Danny?"

"I'd rather hear about the real poisons, please, Doctor Monterra."

The camera whirred on, its focus on Doc. Julie, bored and disappointed by the sudden lack of attention, strolled around the lab, opening everything that could be opened and lifting up everything that wasn't nailed down. Annette reprimanded her, Nick said it was no problem. He followed Julie around, gesticulating, prattling and making her chuckle.

They stopped at a cage with fluffy white rabbits. Annette was too far away to hear their conversation, and she froze in shock at the sight of Gordon charging at them like a rhino. He stopped in the other man's face, almost a head taller and half a foot wider.

"That's inappropriate," he bellowed. "I want an apology."

Annette's heart rolled into a tight ball.

*What had Julie done now?*

She hurried, ready to defend her child, ready to place herself between Julie and danger.

"I'm very sorry," Nick was the one who spoke, his voice steady. "I was way out of line."

Julie stood still, eyes downcast, cheeks crimson. The angle of her shoulders shouted defiance and cold calculated revenge. Annette knew how strong-headed her daughter could be, and she steeled herself to handle the situation.

Danny beat her to it. "Father, let us quickly film the final scene. Please? Julie said she knew exactly what she wanted at the end. Julie?" He pointed the camera.

Julie assumed a smiling face. She didn't smile, she simply put on a happy mask. "Ask me what I liked best."

"And this brings us to the end of our quick foray into the world of special agents, who like it shaken, not stirred. Julie, what did you like best about today?"

"Poisons," Julie sent a grin into the camera, and this time it was a genuine, infectious beam. "They are so cool. I didn't know deadly poisons could be sprayed into the air we breathe, injected into creams we put on our skins, or smeared onto razor blades. But hey, don't try it at home! Someone could get hurt." She shot Gordon a venom-filled smirk.

Danny called out, "It's a wrap."

Annette knew his composure, like her own, teetered on the rim between shatter and hold. His hands, steady enough when filming, now began to tremble.

She caught his eye. "It's nothing, Mom," he said. "My muscles are just tired from holding up the camera. It weighs as much as a baby buffalo."

Her Danny boy, always ready with the right justification. Like mother, like son.

Annette stepped into her own role. A perfect wife and mother taking her children home. "Thank you so much for your time and hospitality."

She touched Gordon's cheek with her lips. A hint of scent, not his cologne, something more floral, registered in her brain. Before she could wonder about it, a warm insistent hand tugged hers.

"I need the toilet," whispered Julie into her ear.

"Upstairs, off the reception area, Copperlocks," Annette whispered back. "Want me to show you?"

"Thanks, I can manage."

Julie didn't even glance in the direction of the toilets. When they'd walked into the office two hours earlier, her Pappa's secretary had been reading a book, which she had dropped into an open drawer as soon as she'd heard them approach. But what Miss Martins, Sally, couldn't hide in the drawer, were her red cheeks.

Curiosity had eaten Julie ever since.

Now, shaking with rage at her father's behaviour, she wanted to read the forbidden text more than ever. She needed a distraction.

*How could her Pappa behave that way? How could he embarrass her in front of a nice guy like Nick?*

She found the book in the middle drawer. The cover alone made her heart beat faster: a dark-skinned young man without a shirt, unfastening the top button of his blue jeans.

*Gulp!*

Across the picture spread an angry red ink stamp:

CENSORED—PROHIBITED.

The pages fell open at a bookmark, a thick paper envelope. Julie pushed it off with an impatient brush of her fingers.

> *"...Tanya liked her men older, seasoned with experience. Men who could still teach her a thing or two about gourmet food, human psychology and the wild ways of sex.*
>
> *She doubted Andy had noticed her in the hotel foyer earlier in the morning, but he was certainly noticing her now. He was no exception: every male between the age of one and one thousand paid attention when Tanya took off her clothes..."*

Julie's heart raced. This was so naughty. She skipped a few pages.

> "...Andy stood behind her, his burnt-sugar skin gleaming with diamond droplets of ocean water, his smooth chest rising and falling. With his wet hair plastered to his skull and his wet jeans he looked good enough to eat..."

"What on earth are you doing?"

Julie jumped up, dropping both the book and the bookmark in the process, before she realised who had spoken. A few dark strips of film fell out of the envelope. She didn't pay them any attention.

"Idiot," she said. "You gave me a fright."

Danny strolled over, picked up the book off the floor and looked at the back cover. "You shouldn't be reading such stuff."

"Well, she shouldn't be reading it, either. It's banned."

"And rightly so. This book is about a white lady and a black man. It's against the law."

"They're not breaking the law, stupid. They're not South African."

"I mean, it's against the law for us to be reading about it." Danny dropped the book back into the drawer. "Come, let's go back downstairs."

They said their thank-you and goodbye in the lab. Julie noticed her father kept standing between her and Nick.

*Silly. Silly, silly, silly.*

Nick was such fun! What was Pappa's problem? Was he jealous of people paying attention to his pretty daughter? At twelve, she was practically a grown-up, and it was high time for Pappa to realise it. He had no right! It's not as though he'd noticed the way Nick had brushed her soon-to-be growing boobs with his shoulder when he was showing her all the cool chemicals, nor the way he'd touched the inside of her wrist when she stood next to him, that brief, wonderfully disturbing, secret caress. Just thinking about it sent a sweet tickle down her back. But Pappa had spoiled it all.

She would pay him back in spades. Whatever *in spades* meant.

In the elevator down to the parking lot, Julie asked the bombshell question she had rehearsed since she'd seen the forbidden book's cover: "Pappa, why is it against the law for white ladies to have sex with black men?"

Bull's eye. Pappa looked as though somebody had slapped him.

"Where did you hear that word?"

Mom, being Mom, spoiled the fun all too soon. "It would lead to interracial tension, Copperlocks, if we started marrying across the colour borders."

Pappa coughed and looked away. "And white cops shooting at black school children on the streets of Soweto is guaranteed to promote peace and harmonious interracial relations."

Julie had learnt about sarcasm at school only the week before, when discussing literary devices in books. It was cool to see it used in an everyday conversation.

Rage simmering in his gut, Gordon waved his family off in the bowels of BRAVO's building. He made sure the grate fell shut behind them, placed his briefcase on the front seat of his BMW, and took the stairs back up.

As usual, he'd take a shower before heading home, to wash the grubbiness of BRAVO and Sally off his skin, but there was something else he had to take care of first.

Nick was in the lab, a test tube in hand, his brow furrowed. He lifted his eyes at the sound of the lab door slamming.

"Easy now," he said. "You don't want to fight me. Back in the army, I spent two years practicing hand-to-hand combat."

Gordon struggled to control his breath, short after running four flights of stairs. *I must take up jogging again*, he thought irrationally, for he knew the reason his heart was galloping, and it had nothing to do with his fitness levels. He stared into the smirking face of the younger man.

"She's twelve," he rasped.

Nick raised his hand in a mollifying gesture. "Look. I was only flirting with Julie to make her feel better about herself. To make her more confident around boys."

Gordon felt a tightening in his chest. Julie, his little girl.

*Flirting? Boys?*

If he weren't so very sure he'd get creamed, he would have punched that smirk right through Nick's face.

He waited until his voice was even. "If you ever as much as think about my daughter again," he said, "I will personally insert a test tube of Hekate up your arse and kick it until the glass shatters."

While Julie drifted in and out of sleep that night, she kept thinking about Nick and the censored book.

*...His burnt-sugar skin gleaming with diamond droplets of ocean water, his smooth chest rising and falling...would you like me to show you my spectrometer? All the ladies I meet want to come here to play. Have another piece of chocolate... With his wet hair plastered to his skull and his wet jeans he looked good enough to eat—look at the rabbits, Julie. Do you know what they love doing best?*

Julie shook herself awake. Even in the darkness of her room, she knew she was blushing. It was all Sally's fault for reading forbidden books and leaving them lying around. As somebody who worked for a special government agency, she should have known better.

It was a dangerous, dangerous book. Thank goodness it was safely back in Sally's drawer, far away from temptation's reach.

Something niggled still. Julie cast her mind back to the events of the afternoon.

*Nick, the rabbits, that humiliating incident with Pappa, Sally's stupid book...*

*Sally's stupid book. Yes, that was it. Whatever had happened to the envelope of negatives that served as a bookmark?*

# Chapter 7—Tuesday, Three Days after the Murder

WITHOUT A WORD, Watson tossed the photo prints onto Sally Martins' desk. They were blown up to ridiculous proportions and still sticky from the photographic fixer.

"What—how—what?" Sally slumped in her chair, her mouth sucking in air like a goldfish. Watson liked the comparison: goldfish were pretty, dumb, aggressive and in the habit of polluting their home.

Sally's face turned pale, then pink, then pale again. "It's not me," she whispered.

"Did I say it was?"

Her mouth wobbled. Obliging tears followed. With her makeup smudged, she looked frightfully young and inexperienced, and yet far from innocent. "I thought he would marry me," she said, her voice swollen with tears. "Gordon was everything I've ever wanted: smart and successful and good-looking."

"And old enough to be your father."

She sniffed. "So? He was a gentleman. Not like the guys my own age who only think about themselves." A tissue appeared out of nowhere. "Nick would never dream of opening a door for me or asking me about my ambitions. Gordon wanted to get to know the real me."

*Yeah, right.*

"How often did you and your boss…" he paused tactfully, let her come out with the details.

Halting every five words, she told him what he needed to know and far more than he ever wanted to find out.

"All right," he cut her short. "How did you take the photos?"

"With a hidden camera, set on a timer."

"Which you got where?"

"I—borrowed it from the storeroom. I wanted—he said he wouldn't leave his family, and I wanted…" she trailed off.

Watson couldn't help finishing the sentence for her. "To blackmail him."

"No!" Too loud, too indignant. "I wanted him to," she bit her lip, an action Watson had learned to distrust, "to—to—realise what he'd be missing, to see how much fun we have together. Men like looking at such pictures, right?"

She cast him a look. The involuntary twitch of his lips must have encouraged her, for she straightened her shoulders and sent him a conspiratorial smile.

"His wife is frigid," she whispered, oblivious of the anger her words awakened. "She would never make love on a desk or on the floor. And she would never take photos."

Watson curbed his emotions and slowly counted to ten. "Go on."

"If Gordon realised we're on the same wavelength, you know, in that way, he'd forget his family obligations and marry me. I'd never blackmail him, I swear!"

He pretended to believe. "When did you show him the photos?"

"I didn't. I used the company's darkroom to develop the film last week, but I couldn't get access to the printer. It's in the main reception area, and people forever walk past it. I couldn't risk it."

"Your boyfriend," Watson tapped his notebook to centre her attention. "Did he know about your *arrangement* with your boss?"

Sally's shrug emphasised the dismissive words. "Nick is a nothing. He talks dirty and only sees me as a pair of boobs to fondle."

Watson doubted Gordon Pretorius had ever seen her as anything more.

Madam Annette had to spend the night in hospital, so Hester cleared the breakfast table with Beth wrapped in a blanket and fastened securely onto her back African style. The baby dozed on and off to the sway of Hester's hips. Hester could get her work done without letting Beth feel abandoned or emotionally distanced. Bad enough her mother was far away…

"Heavens." Hester heard the old madam's voice. "What in the name of the Lord are you doing with the baby? She could fall out of the blanket and get hurt. Take her off at once."

In all her life, Hester had never heard of a baby falling off its mother's back anywhere in Africa. This was the traditional way, far more natural than the cold prison of a baby stroller so favoured by the madams. What next, fumed Hester silently, she'll forbid me to carry shopping bags on my head?

"Yes, missus," she replied. She bent over, took a firm grasp on Beth's arm and swung her effortlessly forwards straight into her pillow-like arms. Beth cooed, the old madam gave a shriek of concern. Real or for show, Hester couldn't tell.

"Give her here," demanded Mrs. LeRoy.

Beth started squealing the moment her grandmother took hold of her. Hester stretched out her arms in an instinctive effort to soothe and protect.

"Go wash the dishes," commanded the old madam. "I'll put the baby to bed. She needs to cry herself to sleep. She's clearly tired."

She's clearly terrified, thought Hester.

The Minister With No Official Portfolio looked at the latest security tapes. Mrs. Pretorius was supposed to be looking for the top secret documents. Instead…

His patience slithered from him, slippery like a good diplomat. He placed a call. "What do you fucking mean, she's in a hospital guarded by the fucking police?"

He listened. Interrupted. "When are they releasing her?"

"Sir, they want to keep her for at least a couple of days…"

A couple of days wouldn't do. He wanted to spend time with his family, not sorting out this sorry mess. "Arrest her. Section 6. Now."

If she could think of a place her husband hid the documents, she'd tell him. The interrogation room was ready, washed down and empty. The lawyer's secretary had apparently left a note citing boyfriend trouble as reason for her sudden departure. Her body would never be found. His people knew ways safer than entrusting a corpse to the South African post office system.

"Where am I?"

At the back of his mind, Watson wondered why people who regain consciousness always wanted to know where they were. Not: *what happened, am I hurt, where is my wallet*. It's always *where am I*, as though something primordial inside them needed to assess immediate danger.

He touched her hand. "In hospital. You've had a shock and been sedated, that's all."

*That's all, except for a severe case of malnutrition, according to the attending medic.*

"The children?" Raw panic in her voice now, eyes dilating as she attempted to sit up in bed, shoulders already uncurling for a fight with an invisible enemy.

"They're with your mom. She's staying in one of the spare bedrooms while you're getting well. We reckoned it was better than to move the children to her house. A policeman was on duty all night at the mansion, too. He's just been replaced by another. We're keeping a 24-hour watch over your family."

*And on you.*

Annette hoisted herself onto her elbow, her skin paler than usual.

"I have to go home. Now."

"In a few minutes. Lie down flat for now. We'll get you home as soon as you're better. The doctor won't sign the discharge papers while your cheeks are green."

He kept talking. It was better than the alternative. The alternative was to tell her the truth: she may not be going home at all.

As of the previous day, when she'd been caught trying to burn those negatives depicting her dead husband in a compromising situation with his secretary, Annette had officially become the prime suspect in her husband's murder investigation. The brigadier wanted her arrested.

Annette fell back onto the bed, whispered, "The photos."

"I have them," he replied, hating himself for misleading her. "They're safe."

He did have them. The negatives were evidence, marked and catalogued and locked up in the police safe.

"The drawing," Annette tried again.

That was a bloody good drawing. They had already compared it with samples from Danny's room, other drawings, although none of them remotely on the same topic. The lad had talent, all right, and he was a normal, red-blooded thirteen-year old, judging by the charred remains of *Bunny Girl*. When Watson drew naked women, he never achieved that level of realism. Sure, he had never been a great artist, but Danny's sketch showed more than talent, it showed knowledge that could only have come from having seen those negatives.

Which meant Danny had known about his father's infidelity, known about it not as an abstract concept, but a harsh reality. The boy's devotion to his mother Watson had witnessed personally.

*Was Danny capable of murdering his father?*

"What about the drawing?" he asked.

"It's not the same thing." Annette's voice was no more than a breath now. She was lying back, her red locks spread over the pillow like copper wire lacework, her eyes shut.

"I found the drawing—elsewhere. Not with the photos. Was going to shout at Danny for drawing naughty pictures—waited for a good moment—then I found the negatives—somewhere else."

She was so transparent in her lie, so vulnerable. Something

tight and heavy inside Watson's chest yearned to protect her at all cost. The medical examination she underwent while sedated had revealed bruises on her arm. The pig of a husband must have been taking out his frustrations on her. Not regular beatings, just a shove here or there, a restraining squeeze on her arm perhaps—bloody bastard. Who could blame her for exacting revenge?

*Oh, yeah, that's right, the law would.*

"Danny…"

"Danny's safe and sound. I'll look after him. Try to get some rest."

"You caught me."

"Hey?" What was she talking about? That he had caught her destroying the evidence of Gordon's extramarital affair? That he had caught her, the culprit responsible for her husband's murder?

"You caught me," she repeated. "I fainted and was falling, but I didn't hit the ground. You caught me."

Her face looked small in the cage of hair. She was Annette, Annette LeRoy, his high school sweetheart.

"I'll always catch you," he said, his body drawing to attention, as though swearing an oath of allegiance. "I will never let any harm come to you or your children."

Annette inhaled the deep breath of somebody asleep. Watson wasn't sure she'd even heard him. Her face was relaxed now, still under the influence of the tranquilisers trickling through her body.

He stuck his head into the corridor. "Find Jones for me," he called out to the first subordinate uniform he saw.

Jones reported to him in less than five minutes. "HQ would like an update, sir. They are asking whether we are ready to close the investigation. The newspapers are panting for a Daisy de Melker story."

Daisy de Melker, the woman who, half a century before, had been found guilty of poisoning three men for insurance money. The evidence had been flimsy at best, but the public didn't care. She had been hanged proclaiming her innocence, her name a synonym for husband-killer. A Black Widow.

Annette would not become another Daisy, even if he had to break every rule in the book.

"Captain. Are we arresting Mrs. Pretorius, sir?"

"Negative, Jones. Tell HQ we'd like a background check on Doctor Monterra. Army records, if he's been in the army. A financial assessment. Our own archives. He must have undergone a security clearance interview before he joined BRAVO, so get us access to that. University friends, school teachers, family—see whether you can trace any of them."

He was going way over the top. If this was the wrong call, his career was over. He didn't care—much.

Today was Pappa's birthday, Julie realised as soon as she woke up. His forty-second birthday. Only, he wasn't here to celebrate it. Somehow, it made the whole horrible situation even more horrible.

She stared at the card she'd made for her father the week before until she thought she'd go blind. Her eyes smarted, yet tears wouldn't come. Drawings of hearts, balloons and a birthday cake with forty-two candles. Too colourful. Too cheerful. Too alive.

Her mouth tasted salty. Today was Pappa's birthday, and nobody had remembered, except Julie herself. Nobody cared. Nobody had loved him the way she did. She ripped the card in half, then into quarters and eighths.

The suitcase was packed and ready. One phone call to Nick and she would be out of here. But not on Pappa's birthday. She owed his memory at least that much.

She wondered why her mother had stopped coming by her door to check up on her. Danny and her grandma tried to talk through the door, but Julie put on her headphones to drown out their voices. Her mom hadn't even bothered, though. Her sudden indifference hurt.

Julie tiptoed to her bedroom door and flung it open.

"Mom," she shouted into the corridor. "Mo-o-o-o-m."

Silence.

\* \* \*

Danny must have found the negatives in Gordon's study at home, thought Annette drowsily. Or perhaps at BRAVO when he went in to make the film. Either way, he realised what he was looking at, because he had used Sally's photos as a blueprint for the nude figure he had drawn.

Her boy had seen those images. Took a pencil, his blond head at an angle, his steady hand forming the lines of upper body, thighs, breasts...A trickle of thin, sour saliva, pooled in her throat.

*Why would Danny want to draw the woman who was his mother's rival? And how did he come across the negatives?*

Danny was no snoop. He would never open Gordon's briefcase without permission. Snooping was Julie's domain...

Annette couldn't follow a straight line of reasoning.

*Gordon's briefcase?*

The medicine was still working its way out of her system, muddling her brain, playing with her emotions.

*Where was Gordon's briefcase?*

I have to find, she thought, not entirely certain what it was she had to find.

"You can't arrest any of my patients," the hospital director told the special team that worked for The Minister With No Official Portfolio. "Not without a warrant signed personally by the Minister of Law and Order."

Normally, the director detested the South African bureaucracy. Looking into the gangster faces of the two gorillas who wanted to execute the horror-laden Section 6, however, he felt smug beyond words.

Watson could've kicked himself. For Annette, for the sake of their history together, he was going against procedure, breaking the very law he had sworn to uphold. No fool like a sentimental fool, he thought.

Annette was a symbol of what they'd once had. Now he was through with love. He was not in love with Annette Pretorius the way he had been with Annette LeRoy. Anything he felt now had to do with the age-old instinct of a caveman ingratiating himself into the sleeping hides of an attractive female. Perhaps he should hunt a woolly mammoth, too.

"Jones?"

"Yes, sir."

"Any more forensic results?"

"No, sir. I've just checked with the lab. We should have chemical analysis within an hour. The autopsy, however, is somewhat tricky—their word, sir, not mine—and the pathologist is asking for more time."

"Hell." That's not what he wanted to hear. He was damned if he knew why, but he wanted all his facts together before he started forming theories. A vague feeling he was missing something flitted around his tired brain.

*Suicide, car fumes, timing.*

"Jones, you know how last week we got called out to that bastard who shot his family and then tried to gas himself in his garage?"

"Yes, sir."

"How long would you say before the emergency unit got to the scene?"

Jones screwed up his eyes. "More than half an hour, sir. It's because their stupid maid didn't call us straight away—"

"Yes-yes. The point is, it took another five minutes before somebody checked the garage and found him, right? So that's close on forty minutes, and when they dragged the guy out of his car, he was still alive."

"Fat lot of good it did him, sir. The carbon monoxide made him a vegetable for the rest of his life."

"And yet Gordon Pretorius was missing from the party for— what? Twenty-thirty minutes tops. How come he was dead when his wife found him?"

Jones creased his brow. "Thought the wife's not our culprit, sir."

Some people, like Watson, joined the police force because they loved solving who-dun-it riddles. Others, like Jones, simply joined.

"Remember Pretorius recently filled his BMW? Find out how much petrol was gone and how long it would have taken to burn. And don't just say *yes sir*. Use your head, man, think, ask your own questions."

"Yes, sir."

Annette woke up again to the gentle feel of her mother's fingers stroking her hair. A moment of calm cocooned her, before worry broke through. "Who's looking after the children?"

"Hester's giving them lunch, and the house is guarded by the police."

"Can I go home?"

"Soon. How do you feel?"

Annette closed her eyes. How did she feel?

*Gordon had an affair.*

She tasted the words in her head. Nothing. No jealousy, no surprise even. Gordon and Sally in his office together. Still no pain. Sally bent over his desk. Sally arched, her face in the shadows...

A woman with no face or arms. Danny's drawing. Danny.

*Ah, yes, here was the pain, all right.*

She opened her eyes. "I'm fine, Mom. Just get me out of here. I need to be with the children."

Her mother patted her cheek. "They're safe, safer than they've been for years. Everything is as it should be, now."

This was the first time ever her mother admitted she knew not everything had been rosy in Annette's marriage, as close as her mother would come to admit she and Dad had made a mistake all those years ago when they compelled their daughter to marry Gordon.

She wanted to go home. Sat up. "I need my clothes." Something didn't feel right, yet she couldn't figure out what. "At least Beth is too young to remember—" She caught her breath.

*Beth.*

The image of the baby's face should have caused an embarrassing gush of milk. Having gone through an afternoon and a whole night and a morning without feeding, her breasts should have been engorged and aching. Instead, they hung from her body like two empty sacks.

A howl lodged in her throat, too bulky to escape. She croaked, "I've lost my milk, Mother."

"That's all right, Annette. Beth is old enough to be weaned. I asked the doctor to give you a special injection."

The room started to spin. "You what?"

"Annette, listen. You couldn't go on breastfeeding under the circumstances. It would place too much of a strain on you. And with your body full of medication..."

The pain in her temples overwhelmed her thinking processes. "I don't remember signing any forms."

"Don't worry, I signed the medical release forms for you." Her mother looked self-satisfied, actually pleased with her ingenuity. "What you need now is..."

"What I need now is a mother who doesn't always interfere in my life," Annette burst out. Amazing, she had stood up to her mother and the sky wasn't falling down on her head. "It wasn't all right even when I was seventeen, but how dare you decide what's right for me when I'm almost thirty-three?"

"Love, it's the hormones from the injection that have a hold over your mouth. Calm down. If the doctor comes in here to discharge you and finds you in this state..."

Annette buried her face in her hands and tried to take deep, even breaths. When she failed, she forced herself to take shallow ones instead. It didn't help, but it was a start.

She glanced at the watch.

9:20.

Just over two and a half hours till the appointment at the House of Coffees.

How was she to get out of this damned hospital? Find the

documents?

She flinched when her mother touched her shoulder. "Remember. I *always* know what's best for you. I would move heaven and earth to help you get it."

Annette wondered why the words made her shudder.

She looked at the clock. 9:30.


"Trevor Watson. Just the man I wanted to see."

"Mrs. LeRoy," Watson acknowledged. His least favourite person on earth. "How can I help?"

"You'd better figure out exactly how you can help, young man. My daughter's life is in danger, what with all those threatening letters. What steps are you taking to protect her?"

"We have a policeman inside the mansion around the clock, ma'am. A patrol car drives by regularly. While Annette's in hospital, a constable's on duty outside her room…" Then Watson's brain caught up with his mouth. "What do you mean, *all* those letters?"

"This was in the post box this morning."

Another birthday-card envelope with Annette's name scribbled on it. This time, Watson handled it through his hankie. The text talked about a wife paying for her husband's sins.

"Jones," he called out. "Place the patrol car outside the Pretorius property permanently, then have this analysed. Prints, type of pen used, handwriting."

He felt a hand on his shoulder, looked into the eyes of the hospital director.

"A word in your ear, Watson. Before the lady gets discharged."


The clock ticked through the seconds, minutes, hours. Panic rising acrid in her chest, Annette watched the hands move past ten o'clock, then eleven. Noon was less than fifty minutes away, and she didn't even have the documents.

"Sorry to disturb you," she called out to a passing nurse. "Is the doctor…"

"Still in a meeting, Mrs. Pretorius."

*Drat.*

The clothes she'd arrived in were folded neatly on a chair in the corner of the hospital room. Her handbag, slung over the chair's backrest, swayed in the gentle breeze. Annette shucked off the hospital shirt. A minute later, she sneaked out of her room.

A pimply policeman positioned in the corridor stood up to attention when he saw her.

"Ma'am? You can't leave."

Annette put on her bubbly guise. "Oh dear. Oh, no, wouldn't dream of leaving. It's just that I've remembered something. I need to find Captain Watson right away."

"Ma'am, I'm afraid I can't let you——"

"Of course not. But would you mind terribly much looking for him? I'll just go back to my room. Feel quite woozy." She put one hand flat against the wall. "You go. Bring Trevor. Captain Watson."

As soon as his back was turned, Annette tiptoed to the nearest door, marked Staff Only, and found herself in a small room. An iron and an ironing board, a tea urn, a hanger with white uniforms. The nurse's cap didn't quite manage to cover the mass of her red hair, so she twisted the bulk and tucked it under her collar. She left via the sliding door leading to the garden, waved to the guard at the main gate and hailed a taxi.

"The House of Coffees, please."

"Pretorius Street?"

"Yes."

Julie had once asked whether one of the main streets of the city was named after her daddy. The memory reached its tentacles around Annette's heart and squeezed.

Watson took twenty seconds to process what the doctor had told him. Severe malnutrition, probable anorexia. Numerous bruises, position suggestive of domestic violence. As though money and jealousy hadn't been enough motive to murder her husband, they could now add abuse victim to the list.

They couldn't have done a better job if they were trying to frame her.

"One more thing," the doctor said.

"*Ja?*"

"Just had a visit from two gentlemen. Big, burly, you know the type."

Watson did.

"They pulled Section 6 on your lady."

"The fuck they did."

The doctor raised a calming hand. "Fortunately, this is a medical facility. Can't extract ill people, not even under Section 6. They're jumping through the legal hoops now, but it's only a matter of time—"

Watson's mind worked with the speed of a cheetah.

*Hide Annette at his place? Absurd. At her mom's place? They're sure to look there, too.*

"Can't you tell them how sick she is?"

The doctor shook his head. "Not if they have the paperwork, no."

Only one thing to do. Arrest her for the murder of Gordon Pretorius and get her tangled up in the criminal justice system. You couldn't arrest someone under Section 6 if they were already arrested. Sure, you could interrogate—Watson felt dread slide down his spine—but you couldn't hold them indefinitely.

"Ok, thanks, man," he said.

Outside the doctor's office, one of the pimply policemen clicked his shoes. "The lady's looking for you, sir."

Watson hurried to Annette's room, the young policeman, Watson noted with satisfaction, unable to keep up.

He knocked, knocked again, entered.

The room was empty.

Watson searched the hospital. Had the special agents already arrested Annette under Section 6? Panic filled his brain in handfuls of sharp bright red spots.

"Captain Watson," a uniformed man said. It wasn't a question.

"That's right." Watson peered at the uniform. Not police. Not army. Not air force or navy.

*Which left—what?*

"Where is Annette Pretorius?"

"Why are you asking?"

A badge flashed in front of Watson's eyes. "Where is she?"

Watson shrugged. Said nothing.

"Captain," the uniform tried again. "You don't want trouble."

"Why? Do you?"

"Captain. Your career depends on your cooperation here."

"My career," Watson sucked through his teeth with deliberation, spat on the hospital floor, barely missing the other guy's shoes, "is so far down the latrine, you would have to get your eyebrows dirty to rescue it."

The coffee shop was almost full and Annette struggled to find the last empty table. The clock said 11:57. She ordered a filter coffee with milk, and, when pressed for details about the beans, read out the first label on the cylindrical containers, without taking in the name.

11:59.

She scrutinised the faces of her fellow coffee-drinkers. Groups of businessmen, all of them in suits and neckties despite the oppressive heat outside. Not a single female, apart from herself and the black waiting staff. And no wonder—most women only ventured into the city to shop, and they wouldn't waste time meeting for coffee when they could do it at home on any other morning.

Midday. The door opened and two more business suits came in. Their necks moved as they inspected the tables, all of them occupied. The taller of the two zeroed in on Annette.

"May we join you?"

Annette swallowed a ball as prickly as a porcupine. "I'm waiting for someone."

"Perhaps you're waiting for us?"

"Perhaps." Her throat was tight. She ran her dry tongue over her lips. "I don't have them yet. I've—been ill. I'll get them to you as soon as..."

"Pardon?" Total incomprehension in the suit's face. "I just thought you might like some company, a pretty thing like you."

The two men sat down. Annette didn't know what to make of it. Were they acting?

"Your coffee, ma'am," the waitress arrived at her elbow, placed a steaming cup on the round table in front of her. "Will there be anything else?"

"Get lost, *kaffir*," the man waved the waitress away. "White people talking."

Annette took the coffee cup in her hands, leaned over and poured the contents into the man's lap. "Manners," she said in her best mommy-tone and walked out of the shop.

"If you find her alone, arrest her," The Minister With No Official Portfolio ordered. "If she's tailed by the foreign press, it's back to Plan A. Make her find the files. Set up another rendezvous."

Secretly, he was hoping for the latter outcome. Enough blood had been shed already. The pretty face of Vermeulen's secretary had haunted his dreams the previous night. He was counting the days till he caught up with his wife and daughter in Mauritius. Hoping a holiday far away from all this mess would bleach away the nightmares.

As soon as she arrived home and checked up on Julie and Danny, Annette took Beth upstairs to the master bedroom. No, she reflected as her gaze skimmed Gordon's side of the bed, not the master bedroom any more. Her own.

The feeding armchair was still there. Thank goodness her mother didn't think to order it removed. Annette settled down into it and unbuttoned her blouse.

Gordon had forbidden her to breastfeed baby Danny and baby Julie, so that her body wouldn't get ruined. With Beth, a late lamb of a surprise after an almost twelve-year gap and all the miscarriages, he'd said nothing. In hindsight, Annette realised he must have been too distracted by Sally. At the time, though, Annette had simply been grateful, lost in the beauty of the additional bond between her and her baby.

The bond was broken now. Beth's miniature face twisted in bafflement, as though to say, *"Why are you putting that in my mouth?"* She refused to latch onto the empty breast. Annette rocked the baby to sleep with a bottle of formula. Crying would have helped, except Annette was done crying.

The phone rang, and she answered, Beth still in the crook of her arm.

"The documents," said the androgynous voice.

Something exploded in her head. "Screw you," she hissed into the receiver. "I don't have your stupid documents. Leave. Us. Alone."

Watson spent ninety-two nerve-racking minutes searching the hospital grounds for Annette. In the ninety-third minute, he received word from his team at the crime scene. She was home, safe.

He returned to the mansion, debriefed the squad car, found Annette in the lounge. Huddled over a cup of coffee, she looked small, shattered and scared. Not the best time to take her to task over slipping out of the hospital.

Does she know, he wondered. Does she know that she's facing arrest from two factions? He could protect her from the criminal police. The other—he wasn't so sure.

He wanted to tell her it was good to have her home, thought better of it. The words would have come across too intimate, something a husband would say to a wife. "How do you feel?" he asked instead.

Annette squared her thin shoulders. "Thank you. Everybody's been so kind, worrying about me." She gestured towards a mass of ribbons and cellophane on the coffee table. "Doc has just brought me this basket. So thoughtful."

Come to think of it, there was a car parked outside the

mansion. Watson had assumed it was the press. "Where's the thoughtful Doc now?"

"By the pool. Giving Julie some tips on improving her mental game during a race."

*Right.*

Watson wondered what the hell was going on.

Julie felt the heat of the sun on her scalp and the wet of the pool water on her face. It wasn't right that her father could no longer feel anything. Not the sun. Not the water. And not how much she missed him.

"Julie." Danny's voice was casual. Too casual? "What do you think he wanted?"

"Mr. Monterra? To show me how to use drafting to conserve energy in a race."

"He came all this way to teach you that?"

Julie didn't see why not. "Sure. What do you think?"

"I think," Danny always spoke slowly, but now his words moved like snails to Julie's impatient ears, "I think Mr. Monterra has a crush on Mom."

"Surely not." If her heart hadn't already been taken by Nick, she may have felt jealous. Instead, she was confused. Why would anybody have a crush on the mother and not her almost teenage daughter?

"What are we going to do about it?" Danny asked. "I don't want Monterra for a step dad."

Step dad? Julie felt the bottom drop out of her stomach. "Nobody," she hissed, "nobody is going to replace Pappa. Deal?"

"Deal."

It took a while to get rid of Monterra. When the door closed at last behind the tiresome Doc, Watson raked through his crew-cut hair. Damn, his nails needed trimming. He looked at Annette. "I have enough evidence to put you in jail. Please give me one good reason not to."

She gave him level eyes. "Very well, then. Ask away."

Whatever game she was playing, Watson hoped he would end up her partner, not her opponent. "Yesterday you found out your husband of fourteen years was having an affair with his secretary," Watson used the clichéd term on purpose. He was after her reaction.

"Excuse me for a second." Annette got to her feet and lifted one of the seats in the leather sofa.

Hidden between the frame and the back support was a white box. Chocolates. She opened the lid, selected a round praline, passed the box to Watson. The top layer was already gone, the second one well underway. He didn't like sweets, took one anyway. "Well?"

"You're making assumptions, Captain. Whatever makes you think I only found out yesterday?"

He almost choked on the hazel cream. "I beg your pardon?"

Not for one second had he considered the possibility that Annette might have stayed married to Gordon had she known the truth. She was too straightforward for that, too honest. That's what you get for investigating a case where you know the suspects, or only *imagine* you know them.

Annette twirled one of her red locks around her finger. "Just saying, don't jump to conclusions. As it turns out, I did find out only yesterday. You want to know what I felt? Nothing. I've been suppressing my feelings for so long, I don't think I have any left."

She said it so lightly, he believed her. The statement threw him off balance, and suddenly he couldn't formulate a single question. What could you ask a woman with no feelings?

'Facts are facts, dear Watson', as Sherlock Holmes would have said. Stick to facts.

"Where did you find the negatives?"

Annette placed another chocolate in her mouth, swallowed it without chewing. "In my husband's desk. After you told me about the fake drawer, I wanted to see it for myself, and I started to rifle through the documents. The envelope with the negatives was stashed in-between the electricity bills."

Watson was pretty sure his team would have found the

negatives had they been hidden in Pretorius's desk. "Why would your husband keep them at home? Anybody could have seen them."

"Nobody ever went near that desk, Trevor. We respect privacy in this house."

*They may respect privacy in this house, but not a woman's right to eat chocolates in the open.*

"Gordon liked his things just so, and he could always tell if anything had been disturbed. I had to teach Hester not to move anything in his room, to just dust around the objects with a feather duster. It avoided—stress."

*Stress. An interesting word to use.*

"How do you mean?"

Annette interlaced the fingers of both her hands. "Gordon was a good man, but if things did not go his way, he would get—edgy. So it was easier to just make sure things went his way."

Watson thought about this. "You're a zebra."

Her laughter sounded hollow. "A zebra?"

"Striking at the first glance, but meek and so very good at blending into the background for safety."

But he knew he wasn't telling the whole truth. She was not a zebra, she was a quagga, an extinct subspecies with stripes only in front, the camouflage failing unless you met head-on.

And he, Captain Trevor Watson, was the hunter about to deliver the fatal arrow, straight through the heart.

"Tell me about the drawing," he said.

She was good. Not a blink. "What drawing?"

"The one of a naked woman," he said. He had to be brutal. Annette was slipping away from him, twisting him around her little finger the way she twisted her magnificent hair. "Of Sally."

She did blush then. "Oh, yes, that. I quite forgot."

*Liar.*

"Tell me about it."

"It has nothing to do with—with anything."

"All the more reason to tell me." Watson poured steel into his voice.

"Please don't put it in the report." She looked away. "I'd be mortified if—if anybody found out. I'm mortified as it is. Don't look at me."

He pretended to look away.

"The picture," she said at last. "I—it was me. I drew it."

The bottom fell out of Watson's world. "You what?"

Men would draw nude pictures to masturbate over, given that porn was difficult to get, and hell, boys would always be boys, no matter how much the government repressed their urges, but *women* drawing such stuff. Unthinkable.

"I saw the negatives and, well, as I said before, I didn't feel anything. So I thought maybe if I were to draw—her—maybe I'd feel something. Jealousy, or even plain envy. She's so young, with a belly that never grew children, and breasts that..." Annette hid her face in the crook of her arm.

"Earlier today you said it was Danny who drew the picture."

She lifted her face. Her cheeks were pink. "No, I didn't."

"You did. You said you were going to punish him for naughty drawings."

"You must have misheard."

*This* was what he got from the woman for whom he was risking his job? He would never understand women. Did she really think she'd get away with blatant fibs and denials?

"Annette," he said patiently. "We compared the picture to samples from your son's portfolio."

"Have you compared them to samples from my portfolio?"

"Hey?"

Annette got up again, searched the drawers of a display cabinet until the crystal glasses rattled. Eventually, she produced a paper napkin and a laundry-marker pencil.

"Gordon marks—marked—the level of the alcohol bottles," she said, wiggling the pencil in explanation. "Hester is a gem, but he said you couldn't trust anybody."

She knelt down by the coffee table, right next to Watson, and began to draw. Firm, confident outlines came first, then colouring-in, artistically smudged by letting the napkin absorb the marker. He could feel the heat of her shoulder, he imagined he could smell her skin underneath the perfume, and from under her fingers, like Venus out of sea foam, emerged the torso of a naked woman. He was no art expert, but it seemed similar enough to the one he had seen before, if you made allowances for the differences between pencil and felt tip.

A naked woman, drawn shamelessly by a woman he longed to see naked. His only escape was to shift away and cross his legs.

His brain was a mess.

Hiding behind the door, Danny couldn't believe his ears. He sometimes saw his mother avoid a difficult topic or give an answer that could, would, be misinterpreted the way she wanted it understood, but he had never before heard her tell an outright lie.

For him, Danny knew straight away. Mom had lied for him, to protect him.

*But from what? Drawing illegal pictures? Possession of stolen negatives? Playing with yourself in the shower? What?*

*Mrs. Pretorius is our prime suspect.*

The words had a dull, persistent ring to them. Day and night, they stayed with him like toothache.

He was relieved to see the cop wouldn't be arresting anybody any time soon. Not with the boner in his trousers Captain Watson was taking so much trouble to conceal.

Annette clenched her fists and waited. Had Trevor bought the lie? She didn't dare look him in the face and yet she had to know.

"Trevor?" she whispered.

*Drat.*

The other policeman, whose name Annette couldn't remember, walked into the room.

"Sorry to interrupt, Captain. The reports are ready and waiting at the office. Shall I drive to fetch them?"

"We'll go together, Jones. I've got everything I need."

Trevor stood up—a bit clumsily—and put her drawing in his pocket. "Thank you," he said, addressing Annette but not looking in her direction. "In addition to the policeman on duty inside the house, a patrol car will be parked outside until we're confident there is no more risk to the family. Good day."

"Good day to you, too." She hid her thoughts behind a farewell smile. What did Trevor mean, he had everything he needed? Everything he needed to do what? Did he really think she was guilty?

Not that she cared what Trevor thought. She only cared about her children.

When the policemen were gone, she said, "You can come out now, Danny. I know you're there."

The phone was ringing when Watson reached his office.

*Damn.*

The last thing he needed now.

"Well, hello there, stranger," he heard as soon as he picked up.

Charlene. Of all the moments to call, she had to choose right now? The case reports were scattered all over his desk and his hands itched to get started.

Still, he owed her. When the call-out to the Pretorius mansion came last Saturday night, Watson had left Charlene in his bed, only half undressed and fully unfulfilled, with her husband out of town. He'd never spared her a thought since.

"Char, I'm sorry. No time to talk. Fieldwork. Only came by my office to sort out the papers."

"I understand."

Judging from her tone, he was telling her nothing new. Watson imagined Charlene ringing his office every fifteen minutes for the last two days. Charlene knew exactly what she wanted and she wasn't shy about getting it. When she'd picked him up at the Policemen's Ball, her rules were as clear as the sky during the dry season: she was married, she was up for some fun with no strings, she found Watson attractive and she was willing—if he wanted her. It had taken him three violent heartbeats to find his tongue, dry-glued to his palate, and say "sure".

Now, six months and nineteen sexual encounters later—he did keep track—the voice on the phone vibrated with the familiar innuendo. "So is your fieldwork likely to interfere with my plans for tonight?"

Watson rubbed his forehead. What now? He was still horny as hell, thanks to the image of Annette's felt tip shading the round breasts of the faceless woman. Yet he could delude himself no longer: Annette LeRoy may have left his life fifteen years before, but she had never left his heart.

"Char, I honestly can't say. Let me call you later."

"You know you can't call me."

The reality of dating a married woman. Don't call her, don't fall in love with her, be happy with what you get. And then there was the guilt....

"Charlene," he began.

At that moment, Jones walked into the office with another manure-green folder. He did an about turn when he saw Watson's face.

"It's all right, Jones, stay," he called out. "I need that file." To Charlene he added, "You will have to excuse me. Perhaps—"

The phone went dead.

"That's great," Watson said into the silence.

*That's just bloody great.*

"Speak to you then. So long."

He replaced the receiver and pulled the phone jack from the wall.

"What reports do we have, Jones?"

Jones pointed to the file in his hand. "With this one, everything."

"Bloody hell. When it rains, it pours, hey?"

Jones shot a glance at the open window, through which the hot breeze puffed in swirls of orange dust. He mopped the marbles of sweat off his neck.

"Wishful thinking, sir."

With Char's phone call, Saturday night came back to Watson. Somebody had taken a shot at him. At the time, he'd assumed it was an accident. Now he was beginning to think otherwise.

Utterly mortified, Annette wished she could crumple up the picture she had drawn, erase it from the surface of the earth and from her memory.

No such luck. Trevor had taken it with him. What would he do with it? Send it away to be analysed? Would an expert be able to tell a son's drawing from a mother's?

Better, much better, if Trevor were to keep it for his own amusement. She blushed when she realised exactly what his amusement might entail.

Watson forgot all about the picture as soon as he opened the first folder. He skipped the autopsy preliminaries.

## Findings

1. Small but deep puncture wound on the outside edge of right palm.
2. Resolving subungual hematoma, right shin.
3. Fingernails bitten to the flesh. Note: because the nails are not deformed, suggestion this was a recent habit, potentially due to anxiety.
4. Scars from 1 smallpox vaccine and 2 tuberculosis vaccines.
5. A crude tattoo of a unicorn between the fifth and fourth toe of the left foot, concealed in the natural folds of the flesh.
6. No surgical scars.
7. The penis is uncircumcised.

*Jeez*, thought Watson. When it came to the ex-husband of the love of your life, number 7 was way too much information.

He passed the sheets to Jones. "*Resolving subungual hematoma* is a *healing bruise* when you say it in English." Let the boy learn.

Watson leafed through the typed sheets of the internal examination, the jargon about Virchow techniques and Y-shaped incisions, the weight of individual organs and the examination of each body part. He noted the changes in the respiratory system and the lack of evidence of cardiac arrest.

He turned to the last page. The cause of death was stated as chemical asphyxiation, but the pathologist reported discrepancies. Some indicators, like the bright cherry red livor mortis, pointed to carbon monoxide poisoning. The colour of the victim's organs wasn't consistent with carbon monoxide inhalation. The drug and poison tests all came back negative. Watson read the personal note to the officer in charge: give us an idea what poison to look for, and we're in business, currently chasing needles in kikuyu grass.

And then, the clincher: Based on the circumstances, the manner of death cannot be classified as natural causes or suicide.

*Hell.*

No chance of it being a suicide, then. So much for wishing the investigation away. This left Annette still very much a suspect as well as a murder target.

Watson stared at the unadorned walls of his office. Where did his loyalty lie? With his job, with his high school girlfriend, with the desire to see justice done?

Too much introspection. Watson plugged the phone back in, dialled Pathology.

"Talk to me," he said without a preamble.

"Ah, Watson, good afternoon to you too."

Watson waited. Why waste words?

"We have a problem. Generally, as the victim inhales more carbon monoxide, the body shuts down. At a twenty percent carbon monoxide level in the bloodstream, the victim will experience dizziness and confusion. At the thirty-five percent comes muscular weakness, and disorientation. At levels greater than fifty percent, the victim loses consciousness and dies."

Watson waited some more, but nothing happened. He opened his mouth, "So in Gordon Pretorius' case, how much carbon monoxide level in the blood are we talking about?"

A click of the tongue from the pathologist. "That's the thing man."

"How much?"

"Less than ten percent."

Watson replayed the figures in his head. "So there is no way this is a case of carbon monoxide poisoning?"

"Let me put it this way," the voice in the receiver sounded cautious now. "While some carbon monoxide poisoning did occur, no way was it severe enough to cause disorientation or death." A pause, then, "Like I said in the report, man, find me the poison."

The knife cut deep and hard into each potato. Ella LeRoy swore under her breath. It was not unladylike if nobody was there to hear it, so she repeated the word louder and louder, until it echoed off the walls and fed the fire of her resentment.

Trevor Watson. After all these years, the danger she had averted fifteen years ago was back. Ella gripped the knife tighter.

Her kitchen was much smaller than her daughter's, and a domestic servant only came to this house three mornings a week, leaving Ella to wash her own dishes and make her own food on Tuesdays, Thursdays, Saturdays and Sundays, while Annette had her Hester full time.

Not that Ella was complaining. One should not expect gratitude, nor consideration, from today's youth.

Take this morning, for instance. As soon as they'd arrived back from the hospital, Annette thanked her, said she'd manage the household herself from here, and would her mother like a lift back to her own house now or after a cup of coffee. Ella was so offended she refused the lift altogether, claiming that *at her age* she needed to exercise her legs from time to time, and that she would walk, *thank you very much*. Besides, it's not like she'd never done it before.

If her daughter had picked up on the sarcasm, she'd given away nothing. Annette had simply nodded and promised to call later. She hadn't, and her mother knew why.

Back home, Ella had watched Trevor Watson as he made his

way to Annette's house. Anger had gripped Ella's senses, yet she could do nothing but watch. Trevor was the investigating officer in charge of the case. He had every right...

The last potato hit the pot when Ella had a brainwave. She dried her hands on the apron and took out the telephone directory.

"Yes," she said into the phone when the duty desk answered. "I'd like to speak to Captain Trevor Watson's supervisor."

Jones was still reading conscientiously, the desire to please radiating from every pore. Watson closed his eyes and tried to order his thoughts.

*So, definitely murder.*

By now he had got used to the idea. The cause of death looked like carbon monoxide poisoning, except for the insufficient blood levels.

A tattoo of a unicorn. Bloody unicorns wherever he turned. The unicorn statue in Gordon's fist, in his study, by his father's body, in Professor Adelbrecht's office.

*What the devil was that all about?*

A shiner on his shin—probably bumped into something. Irrelevant, as it had been healing already at the time of death.

Bitten fingernails—*ja*, that was interesting enough. Watson scrambled around for a pencil and a sheet of paper. "Ask Annette about the nails," he scribbled.

*Annette, no, he was not going there.*

*Nails—nail—the nail in the door to the wine room.*

"Where is the bloody lab report on the nail?" he yelled.

Jones started in his seat, fanned out the papers on the desk and selected a single sheet.

"Right here, sir. Sorry, it..."

Watson snatched the report. The name of the officer preparing the report caught his eye: Charlene's husband was the forensic expert assigned to the case.

*Bugger!*

Three deep breaths later, Watson focused his eyes on the

transcript.

> One nail recovered from a door interconnecting garage
> and wine cellar—ordinary oval wire nail, length
> 50mm…

Right, here it was:

> External examination revealed the head was filed to a
> sharp point once the nail had been hammered in. The
> nail was positioned just above the door handle in such a
> way that it would pierce the skin of a hand that gripped
> the door handle. Although there is fluorescent light in
> the garage, it doesn't reach the door of the wine cellar,
> leaving the handle in shadow.

> Note 1: Tests uncovered traces of blood on the
> sharpened end of the nail and the blood type matches
> that of the deceased.
> Note 2: Traces of various chemicals, e.g., a derivative
> of $C_{34}H_{47}NO_{11}$, were also found on the nail.
> Note 3: There were no surfaces suitable for
> fingerprinting.

The guy was fucking with him. No conclusion, no explanation of
what $C_{34}H_{47}NO_{11}$ was, no personal remark offering guesses or
suggestions. Tension fused Watson's teeth together. This was
war.

Frustration peaking, he tossed the sheet back onto the desk
and watched its erratic downward trajectory.

He never felt very proud of himself for sleeping with married
women. Still, what options did a single male have in this damned
country? Social pressure and religious brainwashing kept girls
virgins until the wedding night. Divorced women were rare and
widows even rarer. Paid sex—not for him. Sordid enough to be
sexually intimate with a stranger, even more so having to hand

over money for the privilege. He knew some of his colleagues went into serial engagements: give a girl a promise and a ring, lure her into bed, stall on setting the date, break up and start all over again. Watson couldn't see himself doing it.

And thus, married women it was. A peculiar morality, and he still had to live with the guilt, but at least he, Watson, was not as hypocritical as some—as Gordon Pretorius, to be exact. Pretorius had gone to church every Sunday morning and screwed his secretary every lunchtime Monday to Friday, if Sally's version of events were to be believed. Personally, Watson had given up on God that fateful day in Soweto, but Gordon had pretended to live by the Ten Commandments...

"Captain?"

Watson gathered his thoughts. "What is it, Jones?"

"I think whatever killed Mr. Pretorius was on that spike in the door, sir. The car's exhaust fumes were a ruse. As you said yourself, sir, it takes longer than half an hour for a man to die of carbon monoxide poisoning. I think Gordon Pretorius was poisoned by those chemical symbols on the spike. Sir."

*Not just an ugly face, then, Jones.*

"Go on."

"The spike was deep in the door. Our perpetrator must have hammered it in after he'd killed Mr. Pretorius. Or perhaps Mr. Pretorius did it himself after he'd cut his hand on it?"

"Jones. Why didn't you go to university after school?"

"With respect, sir, the academia sucks. They never teach you anything useful."

"And you thought the police force would be an improvement?"

A shy grin. "No sir, I knew it would be mind-numbing. But from what I'm told, sitting at the border waiting for an air strike is even more mind-numbing. And potentially fatal."

"You don't believe in dying for your country, Jones?"

"You don't win the war by dying for your country, sir. You win it by making the enemy die. And that's a problem for me, sir. I'd rather arrest killers than become one." Jones caught his eye, faltered, stood to attention. "With respect. Sir."

The words echoed along familiar neurons in Watson's brain. He cleared a sudden build-up in his throat. "At ease, Constable. So what's your plan when the four years of compulsory service in the police force are up?"

"My father has a piece of land in the Cape, sir. I'll help him work the farm, and one day I'll meet a decent girl, get married, have children."

"And that's not mind-numbing?"

Jones stared at him. "It's the only thing in the world that's not mind-numbing, sir. Having a family is—it's the meaning of life."

Watson wished he could disagree.

Julie didn't understand what was going on, and what she didn't understand scared her. Why had Mommy gone to the hospital? Was she ill? Was she going to die like Pappa?

The pain pierced right through Julie's heart.

*Pappa, Pappa, Pappa.*

She missed him so much. True, he did lose his cool now and then, but didn't all fathers? The braid—she didn't care one bit about that. Short hair was much more convenient for swimming, anyway, even if it did look very curly now. Plus, she no longer needed the stupid hair ties for school.

*Pappa.*

She was not his little girl anymore. Pappa, the most special person in her world, was gone. And now Mommy—

It's all my fault, Julie thought. I wanted her to worry herself sick, and now she is sick and it's all because of me.

Tears collected in her eyes and she blinked them away. Crying would only make the guilt worse.

At least Mommy was back home. Julie longed to go to her and seek comfort in her embrace, but she couldn't. She didn't know how to take the first step.

At least she did know how to unpack her school case. She would not be running away to Nick. Not right now, anyway.

"Let's move along, Jones." Watson tapped the report files. "What else do we have?"

"The background check on Doctor Monterra. You were dead right to zero in on him, sir. Something's fishy there."

Watson stretched, his joints snapping back into place with a loud click. "I'm listening."

"At a first glance, everything's flawless. He's well off financially, with assets in property and blue chip shares. No bad habits like sneaking off across the homeland border to Sun City for a spot of gambling or naughty movies." Jones went red at the mention of the latter.

Watson had gone to Sun City to see a porn movie. One. Out of sheer curiosity. It didn't have any stars strategically covering the nipples, and it had a lot of nipples. He cleared his throat. "But?" he prompted.

"Sir. He's listed as married at his bank and at work, and yet I can't find a marriage certificate."

"You know the department of Internal Affairs," Watson said it lightly, even though he was already tasting the familiar buzz of adrenalin. "They've never heard of cross-filing. Sometimes I wonder whether they've even heard of filing, period. What does his security clearance say?"

"Conducted twenty years ago, and it has him noted as single."

Watson took the report. It was a raw transcript of the security clearance interview, together with the conclusion that Monterra was "a trustworthy man of upstanding morals" and "a valuable asset to any government enterprise". A few lines caught Watson's eye.

> *"Do you drink, Doctor Monterra?"*
> *"Doc, please. And to answer your question, only socially."*
> *"Do you smoke?"*
> *"No."*

> *"Have you ever tried drugs?"*
>
> *"I wouldn't even know how to start, my dear lady, where to go or what to ask for. Not that I would ever want to. Drugs are the invention of the devil."*

*Now, what was wrong with that picture? Oh, yes. The smoking. The Cuban cigars in Doc's office.*

Monterra had either lied in his security clearance interview, or he'd taken up smoking since. The stress of the job, perhaps, or the lure of luxurious cigars. Watson turned back to the transcript.

> *"Are you married?"*
>
> *"No, but I'd like to be. So far, I haven't found the right woman."*
>
> *"Do you have a girlfriend?"*
>
> *"Not at the moment."*
>
> *"Have you ever had one, Doc?"*
>
> *"Oh, of course. I went out with my high school sweetheart for two years, but our paths parted when I went to university. I lived in a dorm, studied hard for my degree and didn't have much time for parties. After that, I went out with a few girls I met at work or through a friend, but nothing important."*
>
> *"Would you ever have an affair with a married woman?"*
>
> *"No, I would not. That would be degrading for her, unfair to her husband and unsatisfactory to me. I don't like sharing."*

*Degrading for her, unfair to her husband. I don't like sharing.*

Is that how he, Captain Trevor Watson, saw his relationship with Charlene?

Charlene was a—convenient arrangement. He didn't feel he was using her, he didn't feel used, and sharing didn't bother him. Her marital status had implications both for his conscience and for his work life, particularly when it came to cooperating with

Charlene's husband on a case. Or *not* cooperating on a case, as evident from today's lab report.

Before Soweto, he wouldn't have done it. That day, though, ripped through his loyalty and warped his principles. The good, the bad and the hideously ugly had all meshed into one in his armoured vehicle...

*Enough.*

Watson compressed his thoughts deeper into his gut and returned to Monterra. The section of the security clearance interview dealing with the applicant's attitude towards blacks, communism, the government and South Africa, was textbook. Even the explanation of his outlandish surname sounded good.

> *"My paternal grandfather was half-Italian, half-Portuguese and he settled in Mozambique as a young man. He married an Afrikaans girl and they moved to South Africa. My father and I were both born here, and my mother's roots go back to Gerrit Maritz of the Great Trek. I am a proud white South African and I love my country..."*

A theory began to form. Monterra loved his country. Loved it enough to commit murder?

Watson paged through the other security police reports. His exasperation magnified.

Sally Martins. Not much there: mediocre school results, secretarial college, nothing of note in her attitude towards communism or homosexuality, standard "against" answers that scored well with the security clearance department.

Nick Haddow had arrived in South Africa from what was Rhodesia five years ago, got drafted into the army, sent to the border. Studied chemistry at the University of Pretoria and was currently doing his doctorate part time.

Lula's background check surprised him: no love affairs, even though her husband was away more often than at home, no children, a good double income invested in a wild game farm, spending well within means.

The facts simply didn't add up. Watson got up and started pacing. Two steps towards the window, about turn, five steps to the door. Just like in this investigation, two steps forward, five steps back. He couldn't see how to put the jigsaw together. A Conan-Doyle quote came to him: *On the contrary, Watson, you can see everything. You fail, however, to reason from what you see.*

"Thanks heaps, smart Alec," he said aloud.

"Sir?"

The phone rang and Watson chose not to explain. "Watson speaking."

"About tonight." Charlene sounded business-like. "Have you made up your mind?"

Watson glanced at Jones. The boy was pretending so hard not to listen in on the conversation the tips of his ears had gone crimson.

"It's an honour, Colonel," Watson said into the phone. "Thank you for calling. We're still going over the reports, and the one from Captain Smit is particularly puzzling."

Charlene was not a dumb woman. "From *my* Captain Smit?"

"That's correct, sir." Watson was beginning to enjoy the ruse. "Because of certain comments in the report, I am led to believe Smit knows more than he's prepared to put down on paper." He paused and listened to Charlene take shallow, greedy breaths on the other end of the wire.

"You're joking," she managed at last.

"Negative, sir."

"Oh, shit."

"My thoughts exactly, sir."

"Listen, Trevor," Charlene spoke fast, urgently. "He can't know for certain. It must be a fishing expedition. Just act normal, don't rise to the bait, and everything will be fine."

"Yes, sir." Watson fell into mimicking Jones. So easy: yes sir, no sir, and you just sit around waiting for others to make the decisions.

Charlene said, "Still. Just to be on the safe side, I'd better really go to that church meeting tonight, instead of your place."

That word again, *church*. Here was another regular churchgoer who failed to hear the message.

"Reading you loud and clear, sir. Thank you, sir. Goodbye, sir."

*Was that all you could say at the end of six months? Thank you and goodbye?*

Perhaps that was enough. Fifteen years ago, he and Annette hadn't even got that much.


Annette knew Danny couldn't have had anything to do with his father's death. *Murder*, she shuddered at the sound of the word. Even though the police hadn't explicitly ruled out suicide, the way they'd been acting could only mean one thing: they needed a scapegoat to throw to the media. Once they had a potential culprit behind bars, the press would back off.

The press—she hated the way they parked in the street directly across her lawn, now they'd latched onto the big story of father and son, both scientists, dying in mysterious circumstances. Still, it was better than having them hammering on her front door. Trevor had seen to it that they didn't trespass onto her property any longer.

Trevor. Annette was sure any affection he might still hold for her would not prevent him from going after Danny if the clues lined up all wrong. Her heart filled with fear, the primeval fear of a wild animal fighting for the safety of her cubs. She would lie for them, perjure herself in court and swear she herself had done it if there was no other way out. Anything to keep her children out of it.

And yet, she didn't want Danny, Julie and Beth to grow up with the stigma of their mother imprisoned, or possibly even hanged, for the murder of their father.

Only one thing to do: find the killer. And, in the impossible case the evidence pointed anywhere near her children, frame somebody else.

If this kind of thinking made her a bad person, she was

prepared to live with it.

The phone rang again.

*Bloody hell, who was it now?*

"Watson speaking."

"Watson." The brigadier's voice was neutral, always a bad omen. When on your side, he yelled happily, but when he was about to drop a bombshell, his voice went all detached. "A certain matter has come to my attention."

*Shit. Shit, shit, shit.*

*Smit had turned tattletale. Sprinted straight over Watson's head. What an utter...*

"What matter would that be, Brigadier?" Smooth. That's good. Deny all charges.

His boss *ahem-ed* into the receiver. "I've just had a phone call from a Mrs. LeRoy."

*Not about Charlene then.*

Watson breathed out with relief, but the respite lasted only a fraction of a second. He guessed what was coming.

"Mrs. LeRoy is alleging you've had previous involvement with the family and are therefore unsuitable to lead the investigation."

Watson made sure to polish every word in his mouth before he allowed it out. "That's true, Brigadier. I went out with Annette Pretorius, who was then Annette LeRoy, when we were both in high school, and during that time I briefly met Mrs. LeRoy on one or two occasions." One of those occasions Watson could recall in exceptionally vivid detail. "Annette Pretorius and I lost touch shortly after high school." The understatement of the century. "I didn't think it was pertinent to mention it, sir, because the victim, Gordon Pretorius, was unknown to me."

The brigadier's voice rose. A good sign. "You are investigating the death of your girlfriend's husband, man, and you don't think it's pertinent?"

"Ex-girlfriend, sir. The first time in fifteen years I had contact with Mrs. Pretorius was when called to her house to investigate her husband's death."

"Watson," the brigadier was shouting now, and Watson exhaled with relief. "Have you any idea what the newspapers will make of it?"

"Sir, with all due respect to the newspapers," *and nothing more than is due*, he added silently, "Pretoria is not a big city by international standards. Everybody knows everybody else. I've had my share of girlfriends," a whopping big lie, "and if I were to be forbidden to investigate any case involving women from my past," he produced a jovial between-us-men guffaw, "I'd be relegated to the backroom for admin."

*Had he gone too far? What if the brigadier decided to make good on the hypothetical and demote him?*

The brigadier's mirrored the guffaw. "You and your little women, hey, Watson?"

"Yes, sir."

"So, just between us then, what does Mrs. LeRoy have against you, son? Did you screw her daughter's brains out at the school dance?"

*If only.*

"Mrs. LeRoy thought a future policeman was not fit material for a son-in-law, sir."

That got the brigadier's attention. "A bit of a bigoted bitch, hey, Watson?"

"You said it, sir."

"Right, son, here's what we'll do. You will remain the de facto head of the investigation, but I'll tell the press and Mrs. Bigoted Bitch I'm stepping in because of the case's high profile. Whether they commend me for my diligence or condemn me for usurping your glory, either way, the heat will be off you."

Watson wasn't sure what to think, particularly the part about the usurping his glory. "Yes, sir," he said.

"Good-good, man. And those little women of yours, keep them in the past."

Was the brigadier telling him to stay away from Annette emotionally? The next sentence cleared it up.

"It's no good to have workflow in the office disrupted, son. Find a way to get along with Captain Smit. We don't want him taking any more pot shots at you."

The click of the disconnected call detonated in Watson's ears.

*The brigadier knew.*

And, was he saying it was Smit who'd fired at him last Saturday night?

Watson jumped to his feet. Jones had his eyes fixed on the paperwork. Only the redness of his ears gave him away.

"Jones, I'm going to see Smit now. See if I can pump him for information."

"Would you like me to accompany you, sir?"

"No. Arrange a second bout of interviews with BRAVO for tomorrow morning."

The phone began to ring before Jones could get in the "Yes sir."

Watson waved off the noise with a gesture reserved for flies. "Answer it and take a message. And if it's from a lady," he winced at the mere thought, "tell her I'm out in the field for the rest of the week."

"Captain Watson, please." Annette squeezed the phone so tight it slipped in her damp fingers like the inside of a banana.

"I'm sorry. The captain is out at present. It's Mrs. Pretorius, isn't it?"

"Yes."

There was a pause. "Um, ma'am. I'm under orders from Captain Watson to tell all the ladies who phone him that he'll be out for the rest of the week, but…"

*All the ladies?*

A spiky ball grew inside Annette's chest. "But what?"

"But I don't believe the captain meant the message for you."

Annette caught her breath. "Why—it's Jones, isn't it? Why do you say that?"

"Mrs. Pretorius, you're not anything like the um—ladies

who call the captain."

*The um-ladies, hey?*

For the first time since the nightmare had begun, Annette wondered about Trevor's personal life. He wore no ring and various *um-ladies* were in the habit of calling him to such a degree, he had to instruct Jones to sort them out...

*Why did that bother her at all?*

"Mom."

How swiftly her thoughts snapped back to reality. She bid the policeman a hasty goodbye and turned to her son. "What is it, Danny?"

"Hester says Beth won't settle for her nap. Probably misses you."

A pain, right there, straight in the soul. Her children needed her, and all she could do was stand there and mull over a policeman's love life.

She put her arm around Danny. "Come with me, my boy. Tell me how you've been."

He yielded to her embrace but stiffened at the question. "All right, I guess. A part of me still can't believe Father's gone."

Annette couldn't judge whether Danny had said it with sorrow or relief.

"I know. Can't believe it either." Was it sorrow or relief she herself felt?

They reached the nursery and Annette took the baby in her arms. She rocked back and forth on her feet, kissing her soft feathery head. Beth grabbed her finger and looked up at her with solemn reproach. Her baby girl.

"We'll take it from here, thanks, Hester."

"Yes madam. What can I make for dinner?"

Dinner. A sombre family affair around the long imposing table in the long imposing dining room, where Julie had lost her braid. They'd managed to avoid going back since then, but, sooner or later...

*Wait. Why, sooner or later?*

This was her house now. Her rules.

"Never mind, Hester. I'll take care of it."

The astonishment in the black woman's face was well justified. Annette had never done more than plan the meal, then season it at the end. She could start today. Or not. Did turning a new leaf mean slaving away at the stove?

"How about popcorn and ice cream tonight, instead of a regular meal?"

Danny brightened. "And a movie, Mom? Could we hire a projector and watch a movie?"

They had a video cassette player, brand new, but very few films. Most rentals still came on gigantic spools.

"What would you like to see?"

Her son peered at her with a mixture of defiance and wit. "How about *For Your Eyes Only*?"

"Hmmm." She pretended to consider. "Appropriate for your sister, you reckon?"

Danny looked like his old self for the first time since Gordon's death. "Don't worry, Mom. The inappropriate bits will go right over her head. And if they don't, well, then she's old enough to see them, right?"

Watson didn't knock. He simply walked into Captain Smit's office. What he was looking for was a fight. Man to man, fist to flesh. God, he would even let Smit win, if it came to that, to make it all fair and honourable. They both deserved no less.

"Smit."

A heavy silence. Then a sarcastic, "Well, what can I do for you? What *else* can I do for you? Would you like my house? The shirt off my back? What?"

Watson's admission of guilt and a punch-up would've cleared the air, but he had no right to ease his conscience by mucking up Charlene's life. Her husband, her marriage, her rules. Time to compartmentalise.

He chose to play dumb. "Huh?"

Smit stared hard into his face. From the years spent interviewing criminals, Watson knew it would be a mistake to stare back. He kept eye contact just long enough to pull a what-the-hell expression, then walked to the only empty chair in the room and plonked himself down squarely in front of the other police officer.

"I don't want your stinky shirt, Smit. Take you up on the house offer, though. My one-bedroom apartment is bang in the centre of the city." If Smit had been the one firing the shot on Saturday night, he would already know this. Watson continued. "The air outside smells even worse than your shirt."

The carefree banter must have worked. Smit's suspicions wobbled. "Lay off my shirt, Watson."

Watson pushed on. "You found a derivative of," he consulted his notes, "of $C_{34}H_{47}NO_{11}$, on the nail?"

Smit drew up in his chair. "As far as I can tell, we're dealing with a derivative of aconitine. Aconitine acts by entering the blood stream. The medics will be able to give you the exact mechanism, but it causes death either by paralysing the respiratory system or by paralysing the heart."

Watson said nothing. The post-mortem report showed no cardiac arrest, and death due to asphyxia. Consistent with respiratory system paralysis.

"Upon introduction of the toxin into the blood stream, the victim experiences a feeling of warmth, a tingling in the fingers and feet, moving upwards. Sharp pain, panic and nausea may follow. Death occurs within twenty minutes—"

"Is aconitine another name for curare?"

"You've read too many Sherlock Holmes stories, Watson. Curare comes from South America. Difficult to find in Pretoria. Especially now with all the bloody sanctions, hey?" Smit laughed at his own joke. "South Africa is totally self-sufficient. Let them bring on the sanctions. We don't need their silly Pepsi, McDonald's or curare. We can make our own."

"We can make our own curare?"

Smit's expression grew serious. "From what I can see in the lab tests we ran on that nail of yours, pretty much. The chemical we found is an unknown derivative."

Watson chewed on that. "So if I were to postulate the victim died of a puncture wound caused by a nail dipped in an aconitine-like toxin, that would be consistent with your findings?"

"Whoa! You need to check with the medics, but I won't contradict your choice of poison."

On the way back to his office, Watson reckoned he'd won the battle, at least on the professional level. His satisfaction died, though, as soon as he saw the memo scribbled by Jones.

> *There were 7 calls to your number, sir, in which the caller hung-up without saying a word.*

*Bloody hell.*

Charlene was not finished with him yet.

> *Also, Mrs. Pretorius phoned. She did not leave a message.*

It couldn't be urgent. A constable inside, a patrol car outside. Annette was safe, yet he dialled the number straight away. If his heart were a racing car, it would win the Formula 1 Grand Prix.

The phone call came when Annette and the children were halfway through *Moonraker* (*For Your Eyes Only* wasn't available). She let the projector run without her.

"Sorry, can't talk now," she told Watson. "The kids and I are having family time. Come to the house tomorrow and I'll tell you everything I know. Please. I need you to catch the killer, Trevor."

She stared at the wooden bowl next to the phone. Fourteen years ago, when she'd agreed to marry Gordon to escape her parents' house, she'd put Trevor out of her mind, turned into a dutiful spouse.

Now Trevor was back in her life, this time as a potential enemy. If he tried to pin Gordon's death on her son, Annette wouldn't hesitate to break his career, or his spine, or both.

And yet she couldn't stop thinking about him. With a deep

sigh, she walked back into the TV room, to a movie about a madman who wanted to poison everybody on the planet. Only James Bond could stop him. Did South Africa have a James Bond?

"Mom, Mom, you've missed the coolest bit," Julie said. "Bond's just made Chang fly through the clock face and crash head-first into a piano! Please can we watch it one more time?"

This, thought Annette as James Bond climbed a rope into a clock tower to the accompanying music of a piano somewhere in the distance, this is a lesson in how to deal with enemies.


Watson had barely sat down when his door opened and Captain Smit walked in. The muscles in Watson's arms tensed for another confrontation.

"Sorry," Smit said, smacking another slim folder onto Watson's desk. "Must have slipped my mind."

His eyes said otherwise. Watson chose not to challenge him. "Thanks."

"It's the chemical analysis of those blue vitamin pills." Smit pointed at the folder. "Nothing vitamin about them. They're a female oral contraceptive. Work about half the time to prevent a pregnancy altogether, but when swallowed by a pregnant woman, will most likely cause her to abort the foetus."

"Most likely?"

"It's a mixture of hormones and chemicals. Officially, it doesn't exist, so there's no literature about it. Given its composition, I'd say abortion would take place in nine out of ten cases. But here's an interesting fact."

As though the implications of a South African scientist being in possession of a newly developed contraceptive abortion agent weren't interesting enough. "*Ja?*"

"I found hand-written notes inside the box. Diary entries, if you can call them that. Van der Merwe confirms they're in the victim's handwriting."

Patience, Watson reminded himself. Patience. "And?"

"The victim had a theory the pills could also be a female aphrodisiac."

"What?"

"Cool it, Watson. I get first dibs. Let's just say, all the pills were destroyed during the chemical analysis."

Smit cackled and banged the door shut behind him. Watson sat paralysed. It wasn't the prospect of Smit testing out the pills on Charlene that made the hair on Watson's neck bristle. It was the image of Pretorius feeding Spanish fly to Annette.

*An aphrodisiac that made you lose your babies.*

The Minister With No Official Portfolio sat at his desk. His office was the very essence of luxury and comfort. It was also the last place he wanted to be.

All his adult life, he had put his work first, before himself or his family. He'd served in the army, fought on the Angolan border, got nicked by shrapnel. Studied political science at university, climbed the sticky ladder of career success, missed his daughter's birth while on a diplomatic mission in the States, missed her first birthday because of a covert operation in Lusaka.

And now he was missing a holiday in Mauritius.

All because of a waiting game.

He hated waiting.

Action. He needed to get busy.

# Chapter 8—Wednesday, Three Days before the Murder

WEDNESDAYS WERE HESTER'S days off. Funny that. She still had to cook breakfast for her employers and straighten their house. But if she hurried, the madam would let her go before lunch. Hester was counting on it today. She didn't want to be late for the cell meeting.

The night before Hester had left the kitchen spotless. This morning the sink held two smudged whisky tumblers, an oily pot encrusted with burnt popcorn that would take forever to scrub, a greasy bowl, and two mugs with dregs of milky coffee.

The madam and the master must have had one of their good evenings together. Shared popcorn, whisky and coffee. Alcohol to make her more agreeable and coffee to make him stay up. Hester sniggered. The master sure got a bargain last night, in contrast to that time he entertained his mistress at home while his wife and kids went to the seaside. That night, he had served lobster with sparkling wine.

"Good morning, Hester. The children will have soft-boiled eggs with toast for breakfast."

"Yes, missus. What will the master have?" She knew the madam never ate breakfast.

The madam moved her mouth into a tight smile that faded before it began. "Probably nothing, Hester. He's running late this morning. I'll just pour his coffee."

Perhaps if the master took as much trouble with his wife as he had with his mistress, the smile would've been genuine.

Heavy footsteps on the stairs didn't bode well. The master stomped in like a buffalo with tight testicles. A sense of sisterly triumph bubbled in Hester's throat. Good for the madam not to have been seduced with a bowl of popcorn.

"I'm late," the master's growl was all buffalo too, "and the coffee's bloody hot."

"Sorry. Let me put some more milk in it."

He took another sip. Scowled. "That makes it too weak."

"I'm very sorry, Gordon." The madam handed him a paper bag. "Dry sausage and fruit for your breakfast. Would you like to take a lunch sandwich as well? It's ready."

"No, I'll get something at work."

Hester was sure he would. Not once and not twice had she laundered traces of lipstick off the master's business shirts.

"I'm late," Gordon said, "and the coffee's bloody hot."

Annette felt her stomach cringe. It was all her fault. She should have got up earlier. "Sorry. Let me put some more milk in it."

"That makes it too weak."

Annette still hoped to make amends as she handed him a paper bag. "I'm very sorry, Gordon. Dry sausage and fruit for your breakfast. Would you like to take a lunch sandwich as well? It's ready."

He didn't want it. Perhaps he realised she hadn't made his lunch with as much love and devotion as a wife should. When they were newlyweds fourteen years ago, she would hide little "I love you" notes in his sandwiches, but Gordon complained he kept biting into the pink paper, so she'd stopped.

When they were newlyweds fourteen years ago, Gordon would have this contagious laugh that started in his belly and burst out like gunshot from his mouth. What had happened to that laugh? Had she killed it?

"Bye, doll." Gordon called out.

Yvonne Walus

For old times' sake, Annette wanted to say, "Bye, honey."
She couldn't.

"Bye, doll."
*Doll.*
The madam did look like a porcelain doll, and she certainly
acted like one, too, whenever the master was around.
With the puppeteer gone, the doll regained control of her
own strings. "Hester, I'm going grocery shopping later. What do
we need?"
Hester recited a long list of foodstuffs and cleaning products,
and the madam wrote it all down. The whites couldn't remember
things, which explained why they had to be so good at reading and
writing.
The clock hurried on without mercy. Hester changed the
baby's nappy, washed up after breakfast, straightened the beds,
picked up the dirty clothes, changed another nappy. Beth was
getting hungry. Hester was getting restless.
"Shall I make up the bottle, Missus?"
"No, I'll feed Beth myself. You may go now. Take the
sandwich from the fridge, if you like."
"Thank you, Madam." Master Gordon's rejected sandwich
was bound to contain something more interesting than Hester's
usual apricot jam with a slice of pink Polony sausage.
Free at last. The madam would make her own lunch and
gobble it all up, away from the master's controlling gaze. For
dinner, the family would go out to a restaurant in order to relieve
the white woman's *workload*. After all, the madam was bound to
be tired from lying by the swimming pool all day, painting her
nails and pretending not to gawk at the gardener's muscles
covered with forbidden black skin.
Hester glanced at the clock. Just enough time to catch a taxi
van to the illegal political meeting.

Annette glanced at the clock. Just enough time to drive into the
city for her meeting. As the garage door closed behind her, she

193

could feel the metal band around her throat loosen.

Lula stared into her cup, wishing she could read her future in it. The House of Coffees, one of the few coffee shops in Pretoria that served coffee made from real coffee beans, was almost empty at this hour. Too late for morning coffee, too early for lunch—a perfect time for a discreet meeting.

Careful, she reminded herself. Make it sound natural.

She took a long sip, careful not to disturb the whipped cream topping, and raised her eyes to Annette. "How's your coffee?"

They had already complimented each other's lipsticks, discussed the new potato-water diet which involved serving boiled potatoes to the family and eating only the cooking water for two days, and reviewed, in detail, the previous night's episode of *Dallas*. No point talking about the weather in Pretoria, there were only so many ways to utter: "Hot today, isn't it".

Annette plucked a fold of her thin blouse. "You didn't ask me to come here to talk about coffee, Lula. Go for it."

Lula sighed, still unsure how to find out what she needed. "It's about Gordon, I'm sure you've guessed as much. Lately he seems to be—please don't take it as a criticism—different. Not the Gordon I know. Have you noticed anything unusual?"

"Unusual?" A shadow crossed Annette's face and settled there. "No." Her tone was firm, discouraging further questions. "Downcast after his father's death, that's all."

"Downcast?" Lula feigned surprise. Getting closer now. "What about the opportunity to be involved in the latest project? Doesn't it excite him? Is he going to give it a try?"

"I can't say for sure…" The sentence dangled unfinished.

Lula waited.

"Honestly, Lula, I'm the last person you should ask," Annette burst out. "Gordon doesn't talk to me about his life."

Disappointment gnawed at Lula's gut. Annette knew nothing. Pointless. All pointless. Then curiosity took over. "Does it worry you?"

Annette spoke slowly, pausing between phrases. "As long as

Gordon's happy, I'm happy. If he chooses to leave work at work, I'm there to help him achieve that. It's always been my ambition to be a good wife and a good mother. Not the best, just good enough."

*Damn.*

She should have seen it coming. It was the heartache that spoke the next words. "Perhaps that's your problem, Annette. Are you more of a mother than a wife? Men need to feel they're the most important thing in your life."

Annette's expression couldn't have looked much different if Lula had suggested stripping down to their panties and dancing on the coffee table. "I would never put my husband before my children, Lula. You'll understand it one day when you have your own—"

The pain blocked out everything else. "I won't," Lula interrupted, pushing the chair back and springing to her feet. "I'll never understand."

"Lula?"

She blurted, "I can't have children."

Instant relief to have it out in the open. But, bloody hell. Instead of getting information, she was giving it away.

Gordon's face had developed a new wrinkle. Today, more than ever, he showed his age. "Sally. We can't go on. I have a family. Responsibilities."

Sally forced herself to keep compliant. "I understand."

*Then marry me, fool, if you're tired of feeling guilty.*

"You are wonderful, the way you always put them first, Gordy. I mean it. Truly a good person."

"So you agree. We have to end it."

She deliberately sucked in her lower lip with her teeth. Men liked that. "Of course", she whispered. "Whatever you want."

Sad face, check. Amenable voice, check. Cleavage…She leaned forward, forcing her dress to slide down her shoulder.

"Whatever you want," she breathed into his neck, "whenever you want. Your choice. Always."

Men were all the same. There were only two things they craved: flattery and the illusion of power.

*Make that three things*, she thought when Gordon slid the dress all the way down.

Before he knew it, she would be the new Mrs. Pretorius. Sally Pretorius. It had a good ring.

The remnants of a burned body, with an old car tyre around its chest, stopped Hester in her tracks. Her stomach heaved. This was black-on-black violence, something far worse than what they'd been taught to fear at the hands of the white man. This poor person must have been accused by the mob of being an informer to the police. Tortured for a confession. Lynched. All in the name of the struggle against apartheid. Suddenly she wanted no part of it.

The peeling door to the nearby shed creaked open. "Welcome, sister."

She couldn't turn away now. If they thought her untrustworthy—if they thought her a spy…With a backwards glance at the blackened skeleton, she entered the meeting shed.

The summit began with the leader paying tribute to the victim of necklacing—the fiery tyre's gruesome nickname—and warning the members to stay true. "It may look horrific," he said, "and it *is* horrific. A horrific reminder of our fight's significance. Those who aren't with us are against us."

Hester took a while to digest this. The words were hypnotic, the leader's eyes willed her to let go and be swept along for the ride. And yet, and yet. Could one horror be justified because it's helping prevent another? Who got to set the price of freedom?

"Can you help us, sister?" The leader's voice reverberated inside Hester's heart. "We need to know what the people at BRAVO are scheming. Gordon Pretorius is an important cog in the racist machinery. Can you—will you—help us?"

She'd only joined the banned political movement for a bit of fun, to meet people, drink sweet tea and pretend she was doing her share for the freedom fight.

What the leader was asking her to do was a different pot of stew altogether.

"Sister?" His eyes were black like the bushveld night.

She heard her own voice saying, "You can count on me."

"Good. People like that have to be stopped at all cost. The end justifies the means. Understand?"

"Yebo."

On the green bus back—not back home, home was in the township where her three sons were growing up without her—on the bus back to a room at the back of her employer's mansion, Hester wondered what had possessed her. The way the leader had talked—had he wanted her to do more than steal Master Gordon's files? Had he asked her, in that veiled way of his, to remove Master Gordon from the equation?

She looked around her. The bus was almost empty. Most black people were travelling in the opposite direction now, away from their employers and towards their families. A twinge of pain inside her warned her not to think about it, but not thinking about it meant pushing her children to the outskirts of her mind.

Her children. Kabelo, Thabo and her baby Siyabonga. Because she had a job, they had a future. One day, they may be bus drivers, like the one two rows in front of her, shut securely in his driver cage together with the fare money. One day, they may be famous soccer players or even politicians…A black politician. That would be the day.

She disembarked and walked straight into two patrols checking that no unauthorised blacks ventured into the white suburb.

"Pass book," the fatter one said.

No *please*.

Hester handed over her ID document. Like handing over your dignity.

"Seems in order." Was that a glint of disappointment in the cop's face? "Make sure you don't make trouble now, you hear?"

She hid her scorching rage behind the safety of, "Hau, *Baas*."

At the party meeting, the leader shouted many inspirational

slogans about freedom and the right to vote and free houses and jobs for everyone.

She didn't believe a word of it. But after the pass book incident, she would do as he'd asked.

Eyes on the clock, Annette filled a pre-frosted glass with cold pilsner. As expected, Gordon walked into the house exactly at half past four in the afternoon. Fourteen years ago, she'd admired his punctuality. What was it about marriage that changed the quirky and cute into quirky and annoying?

"We're eating at the steak house tonight." He sounded tired. "The one that serves ostrich."

Julie flung herself into her father's arms. Daddy's girl, never this forthcoming with Annette. "Pappa, the one with the big wheel in front? Cool."

"The very same. Aren't you all excited?"

Danny lurked in the corner. Silent. Unsmiling. She knew she had to intervene before Gordon noticed the attitude. "Thank you, honey. Beth's with my mom. Ready when you are."

Gordon's hopeful eyes met hers.

Men need to feel they're the most important thing in your life.

"Mom says Beth can stay there the whole night if we like." Her tongue tasted of metal.

Gordon bent down to kiss Annette's cheek. He smelled of soap and mouthwash, fresh, the way he always smelled after a day at the office.

"I'd like that," he said.

Annette handed him the icy mug of beer and tried not to think.

Gordon always showered before leaving the office. It never helped. The guilt stayed with him no matter how hard he scoured.

He wanted to make it up to them. Make up for everything he'd always been and everything he'd recently become.

"Dan, Julie, let's do something naughty. How about an ice

cream cone before we go to dinner?"

"Yippee, Pappa. Who's your favourite girl?"

"You are." Gordon stroked his daughter's braids. Silky and hard, still damp from being in the pool half the day. "Annette, get us all some ice cream."

His wife didn't move. "Is that a good idea, Gordon? They won't eat their food if they have sweets now."

The familiar rage welled up inside him, as always whenever he met with opposition. "They are my kids, too. I have a say. And I say we should all have some fun in this house every now and again."

Damn the hurt in her eyes. Why couldn't he ever get anything right? Trying so hard to do his best by everybody, to meet their expectations, to protect them. His guilt amplified. "It's all your fault," he hissed, aware his logic didn't make sense to her. "Stop contradicting me. You're undermining my authority."

Annette took out a square box of Dairy Maid ice cream.

"Cones or bowls?" she asked.

"Cones, Mom, please," said Julie.

"Not for me, thank you." Dan's face was emotionless, like Annette's. "I don't really feel like ice cream today."

"Nonsense, man." Resentment stabbed deep. There he was, trying to be a good father, and Dan refused to play along. "It's sizzling outside. You do want an ice cream."

His son gave him a level stare. "Sorry, Pa. My stomach doesn't feel that great."

"In that case you won't be wanting to go out to dinner with us."

"Gordon…"

"Stay out of it, woman. Dan?"

Danny's voice matched his steady gaze. "Absolutely. Best I stay at home."

Disappointed, Gordon jingled his car keys. "I'll give you a lift to Grandma's."

"I'll go over the wall, thanks all the same, Pa."

Gordon paused. Danny looked as unconcerned about missing

dinner as only a teenager who's never gone without could possibly be.

"I've changed my mind." Gordon was aware how ridiculous he sounded. "You'll go with us. Julie, go get into the car."

"Shouldn't she wait till she's finished her cone?"

"Annette, stop fussing. You are the most annoying person I know. I said, get into the car. All of you."

They traipsed to the BMW silent and unsmiling.

*What on earth had he done wrong?*

He shrugged and sounded the horn. Within a minute, the big flap-door began to rise, lifted by the garden boy, his grin full of white teeth. At least somebody was happy.

They drove out in silence.

"Oh, sh—sugar!" exclaimed Julie from the back seat.

"What is it, Copperlocks?" asked Annette at the same time as he said, "Don't say, *oh sugar*, Julie, it's ugly."

"My cone fell onto the seat."

Gordon stood on the brake pedal and spun his head back. White creamy streaks ran along the seams of the beige leather.

*His car? His pride and joy?*

"Julie, you dunce—you're disgusting." The words tore out of Gordon's throat without warning. He didn't really mean to say it. Something inside him said it for him.

His daughter gulped and burst into tears. She cried with her mouth wide open, like a toddler.

"Gordon."

It was the way Annette had said it, so quietly and so distantly. Red spots whirled before his eyes. He grabbed her arm, squeezed all his pent-up frustration and anger into her flesh.

"We are supposed to be a team. Don't you defy me."

"Gordon. You should apologise."

He looked down at his fingers biting into her skin, the knuckles white from the pressure.

"I'm sorry, Annette. I didn't mean to."

"Not to me," she murmured, rubbing her arm where a blue welt was already forming. "To Julie."

"Are you out of your mind? I'm not going to apologise to a child."

"It's the right thing to do."

More red spots. "Shut up. Children, we're fighting because Mommy is wrong and I'm right. Mommy doesn't know what she's talking about."

His wife spoke so softly it was hard to make out the individual syllables. "Let's not involve the children again. Please. Let's just go to dinner."

*Go to dinner?*

*Why?*

The people in the car, his only family, were all strangers. He didn't belong with them.

"Maybe you should all go without me. That'll make you happy, won't it?"

"How can you say that?"

*How?*

The world was collapsing all around him, covered in floating red spots, and nobody had noticed a damned thing, not even his oh-so-perfect wife. He heard himself say: "It's all your fault. Your idiotic criticism challenges my authority in front of the children. You behave as though I'm not even their father. I despise you and I may as well have nothing to do with them. I can't tolerate spoilt children. And I really can't stand scheming adults."

The red spots had disappeared with every word he uttered. It was like playing Asteroids. Bang, bang, boom. All his wrath was gone and the air felt much cleaner now, his chest lighter. He wasn't sure that he felt better though.

"Let's go," he said. "The ostrich steak awaits."

He eased the car into *Drive* again. The outburst had made him hungry. Besides, they had a reservation and Gordon was done with breaking promises.

In the restaurant Danny had a chance to see his mother's face for the first time since the incident in the car. She looked beautiful, even with reddened eyelids and a mouth that dipped at the corners. When he met her gaze, he saw anguish.

Disgusting—Father's word, not his—that another human being could reduce his unfaltering mom to that. By nature, Danny preferred pacifist solutions to confrontation. This time, though, his father had gone too far.

"What will you have?" the waiter asked.

Mom's voice hooked in her throat when she spoke. "Just a salad for me. I'm not very hungry."

Usually she would order a lady's steak with pepper sauce and no sides, and when it arrived, she would spend the evening cutting the meat into miniscule bits. Danny watched her every Wednesday. Every Wednesday, she would swallow a few pieces and spread out the rest to make the plate look as though she had already eaten.

She always said she wasn't very hungry. Today, Danny believed her. His father could suck the fun out of a funfair.

Pa, meanwhile, nodded his approval of Mom's diet. "Ostrich steak with a baked potato for me," he said. "And cheese sauce."

"Me too, Pappa, me too," Julie's laughter chimed in the air, the car scene evidently long forgotten. "I love ostrich. You and I like the same things. We're the same, Pappa."

Crap, he hoped not. One Gordon Pretorius in the family was enough. More than enough. God, how he hated the son of a bitch.

"What will you eat, son?"

"Just a salad for me," he echoed. "I'm not very hungry."

The thought bounced around in his head.

*One in the family was one too many.*

Annette had thought the dinner would never end, but when they came home, the atmosphere remained leaden. More than anything, she wanted to escape into unconsciousness. Normally by this time of the evening, she'd be starving, sneaking a large chunk of cheese or two sticks of dry sausage from the kitchen.

Not tonight.

Beth had stayed with the grandma for the night, after all, because Annette found it near impossible to function. Her mind was shutting down her body, telling her to sleep. Sleep equalled oblivion. Children first, though.

She found them in Danny's room, engrossed in a discussion, and she stopped to listen.

Dan's adolescent voice had climbed a few tones. "Stupid! Do you know how rare and expensive the computer is? What if you break it?"

"I'll be careful."

"It's in a special room, and it's as big as an elephant. It's not a toy, Julie. Pa will never let you touch it."

"Will too."

"Will not."

"So he's letting you use his precious video camera because you're a boy? Is that it? I can't have fun with machines because I'm a girl?"

"Children." Annette had no energy for more than that single word. What could she say? Julie had it right: it was not about the age difference. Gordon wouldn't allow his daughter near a computer precisely because of gender discrimination.

Julie's voice beamed cold fury: "Mommy, Danny is annoying me. Arrrrgh. You have no idea how annoying it is to have a big brother."

"Danny is right, Copperlocks. Your father won't let you play with computers. Not for a school project, nor for any other reason."

"Then I'm not doing it; I'm not helping him with his stupid project. Not if I can't play with cool stuff."

"Julie." Signs of cracking in Danny's patience. "You wouldn't know cool stuff if it stood in front of you and stripped itself naked."

Tears gathered heavy under Annette's eyelids. When did her little boy grow up? When did he start using words like *naked*? She chose not to react.

Julie's choice was overreaction. "Ooo—you're so disgusting."

Annette couldn't ignore it. "Julie, honey, we don't talk like that."

"Well," Julie put her skinny arms on her hips. "Pappa does."

"I'm sorry he called you that, Copperlocks. Now it's bedtime."

She kissed them both goodnight, hoping the brush of her lips said what her tongue could not: how very, very sorry she was that Gordon was their father.

Back in the main suite, she took a long cool shower. Her anger could still scorch asbestos. She yearned to pack their bags and take the children far away from all the insults and heartache. Or better yet, pack Gordon's bags, together with the insults and the heartache, and leave them out on the driveway.

What was Gordon's behaviour doing to the children's self-esteem? If girls married men who resembled their fathers, what sort of monster would Julie end up with?

A weight crushed her lungs, each breath painful.

When she walked into the bedroom, she saw Gordon in bed. Sitting up, waiting. He didn't have his pyjamas on, and Annette knew exactly what that meant.

His wife looked dazzling in her see-through nightgown, her curves tantalisingly concealed yet outlined by the play of light and shadows. Completely unaware of her sexual allure, completely unaware she was the woman of his dreams. Not the slut-like Sally, nor the perplexing Lula, only Annette. His Annette.

The apathy lay bare in her eyes.

*Why? What had he done now?*

*Well, okay, to be fair...*

Still, Annette didn't know about Sally, and he had apologised for his earlier outburst. It was just like a woman to hold grudges.

His rage ballooned. "You don't love me." He didn't know where that came from, but as he said it, it sounded exactly right. "You've never loved me."

After Gordon left to sleep in the spare room, Annette dissected the latest accusation. Had she ever loved Gordon? Fourteen years ago, he had been the way out of her parents' house where she'd had to watch her every step lest her behaviour lead to family quarrels and, ultimately, to her parents divorcing. And, even more importantly, he had promised she could go to university once they were married. They'd wanted the same things in life: children, a house on a hill, a quiet life.

What was love, anyway? Annette couldn't get "Love is…" stickers out of her mind, with their obese love hearts, a cartoon freckled blonde and a cartoon dark-haired boy. Both she and Julie collected them, glued them into A4 booklets according to their number, read the captions out loud to each other. You could get a packet of four "Love is…" stickers for ten cents. Lucky dip, you never knew which ones were inside.

"Love is—when you're his beauty queen."

"Love is—wanting to give her the stars and the moon."

"Love is—your secret weapon."

Tonight her secret weapon had been the fight between her and Gordon.

"Marriage breakdown is—when you'd rather argue than have sex." Now that would make a good sticker.

How far was she prepared to go not to go to bed with Gordon ever again? She thought about it. The answer petrified her.

# Chapter 9—Wednesday, Four Days after the Murder

THE BRIGADIER WASN'T a happy chap, Watson realised as soon as he'd walked into his superior's office. For sure, that was the norm, but Watson tried to minimise the number of times the brigadier wasn't happy with him.

This was one of those times.

"Did you know," the brigadier said in a calm, conversational tone that made foreboding blossom right at the base of Watson's spine, "that Mrs. LeRoy has a record?"

"No, sir."

*A record for what? Malice? Bigotry? Bullying?*

"Interesting." The word swished through the room. "Why not?"

*Because I'm too busy trying to protect Annette from being arrested?*

That wouldn't fly.

"Sorry, sir. The paperwork on my desk is higher than Kilimanjaro."

"That a good enough excuse, Captain?"

"No, sir."

The brigadier shoved a file into Watson's hands. "Read it. Tell me what you think."

Still standing, Watson opened the file. No mug shot, because Annette's mother hadn't been arrested or formally charged with any crime. The job sheet, dated a decade earlier, raised questions as to whether Mrs. LeRoy had indeed thought she was shooting an intruder when she discharged the handgun that killed her husband. The neighbours had described the couple as quiet and loving, though of course you never knew. There was no life insurance policy, no sign of another man or woman, and so the investigation died before it began.

"Like mother, like daughter, hey, Captain?"

Watson's jaw muscles ached. "No sir, I don't believe so."

Annette knew it was time to act. Julie still refused to talk about Gordon but this morning her pillow was wet with tears. Again.

She dialled. "Good morning, Doc," she said.

"Annette. Glad you called. Everything is organised and ready to go, my dear, as soon as the police give us the go-ahead."

Annette knew what Doc meant. As soon as they release Gordon's body. Gordon's body. Dead. Cold.

She blocked the images. Right now, she needed to focus. "Thank you, Doc. Just one thing, if it's not too much trouble."

"Nothing is ever too much trouble for you."

"We need closure, the children and I. If we could possibly hold the memorial service already? And have a quiet funeral when—when a funeral is possible?"

"Of course."

She captured her thumbs in her fists for luck. "How about this afternoon? Is that too little notice?"

Doc's voice rang with strength and confidence. "I'll make it happen." He paused for a fraction of a beat. "Have the police come to any—conclusions?"

"I believe I'm suspect number one," she said lightly. The sound of the doorbell interrupted Doc's reassurances and Annette bid a hasty goodbye.

"I'll get it, Hester," she said. "It's Wednesday. Go enjoy your day off."

The black woman shook her head. "I'll stay, Missus. You need looking after."

A simple kindness, yet it made Annette cry, a short sob with tears welling up. Hester's squashy arms held her steady until she composed herself. The doorbell chimed again.

Trevor stood on the front porch, his finger still raised to the bell. At six foot three, he crowded the door and Annette felt something stir inside her, something she had believed gone for good.

"How are you?" His voice reverberated in her ears warm, focused, concerned.

"I'll feel better when you find the killer."

His eyes darkened with a fire so intense, she flinched. Trevor's hand on her cheek, tilting her chin, burned her skin. "Why, Annette, what happened? Has something frightened you?"

"No," she replied slowly. An idea formed in her mind.

The bruise-coloured shadows under Annette's eyes set off alarm bells in his heart. She led him through the lounge onto the terrace, gestured to one of the wicker armchairs, sank onto another.

"Nothing specific's happened to frighten me. I just need the nightmare to go away. You think Gordon was murdered. I'm a suspect. The wife always is. No, hear me out. You must have seen the insurance policy. The sooner you finish the investigation, the sooner we can all get on with our lives."

He wanted to ask her what she proposed to do.

"I'll help you solve this case," she said. "Before—well, I didn't see the point of all the questions, so I didn't think very hard about the answers. Maybe it was the shock." She was babbling now, her hands fluttered around her chest and throat, and Watson bit his lip to rein in his suddenly raunchy mind. She was a widow. He was a horny jerk.

"Let me get this straight," Watson held up his hand to halt her. "You will help the investigation by answering my questions."

"No," she interrupted. "More than that. I'll tell you everything I think is relevant, things you have no way of asking."

He made his voice hard. "And in return?" If she asked for immunity or special treatment...

"And in return you arrest the killer. That's all I want."

The policeman in him relaxed even as disappointment rose bitter. *Ja*, that's all Annette wanted from him, all right. In the past fifteen years, she had built a life and a family, while he screwed married women and took care of rioting black school children.

"You have a deal," he said.

The bloody policeman was back. Danny had seen him approach the front door and now he heard him picking on Mom. Questions, questions, questions. Mom always hated questions.

Danny knew he had to protect her, now that Pa was gone. The decision came—instant and easy.

One question blazed in Watson's brain. "What's with the unicorns?"

"The secret order." Her words oozed contempt. "Call themselves the Order of Unicorns. They believe their mission is to keep South Africa white."

"How?"

"Cloak-and-dagger meetings. Riding around the suburbs at night to make sure all's safe. Big boys, dangerous toys."

"Do they ever achieve anything of political importance?"

Annette shrugged.

"Who belongs to the society?"

She didn't know that, either, and the flicker of hope in Watson's investigation began to dim.

"Did you ever drive your husband's car, Annette?"

She shook her head.

"When was the last time you were in the BMW as a passenger?"

"Last Wednesday." No hesitation. "We—Gordon and the children and I—had dinner at a restaurant that night. We always take Gordon's car when we go out as a family."

That would explain the chlorine and ice cream stains, as well as Annette's fingerprints on the passenger door. What about the prints on the driver's side?

"Do you think it's possible you opened the driver's door and switched off the engine on Saturday night? Maybe also checked whether Gordon was still alive?"

Annette couldn't remember.

Watson believed her. Traumatic events had that effect sometimes—the mind would block them out as an act of self-preservation. Perhaps she would remember it all one day. Perhaps not.

"All right," he said. "Let's take a break. No, don't get up. I can find the kitchen. Do you still take your coffee with milk and two sugars?"

"You remembered." She tried to smile, the effect forlorn. "But it's just with milk nowadays. I'll go check on the children. The memorial service is this afternoon."

*Just milk, hey?*

Watson flared up at yet another manifestation of Gordon Pretorius' influence over Annette. Pretorius had taken a carefree seventeen-year old with dimples and turned her into a starving nervous wreck.

The Minister With No Official Portfolio put down the phone. One more day in this office, the minister thought, and I'll be as cuckoo as a clock. "We're going to a funeral," he told his assistant.

The other man winced. "I thought the muscle usually took care of that, sir?"

"No, man. The Pretorius funeral. Reckon the reporters will give us a break after the service, go back to file their copy or eat doughnuts. We'll get Mrs. Pretorius then."

"Very well, sir."

Annette found Julie and Danny playing TV games. Gordon had bought the Atari for his son's thirteenth birthday, and Danny used it at every opportunity. Apart from improving his reflexes, Annette couldn't see any benefit. Gordon, however, had liked arcade games too, and kept bringing more of them home. Space Invaders, Defender, Night Driver. The realistic pictures on the boxes looked nothing like the blockish shapes moving around the

TV screen. The players didn't seem to mind.

"Danny, Julie."

Neither child responded, their hands glued to the joysticks, their eyes fixed on the action. Julie's profile resembled her own, Danny's concentrated expression was all Gordon.

"Excuse me," she tried again. "I'm talking to you."

No reply, only the irritating beepy-boppy-beep and pow-pow-pow of the colourful blobs on the TV screen. Aliens? Aeroplanes? Bunny-eating whales? It could have been anything. And now the anything was sucking her children right into the imaginary world of what in her childhood would have been science fiction.

Annette wanted to pull out the plug. She wanted to hug her children tight and never let go, and she wanted to yell at them for abandoning her in this reality. This reality stank.

"Listen," she began. Checked herself. Walked away.

The children were better off in the world of shooting blobs. They would find out about their father's memorial service soon enough. For now, they were happy. Happy and safe.

Before going back downstairs, she prepared the outfits for the afternoon. The black dresses they'd bought at the Carlton Centre last Friday night would do for her and Julie. Would they be appropriate? The cut was conservative enough. The fabric only shimmered in artificial light, it would look totally black in the afternoon sun.

She didn't have any other black clothes. Besides, this was the only dress she'd bought with her own taste in mind instead of Gordon's. It seemed fitting to attend his memorial service without all her emotional baggage.

Yes, she mused as she walked back to the lounge, following the smell of roasted chicory and Trevor's aftershave. Those twin dresses would do very well indeed.

Danny made sure his mother was pfaffing around in her wardrobe before he made his way downstairs. He found the policeman in the kitchen, poking into cupboards. Looking for the poison that had killed his father? Or—planting it? Danny had heard the stories of police frame-ups.

No way would he let his mom go to prison. Too frail. Too precious. Too—mom.

"Captain Watson?"

"Danny. Would you like some coffee, too?"

*Huh? A policeman making coffee?*

The only thing policemen ever made were arrests. Speaking of which.

"Captain. I want to confess to the murder of my father."

A heavy hand fell onto his shoulder. He cringed. This was it, then.

"Danny." The policeman's voice was surprisingly gentle. "I know what you're doing. Don't worry. Nothing bad will happen to your mom. I promise."

*Could he trust a policeman's promise?*

*Nah.*

"You don't understand, sir. I did it. I killed my father." He felt better for saying it.

"Go back to your room and be a child. Read a comic book or break a window. I'll protect your mother."

Danny's resolve waned.

"All right, son?"

"Only if you pay for the broken window."

"Deal."

They sipped their coffee in silence. It was another sizzling dry February day, the sky an impossibly perfect blue colour with not a wisp of cloud in sight.

Time to break the spell. "After you found your husband dead, you sent the guests away. Why?"

Annette made a helpless gesture. "I couldn't think what else to do. Gordon was in his car, dead. I didn't want people to see him. It would have been undignified. And," Annette faltered, "I know it seems petty, but I didn't know how to tell them. The etiquette rules my mother taught me didn't include announcing the sudden death of the host."

Watson did a mental shaking of the head. Only Annette would worry about manners at a time like that.

"Then you went to bed," he said.

"I didn't go to bed." It came out soft, resigned. "I went upstairs to lie down. My head was spinning and I—I thought I was going to faint. I felt ill."

Watson remembered the maid's testimony about the madam vomiting.

"That's all right," he said as gently as he could. "Can you tell me exactly what happened on that day? From the beginning."

"From the beginning." Annette drew her brows together. She still looked as tempting as the Seven Sins combined. "On Saturday morning, Gordon told me he'd invited a few people for dinner. He didn't say, but I assumed it was to celebrate his birthday. His birthday would have been yesterday," she added, a factual statement untainted by emotion.

"Who was the first to arrive?"

Annette chewed the end of a strand of hair that fell across her cheek. "I remember Lula was last," she said. "The others? Let's see. Doc got here first. Then Sally and Nick, followed by Professor Adelbrecht. We all had drinks and snacks. When Lula appeared, she suggested playing a party game—" she broke off. "We ate shortly after that—"

"What party game?"

Annette shook off his question. "It's not important. Just a silly party game. Gordon had the roast on the coals by then, the sausages were done, so all he did was blacken a few eye fillet steaks while we all helped ourselves to salads and bread—"

"What party game, Annette?" Watson repeated. The more he knew, the clearer the context.

She told him and he pretended not to be shocked.

"You must understand," she said. "Lula is like that. She enjoys insinuating things and watching people's reactions. She'll put on the most innocent expression and say ambiguous things, double entendre. Attention-seeking. I imagine she's quite lonely, no children and an absent husband."

"If her husband's away a lot, she has plenty of opportunity to play around. Perhaps her act is a cover?"

Annette winced. "It's not her photos I found with my husband."

*Touché.*

"Sally dresses like a convent girl and sounds like a nun," continued Annette in that factual, detached tone of hers. "Yet she's capable of having an adulterous relationship with a man twice her age. In broad daylight," the last three words quavered a little.

Women, Watson thought. It's the detail they mind.

"Lula is not two-faced like Sally. With Lula, what you see is what you get."

"Sally's guilt in this matter doesn't prove Lula's innocence." Watson hated provoking her. No choice, though. Police investigator first, star-crossed ex-boyfriend maybe a distant second.

"Don't confuse yourself with logic and semantics, Trevor. Look at the person behind them. Lula is not the cheating type."

"Was your husband?" It was his job to be a jerk.

Annette took it well. "No. Sally may have been a midlife crisis for Gordon, a trophy he just couldn't resist. Our marriage," now she coloured slightly, "was far from perfect, despite what I kept telling myself. Ever since my last pregnancy, I..." she coughed, tried again. "He needed, just like every man needs..." Her blush covered her throat now, all the way to where her breasts started.

"That's no excuse," Watson began.

Annette narrowed her eyes and looked him straight in the face. "Have you never broken any rules in order to satisfy your sex drive?"

Watson looked away.

*Charlene. Charlene, and those before Charlene.*

"No, don't answer that. All I'm saying is I don't blame him."

Watson bit down the first words that came to his mind,

toned down the second. "You should blame him," he said. "When he married you, he made a vow before God." That last part meant nothing to Watson, but it should have meant the world to somebody like Gordon Pretorius. "He was a religious man, wasn't he?"

"Even religious men lose their way, Trevor. I'm as guilty of breaking the marriage vows as he was."

"What?" Watson felt little ants of numbness tickle his lower lip, like local anaesthetics at the dentist. He rubbed his skin to get some feeling back. "You had an affair, too?"

The implications were paramount, another motive for getting rid of her husband. A divorce would have been out of the question, she would have walked away with no house, no money, perhaps not even the custody of her children, for Gordon Pretorius was a powerful man with friends in powerful circles.

His jealousy obliterated his train of thought. That she'd been married was hard enough. But a lover?

Annette kept staring at him. "Tell me you haven't just accused me of infidelity."

"But you said—" He replayed her words. "All right, so you broke the vow by—what? Failing to love and obey?"

He said it flippantly. The look in her eyes told him he'd hit a nerve.

"Let's move on, shall we?" he suggested. "Saturday evening after the key ring game. You had dinner. Anything significant happen?"

Annette squeezed her temples with the palms of her hands. "All the while we're talking, I have a sense something's slipped my mind. Something about the party."

Ella LeRoy sat in the bay window of her lounge. It was her favourite spot, with a panoramic view of her back garden. Red tangles of bougainvillea, basket-like finch nests, the birdbath where the birds came to drink in the dry February heat....She lifted her binoculars to observe a solitary bee-eater, with its pale green belly and tawny head.

Out of habit, she directed the binoculars towards the towering mansion where her daughter lived. There was no need to do that any longer, yet Ella checked out the abandoned pool and wondered where Julie-Ann and Danny were. She scanned the windows and the terraces...

Incensed, she dropped the binoculars. Annette and Trevor. Together outside. Talking.

Ella hadn't approved of it fifteen years ago. She didn't like it any better now.

Trevor's embarrassment when discussing his sexual desires was palpable. Annette grew acutely aware of the space that separated his body from hers. The space between them, the space in-between, was less than a metre. At the same time, it measured more than fifteen years, a chasm she had no way of crossing.

"What was it, Annette?" he urged, oblivious of her confusion. "Try to remember."

*Something significant. Something significant.*

"After the key ring game..." she tried to concentrate on the events of the party, yet her thoughts kept slipping to Trevor. What did he carry on his key ring? "After the game, we all moved to the pool area where the barbecue is, and after we'd eaten, Lula suggested we all go for a swim."

"Let me get it straight. Lula put forward the idea of the key ring game, she proposed the swimming..."

"Lula's spontaneous. Unconventional. When she feels like something, she makes it happen. It never occurred to her how it might look."

"Quite selfish, then."

"No, Trevor. Self-centred."

"And all the time you were drinking, playing and eating, were you all together or did anybody leave the group?"

*If only it were as easy as checking people's alibis!*

Of course we weren't always together," she said. "The ladies would leave to, you know, check their makeup, and the men went off to—er—check their makeup too. Nick and Sally disappeared together for a good ten minutes to admire the flowers in my garden," she didn't allow herself a smile, "and when they came back, there was lipstick all over Nick's face."

"In Gordon's…" Trevor broke off.

"You're wondering how far Sally went with her boyfriend, right under Gordon's nose, in his very own garden? Not very far, I assure you."

"How do you know?"

Annette remembered the revealing bulge in Nick's trousers. "A woman can tell these things."

Trevor's expression remained sceptical.

She tried again. "When they came back to join us, Nick did not look," she lowered her gaze, "*satisfied*. In fact, he was acting rather uncomfortable, physically uncomfortable." She stared pointedly at the place below Trevor's abdomen. "Sally joined us straight away afterwards, while Nick went for a solitary stroll in the garden to, ahem, cool his desire."

When the last asteroid on the screen exploded into a rainbow, Danny pushed away the joystick.

"Talk," he said to his sister.

No effect.

"Julie Ann Pretorius."

Julie shrugged. "There's nothing to talk about. Let's play another round. My turn now."

Danny felt the muscles of his jaw harden, and he made a conscious effort to relax them. "I know you went out into Grandma's garden after dinner on Saturday. You had her binoculars around your neck. Tell me what you saw."

Julie squeezed her lips together and hunched over the joystick.

Watson blanked his face. "How long was Nick alone in the garden?"

"Ten minutes, maybe?"

Enough time to bang the poisoned nail into the wine room

door.

"Was that before or after the key ring game?"

"Before. We went to dine straight after it—hang on, I remember now." Her face cleared. "The thing that could be significant? Gordon said he had an announcement to make after dinner."

"Did he?" Watson asked the question without much hope.

"No."

"And do you have any idea…"

"No."

Watson drew a triangle in his notebook. Pretorius throws a party. Says he has an announcement. He's murdered before he can say anything. Typical.

He decorated the page with a head of a unicorn. "All right. Is there a way to get into your garage directly from the garden?" Damn, he should know this already. The sketch of the murder scene was in the case file.

"Other than the tilting door for the cars, there is also a side entrance we never lock in case Johannes, the garden boy, needs a tool from the garage bench."

Another strand of hair fell across her face in an unfamiliar way. Her old hairstyle had been a ponytail, and even though she wore it loose now, in his mind's eye she was always the girl with the red ponytail.

Too much past. Too much of what could have happened and hadn't. Watson looked at Annette and saw the path untaken. The might-have-been would have sliced open his soul, only he didn't have a soul. He'd lost it on that fateful day in Soweto.

*Don't think about it.*

"Of the people present at the party, who would know that your husband," the term's edges still felt serrated in his mouth, "was the only likely person to open the wine room door?"

Annette spread her hands. "Everybody? No-one? It's customary for the head of the household to be in charge of the wine."

The phone rang. When Annette went inside to answer it,

Watson caught his breath and found his thinking head again, though he didn't like what his thinking head was saying.

Could he believe anything Annette had told him?

He shook his head to dislodge the uncomfortable idea, tuned his ears to Annette's voice.

"Oh, hi, Mom." Watson thought she sounded a little off-balance. "We'll have to keep it short now, but I'll pick you up on the way to church—"

Then, all traces of irritation gone, "What sort of pains?"

Watson started moving. He heard, "I'll be right there."

"Chest pains?" he asked. "You go ahead, I'll call the ambulance."

"She said no ambulance, just a cup of tea."

"I'll drive you."

They were already in the car when Watson put together the facts. Aconitine, chest pains.

"Shiiiii—," he broke off the swearword, conscious of Annette in the passenger seat. His fingers were already working the radio. His mouth caught up and requested medical assistance at Mrs. LeRoy's address. Annette had question marks in her eyes, but he remained silent, the car squealing around the two corners to a standstill outside Mrs. LeRoy's house.

Barely aware of the hot rubber stench, Watson yelled at Annette to stay back. For all he knew, the killer was still hiding there.

Ella LeRoy reclined on the couch, cursing her bad fortune. When she faked her chest pains, she had not counted on Trevor Watson accompanying Annette to save the day. All she'd wanted was for her daughter to stop looking so darned cosy sitting outside with her erstwhile suitor.

"Mom." Annette ducked under Trevor's blocking arm and burst into the room.

Ella fanned her face with yesterday's newspaper (more front-page articles about Gordon's death, though the paper contained nothing except speculation) and hoisted herself up onto her elbow.

"I'm fine," she said a bit more sharply than she'd intended. "Just some jabbing in my chest, and I couldn't breathe. No need to worry."

"Mommy." Annette looked grey, as though she was really the one on the verge of a heart attack.

Trevor Watson put his hand—he actually put his hand—on Annette's arm. "Allow me," he said. He turned to Ella. "Ma'am. It may be a false alarm. However, we have reason to suspect that your condition may be the result of foul play. A medical expert is on his way—"

"Call him off." This time the sharpness was deliberate. "There's nothing wrong with me. Foul play, my foot. First you insinuate there's something suspicious in the fact that my unfortunate son-in-law took his life, now you're chasing the boogieman because I felt faint."

"Nevertheless, ma'am—"

"Nevertheless nothing, Trevor Watson. Do as I tell you."

"No, ma'am. Not this time."

Their eyes met. Ella felt a sting—a genuine one—straight through her chest.

"The killer's out there." Trevor Watson's posture was all authority. "We don't know his motives, but we know the poison he uses simulates a heart attack. Mrs. LeRoy, have you consumed anything that tasted off? Sustained a small cut? Used hand cream?"

Annette's heart slowed down to its normal pace only after the police doctor had pronounced her mother "as fit as the proverbial fiddle". As irritatingly meddlesome and know-it-all as the woman was, Annette would never be able to stop loving her. Wouldn't want to, either.

"You gave me a scare." She squeezed her mother's fingers. "I don't want to leave you here all by yourself. Let me hire a nurse."

"And pay her with what money?"

Nothing escaped the old lady. "Don't worry about it, Mother. There was cash in Gordon's safe. Lots of cash. The policemen have taken it as evidence but I'm sure—"

"You'll get it within the hour," Trevor interjected.

*Dear Trevor.*

"Isn't it easier for me to move into the mansion? We can sell this house. With Gordon gone, the children need another adult around."

That part about never being able to stop loving my mother, Annette mused, I didn't know how wrong I could be.

Watson wondered what made fiddles particularly fit as he watched the medic pack away his gear.

"A moment longer of your time, Doctor?"

"Sure."

Watson led him outside, raised a questioning eyebrow.

"Not a single sign indicating aconitine poisoning or carbon monoxide inhalation," the medic said. "No visible cuts or prick marks on her skin, either."

Watson thought for a bit. "So—what is your professional opinion? A panic attack?"

"In my professional opinion," the medic gave a short bark of a laugh, "it was a cry for attention. Lonely people will stop at nothing to get noticed. Mostly the elderly. This one here is only in her fifties, but it takes all sorts."

Watson thought some more. "She told her daughter not to make a fuss. That doesn't tally with your explanation."

"That's not my problem, man," the other man said, not unkindly. "You're the detective. Work it out. The symptoms she experienced, correction, *said* she experienced, are not consistent with a heart attack or a panic attack or any affliction known to medicine apart from one."

"Being?"

"Hypochondria. Practically incurable. This was as classic a faking of a heart attack as I've ever seen. Best of luck to that foxy daughter of hers."

*Foxy.*

Watson made a scornful face. "And you a married man."

"The emphasis is on the word *man*, not on the word *married*. I'm a man. I can't help noticing perfection."

"Aren't you a church goer?"

The doctor winked. "The Ten Commandments talk about not coveting your neighbour's wife. Nothing in there prohibits a married man from coveting, or indeed from taking on, an unmarried woman. Look at Abraham, look at Jacob."

And there you had it, Watson thought with a bitter taste in his throat, Gordon Pretorius' excuse for bonking his secretary. The logic would appeal to a man like Gordon. It might also explain why he hadn't gone after the married Lula.

Annette appeared in the doorway of Mrs. LeRoy's house. The greyness in her face had already faded away to her usual porcelain white. "Does your van have a stretcher, Doctor?" A pleading look lit up her face. "I'm so sorry to impose, but it's not a good idea to leave my mother alone. Would it be possible, in her condition, to move her to my house?"

*Great.*

The hypochondriac mother, once upon a time suspected of killing her husband, was moving in with Annette. How much worse could the day get?

There were many more things Annette wanted to tell Trevor. About Gordon's brother killed in Angola and how it had affected Gordon's ultra conservative father. About Gordon's stillborn sister. About his mother.

Presently, though, Annette's own mother was moving in and Annette's emotions swayed between bad and worse. The immense guilt conflicted with the almost equal sensation of dread. Her mother had meddled with Annette's life often enough, most recently the injection that had stopped Annette's milk. There had been others. Offering to mail Annette's university application and dropping it into the rubbish bin. *Women don't need to scare men off with fancy degrees, darling.* Getting rid of Trevor. Accepting Gordon's marriage proposal on Annette's behalf.

Tension gripped Annette's spine. She made a conscious

effort to breathe.

"Hester," she called out as soon as she reached her own front door, "please prepare a room for my mother. She'll be staying here a while."

Compassion washed over the black woman's face, hastily hidden by a polite nod. "Lunch is ready to be served, missus."

Annette had an idea. "My mother will have a tray in bed. She is feeling poorly today. Doctor's orders."

"Very good, missus."

*Yes*, mused Annette, *very, very good.*

Watson itched to get back to the case. Mrs. LeRoy's call had come just as a vague shape of the culprit was forming in the back of his mind. Now the solution had scuttled away and he had to start from zero.

At the lunch table, the conversation bordered on dull. Julie asked whether they could go back to school soon. Annette said as soon as they were up to it. Watson announced that for the sake of safety, a police car would do the school runs.

Danny perked up. "With the siren on?"

It would be against the law. Hell alone knew how many rules he'd broken in this case, more in the last four days than in the last four years, for sure. "Sure," Watson nodded, "why not."

He was pleased to see Julie spear a cube of cheese onto her fork and pop it into her mouth.

"Daniel, Julie," Annette's tone sounded official. "After lunch today, we will all go to church to say goodbye to your father."

"A funeral?" Julie's chin trembled. Watson watched with concern as she lifted a napkin to her mouth and placed the semi-masticated cheese cube in its fold.

"Just a memorial service, honey. We'll all say a few words about Pappa, remember the good times, share our grief with others."

Danny spoke for the first time. "I don't want to go."

"It's the right thing to do, Danny."

"Mom, I'm sorry. But no."

Watson looked at the boy, at the golden fluff outlined against the sun on his cheek, at the muscles set in the adolescent jaw. A boy. A man. Thirteen was such an awkward age.

He expected Annette to push the issue, if not for her son's psychological wellbeing, then at least for the sake of appearances, and was surprised when she gave in without another word.

"I need to speak to you," he said when the children had left. He didn't only mean about the case.

She touched his sleeve. The single gesture sucked all the oxygen from the room. "I need to speak to you too. Did you really say Gordon was poisoned?"

*Damn him and his big mouth.*

"I'm not at liberty to—"

Annette's hand moved from his arm to his lips. "BRAVO has a piece of equipment to analyse the chemical composition of substances."

Captain Trevor Watson, the sharpest detective in South Africa, should have realised it himself. No fool like a fool in love.

*There. He'd admitted it.*

*In love.*


Annette stood at the pulpit beside the vicar, waiting for everybody to take their places. *The murderer always comes to his victim's funeral*, the phrase kept pounding out a pattern of pain inside her temples, thud-thud-thud-thud, *the murderer always comes to his victim's funeral.* Even if, technically, this wasn't a funeral. *The murderer—*

"Annette?"

"I'm all right, Mother. Please go sit down." No reaction. "Don't gamble with your health. Perhaps you should have stayed at home with Danny and Beth, after all."

"Nonsense, child. How would it look if I stayed away? What would everybody think? It's bad enough Danny's not here to say his last goodbyes."

"Danny's saying goodbye in his own way, Mother." Annette scanned the room, desperate for an excuse to end the exchange. "Oh, dear, I see Doc's heading over this way. Mother, could you possibly steer him away? I can't deal with condolences right now."

Annette almost felt sorry for Doc as he escorted her mother to a pew and remained there, pinned down by the older woman's stare.

Nick Haddow entered the church next, wearing his usual look of an adorable bad boy who would empty the cookie jar knowing he'd get away with it every time. If he was still bearing a grudge against the dead man because of the punch-out, his body language concealed it.

*Gordon. A dead man.*

After four days, it still sounded incredible.

Sally Martins, all in widow-black yet dry-eyed, walked a few paces behind Nick. Together and apart.

The other mourners—Julie—no, Annette couldn't look at Julie's small crumpled figure clad in a smaller version of her own dress. Julie's desolate expression was everything Annette's should have been.

Lula's face, unusually serious with red swollen eyelids—gosh, had she been crying?—reflected the colour of her cinder twin-set. Lula's expression was also closer to what Annette's should have been. Alongside her, professor Adelbrecht, in a well-fitting black suit and white shirt, looked so much like a penguin Annette expected him to hold up a slogan advertising Eskimo Pies.

Of all the things a widow would think during her husband's memorial service, she rebuked herself, ice cream shouldn't be on the list. A pang of hunger twisted her insides. Good. Hunger was good. Hunger meant your arms were slim, your stomach flat, your body attractive.

She cast her eyes over the pews of forty-something men. Gordon's classmates? Buddies from university? She knew so little about his life before their marriage.

*The murderer always comes to his victim's funeral.*

Thud. Thud, thud, thud.

Her gaze caught Trevor's and she lowered her lids for the briefest of moments. It was like a sip of lemonade on a summer afternoon. She rolled her shoulders to release the tension in her neck. She would go through with it, if not for Gordon's sake, then for Julie's.

The vicar leaned towards her. "It's time to start," he whispered. "Are you ready?"

*Ready to say what a good husband and father Gordon had been?*

*Ready to send him off shrouded in honour and grief?*

*Ready to send him off?*

She nodded. "Ready."

The murderer watched Annette as she delivered Gordon's eulogy.

"Gordon, thank you for our years together," she began. "Thank you for our three wonderful children. I can't bear the thought," her voice fractured into a choke, "that you won't be here to watch them grow——"

She was good, the murderer thought. Her distress sounded genuine enough, and the way she had pinned up her decadent red locks out of sight made her look almost inconsolable. *Almost* and *sounded*. In reality, she was no bereaved widow.

So much the better. When presented with the evidence, the cops would have no trouble accepting her guilt.

The refreshments were served in the church hall. Watson followed Annette as she moved from group to group.

"I'm confident the police will find the culprit, Professor," she said.

Watson wished he could go halves with her on that belief.

"Are they sure it was not—natural causes?"

*Since when was "natural causes" a euphemism for suicide?*

"I'm positive it was murder."

He didn't like the way her voice had changed. From feather to flint in a fraction of a second. He looked straight at her, surprised. Her eyes gave away nothing.

Annette moved towards Lula and the two women embraced. Lula didn't say a word, her crushed expression out of place against Annette's blank one.

"I'm going to find the person who did it," Annette repeated. "I've found something—"

Watson steered her away. "What on earth do you think you're doing?" he whispered.

"That's very kind," Annette replied at full volume. She leaned towards him. "Trust me," she breathed into his ear.

He knew it was the last thing he should do, but the almost-kiss sent his hormones haywire. Half an hour later, he cursed himself for the lapse of attention.

Half an hour later, a high-pitched scream tore the afternoon air. People milled around the interconnected church courtyards, each landscaped in a distinct theme, from an enchanted garden and a waterfall grotto to a desert rockery and a wildflower meadow.

The high-pitched scream arose from a mini-maze of hedges. Watson elbowed others out of the way and ran.

When he got to the scene, the first thing he spotted was the knife. A big, sturdy, silver knife with an elaborate handle and a glinting blade, the one used to slice cakes for their afternoon tea.

The knife lay in the orange dust. Two steps away from it, Julie sobbed hysterically in Annette's arms.

Watson clicked into his police-officer-in-charge mode. "Who's hurt?"

"Nobody got hurt." Annette didn't even look up. "Julie got a fright, that's all."

"The kn-kn-knife," managed the girl. "I heard someone behind me and I t-turned around and I saw it."

"What did you see?"

Julie moved her chin in the direction of the knife.

"The knife?"

She nodded.

A flicker of hope pierced Watson's self-reproach. "Did you see the person who held the knife?"

"No. The knife was on the ground."

"All right." Goodbye, flicker. "What did you do?"

"I screamed."

Watson thought fast. "Julie. Did you see anything else besides the knife?"

The little girl looked surprisingly like her mother, with her shiny black dress. Her speculative mien told him exactly how big a part of the hysterics she'd acted out for the spectators.

She lifted her chin. "I didn't see the man who threw it."

A jolt of adrenaline. "Was it a man?"

"Must have been. He had a knife."

*Right.*

Girls of Julie's age were taught not to talk to *men* they didn't know, and that some *men* were baddies. Statistically speaking, the gender discrimination was justified. In this case, though, Julie's hard-wired prejudices were not helping.

Watson guessed what must have happened. The murderer was targeting Annette—perhaps because she'd been threatening to find out the truth about Gordon's death—and ended up following Julie by mistake. The two were very much the same height and shape. As soon as the girl had turned around the murderer realised his mistake, dropped the knife, fled.

"Julie?" he tried again.

Annette stepped between them. "That's enough, Trevor. Julie's had a shock. She needs to rest now."

"I didn't see anything, mister." Julie looked him straight in the eyes. "Not a single thing."

"Apart from the knife, you mean?"

A pause. Then, "Yes. Apart from the knife."

Annette knew that lilt in her daughter's voice. Julie had told a fib. Now, however, was not the time to draw attention to it. Although the girl had milked it for all it was worth, exaggerating and dramatising her experience in order to get more attention, the regrettable event had spooked her.

"Come back inside," Annette said. "Granny must be worried sick. I'll give you some sugar water for the shock."

"Coke, please, Mommy?"

Negotiating treats. A sure sign Julie was all right. A flood of relief displaced the guilt.

"All right, honey. Only this once, though. Because Coca Cola actually contains even more sugar than sugar water."

"I know, Mommy. Mommy?"

"Yes, honey?"

"I really didn't see anything."

That lilt again. Annette's heart lurched.

"What didn't you see, my darling?"

The trick might have worked six years ago, but Julie was not a little girl anymore. "That's what I'm trying to tell you, Mom. I. Did. Not. See. Anything. No matter what Danny says."

*Danny?*

Annette felt the familiar tightening of her heart.

*What did he have to do with it?*

A stroke of good luck he wasn't here. By staying at home this afternoon, he'd received an automatic alibi.

Ella LeRoy reclined on an armchair, dabbing her face with a napkin. When she'd heard the scream, the blood in her veins froze, and she'd felt sure God was punishing her by giving her a real heart attack this time. She had recognised Julie-Ann's voice instantly, wanted to rush to her granddaughter's aid—and couldn't move a muscle. Like Lot's wife. Yes, punished for sure by an omnipresent and omniscient God.

"I'm all right, Granny." A small hand covered hers and gave it a light squeeze. Julie-Ann was smiling, the rims of her eyes still a little raw, the eyes themselves cloudless. "A big bad man came after me with a carving knife, and I scared him off."

"Goodness gracious, child. My poor darling little girl. My brave, wonderful Julie-Ann. Let me look at you. Are you all right?" She squeezed the precious girl to her chest.

"Stop it, Gran, you're embarrassing me."

"But, heavens, a carving knife?"

"Actually, it was a cake knife," Annette interjected.

Ella waved her off. "You must be ever so careful, Julie-Ann. South Africa is not as safe as it used to be. All those liberals stirring up the bad element, you mark my words. If we don't put a stop to it, the streets won't be safe from blacks brandishing carving knives—"

"Mother, it happened in a church garden, not in the street. It was one of the white people who came to the memorial service. And for the last time, it was not a carving knife!"

Her daughter's outburst was so astounding, Ella forgot to ask why the type of knife mattered.

The reporters, already scattering as the tea was being served, now came back, buzzing like fat, blue flies. The American journo was with them. The Minister With No Official Portfolio felt something snap in his fingers. He looked down. A pen he'd picked up from the church's visitor book, was bleeding its black blood onto his shoes.

"We could simply arrest her in front of an audience, sir," his assistant murmured.

Tempting. Oh, so tempting. Just as well he was good at fighting temptation.

"Negative." He broke the pen halves into halves again.

"Sir?"

"Yes."

"There's this place in town. Excellent at helping men who work too hard. Topless dancing. Private shows. If you know what I mean."

The minister did know. Many of his colleagues dealt with the stress of the job by visiting such clubs. They perused their Bibles and found no verse that would forbid it. But he, he loved his *Bokkie*. And he could tell right from wrong even if the wrong was not explicitly mentioned in the Holy Book.

"No," he said. It came out good and strong.

Watson considered calling a dog handler with a sniffer. Decided against. Everybody had rushed out to follow Julie's shriek and mucked up the scene in the process.

The knife itself, though—he hesitated, looking at the silver contour sealed in a plastic bag. Detector dogs could sniff out traces of blood on weapons that had been thoroughly washed. In this case, of course, there was no blood, just crumbs of cake. Still, would the metal absorb the smell of the perpetrator? Worth a try.

"Jones?"

"Sir."

"Get everybody who's still here to give you something personal, a hankie or a sock, and send it to the dog unit together with the knife. In separate bags," he added. "That's before you dust the knife for prints."

"Yes, sir." The stock reply came out sceptical.

Watson couldn't agree more. But hey, no stone unturned. This case was going to cost him his career. May as well go down in style.

He instructed Annette, Julie and Mrs. LeRoy to be driven home by one of the policemen, with another sitting at the back. He didn't know what good the extra precautions would do if the murderer risked an open attack.

Everybody else he kept back. Most of Gordon's friends from his youth had left straight after the service and Jones would interview the remaining few. For himself, Watson reserved the main suspects.

Professor Adelbrecht. Doc Monterra. Nick Haddow. Lula, whose last name he still had to look up in his notebook every time. Sally Martins.

He conducted the fresh wave of interviews in the vestry, a large empty space with oversized armchairs and a large abstract suggestion of a cross hanging on the wall like an indictment.

Professor Adelbrecht hadn't seen anybody sneak after Julie with the cake knife.

"Tell me about the Order of Unicorns, Professor."

"Don't see how that's relevant."

The brigadier had made sure the press was kept in the dark about the ivory figurine clasped in Gordon's dying fist.

Watson gave him a hard look. "With respect, Professor."

"The Order goes back a long way. My father fought in the

Boer War for the Afrikaner's right to run our own country. Patriotism meant everything to him."

That word again, *patriotism*. Capable of making heroes, of making cowards, of causing good or evil depending on your side of the political divide.

"Was your father the founder of the Order?"

"No." The professor took out a large white handkerchief and began the slow process of cleaning his spectacle lenses. "My father taught us, Piet Pretorius and myself, to love our country. Piet was the one who instituted the Order way back when Gordon was still a child. He wanted to ensure a patriotic environment for his sons. Gordon got involved in the Order in earnest after the bloody communists killed his brother. He needed Stuart's death not to be in vain. To change—all this."

"By *this*, you mean?"

The professor frowned. "Look around you, Captain. There are people out there, white people, who shout for democracy alongside the blacks. Some, I believe, even join the banned ANC rebels. What next? One man, one vote? A black Prime Minister? What?"

Adelbrecht spoke fast, spitting saliva, the words jostling in his mouth in a race to get out first.

"What's the alternative, Professor?" Watson asked. "Violence? Riots? A civil war?"

*Shooting black children in Soweto?*

"Nothing wrong with that. War, even a civil war, is the honourable way."

Something inside Watson snapped. "Poisoning a township's water supply. How is that honourable?"

"It's all about numbers." Adelbrecht's eyes were steady. "At present, our country is ruled by a minority, a very worthy minority, but a minority nonetheless. Global powers like America have a problem with that. If we change the numbers, though, if whites become the majority—"

The guy really believed it. A frozen prickly pear of dread blocked Watson's airways.

Ella LeRoy held her tongue all the way home. Once the children were out of earshot, Julie-Ann treating her brother to a full retelling of her adventure with a carving knife the size of an elephant's tusk and growing, Ella cornered Annette in the nursery.

"I need to talk to you——" She paused. Beth was face down on the carpet, not liking the position one bit. The baby craned her neck and wriggled her body in a vain attempt to flop over.

Her beautiful Beth. Her love. Ella would give her right arm in exchange for Beth's happiness. She would steal and kill and remove every obstacle. Her lower back protested when she stooped to turn the baby onto her back. Beth delivered an effervescent squeal of delight.

"Mother. I wish you wouldn't. Beth needs to exercise her muscles."

"Nonsense. I never put you or your sisters on the floor, and you turned out just fine." She shouldn't have said it. Annette got a bit funny whenever her sisters were mentioned.

"*Just fine*, indeed." The snort escaping Annette's throat was not at all ladylike. "With Jeanette in England and Lynette in the Cape. Such loving daughters. When was the last time either of them phoned you?"

Unexpected tears blurred Ella's vision. "It's expensive to call long-distance."

"A Christmas card never broke anybody's budget. But they are in no hurry to communicate with you, Mother. They're too busy enjoying their freedom."

"Annette!"

Annette tickled Beth's bare foot before easing her baby onto her tummy once more. "The Three Sisters. Annette, Jeanette and Lynette. Carbon copies of one other, right down to our first names, the sports we did and the opinions we were allowed to have. Nobody ever thought of us as individuals, we were always the LeRoy Sisters, the conservative, stuck-up LeRoys people never bothered to invite to parties."

Trevor didn't see the LeRoy Sisters, Ella remembered, her teeth clamping. He'd only had eyes for Annette.

That's why he'd had to go.

Monterra shook his head. "Sorry I can't help you, Captain. Haven't seen anything even though I stayed with Annette throughout the afternoon tea. She's very vulnerable at the moment. Gordon's death was a big blow."

Watson doubted it. "So you were with Mrs. Pretorius when you heard the scream?"

"Not quite. When Annette finished her tea, she asked me to make sure the guests were properly looked after. She didn't want to give people the wrong idea, my playing host at Gordon's memorial service, but she absolutely had to check up on her mother. Mrs. LeRoy has a heart condition—"

"We're aware of that," Watson interrupted. The thought of Monterra playing host with Annette chafed him. "But surely people wouldn't get the wrong idea? A respectable married man like yourself..." Watson let the sentence hang in the heat of the afternoon.

"Indeed." Doc rose from his chair. "If there's nothing else..."

"Sit."

Monterra sat down like a trained puppy. Watson took one look and knew he was going to enjoy the next ten minutes.

"Let's start with your wife," he began. "We've noticed some inconsistencies within your official records—"

"All right, you got me there," Monterra raised both his hands, palms outwards. "I'm not married, though I tell people otherwise. You see, in certain lines of business, particularly working for the government, it creates a better impression to be married. A family man seems more reliable, more stable, more rooted in the community. Personally, if I ever ran a company, I'd only employ single men, like Nick Haddow, who don't have to be back home in time for dinner with their children every evening. Single men work harder, they are more focused..."

Watson couldn't resist asking. "And single women?"

"Hey?"

"Are single women good workers? More focused than married women?"

Monterra laughed. "Ah, I see what you mean. And the answer is no. Single women don't care about their careers. They are all after one thing."

So are men, Watson thought without humour. Single or married. "And what might that one thing be?"

"Getting married, of course. That's what they all want. A woman is nothing without her husband."

He really believes that, Watson thought incredulously. It was bad enough to live in a country where the law discriminated against women and even worse to hear the discrimination justified in a casual remark.

"So tell me this, Doctor Monterra. Why didn't you simply solve your career problem by getting married to some lucky girl and making her a not-nothing?"

If Monterra had picked up on the sarcasm, he didn't show it. "You mean, do what Gordon Pretorius did? Get myself a trophy wife, ten years my junior, with good genes and good breeding potential, an excellent homemaker and hostess? And when I realize how little I care about her, get myself an even younger trophy mistress to pay tribute to my aging manhood? No, Captain. I simply didn't find a woman I loved enough to make my wife. As you surely understand, having never been married yourself."

A certain something in Monterra's tone seized Watson's attention. "Is that a shot in the dark, Doctor Monterra, or have you been asking around about me?"

"I'm a government employee, Captain. A *special kind* of a government employee, with access to," he paused, "*information*. Don't worry, I won't tell your superiors about your past involvement with Mrs. Pretorius. As long as it remains in the past. Do we understand each other?"

Watson suppressed a grin.

*Thank you, Mrs. LeRoy, for your timely phone call to the brigadier.*

"We understand each other perfectly, Doctor Monterra," he

said. "You'll be disappointed to hear my superiors believe there to be no conflict of interest. On the other hand, the penalty for attempting to bribe, blackmail or obstruct a police officer is—is something I'm prepared to overlook if you allow my men to analyse a substance in BRAVO's lab before we get the official go-ahead."

Annette hoped a smile would soften the words she had to speak next. The smile wouldn't happen. "I've always wondered," she said slowly, waving a red-and-white rattle just out of Beth's field of vision, forcing the baby to lift up her little head off the carpet, "what you had against Trevor. Why you made me split up with him."

The temperature in the room plunged despite the heat of the afternoon.

"Trevor was a fine young man," her mother said in a voice painted over with *do-not-enter* signs.

Annette ignored the warning. "I was so stupid back then." Her dry throat made speaking painful. "So very, very stupid. I really thought you knew better. And when you said I was young and naïve and couldn't tell when a boy only wanted to 'do his thing' to me, I believed you. I believed all his wonderful words were just a way to make me open my legs for him—"

"Good. I hope you believe me still. Trevor Watson may be wearing a uniform today and he may be fifteen years older, but underneath it all he's still a man, and the only thing on his mind is how to get into your knickers."

The room started hurtling, plummeting through space and time. "I wish." Annette didn't mean it the way it sounded, only that Trevor had other things on his mind, like arresting Danny. She wasn't going to clarify, though. Not when she knew her mother's interpretation was equally valid.

Her mother took a step back. "Annette, poor Gordon's not even in his grave yet. Don't you have any shame?"

Annette considered the question, though she knew it to be rhetorical. Deep breaths, in and out. Did she have any shame?

Plenty. Would she hesitate to use her sexual power over Trevor to bargain for her son's freedom?

"Not one bit," she said aloud.

"I'm sure our Doc has a crush on Annette, the way he's been tangoing around her all day," Nick Haddow said with a wicked grin. "She doesn't see it, of course. Annette puts people in boxes and expects them to behave accordingly. As Doc is married, his attention must be kindness, not flirting. By default."

Watson thought Nick was not only a brilliant scientist, but also an acute observer. In his experience, the two seldom went together. Super-intelligent people often sucked at practical life. Still, he didn't want to talk about Monterra's flirting, especially now he knew the guy wasn't actually married.

"Whom do you suspect of today's prank with the knife?" he asked instead.

The shrug Nick gave was larger than life. "Sorry, no clue. Though I think you hit the nail on the head," his voice faltered, "oops, a cliché! I mean, you got it right when you called it a prank. Julie's a good kid. Nobody'd want to hurt her."

"What about the theory that the knife-bearer was after Julie's mother? They did look pretty similar this afternoon, what with Mrs. Pretorius' hair pinned up."

Nick chewed on some imaginary tobacco, poked his tongue into one cheek, then into the other. "Last time I saw Julie, she had long hair. The haircut is less than a week old. It's possible whoever's behind the knife episode didn't realise." He chewed some more. "No, wait. Everybody saw Julie's new look in church today. They would have made extra sure they were following the right woman. Plus, why would anybody like to kill Annette?"

If Nick hadn't figured it out, Watson wasn't going to enlighten him. Emphasising Annette's bizarre comments would only expose her to more danger.

"Right," he said. "What about why somebody would like to kill Gordon Pretorius?"

"I don't know, Captain. When a prominent scientist dies in

suspicious circumstances, it pays to broaden your thinking beyond the usual the-wife-did-it scenario they are so fond of in murder mystery books."

"Are you trying to do my work for me?" Watson tried for bullying. Difficult when you have to suppress your smile.

"Wouldn't dream of it. I know an intelligent person when I see one—which is not very often."

Watson realised he was being flattered. It didn't change the warm feeling that spread inside his chest like butter left in the full blast of the February sun.

*Buttered up.*

"Speaking of books, have you read *Gone with the Wind?*"

Watson shook his head. "I don't do romances."

"*Gone with the Wind* is not a romance novel. It's a history textbook on South Africa's future. 1982 is our crossroads. Which way will we head? Will we learn from the past? Will we learn from other countries?"

"You mean, learn from America? Win the civil war?"

Nick pulled a face. "In *Gone with the Wind*, the South fought for their way of life. What they didn't realise was that their lifestyle as they knew it was over as soon as the first shot of the Civil War was fired. It didn't matter whether they won or lost the war, because everything they had cared about was already obliterated by the very act of fighting."

Was it too late for South Africa, too? Watson couldn't answer.


Annette's eyes avoided Ella's. "I think you'd better go to your room, Mother. We have nothing more to discuss."

Every word like a dagger straight into Ella's heart. Children were so ungrateful. You slaved away your whole life, you denied yourself, and suddenly your children were their own persons who didn't send Christmas cards, or who said, "We have nothing more to discuss."

"Oh yes, we have," she retorted. "We have plenty to discuss. I'm your mother. Julie-Ann's grandmother. I need to know what really happened at the memorial service. Who attacked the poor girl? What happened?"

Annette drummed her fingers along her bottom lip. "Nothing happened. Someone mistook Julie for me."

"But why would they want to chase *you* with a knife?"

"You know why. The anonymous letters."

*The anonymous letters?*

Ella LeRoy backed off, mystified.

Lula's voice was breathy. "What can I do for you, Captain?"

It came across suggestive. Lula sent out sexual messages, as though she pulsated out raw primeval sex.

Annette didn't pulsate. Annette was a constant, she was tranquillity and composure. Of the two women, Annette won hands down.

"We're trying to establish who followed Julie Pretorius through the church garden with a cake knife," he said to Lula, thoroughly sick of repeating himself. A yawn threatened to force his jaws apart, and he clamped them together. "Did you notice anything that might shed some light—"

"I believe I may have, Captain."

Watson sat up, the yawn vanquished.

"I don't know anything about the knife," Lula said, "but I did see Doc follow Annette out of the gazebo where tea had been served, and walk after her deeper into the gardens."

*Doc!*

"And you're sure it was Annette he followed? Not Julie?"

"I *thought* it was Annette," Lula said, "I *assumed* it was her. Doc always keeps close to Annette at parties. It's quite sweet, really. He may style himself on James Bond but around Annette he's a faithful Don Quixote."

*Or a donkey, at any rate.*

Watson held back a snort. What was it about the mating ritual that brought out the worst in men?

He asked a few more questions, probing deeper into what Lula had witnessed. No use. Time for a new topic. "What do you know about the Order of Unicorns?"

"Is that what they call themselves?" Lula's smile was all scorn. "They pretend to be God's gift to South Africa, one step away from putting white sheets over their heads and lighting crosses."

"You're sore because they didn't let you in?"

Lula surprised him once more. "Yes. It's no fun to be left out. I'm fed up with the way women are excluded in this country. Because of my gender, I'm forbidden to walk into a bar, or even belong to Toastmasters, or have a stupid figurine of a stupid unicorn on my stupid office desk. Discrimination is what South Africa does best."

Watson couldn't argue. Tried anyway. "Discrimination is part of human nature. Think tribal warfare, think class distinction. The French bowed to their aristocracy until the French revolution. The British revere it today still. If it's acceptable to consider someone superior based on his birthright or surname or because his great-great-great-grandfather sucked up to the king of England, why is discrimination along gender lines more difficult to swallow?"

"Perhaps," said Lula softly, "because of the absolute belief that if a person is female, she has a lesser brain? That she can't possibly amount to anything thanks to her gender? Women are earmarked for nothingness from the moment of birth."

"The same argument is valid for discrimination across the colour-divide."

Lula fell silent.

Watson pressed on. "Who, at BRAVO, has a statuette of a white unicorn?"

"The professor and Doc."

"What about Gordon?"

Lula shook her head. "I've never seen one in his office."

A light flashed in Watson's brain. Better late than never. He was cocking up this case big time.

*A unicorn with a broken horn in Gordon's study at home. A unicorn inside Gordon's fist, now safely in evidence. Not the same unicorn, clearly.*

*Whose?*

He'd seen a figurine of a white unicorn in Adelbrecht's office. He hadn't seen one in Monterra's. Monterra. Funny how his name kept cropping up.

Even though Julie relished all the attention she got from the knife incident, Annette's heart contorted whenever she remembered.

Scalding her lips on her coffee, she analysed her motives once more. Could she have done it any other way?

*No.*

*No.*

*No.*

"Missus," Hester stood over her, a plate of sandwiches and fruit in hand. "You must eat something. Please. Julie's already eaten hers."

"Thank you, Hester." Annette placed the dish on the coffee table. "A little later, perhaps."

"Not later, Missus Annette. Now."

Feeling like a little girl, she obeyed, forcing a triangle of bread with honey down her throat.

"Now a few grapes, please, Missus."

The grapes were of the dirty-red variety, with bitter skins and large pips, not as flavoursome as the small black Catawba ones that slipped out of their skins when squeezed. Today, though, Annette couldn't taste anything anyway. She swallowed the glutinous flesh.

"That's enough for now, Missus. Eat more in half an hour. Small snacks often. Let your body heal. Master Gordon may have been clever with poisons at his work but he didn't know about women."

Annette couldn't hold back her words. "Isn't that the truth."

She closed her eyes. Something niggled. She let her mind drift, playing back the conversation.

The sudden realisation propelled her upright.

*How did Hester know what Gordon did for a living?*

\* \* \*

"You've left me till last, Captain," Sally Martins said. "Didn't you think I had anything important to tell you?"

She was only a child, Watson reminded himself, a nineteen-year old child with so much growing up to do still. "What is it that you have for me, Sally?" he asked in a mild voice.

Sally thrust something into his hands. "This is not my handbag."

He didn't understand. "All right," he said slowly. "Whose is it? Why do you have it?"

"It's Annette's."

Even before Watson's brain produced the *so-what* question, his heart was hurtling down into a rocky abyss. "And you are showing me Annette's handbag because..." he left the sentence dangling.

"Look inside," Sally said. "I thought it was my own bag, they look exactly the same, and when I opened it to get my keys... Go on, have a look."

Watson did. It was an elaborate handbag made of soft leather, with fancy zips and pockets. The main compartment was empty except for a small laboratory test tube half-filled with an angry-red powder.

The test tube looked so obviously like poison that the walls of the room rushed towards him and crushed his chest before he realised Annette was incapable of killing anyone. If she'd been a policeman, nothing would have made her fire a weapon in Soweto.

"Tell me how you happened to swap bags with Mrs. Pretorius today."

The African night sang softly around her as Hester approached her quarters. She felt somebody's presence and froze. Couldn't be Johannes, he was spending the night back home, and his room was on the other side of the garage.

"Hester," the leader's voice came from behind her. "We worried about you at the meeting."

She turned to face him, pressed her beige palm to the black skin of her throat, felt the THUD-THUD-THUD of her heart as her eyes met his. "I couldn't get away."

"What information have you for us, sister?"

Hester hesitated. She didn't support all the methods employed by those who resisted apartheid: not the random bombs, nor the landmines on South African roads, nor the necklaces of burning rubber.

"The time comes in the life of any nation when there remain only two choices—submit or fight," the leader quoted Nelson Mandela. "We shall not submit and we have no choice but to hit back by all means in our power."

She gestured. "Come inside."

When he was seated on her bed, elevated by the bricks, she leaned against the door and told him everything.

# Chapter 10—Tuesday, Four Days before the Murder

TUESDAYS WERE RESERVED for Annette's tennis club, a game followed by lunch. All her friends were married. Some didn't have children. Annette often wondered how the childless women occupied themselves while their husbands worked. Swam? Shopped? Had their nails done? Surely that couldn't take up all their free time?

"Hester, is Beth still asleep?" Annette asked as she passed the maid. As much as she enjoyed the tennis mornings, she missed the baby.

"Due to wake up any moment, Missus."

"I'll go get her." Annette touched her full breasts. Just the thought of Beth threatened the milk to spill out. "You go on and serve the coffee. We'll take our lunch by the pool, I think. "It's too hot not to take a dip."

"Yes, Missus."

"We'll take our lunch by the pool, I think," Madam Annette said. "It's too hot not to take a dip."

It was too hot, indeed, for the madams and for the maids alike. The ludicrous image of Madam Annette suggesting a shared swim with her maid made Hester lower her head to hide the smile. "Yes, Missus."

When she brought out the coffee carafe, the ladies were

already in their swimming costumes, sitting on the pool steps or wading dignified in the sparkling blue water, careful not to splash their makeup.

They didn't lower their voices when Hester appeared. She was just part of the setting, a robot who cleans floors and serves tea.

"We're going home this Easter," one of the madams said. Her eyes, the eyes of a preening peacock, glared, *Trump that.*

*Home.*

Hester's own love for her land flared up, bright and hot. This madam was born and raised here, she lived in South Africa's luxury and sunshine, but once a year she would take her family and *go back home to England.*

"We were going to go to Mauritius," this from another madam, "but we have season's tickets to all the ballet premieres this year, and the dates clashed. Did you know the director almost considered allowing a *coloured* dancer to perform on stage?"

If the woman had stripped off her bikini bottom to show off her latest wax job, the gasps couldn't have been louder.

"A coloured dancer? Whatever will they think of next? Maids practising the steps of *Swan Lake* while polishing the floors?"

Madam Annette didn't reply. The blonde on her right laughed. "They wouldn't. My maid is so stupid she can't learn a thing. I've told her a million times to take a cloth and wipe the top of the tomato sauce bottle before replacing the lid. No such luck."

Can't or won't, wondered Hester as she handed out the yoghurt and fruit, the food of choice for the rich. If she were rich, she'd eat steak every day. No wonder the madams didn't look happy.

"My maid has such butter fingers, she keeps breaking the dishes whenever she washes up. Really, sometimes I think it would be far easier if I did it myself."

*Easier to break your own dishes, is it?*

"When we still lived in Rhodesia, my parents had five servants. Five. A nanny, a cook, a parlour maid, a garden boy and a chauffeur. That was *the* life. Now we have to make do with two."

Perhaps Missus Annette could employ a cook and a parlour maid too, mused Hester as she returned to the kitchen to clean up after her lunch preparations and do a spot of ironing before it was time to cook dinner while entertaining baby Beth. Hester wouldn't mind just being the nanny. That would be *the* life.

*Dream on, girl.*

Master Gordon would never allow such extravagance.

After lunch, Annette drove to pick up the children from school. Danny came to the car straight away and flung himself into the front seat. Julie stopped by the school gate to chat.

"Mom." Danny furrowed his brow. The crease in his forehead made him look like Gordon. "Mom," Danny repeated. "Does God really exist?"

"Yes." She stole a quick glance at Julie's group. Still talking.

"*Really* really?"

Annette hesitated. What was she supposed to say to that? "Yes. *Really* really."

"How do you know?" Danny's eyes bore into hers. Demanding. Unlocking. Exposing.

She thought for a second. "Look around you, honey. Look at the gold of the sun over the valley. Look at the orange of the soil and the yellow of the grass. Who else would have created this beautiful land?"

Silence. Then, "Mom? What if it was somebody else who created it?"

In effect, he was asking whether the God of the Bible was the same as God the Maker.

"When we pray to God, we pray to the Creator of Heaven and Earth," she said. Her mouth was like sandpaper. She repeated the mantra learnt in childhood. "There is only one God."

Sometimes she wasn't sure she believed it herself. "About the video camera," Annette said, moving on to a safer topic. "I asked your father, and he agreed to lend it to you as long as Julie doesn't touch it."

"Naturally," Julie said as she banged the back door of the car. "As long as Julie doesn't touch it."

Not a safer topic, after all.

Danny asked, "What about doing the documentary at his office?"

Annette hesitated. Danny was only trying to help her manage Julie, she knew, but this was turning out to be a subject almost as treacherous as religion. "Your father and I are still talking," she said diplomatically. "He needs to get clearance from his boss."

"Sure, Mom. Thanks."

A week later, Annette would wonder whether she should have paid more attention to Danny's religion crisis. She would wonder whether by probing Danny's motive for asking about God's existence, she could have changed her family's future.


It was after dinner, that empty hour when the kids were still awake and bound to interrupt any meaningful activity. Gordon switched on the TV, noting with brief approval that Annette had already prepared popcorn and coffee. He sank down into his La-ZBoy and let his mind wander.

"Gordon?"

He made a sound halfway between a grumble and a groan, hating the interruption. Right now, he was staring at a TV advert in which a potato wanted the privilege of becoming a Simba Chippie. Gordon's dilemma was more complex: trying to decide whether to contact the press or his lawyer. The knowledge he had uncovered was weighing him down, tearing at the fabric of his very existence.

"Never mind," his wife said quickly. "Another time."

Never mind? Never *mind*? She had interrupted him and now was dismissing him with a *never mind*?

"What is it?" The TV scene had changed to an idyllic picture of a woman fussing to make a perfect cup of tea. Now *there* went a good wife…

"It's just about Danny's school project," his own wife said.

Typical. Other men had wives who cared about them and

made them tea. Annette's only focus was on the children.

"Forget it," he said, his voice raised, the tone unpleasant even to his own ear. "I've already said yes to the camera. Enough's enough. I don't want him at my office. He can film *your* usual day for all I care."

No way would he let his children anywhere near his place of work. That—that *cesspit*.

He helped himself to a handful of popcorn and turned to the drinks cabinet.

"What are you having?" The atmosphere in the room needed lifting. "A shot of whisky?"

Later, if things went well, the whisky might lead to other things. Gordon missed sex with his wife. It'd been over three bloody months. Sally's inexperienced ministrations were a poor substitute.

Annette was not going to let Danny film her wearing a wet bikini around the swimming pool or breastfeeding his baby sister. The idea of his classmates watching—totally out of the question.

All week she had known she'd call that number. Everything else was a displacement activity. It was wrong. Emboldened by the whisky on ice she'd gulped earlier, she did it anyway.

"Good evening, Doc," she said, beaming her best smile into the phone.

Gordon walked into the bedroom in time to catch the last words.

"Thank you very much for organising it all, Doc. Too kind."

If it weren't for the shock paralysing his wits, he wouldn't have even waited for Annette to disconnect the call.

"You went over my head," he said, his voice like a stranger's in his ringing ears. "I'll teach you never to do that again."

He must have twisted her arm behind her back, he wasn't sure. Annette yelped in pain. Gordon barely registered her cry. The drums in his ears muffled everything: the bang of the bedroom door crashing into the wall, his son's voice, the word "Pa!"

A condensed ray of pain in his shin tore through to his consciousness. He let go of Annette and sat down on the bed, dazed.

*I used physical force against my wife.*

The thought pounded in his head, echoing alien and ghastly.

*Physical force.*

*My wife.*

Annette's steady words filled the room. "Everything is all right, Danny. Sorry we gave you a fright. Your father was— demonstrating the basics of self-defence."

"Of course, Mom." His son sounded very grown-up. "Pa? Sorry I tripped and kicked your shin by accident."

The cover story was transparent enough to be insulting. "No problem, Dan. Go back to your room."

"I'll go with you," Annette said quickly. Too quickly? Gordon couldn't tell.

"Stay," he pleaded.

"I'll be back soon. Just need to check Danny's homework."

Since when did Danny The Golden Boy's homework need checking?

He tried to wait up for Annette. Minutes ticked away until he realised his wife wouldn't be coming back to their bedroom that night.

Perhaps he deserved that. Hell, he definitely deserved that.

It still seemed unfair.

# Chapter 11—Thursday, Five Days after the Murder

WATSON LAY SEMI-AWAKE in the moonlight. The soft hum of Springbok Radio filled the room. He strained to hear the lyrics.

*My heart turns my mind into circles as I lie here all alone in my bed.*

The Ballyhoo song was about choosing between two pretty ladies, which was not the problem keeping Watson's brain alert. The melody stuck with him anyway.

*If there is a man on the moon, can you hear me calling you?*

*Ja*, you man on the moon. Can you help me solve the case? I know the how, you tell me the who and the why.

The man on the moon was silent. Still, now that he had no religion, Watson may as well believe in something. The man on the moon. Moon made of cheese. Cows jumping over the moon...He counted the cows until they morphed into all the murderers he had ever caught.

This anonymous letter was different. Same lined paper and plain envelope, same malformed writing, the words slightly too big and too close together.

> *Stop talking to the cops. For Beth, Julie-Ann and Danny.*

A scream built up in Annette's throat. Silently, it exploded downwards into her chest as her horrified eyes took in the item enclosed inside the paper fold.

Secured with an inch of clear sticky tape, one of Julie's hair ties lay lifeless like an accusation. It would never be used again, even when Julie's hair grew out, for the author of the letter had sliced its shiny fabric beyond repair.

Watson got up early, exhaustion sucking his eyeballs into his skull. His apartment was out of coffee. At the office, he headed straight for the canteen, surprised he wasn't the first. The filter machine was already switched on, drooling out its brown elixir. Its aroma penetrated the cement between Watson's ears. Heaven.

"I'm losing my patience," he heard.

So much for heaven. And not even a *good morning.*

Watson clicked his heels together. "Brigadier."

His superior's quiet voice chilled his bone marrow. "While you're sitting here enjoying your morning brew, a murderer is out there, still at large."

*A few hundred murderers, judging by the police station's archives of unsolved cases.*

"Yes, Brigadier."

"Officially, this is my investigation. Do you know how this makes me look?"

Watson clamped his teeth together, counted backwards from ten. His insubordinate behaviour had never earned him favours before, and now he had more than just his career on the line. One false move and the brigadier would be arresting the most obvious suspect. Take a page out of Jones' manual. "Yes, sir. Sorry, sir."

The older man's eyes accosted his like sharpened steel. The subsequent bellow bounced off the walls of the still empty canteen. "The cat got your balls, man?"

"Yes, sir."

He earned himself a chuckle and a dismissive wave. "Go to it, Captain. Do us proud."

Watson retreated to his office, still clutching his untouched coffee mug. Jones was already there and his expression said

Christmas had turned up late on this February Thursday.

"Captain." No *good morning* from him either. Perhaps it wasn't a very good morning. "You know how you said to dig deeper into everybody's backgrounds? I went through financial statements, birth records and neighbourhood gossips alike, sir. The Ministry of Internal Affairs has an archive room the size of the Kruger National Park, and just as dusty," the tip of his nose twitched. "Good thing it's cold down in their basement. Unlike in the Kruger."

"Are you going to tell me what you've found, constable, or will I have to interrogate it out of you?" Watson took the first sip of coffee. Fresh. The contrast with the usual swill left to brew on the warm plate for hours woke him up more than the caffeine alone ever could.

"No, sir. I mean, yes, sir. I've looked at all the birth records, naturalisation applications and name change forms," Jones took a deep breath. "There is no Monterra anywhere. I've asked the embassies of Italy and Portugal and Mozambique for assistance. No such person. No such surname anywhere in their part of the world."

It was turning out to be a very good morning after all. Watson forgot he was sleepy.

The arrival of the latest anonymous letter didn't change anything. Danny and Julie went back to school that Thursday morning. As much as Annette loved having them at home, they needed the normalcy of their school routine. If you could call being driven in a police car normalcy, but Danny had been elated by the prospect of arriving at school with the siren on.

With Beth fed, changed and asleep in the pram outside, Annette sat on a padded wicker chair nearby, hunched over a cup of tea.

*Who did it?*

She asked herself the question every time she had a quiet moment. Who hated Gordon enough to kill him? Or, who was so afraid of Gordon that the anathema of killing another human being hadn't stood in the way?

She heard the life-long familiar footsteps behind her.

"Was it wise to send Julie-Ann to school so soon after her ordeal?"

"Julie is fine, Mother. We talked about the incident with the cake knife. She can't wait to tell her friends about it. You know how she loves attention."

"If you say so."

"I say so."

A week ago she wouldn't have dreamt of acting this assertive.

Her mother settled herself into an armchair directly opposite Annette's. "I smell condensed milk," she said through her nose.

"That's because I added a spoonful to my tea. Would you like some?"

"Condensed milk is rubbish, Annette. Full of sugar and fat. Think what it's doing to your figure." She reached for Annette's cup. "Here, let me tip it out and pour you a fresh one. Tea tastes so much better without milk."

"Black, you mean." Annette moved her tea out of range.

She didn't think it was possible for her mother to purse her mouth even more. She was wrong.

"There's no need to use that word," her mother said, ice forming around every syllable.

"It's just a word."

"In this country, it's not just a word and you know it. We say *neat*, or *without milk*. What have I been teaching you my whole life?"

If only her mother knew how ridiculous she sounded. Many people saw nothing wrong with racial segregation, but Ella LeRoy embraced apartheid and climbed it to previously uncharted peaks. Nobody else minded *black* as a word.

Annette took a long sip of the sweet creamy liquid. "I don't know, Mother. What have you been teaching me my whole life? To dance to your tune? To not think too much in case men found it undesirable? To marry the man you handpicked for me because the one I had chosen was too dark-skinned for your liking?"

A choke of indignation. "Your Daddy and I never said—"

"—anything of the kind, I know, Mother. You told me it was foolish to wait for Trevor to finish his military service. But the truth was that you didn't want a speed cop for a son-in-law any more than you wanted a son-in-law whose entitlement to the white race might one day be questioned. After all, what would your friends say?"

"What would yours say if you and your children had to go live in Soweto? How would you feel if you had to move out of your comfortable mansion in a white suburb to a shack with no electricity? The only milk you'd drink with your tea then would be condensed, because you'd have no fridge to store fresh milk. I did what I had to do with only your best interest at heart. I always do. As a mother yourself, you should understand."

She snatched the half-full teacup out of Annette's resisting fingers. Tugged.

*Clink-a-link-a-link!* The porcelain cup hurtled to the floor and smashed on the tiles of the terrace.

Annette ignored it.

*I did what I had to do with only your best interest at heart.*

Was her mother still talking about showing Trevor the door, or...

Annette couldn't finish the thought that was hatching in the deepest recesses of her imagination.

*Who hated Gordon enough to kill him?*

*Who else but a disillusioned mother-in-law?*

What Watson wanted to do was to march into Doc's office and cuff him. He fought off the temptation. He needed all the pieces of the puzzle.

Nick was pouring one clear liquid into another when Watson knocked on the door of the lab. The radio placed in the middle of the room was telling him to "get down on it" over and over again. He listened some more. Something about not wanting to dance and standing on the wall. Watson shrugged. Today's music for you.

"The cops again?" Nick raised his eyes from the now clouding test tube, turned down the radio, grinned. "What can I do for you today? An untraceable poison to get rid of your mother-in-law, perhaps? An aphrodisiac that will make any woman putty in your hands? A—"

"I don't have a mother-in-law," Watson interjected, feeling tempted by the poison as the image of Mrs. LeRoy's face floated into focus.

Nick gave a solemn nod. "The aphrodisiac then."

"Another time, perhaps. For now, I have a question concerning your girlfriend's handbag."

"Sally's handbag?"

Watson cocked an eyebrow at him. "You have more than one girlfriend?"

"I wish, but no luck. Hey, if you have any pointers on how to seduce new women while keeping current ones, please share, man to man. South African girls are so prudish, saving themselves for the white wedding. You have no idea how hard it was to get Sally into the sack."

In Watson's experience, girls did not visit *the sack* before the wedding night. While he could just-just understand that Sally would use her sexuality to lure or trick Gordon into marrying her, going all the way with Nick seemed out of character.

"You slept with Sally?"

"No." Nick grinned again. "As I mentioned, it was hard to persuade her. Too hard. For me anyway. I'm not the persistent type."

"Did you realise she was," Watson hesitated, searching for a delicate word, "er, *seeing…*" he broke off.

"You mean, screwing her boss behind my back? Not until the Friday before the murder." Nick's eyes were steady. "I realise that makes me Suspect Number One. My only saving grace is that I told you about it. I could have lied."

Nick was right. It was a revelation Nick had known about Sally's affair with Gordon. A double bluff?

"Tell me about it," he said.

Nick recounted how, on that fateful Friday, he had gone up to Gordon's office at lunchtime.

"The professor wanted me to get Gordon enthusiastic about one of our projects."

"Project Hydra?"

"Aphrodite."

Project Aphrodite. The sketched pyramid of sexual positions. He forced himself to stay on track

"Go on."

Nick shrugged. "I took the stairs up. As I rounded the corner, I saw Sally come out of Gordon's office, her blouse undone and her boobs hanging out. Couldn't believe my eyes. I did an about turn on the spot. Went back to the lab."

Watson waited, his eyebrow raised. When nothing happened, he uttered a concise, "And?"

"And nothing. I remember thinking it wasn't the end of the world. Sally may be a fine-looking woman, but I'm not in love with her. Pathetic to have an old geezer for a rival, though."

"So what did you do?"

"Went back to my experiment. The previous working day was short because Gordon's kids came here to shoot a documentary, and I was glad to have more time on Friday to catch up."

Watson made a mental note to watch the documentary.

"Did you go back to discuss Project Aphrodite with Gordon?"

"No. I never wanted to see him again. Are you going to arrest me, Captain?" Even the most clichéd responses sounded comical in Nick's mouth. The guy had a talent very much wasted in lab research.

"But you went to his dinner party the next day?"

Nick gave him an embarrassed wince. "I'm not proud of my motives. See, I had a good think about it and reckoned if Sally's not a virgin, I could—you know—push the sex issue harder. Get lucky."

Watson nodded. Much as he hated to admit it, Nick's

reasoning wasn't that different from his own. Virgins were taboo, but once they'd lost their so-called treasure…

He got back to the original question. "Tell me about the mix-up with the handbags on Wednesday."

"After the service most ladies put their handbags on the sofa so they could hold a cup of coffee and a plate of cake at the same time. When Sally asked me to fetch hers, I took Annette's by accident. They look rather similar."

"They should," said Watson. "They're identical."

Nick groaned theatrically. "A gift from Gordon, I bet. One designer handbag for each member of his harem."

*Ouch.*

"Please talk me through the security procedures in your lab," Watson asked.

"Consider it done already: there aren't any. And to answer your next question, no, the poison's not locked up. There would be no point—almost everything in my lab is poison, everybody who works here has security clearance, we receive no visitors except via a prior arrangement. Plus, every room gets locked up for the night and the premises are under alarm surveillance."

"Would you notice if poison got stolen from your lab?"

"If all the phials disappeared, sure. I doubt I'd miss one or two out of a dozen." Nick hesitated. "So tell me, captain, does your line of questioning mean that Annette did in fact kill her husband? I recognised my poison as soon as Sally showed it to me."

Watson sidestepped the question. "Do policemen in Zimbabwe share such information," he was going to say 'with the suspects', but amended it, "with the public?"

"Rhodesia." Nick looked him straight in the eye. "Zimbabwe is what the monkeys call the country now they're running it. I," he emphasised every word, "was born in Rhodesia, when it was still Rhodesia."

"All right."

"Remember how I talked about *Gone with the Wind* and that we should learn from other countries?" Nick was on a roll. "I didn't mean The States. I meant somewhere closer. Learn from Rhodesia. In Rhodesia, we thought that if we gave the blacks equal rights, we could co-exist in harmony, black alongside white, ebony and ivory." His smile was different now, broken. "We were fools. What Rhodesia has now is a black president who won the elections in a landslide victory, but we also have uprisings by his opponents. And if anybody thinks Robert Mugabe's reign will be good for Rhodesia in the long run, they ought to have their heads examined—to see where best to put a bullet. On second thought, a bullet would be too good, too pure, for the likes of them."

"You have a lot of hatred in you."

"Let me show you something." Nick pulled out a bunch of keys: car keys, house keys, probably the key to the very office they were sitting in right now. "See this bullet? It's my personal war booty from the Rhodesian bush war. As a teenager, I retrieved it from a gun aimed at me. Retrieved it after I killed the guy who held it. He was younger than me, and probably just as frightened. But when I heard the order to fire, I didn't hesitate. And you know what? I'm bloody glad." Nick tapped the bullet. "He took a long time to die," was all he added. His eyes looked inward, to a moment long ago and far away.

Watson didn't know what to say.

Nick turned up the radio. The room filled with somebody yelling that, "It must be love, love, love". Nick pointed to the speakers. "*Madness*," he said.

"The sentiment?"

"The pop group."

Watson left the room to the sound of "nothing more, nothing less, love is the best."

Madness. Aptly put.

Her mother left the room and Hester came in to sweep up the broken cup.

*Don't think of her as your mom—just another suspect in Gordon's murder—rather her than Danny.*

Deep breath.

So, if her mother had done it, would she have fulfilled the three classical detective-book criteria: means, motive and opportunity?

Motive: to protect her daughter and grandchildren. Although Gordon had always been the hand-picked son-in-law, Annette remembered her mother's reaction to the idea of Danny joining the Order of Unicorns, to Julie's braid having been cut off, to Gordon's outbursts of temper.

How far would her mother go to protect them? Annette winced .

Add to that the financial incentive. Her mother was too young to draw a pension and had no skills to earn money. She lived rent-free in a house owned by Gordon, who also footed all the bills. What if Gordon decided to divorce Annette and marry Sally instead? Not that Annette's mother even knew about Sally's existence. Or did she?

How much of the goings on in the mansion could her mother see from her own house? If Gordon had ever brought Sally home—

"Madam." Hester walked in with the baby. "I can't get Beth to settle. She needs her mommy."

Guilt washed over Annette as she kissed her tiny cheeks and nose. Beth sighed with contentment and Annette cuddled her tighter.

"Hester," she hazarded, "Remember the young madam the master brought home when I was on holiday with the children?"

Alarm mixed with compassion on Hester's face. No perplexity, though. Bull's eye.

"It's all right," Annette said with a smile that was more forced than usual. "I'm not upset."

Not the entire truth. While it was all right, she was very much upset. Repulsed. Revolted. In this house, she thought, probably in my bed. He wouldn't have thought to change the sheets afterwards, either.

Beth stirred unhappily, her drowsy eyes opening wider.

"Shhhh, shhhh, everything's fine." Annette rocked back and

forth on her heels. "I love you, my little one. Now sleep."

Her heart filled with the fierceness of a lioness tending her cubs. In this moment, she'd be perfectly capable of murder if the need arose.

Her own mother, Annette knew, was no different.

Watson found it difficult to keep the interview on topic.

"A pity Gordon missed out on compulsory military service," Adelbrecht raised his finger to emphasise the point. "It's a bonding experience, all for one, one for all. You learn to take orders. You learn to work as part of a group."

Watson knew everything there was to know about taking orders and being part of a group. His role in the Soweto Riots, six years prior, had taught him about reduced responsibility for the atrocities you committed as a team. He did not think of it as a bonding experience.

"So it's acceptable to do a bad thing if it was an order? And even more acceptable if you did it as a group?"

The professor shrugged. "Exactly right. A soldier's not allowed to think for himself. He doesn't get the blame."

No accountability. Some of the worst monstrosities came from following orders.

"Now, about Mrs. Pretorius and her handbag..."

It was hard going. Professor Adelbrecht hadn't noticed any handbags at all. At least he confirmed the lab's security measures.

"We trust everybody who works here," he said, polishing his spectacles. Without them, his eyes looked soft and vulnerable. Watson wondered whether it was a calculated effect.

"Everybody, Professor?"

"Yes."

"Do you trust Doctor Monterra as much as you trust the others?"

"Naturally."

"Are you aware he's not married?"

No change in the professor's face. "What of it?"

"Might not be wise to trust people who lie about their

personal lives."

"I'll be the judge of that." Like steel.

Watson pretended to consult his notes.

"Are you also aware, Professor, that Monterra is not Doc's real name?"

"What of it?" the professor repeated.

*What of it?*

"A person usually changes his name to protect his true identity," Watson said, perplexed. "That doesn't bother you?"

"You should speak to Doc, Captain."

Annette sat with Beth in her arms.

Motive was all very well, she reflected, but how could Mother possibly have done it? Even if she'd left the children asleep in her house, and climbed the wall or walked around the block to gain entry into the house, how would she have obtained the poison?

In Monterra's office, Watson let the pacing, gesticulating Monterra do all the talking.

"The professor's just phoned me. You know Monterra's not my birth name. Would have been better to tell you straight away. I realise it now. At the time, though, I didn't want to complicate what I thought of as a straightforward suicide investigation. All I can say is I'm truly sorry. What can I do to make amends?"

Watson remained unimpressed. "Tell the truth?"

"Fair enough. Most people change their name to hide something in their past. My reason was…" Monterra paused. "This is rather more difficult than I'd expected." He sat down, stood up, sat again. He was still James Bond, but one who thought the head of SPECTRE might win, against all the rules of popular fiction. "Shakespeare had a beautiful line about a rose still being a rose no matter what it was called. I disagree. If a rose had to go by the name of faeces often enough, it would start to stink, at least to the beholder."

Watson's patience had a super-short tether this morning.

Must be the lack of sleep, the dark-hour talking to the man on the moon. He drummed his fingers on Monterra's desk. "The truth."

"The truth is I was unfortunate enough to have the same birth name as one of the most notorious criminals of my time. It wasn't my parents' fault. When the story hit the news, I was already an adult. A budding politician, earmarked for greatness." Monterra broke off again. Watson noticed the transformation from the suave James Bond to a middle-aged man twisting his fingers. "You have no idea, Captain, what life was like for me after that. The teasing, the cruel jokes. They stuck. Sullied. Hurt. When I moved to Pretoria, I had my name legally changed. So it wouldn't happen again, I chose a surname I couldn't find in any telephone directory."

Watson felt his excitement deflate like a used condom. Hell's bells, he had thought the case almost closed. He changed tack, firing the question without a preamble. "Where is your unicorn?"

Monterra stared, his eyes still. "What's that got to do with Gordon's death?" When no reply came, he shrugged. "I noticed the unicorn missing a few days ago. Monday or Tuesday, I'm not sure. Things were rather chaotic here for a while."

"Do you lock up your office at night?"

Monterra didn't. Watson knew this avenue was dead. Time to go and bash the case some more. "Just out of curiosity, Doctor, what was your birth name? The Ministry of Internal Affairs squashed that particular bit of information."

Doc's smile was as sour as a lemon. "Good to know BRAVO still carries weight in government departments."

Watson got up, headed for the door.

Monterra said, "My birth name is Charles Manson," and Watson felt an icy shadow glide into his gut.

Monterra watched him with a resigned expression. "No relation."

Watson took a while. "You're right about that rose," he managed at last.

Not my mother then, thought Annette.

The same argument absolved Danny. Although her son had been to BRAVO's lab, he couldn't have rummaged through cupboards in the hope of finding a bottle labelled with skull and crossbones. And it's not as though you could buy poison at the supermarket. So. Somebody from Gordon's work.

*Sally?*

No, Gordon was more useful to her alive than dead. Even if he didn't want to marry her, there was only one reason for those photos. She would have to be extremely stupid or extremely in love to kill Gordon, and Sally was neither.

*Lula?*

What possible motive could she have?

*The professor? Doc? Nick?*

*Absurd.*

When Watson walked into Lula's office, he almost didn't recognise her. Her face had lost all its usual sensuality. Her right hand toyed with a pencil, spinning it from thumb to little finger.

"Mrs. Nortje?"

She shifted her empty gaze to him. "It's Miss Larsen now. Or will be soon. My husband's left me." A wince of distaste tarnished her feline features. "For an air hostess, of all the clichés."

Watson dithered, wishing he had a female constable by his side. A woman would be naturally good at this. What the hell was he supposed to say now?

"More fool, him," he offered. "May I sit down, Miss Larsen? I need to ask you a few questions."

"About the poison found in Annette's handbag? Sally's convinced it proves her guilt. Annette's, I mean."

"And what do you think?"

Lula's eyes lost the vacant look. "Dim-witted to carry incriminating evidence in your bag. Why not simply throw the poison away?" She paused, ever the scientist who considers all avenues. "Even assuming Annette carried it with the intension to use it, she would never have let the handbag out of her sight."

Lula tapped her teeth with the pencil. "What's more, she wouldn't even put it in her handbag to begin with. There are many places for a woman to hide something on her person…"

Watson felt himself grow hot under the collar.

"…like the bra. Why, what did you imagine?" Lula actually smirked at his discomfort. "A small phial wouldn't show through the dress."

Watson cleared his suddenly dry throat. "So the poison was planted?"

"That's what you wanted to hear, wasn't it?"

The best line of defence is a counter-attack. "Who killed Gordon Pretorius, Miss Larsen?"

"I wouldn't tell you even if I knew."

"You hated the victim that much?"

Lula's eyes met his. "I liked Gordon. He was quirky and scrupulous about details, both of which are compliments in my vocabulary. Everybody liked him. Don't you see? Whoever killed him must have had an imperative motive, something bigger than life, something like the greater good of South Africa. That's why I wouldn't turn the murderer in. Hypothetically speaking."

The phone call disturbed Annette's latest line of thought.

"Mrs. Pretorius, my name is Hendrik Vermeulen. I'm your late husband's legal representative."

Gordon's lawyer. Annette had quite forgotten.

"I cut my leave of absence short when I heard about Gordon's death. Came directly to the office. May I take this opportunity to say how extremely sorry and shocked—"

And so they danced through the appropriate steps of sympathy and upset before Vermeulen got to the point. "There are two items I need to discuss with you, Mrs. Pretorius. When would it be convenient for you to see me?"

After they'd arranged a time, Annette asked, "I'd like to come prepared. Could you tell me the gist of it on the phone?"

Caution in the lawyer's voice. "The first item is simple enough, Mrs. Pretorius, um, just a matter of your husband's last will. My office has dealt with the paperwork in my absence and, as there are no claims against the estate, the bulk should be released to you within a few weeks. Sorry, I should have mentioned that you and the children are the sole beneficiaries. The children's share is to be kept in trust until they turn twenty-one."

All right, then. Nothing like in books, where there is an official reading of the will, at which the inconsolable family discovers the sole heir is the mistress's pet horse.

*Hard luck, Sally. And Sally's horse.*

"And the second item you wished to discuss, Mr. Vermeulen?"

"Ahem, that's a matter of utmost delicacy, I'm afraid. If you don't mind, I'd rather confer in person."

Annette capitulated. Now, Lula's motive for Gordon's murder.


The contents of this letter was so confidential, the minister typed it out himself, not daring to entrust it to his secretary, even though her security clearance was just one level below his. Addressed to his opposite number in USA, the minister outlined the preliminary findings of Project Aphrodite and offered to sell the modified virus as soon as it passed the testing stages. The US government, he guessed, was faced with similar problems to those of South Africa.

And if they were too squeamish to fling a manufactured virus into their population, there was always the Middle East. Saudi Arabia had the money to pay…

A knock at the door. He slid the letter under a document folder. "Enter."

"Minister, the lawyer's back from vacation. He made an appointment with Mrs. Pretorius for three o'clock."

*Finally.*

"Bring him in."


Yet again Watson left interviewing Sally till the end, consciously trying to put off the inevitable. As an officer of the law, he was supposed to be above personal prejudices. Sally, however, rubbed him the wrong way. She was too blatant, too in-your-face. As for her morals...

Hang on, common sense whispered. How was Sally any different from Charlene? They both cheated on their men, except Char had vowed not to, while Sally had intended to wrench a married man away from his family.

Sally broke the silence. "You wanted to see me, Captain?"

*Not really.*

"Yes, thank you, Sally." His mind grasped at straws. "Tell me about Saturday's party."

"I've already..." Sally's pupils dilated in surprise.

"Tell me again."

"Right." She touched her forehead with her fingertips and started to speak. What came out was quite different to her original, bland as bland, account of the evening. "It was Gordon's birthday party. He said he had an announcement to make. I thought—hoped—he'd decided to leave his wife, but hours passed and he never said a word."

"Did he say that before or after you went to admire Mrs. Pretorius' garden with your boyfriend?"

Sally's laugh did not carry a single note of self-consciousness. "Oh, after. In fact, I presumed my little flirtation with Nick was what had made up Gordon's mind. Evidently, I was wrong."

"Why do you say that?"

"Because he never made that announcement. He said he'd do it straight after dinner, and he didn't."

"You all went swimming after dinner," Watson reminded her.

"So we did. Gordon acted like a true hero." Sally brightened. "Of course. I've been so silly not to see it earlier."

What *was* she on about?

"I mean," Sally went on, "Gordon must have decided we belonged together. Why else would he have decked Nick?"

The minister was pleasantly surprised when the lawyer arrived with a large parcel wrapped in brown paper.

"Your envoy was kind enough to explain why you'd like to see me, Minister," Vermeulen said. "I took the liberty of delivering the required documents in person."

Lawyer speak, the minister knew, for: I bamboozled your gorilla with legalese, he spilled the beans, I'm cooperating in full, please don't disappear me.

He needn't have worried. Disappearing white lawyers was much harder than disappearing their secretaries.

He tore open the paper, took his time to scrutinize the documents. All present and accounted for. At last. And with no need of the interrogation room that always left a gory imprint on his soul.

"Good," he said. "You did the right thing, Mr. Vermeulen."

"In that case," the lawyer shifted forward in his chair, "may I be permitted to go back to work? My secretary seems to have quit in my absence," a significant pause, "and I find myself swamped with work."

The minister nodded. Vermeulen was of no further use to him. In a few hours, he'd be on the government plane heading for Mauritius. He hoped his daughter missed him.

"Please let's skip the preliminaries," Annette said when she entered the lawyer's office. "What is the second issue you wanted to discuss with me? No, thank you, no coffee for me," she added when she saw Vermeulen gesture towards the percolator.

"Very well." The lawyer shuffled a few sheets of paper on his desk. "As you may be aware, before he died—the day before he died, to be precise—your husband deposited a parcel with me. An important parcel, because he delivered it personally to my house, while he made his secretary mail out a decoy parcel to my office. What's more, he left two identical parcels with me, one to be handed over to the authorities should they ask…"

Annette was through with politeness. "Can I see the parcel? What's in it?"

"Mostly documents relating to his work at BRAVO, together

with instructions to pass them on to the newspapers should anything untoward happen to him." The lawyer cleared his throat. "The documents are top secret and politically sensitive. Gordon specified the conditions for making them public: a suspicious death, a fatal accident even. But he did not mention suicide. This puts me in a bit of a quandary..."

"It was not suicide," interrupted Annette. "My husband was killed, Mr. Vermeulen. If somebody did it to silence him, you need to make those documents public."

"It's not as easy as that. What if the alleged murder had nothing to do with those documents?"

The question hung in the air.

"Please bear in mind, Mrs. Pretorius, our country's wellbeing is at stake here. If these documents are made public— we're fighting a war on our border and we don't need any distractions."

"War achieves nothing," Annette said automatically. "It only kills other women's sons, for the crime of wearing the wrong colour uniform." She almost added, and having the wrong colour face.

"It kills communists, Mrs. Pretorius. Black communists."

"What about our sons?" Annette wasn't aware of having raised her voice, yet the volume hurt her ears. "What about the boys lost on our side?"

The lawyer's expression turned arctic. "Our losses are minimal. More soldiers are lost during peace-time manoeuvres than during this bush war of ours."

Annette rose from her seat. "I suggest you consult the police officer in charge of the case, Mr. Vermeulen, then carry out my husband's wishes as his lawyer, without worrying about political ramifications. Now, if there is nothing further—"

"Just a sealed letter addressed to you personally, Mrs. Pretorius. It came with the other documents, but as it's marked confidential, I did not open it."

Annette stared at the familiar handwriting. Felt nothing.

"*What?*"

"Oh," Sally cast Watson an amused glance. "You didn't know? Nick got frisky with me in the pool and Gordon punched him one."

*Why did nobody tell him these things?*

"We were all stunned. Shocked. Gordon offered to bring out some sparkly to ease the tension. That's the last time—we saw him…" Sally took a crumpled tissue out of her designer bag, her own and not Annette's, Watson guessed.

"And Nick Haddow?" he asked.

"His evening clothes got soaked when Gordon's blow made him fall back into the pool. He went home to change. Professor Adelbrecht gave me a lift back."

*Must have been some blow.*


Annette opened the letter in the car, parked in the lawyer's covered garage. She ignored the official-looking page about Project Aphrodite and started with the personal message from Gordon. Five minutes later, the order of the world she knew collapsed around her.

> *My dear Annette*
> *If you're reading this letter—well, I realise what it means. I'm sorry. I know I haven't always been the best husband to you, nor the best father to the children. Please forgive me, if you can. I hope one day you'll find somebody to love you the way you deserve to be loved.*

Annette read the words. Still felt nothing.

> *I'm writing this on the Friday before my forty-second birthday. I'm planning to resign from BRAVO and sabotage Project Hydra, which aims to pollute a township water supply with drugs that cause infertility. This is actually a better alternative than the original idea to poison the water supply with Hekate, a lethal*

*and undetectable poison BRAVO's developed.*

    *I have faith in mankind, Annette, and I trust my colleagues to accept my resignation at Saturday's dinner party. Should I be mistaken, however, this here is a way of stopping any further atrocities from ruining our beautiful country.*

    *The most crucial project to halt is Project Aphrodite. Its objective is to modify a virus, which is transmittable only through the sexual act. The idea is to eliminate promiscuous people, especially Whites who break the law by having relations with the Blacks.*

    *Enclosed with this letter are extensive summaries of all the agency's projects: past, present and future; everything from poison-laced clothing to genetics.*

    *I'm not a hundred percent certain what brought about this change in me, me, an avid member of the Order. Hopefully I would have seen the light sooner or later. As it turned out, the catalyst was something I found in my father's papers after his death—*

    *It's not easy to say it to you, Annette. I know it'll be a shock, and I'm so dreadfully sorry you have to find out.*

It's about Sally, thought Annette. Poor Gordon, trying to clean the slate.

The next paragraph was not about Sally. It punched Annette in the chest, blocking the airways. She read until the paper shook so much she could read no longer. The words didn't make sense.

*Dear God, it couldn't be.*

Her throat raw and the familiar world gone forever, she folded the letter. She would finish reading later. Much later.

Maybe.

Lula knocked on Professor Adelbrecht's door.

"Professor. Sorry to disappoint. I'm not the best person to be involved in Project Aphrodite. Virology is not an exact science, and I wouldn't be comfortable modifying a newly discovered highly infectious virus…"

The professor stroked his Voortrekker beard. "Think of all the applications. Like cheating spouses."

*Tempting.*

"The answer is still no, Professor."

"My dear Lula. You're an idealist. If we don't develop the virus, somebody else will. Is a clear conscience really so important?"

"It is to me."

"In that case," the professor shifted in his chair, "you leave me no option. I knew it was a mistake to hire a woman scientist."

She had expected it, yet the injustice stung. "Are you firing me?"

"Perhaps it would be best if you wrote a letter of resignation. Quoting your personal circumstances."

Lula suppressed the impulse to drive her fist upwards through those hairy nostrils. "Perhaps it would be best," she retorted, "if I told you what I found in your strongbox and how I intend to use it if I'm not longer an employee of BRAVO."

She placed a single sheet of paper on his desk. A photocopy of orders issued by the head of the country. "The original is in a safe place, and the safe place is not your strongbox. Not anymore."

The blurred copy of a document signed and stamped by South Africa's top leader lay between them, an island of white on the desk's surface.

"Needless to say, should anything happen to me…"

"Understood. So do me a favour and look after yourself." The professor removed his spectacles and pinned Lula with his pointed stare. "We can't afford another hush-up."

*Vermeulen, Vermeulen,* wondered the murderer as the image on the security camera showed Annette put down the phone and tap her lips with the tips of her fingers.

It only took five minutes of research to get the answer.

Pretorius had left something else with his lawyer. This could be bad. Very bad indeed.

"Give me the murderer, Captain."

At the end of another stretched-out day, the brigadier's office held all the appeal of a prison cell on Robben Island.

"We're getting close, sir."

The brigadier pushed a piece of paper his way. Watson knew the look of an arrest warrant well enough. He leaned to read the name filled in on the dotted line. The words started to spin.

"Brigadier—"

"I need a result, Captain. The press is a bitch."

"Please, sir. Three more days."

The brigadier laced his fingers, his knuckle crack ringing out gunshot style. "Friday," he said bending his thumb. "Saturday," he bent his index finger. "You will work on Saturday to save Mrs. Pretorius from the gallows, won't you?" It wasn't a question. "Very well. You have until the end of Monday." He made an inside-out steeple with his fingers. "Take Sunday off to pray."

If that's what it took, Watson *would* pray.

# Chapter 12—Sunday, Six Days before the Murder

AS USUAL, THEIR local church was packed for the morning service.

"Then all the trees of the forest will sing for joy, they will sing before the Lord for he comes, he comes to judge the earth."

It's time for a new church dress, thought Annette as she recited the words, without taking in their meaning. Everybody has seen this one, with and without the brooch, with and without the shawl.

"Today's sermon," began the vicar, "is about South Africa and the mission the Lord entrusted us with. The rest of the world is shouting for democracy and equality in our country. And yet I tell you the concept of equality is in direct conflict with God's deed at the Tower of Babel. Do not join together that which God has separated."

And a new church hat, Annette decided as her eyes glossed over Lula's elegant silhouette two pews ahead. Lula sat hand in hand with her handsome husband, the pilot.

*A happy couple.*

"God has given separate nations their separate identities and boundaries. The blacks are further divided from us by their barbarity which comes from the curse of Ham...."

Beside her, Annette felt her husband stir. She glanced at him. Gordon's face was pale. He gestured for her to stay as he headed for the side door.

It must be the heat, thought Annette. Odd that it should happen here, though, inside the cool brick interior of the church. Was Gordon ill?

"Listen to the radio and weep," droned the vicar. "Bombs exploding in Durban. Railway lines sabotaged. Recently, a limpet mine was found in Alberton, not fifty kilometres from here…"

Annette tuned out. She didn't want to know. Bad news wasn't real until she heard it. Much better not to know.

After the service, the church ladies always served tea and biscuits in the hall. The intoxicating smell of vanilla mingled with the homey aroma of fresh butter. Annette couldn't resist. With Gordon still out of sight, she turned her back towards the room and dipped one shortbread finger after another in her milky tea, popping them into her mouth with the precision of a well-oiled machine.

After ten pieces of sweet crumbly self-indulgence, her stomach taut, she walked to the ladies' bathroom, locked the cubicle door and threw up the lot into the toilet bowl.

Gordon realised it wasn't the first time the vicar had raised the topic of racial discrimination. This time the message hit home. Leaning against the outside wall of the church, unable to walk another step, he prayed. Prayed the way he'd never prayed before. Silently, without a clergyman, without kneeling down. He prayed for forgiveness, he prayed for his children's future, and— above all else—he prayed for guidance.

"That's where you've been hiding," Lula appeared by his side, her footsteps light as a cheetah's. "The church can get rather stuffy with all the hypocrisy."

Gordon was all too aware how bleak his smile must look. "Rather."

He didn't know what Lula had seen in his face, but she took him by the arm and said, "Let's get some coffee into you. The others are waiting."

Professor Adelbrecht belonged to a different church, but

Doc, Sally and Nick were all inside. Gordon stiffened when he saw Sally and Annette deep in conversation, then he caught the word 'hats' and relaxed.

"Here you go." Lula handed him a cup. "The coffee will do you good. You've been working too hard."

Gordon took a sip, tightened his lips, put down the cup. "Sorry, can't drink this. The milk is old, not even yesterday's. Awfully kind of you, Lula, just the same."

Lula laughed. "Your Annette is a saint to put up with you. Me, I would have poisoned you within the first year of conjugal bliss."

"No, you wouldn't have." Gordon couldn't resist exposing the logical loophole. "You could shoot me, but you wouldn't be able to use poison. My taste buds would save me."

"They wouldn't save you if you drank rooibos tea like Annette does." Sally's face looked as innocent as a child's. "The brew tastes like mud mixed with tobacco. It would conceal anything short of cyanide."

"Since when do you know so much about poisons, little woman?" asked Nick.

Sally shot her boyfriend a look so seductive it made Gordon feel sick.

"Why Nick," Sally stretched out the words. "You're an excellent teacher, darling. You've taught me everything I know."

*Everything?*

Gordon's rage threatened to explode right in his chest.

*Nick's taught Sally everything? Including that thing she did with her tongue...*

His male pride snarled, even though Sally meant nothing to him. He needed an outlet. Turning to his family, he said: "Let's go to the shooting range. It's been a while. Julie, do you still remember how to clean a revolver?"

# Chapter 13—Sunday, Eight Days after the Murder

AS USUAL, THEIR local church was packed for the morning service, and, as usual, Annette found it hard to concentrate.

Everything was as usual, the petty rivalry between neighbours, diamond jewellery and prestigious brands of car tyres. Everything was as usual, except Gordon was not with them and Trevor sat in the pew across the aisle.

*Guarding the family? Hoping the murderer would crack under the pressure of religion? What?*

"Our sermon today," the vicar announced, "will show how God keeps his people united, pure and safe from infiltration by incompatible peoples and their views. Nations and races shouldn't mix. Starting with the Old Testament, in which Jews are forbidden to marry Gentiles, just as today we are forbidden to marry anybody of a different race—"

Annette's memory flashed back to a fortnight before, when Gordon had walked out of church. Suddenly, she understood his behaviour only too well.

The colour of your skin was your destiny. You were your race: White, Black, Indian. Or simply White and Non-white. White and Other. White and You-Don't-Count. Every aspect of your life depended on your racial classification: your suburb and your school, what bus you were allowed to catch and what job you were allowed to take. To be anything but White meant to be restricted in your options, to have no future and to pee in inferior toilets.

Which was all right for the Whites.

Watson had spent the previous day getting nowhere. The more he thought, the less he understood. Why did the victim have a box of abortion pills next to his bed? What did the unicorn in his fist signify? And, most important of all, who was the perp?

He'd come to church not to pray as the brigadier had suggested, but to watch them all. Now he tuned out the preacher and composed a mental list of suspects. Monterra was still by far his favourite, followed closely by Mrs. LeRoy. So much for wishful thinking. In the real world there was also the professor, Nick, Sally, Lula.

One of them.

*Which?*

Surreptitiously, the murderer watched Annette. The look of eureka on her face said everything. Never mind how the aha-moment had happened. The woman suddenly knew too much.

She had to be stopped before she had a chance to speak to that policeman boyfriend of hers. She had to be stopped today. After the service.

Easy. The poison in the key ring was safe from a spot-search yet always readily accessible.

Annette drank rooibos tea. The murderer considered the implications. Poisoning the pot was too extreme. No, it would have to be in her cup.

Gordon's taste buds may have been too sensitive to risk giving him this almost flavourless toxin orally, particularly as he was familiar with its composition. Gordon's wife, however, would be a piece of cake to kill. No elaborate schemes necessary.

"For me? Thank you." Annette accepted the proffered cup. "Rooibos, how perfectly lovely."

She sought out the plate of biscuits and placed three Romany

Creams on her saucer. The biscuits were crunchy, and she knew she shouldn't dunk them in her tea for too long or they'd fall apart.

The first biscuit she dipped was awfully good. She moved to the sofa where Lula sat all by herself, a pariah already because of her impending divorce.

"How are you holding up?"

Lula moved her exquisite shoulders up and down. "Like hell. Every woman I meet is convinced I'm going to steal her husband. A divorcee is worse than a fallen woman."

Annette dunked the second biscuit.

"Surely..." she began. She placed the biscuit in her mouth, swallowed the mush as quickly as she could, crunched up the dry part. "Surely that can't be true. I don't have a husband anymore, either, yet people don't..."

"Oh, but you're different. You're the bereaved widow," interrupted Lula. "I'm a reject who needs to catch a man in order to prove her worth. No husband. No children. No value."

Annette dunked the third biscuit. It fell into her cup with a soggy, dull plop. She set the cup aside and gave Lula a quick hug. "You will always be welcome in my house." She added teasingly, "Fallen Woman."

Lula didn't smile back. "You know it was my husband who didn't want children?"

Annette shook her head. She had always assumed it was the cool cat Lula who hadn't fancied the bother, the responsibility, the permanent imperfections in her beauty that pregnancy would bring.

"Now he's gone off with that sky slut, because she's pregnant with his baby, and he's over the moon with joy. How ironic is that?"

"Men," agreed Annette. "Who needs them, right? If you want a baby of your own..."

Lula's voice was matter-of-fact. "Five years ago, I had an abortion. Not my choice, you understand. He took me to Europe on one of his free air tickets to have it done. We told you all it was our second honeymoon—well, anyway. Something went wrong, as it does, and the net result is I can't get pregnant again. Ever." Still zero emotion.

"Lula?"

"What?"

"If you ever decide to kill the bastard, I'll give you an alibi." Annette wanted to say more, but the two biscuits she had just eaten rose to the back of her throat. "Excuse me," she muttered, trying to keep them down.

She barely made it. The toilet was for whites, which she found ironic as she banged the door shut. The violence of her heaving came as a shock.

Over the years her stomach had learned to reject large amounts of food, particularly "naughty" food. Yet today she'd eaten only two biscuits. What was the problem?

Trevor knocked on the door. "Are you all right?"

Was she all right? In the greater scheme of things, she wasn't. Time to get help. As soon as this was over, she promised herself, she'd see a doctor.

"I'm fine," she called back. "Just give me a minute and we can go home."

She liked the way that sounded.

*Go home.*

*Together.*


After a family lunch of roast chicken, mash and salad, which Annette hadn't even pretended to eat, the children took their bikes and vanished into the neighbourhood. Watson had listened to their plans. First they would jump on the trampoline at so-and-so's house, then go swim at somebody else's, maybe they'd ride their bikes to the only local shop open on a Sunday and buy ice-cream.

Theirs was a good childhood, he reflected, with nine months of summer weather and streets safe enough to play in all day long. Suddenly he understood those who feared a change. Any change, no matter how politically  idealistic, would alter the balance of power, blur the lines between the whites and the blacks, paint the neighbourhoods with an alien streak.

"Trevor," Annette's voice pulled him back into the lounge. "Here's the video you asked for. Best watch it now. Wouldn't want Danny and Julie to see it just yet. Too soon."

Watson nodded. He may as well watch the documentary of the children's visit to Gordon Pretorius' office. Who knows, it might offer a clue. The case was unravelling in his hands. So many loose ends, unrelated threads, holes that needed darning. He knew he was no wizard with the needle, but, damn it, he was a good cop and a smart detective. The murderer should have been behind bars already.

"Ready?"

"Ready."

He slipped the cassette into the VCR, fumbled with the unfamiliar controls of the new technology. The TV screen filled with the face Watson had only ever seen dead. Gordon's shirt, he noticed, was buttoned up skew.

Julie's animated voice echoed in the room. "My father is the coolest guy in the world. He plays with poisons for a living..."

Behind him, Watson heard a sob. He didn't turn around. This was a widow's grief. An ex-boyfriend had no place in it.

He concentrated on the video. When it was over, a sense of disenchantment weighed him down like, well, like disenchantment. It would have been poetic justice if a video made by the children aided in the capture of their father's killer. Alas, the video held no clues. Not a single one.

Joe Flanagan had almost given up hope. South Africa had sounded exotic back home, but after two weeks as a foreign correspondent, he was beginning to find the sun too hot, the story too sluggish, the human relations too alien. He wished for the noise and familiarity of New York.

"You the American newspaper guy?" The voice came out of nowhere and Joe tasted the first tinge of adrenaline on his tongue.

"Yeah."

"Then listen, my brother." The bushes parted enough to reveal a chocolate-brown face and black eyes that commanded total attention. "I will tell you about the dead master of this house. I will tell you about the plague he was prepared to unleash onto our land. I will tell, and you will write. Write in your overseas newspaper."

Annette felt the tears behind her eyes and in her throat. The difference between the Julie captured on tape before Gordon's death and the Julie she saw nowadays was too much. Innocence and joy then. A broken spirit now.

"How do I help her?" Annette didn't realise she'd said it out loud until Trevor turned around.

"You can't," he said. "Be there for her, love her, hold her when she cries. She'll have to cope on her own terms."

Everything in Annette rebelled against abandoning Julie in her hour of anguish. "I'm her mother. There must be something I can do. I want to protect her—"

She broke off. On the screen, Nick and Julie were whispering together in the background, while the camera panned across the rows of computers, spectroscopes and colourful bottles. Her daughter's cheeks were flushed, her eyes huge and sparkling.

Annette looked at the screen. She blinked. Looked again. The image remained unchanged. Her twelve-year old daughter, in her school dress—and Nick's hand resting casually on her bare knee. Above her bare knee. Inching higher.

Bile gathered in Annette's stomach but she knew she would not throw up. Not this time. This time, she was done throwing up. She was done being a victim.

Her child, her Julie, needed help. As simple as that.

She and Danny were in the street, leading their bicycles because the road had too many twists to ride safely.

"Did you see anybody go into the garage?" Danny's voice was casual, too casual.

She stilled the mad beating of her heart. "Today?"

Her brother just walked.

"All right," Julie relented. "Why do you want to know?"

"The swine who took our dad away from us. He must have gone into the garage."

Julie hopped onto the saddle and pumped her legs into the pedals.

"Julie," she heard.

She pushed her body, the way she would in a swimming gala. "Go Julie." her Pappa would shout on the rare occasions he left work early to watch her race. "Julie. Ju-lie. Ju-lie." Curious how her heart could be both numb and excruciatingly sore at once.

"Julie. Ju-lie," Danny shouted.

The car roared around the corner too fast. Julie heard the engine give way to the yelp of the brakes. She didn't see the white hood until she landed on it.

# Chapter 14—Saturday, Three Weeks before the Murder

CRYING AND APPLYING mascara didn't go together. Annette blinked the tears back, swallowed to make her voice sound normal. "Can this discussion wait till after the funeral?"

Gordon's jaw line was set to rigid. "It's not inappropriate. Father would have approved. It's tradition to do the induction on the thirteenth birthday. We'll do it even if my father's no longer here to witness it." His hollow tone scared her.

Annette paused, collecting her thoughts. "While I can appreciate how it's tradition in your family, I'm not comfortable with the whole secret society idea."

"Rites of passage are important to adolescent boys and secrets add a dimension of fun. Every boy needs a sense of belonging."

"Sounds medieval, with all the rituals," Annette shied from calling it Ku Klux Klan-ish. Heavens alone knew, Gordon might see it as a positive.

"Nothing wrong with teaching our son to love his country."

What Annette had a problem with was the brainwashing and the tattoo. That, and the whole idea of a hero's death, dying for your country. She gathered her strength. "I'm saying no, Gordon. You will not taint our son. You will not teach him to lay down his life for South Africa. It's his life we're talking about, Gordon. His life!"

"Woman, you're not making any sense. Our anthem says, *At thy will to live or perish.*"

*So the anthem needed changing.*

She grasped the last straw. "That image of a unicorn. I'm sure the Bible has something to say about tattoos."

Gordon's face appeared in the mirror next to hers. His eyes tracked his fingers as they made a wide knot in the funeral tie. "Leviticus 19:28. *Do not cut your bodies for the dead, and do not mark your skin with tattoos. I am the Lord.*"

A glimmer of hope. "Right." She kept her voice gentle. "We can't go against the Bible."

She should have known better than to argue logic with the most analytic person in South Africa. In the time it took Annette to get ready for her father-in-law's funeral, Gordon had delivered a mini-lecture about interpreting the Bible in the modern context and the importance of understanding the intent, as opposed to the letter, of the law. "This passage in Leviticus," Gordon said, "talks about God's desire to set his chosen people apart from others by forbidding pagan worship and witchcraft which could lead them away from Him. Today, the question we have to ask ourselves is not whether or not it's all right to have a tattoo; the question is whether you are doing it for the greater good and for God's glory."

And a unicorn glorifies God how, thought Annette, though she chose not to agitate Gordon any further.

She still had a week in which to come up with a plan to protect Danny. Not only from the tattoo, but from what it stood for.

"I've already spoken to Danny," Gordon said, making Annette smudge her lipstick. "He's memorising the words of the Oath. I'm the head of the family, Annette, and what I say goes."

Pieter Pretorius' funeral drew a crowd of friends and government officials. A church service preceded political speeches that seemed almost as long, but Gordon would have endured double that if it delayed the procession to the graveside.

When he lifted his father's coffin, his thoughts turned to his brother. Stuart should have been here by his side, sharing the burden. Not the physical burden—Pieter Pretorius weighed surprisingly little for a man of his power—but the emotional anguish that filled Gordon's heart and seeped into every minute of his every day.

"Are you all right?" Professor Adelbrecht carried the coffin on Gordon's immediate left. No way could he have seen Gordon's face.

"I am." Saying it made Gordon feel better. Not by much. His brother was still absent, buried—if indeed there had been enough of him left to bury—up north in the spongy Angolan soil. And their father was still dead.

Afterwards, Gordon sent his family home. He needed to be alone. Slowly, delaying the inevitable, he drove to his father's house and rang the doorbell.

Rosina had retired years ago. The new maid, the same one who'd picked out the suit for Pieter Pretorius' final journey, greeted Gordon at the door.

"Did you switch off the fridge?" Gordon asked.

"Yes, *Baas*."

"And you took the food to your family?"

"Yes, *Baas*. Thank you, *Baas*."

They walked to the dining room, where the carpet had been ripped out. A large brown stain still marred the cement of the floor.

"Were you the one who found Master Pieter?" Gordon asked.

Wariness in the line of the maid's mouth. "He is already dead when I come in, *Baas*."

"Of course. What I meant was…" He didn't know how to phrase the question.

"He wasn't cleaning his gun, *Baas*. The cleaning kit is in the study, not on the dining room table. I don't tell the cops."

So that was that. Pieter Pretorius had committed suicide. The weight crushing Gordon's chest got even heavier. Suicide was a mortal sin.

"Thank you…" he hesitated. What was the new maid's name? He couldn't remember. Probably had never bothered to find out. "Did he have anything else with him? A letter maybe, or…"

"Just the carving of the springbuck with one horn, *Baas*. And the Bible."

The family Bible.

"It's on the mantelpiece, *Baas*."

Gordon leafed through the leather-bound book, turned to the front page, where Pieter Pretorius had inscribed the births and deaths of his children.

Gordon, born 23 February 1940.

Stuart, born 29 October 1942, and then, with a different pen, died 15 January 1981.

Lesley, born 4 June 1945.

Gordon stiffened. Lesley, his sister, had died on the day she was born, yet her death had not been recorded in his father's Bible.

"I'm not doing it, mom," Danny said on the way back from his grandfather's funeral.

Annette kept her attention on the road. Her mother's watchful gaze from the passenger seat made it difficult to concentrate on the driving.

"Danny, won't you give your father a chance to explain?" Annette tried to sound convincing, failed, tried again. "The Order of Unicorns is important to him."

"What's the Order of Unicorns?" asked Julie.

Danny ignored his sister's question. "Mom, it's crazy. They say things like, we *need to protect our womenfolk from rape*, and also something about keeping on the right path. Do they mean the correct path or the Conservative path?"

Annette pondered. "It's one and the same to them, I think."

"What's rape?" asked Julie.

* * *

The radio in Pieter Pretorius' study was tuned into one of the Afrikaans radio stations. Gordon listened with only half an ear to the presenter bemoan today's youth, their lack of moral fibre and the unacceptable lyrics of today's pop songs.

As he searched for references to Lesley in his father's documents, Gordon wondered whether the youth of 1982 was really so much worse than the youth of the 1950s. He didn't think so. Children and teenagers were the cruellest representatives of every generation. Gordon, whose mother was Scottish and father Afrikaans, and therefore a neither-nor in a country obsessed with classification, had learnt that particular lesson only too well. Not that he'd been disadvantaged by the country's law in any way. English or Afrikaans, he was still White, still privileged. Still teased at school for not belonging.

There had to be something pertaining to Lesley in Father's papers. Stuart's birth certificate lay neatly under the death certificate. Where was Lesley's birth certificate? Where, if she indeed had died on the day she was born, was her death certificate?

The radio chimed the hour and started a list of news headlines.

"Attack on the Koeberg nuclear power plant in Cape Town," announced the radio presenter solemnly. "Still no leads in the investigation of the bomb in Soweto yesterday."

Gordon turned the tuning knob to search for another station. Static. A black language he didn't understand. More static. He kept turning.

When he was growing up, radio had formed the kernel of family entertainment. Audio stories for children and adults, music and local news, drama and comedy. Now, six years after television had come to South Africa, out of habit or sheer sentimentality, Gordon still chose the radio. Not that there was ever anything on TV before dinner, in any case—literally nothing, just the test pattern.

The radio static gave way to a signal. "Seven-oh-two," chimed the jingle before it dissolved into music. "*So long*," complained the singer, "*I've been looking too hard, I've been waiting too long.*"

Gordon could relate. His whole life he'd been looking for his place on earth, somewhere he would belong. The Order of Unicorns had given him the illusion. Twenty-nine years later Gordon had to admit the secret society didn't exactly fill the void.

"*I've been waiting for a girl like you to come into my life*," the radio told him.

Who was the one and only girl for Gordon? Not Sally. Annette? No. Gordon had married significantly later than his peers, and he had married an ornament, a woman to show off on his arm during work functions. Had he ever even loved her? Or did the jealousy that clenched his jaw every time Doc looked at Annette stem from ownership, not from love? If his wife died, would he, Gordon, keep a lock of her hair in his wallet his whole life, the way his father had done?

Gordon shook his head. His goal was to find Lesley, and he wouldn't find her among his father's electricity bills.

The radio spouted something dangerously like communist propaganda, so he switched it off and summoned the maid.

"Did Master Pieter keep a diary?"

She looked blank. Oh, why couldn't they all be like Rosina, the domestic servant he had grown up with? After his mother's death, Rosina had practically raised Gordon and Stuart. Sometimes she brought her own baby to play with them, a funny little girl the colour of caramel fudge...

Gordon sighed as he looked at his father's new maid. "A diary," he repeated, "did he sometimes write in a book?"

"No, *Baas*."

"On sheets of paper?"

"Sometimes he writes letters, *Baas*. On pretty paper, with flowers."

"Did he give them to you to take to the post office?"

"No, *Baas*. He puts the envelopes on the shelf. Inside books."

"Show me."

Annette parked outside Mother's house, and walked her to the front door.

"You should stand up to him, child."

Annette opened her eyes wide in mock surprise. "To Danny?"

Her mom paused in the process of turning the key in the lock. "To your husband. No, don't give me the eyebrow, young lady, I don't mean explicitly. A woman's place is to cajole rather than to confront. Be covert about it. Flatter him. Play up to his instincts as the family's protector. Do something unusual and wild in the bedroom…"

"Mother!" This time Annette didn't need to feign the shock. They had never before mentioned—er—*those matters*. And her mother had never, ever, ever, had anything other than blanket approval for her son-in-law.

"Danny is worth it." An odd smile quivered on the older woman's lips. "Danny is worth—everything."

The words went straight to Annette's heart and stayed there, warm and velvety and imperative. Something like the foundation of a bond unfurled its hesitant tentacles from mother to daughter.

"Mommy." Annette reached out, clutched her mother's hand.

"Everything," the older woman repeated. "I'd happily perform indecent acts on Gordon myself if it helped Danny's cause."

"Eeu!" Annette drew back, her whole mind wincing. She rubbed her temples with frantic fingers. The image of her mother in bed with Gordon was not something she wanted to keep. Perhaps not even in a bed—*oh, gross*, as Julie would put it.

"Do it." Her mother swung the front door open and stepped inside. "You only have a week left."

For the rest of the day, Annette thought of nothing else.

Three hours later, Gordon still stared at his father's letters to his mother. All written after her death, so full of love, despair and pain that Gordon felt like an intruder. Still, he had to read them.

Had to find his sister.

The bits relating to how his father had started the Order of Unicorns Gordon skipped, together with flight-of-fantasy plans for revenge on *that savage*. Gordon couldn't work out who *that savage* was, but in the PS of one of the letters was a cryptic message: *Despite what that savage did, I realise your maternal instinct can't be helped, so I asked. Rosina says all's well with Lesley. Rest in peace, my love.*

Gordon had almost choked on the too large a gulp of air he drew in.

*Rosina says all's well with Lesley.*

His sister was alive.

Back home, Julie couldn't settle down. The funeral of a grandfather she'd hardly known hadn't upset her too terribly, the strange dialogue in the car, however, niggled.

She entered Danny's room without knocking.

"Hey," he shouted, "private."

"Sorry." She wasn't. "I just want to know what's going on."

Danny threw a tennis ball against the door of the cupboard. The ball bounced off with a loud thud. Danny caught it almost without looking.

"What's going on," he said through his teeth, "is I'm so angry I could murder him."

His head like a volcano, Gordon read the letters. As far as he could work out, his father had given Lesley away because she was the result of a rape attack on their mother. Gruesome enough, yet Gordon's logic didn't stop there. Why had their father been so sure Lesley wasn't his? And why did he give her away to Rosina?

The answer hit Gordon out of the blue, made his legs buckle and his heart tear open. It explained everything, right down to the Order of Unicorns and Pieter Pretorius' ultraconservative politics.

Lesley, Gordon's sister, his half-sister, must have looked like a coloured.

Gordon's mother had been raped by a black man.

"Don't be silly," said Julie. "He's our father. Sure, he's a pain at times, but everything he does is out of love."

Danny bounced the tennis ball up to the ceiling. "If that's love, screw it."

Gordon found his father's maid in the kitchen.

"Are you sure the only thing Master Pieter had with him were the gun and the Bible?"

"Yes, *Baas*."

He went back to the dining room, leafed through the Bible.

There it was, an ordinary lab analysis report from BRAVO, folded double and hidden inside, bookmarking the parable about forgiveness. His father, Gordon knew, would use BRAVO's lab for his consulting work.

Confirmation of his suspicions, that's all Gordon was after. He didn't expect the report to twist everything he'd ever believed.

Twist. Uproot.

Annette imagined Gordon would take only an hour or two to sort out his father's personal belongings. Most of the furniture and clothes he'd already donated to charity, all that remained were papers, books and ornaments.

After five hours, Annette began to worry. She dialled her father-in-law's number. Already disconnected. No choice but to drive there.

She left Danny in charge of his sisters and opened the door connecting the house with the garage. Gordon was sitting in the driver seat of his BMW, his face an ashen mask.

*When had he come back? And what was he doing in the garage?*

She tiptoed to his open window. "Are you all right?"

"You can stop worrying about your precious Danny."

Gordon's voice was robotic, every word separated by a tinny pause. "He won't be joining the Order."

She wanted to make sure she understood correctly. "No tattoo?"

"No tattoo. We'll never talk about it again."

In the three weeks Gordon had left, they never did.

# Chapter 15—Monday, Nine Days after the Murder

THIS PARTICULAR MONDAY started like any other Monday. Watson brushed his teeth and burned his toast without any inkling the day would wrench his heart inside out.

At the office, he binned a stack of internal memos, read two reports and requested an appointment. It was granted too fast, and he walked into the brigadier's office expecting the worst.

"I know you only gave me three days," he began.

The brigadier waved away the three days like a particularly pesky mosquito. "Walk me through what you have so far."

Watson spoke for fifteen minutes.

"So, to summarise," his boss said. "Gordon Pretorius had an affair with his secretary who was blackmailing him, or about to blackmail him, into marriage. His project at BRAVO was going to decimate the black population of this country. The day before he died, he invited all his co-workers to his birthday party and shredded most of his work, sending the remainder to his lawyer. We now have the paperwork in evidence and I'll be buggered if I know what to do with it. This case is highly political, Trevor," the brigadier used his Christian name, a sign of distress if ever there was one. "I've had pressure from all directions to lose the project documentation and arrest somebody—anybody—not connected with BRAVO."

*Anybody not connected with BRAVO. Annette.*

"The evening of the crime," continued the brigadier, "Pretorius doesn't make his announcement, doesn't quit BRAVO, doesn't threaten to expose their secrets. Instead, he quarrels with Nick Haddow and punches him into the pool. He gets cut by a nail, which we know was meant for him because only he ever entered the wine cellar. The nail is laced with a new secret weapon developed by BRAVO. What I can't figure out is how the murderer could predict *when* Pretorius would spring the trap, because the trip to get the bubbly was spontaneous."

Watson had a few theories. "Maybe he counted on Pretorius fetching a bottle of port to go with the coffee. Or he was going to suggest opening a sparkling wine to celebrate the birthday. If all else failed, Pretorius would have died the next day, selecting the wine for his Sunday lunch. With no improvised suicide in that scenario, we would only have had the poison's symptoms to go on, and the death may well have been ascribed to natural causes."

The brigadier's wince indicated he considered them smarter than that. "Take me through the arranged suicide, Captain."

"The murderer slipped into the BMW with Pretorius still in the wine cellar. He lured Pretorius into the car on the pretext of a discussion. Or *she* lured him in on the pretext of hanky-panky. Either way, the murderer waits for Pretorius to pass out from the poison, then arranges the tube, plants the unicorn and starts the engine."

"I understand all that." The brigadier leaned back in his chair. "It's what comes after that bugs me. Anonymous letters to Mrs. Pretorius? An attempt on her life?"

"That's when it gets even more interesting." Watson opened a report. "This came from the sniffer-dog team earlier this morning. I instructed Mrs. Pretorius to put the anonymous letters into a zip-lock plastic bag. The dog picked up her scent, naturally. As well as one other."

The brigadier glanced at the results and tut-tutted his surprise. "Now that I would not have suspected. Not in a million years."

"You don't know the lady in question, sir. It's perfectly in character for her to write anonymous letters. As to the motive—"

"The motive is obvious. But how did she stage the cake knife incident?"

"Oh, that wasn't her." Watson handed over another report. Sniffer dogs were a godsend to the police, now that every layman knew to wipe off fingerprints. Fortunately, not many TV shows mentioned sniffer dogs. Watson pointed to a sheet of paper. "Now this one, I confess, was a bit of a shock."

"I bet," murmured the brigadier. "Give me one good reason I shouldn't issue an order for Mrs. Pretorius' arrest."

Because I love her, thought Watson. "Because she didn't kill her husband."

"You sure?"

Watson put everything he had into this one word. "Positive."

The brigadier stretched out in his chair until his joints popped. "Any idea who?"

"We're following a number of—"

"Enough." The case folder closed with a crocodile-like snap. "This is one hell of a case, Captain. The more we analyse fingerprints, anonymous letters and knives, the cloudier it gets. Even the latest technology in poison breakdown yields one big ef-all. It's time to get back to basics. Do what you do best, Trevor. Think."

Watson thought it prudent to settle for the all-encompassing, "Yes, sir."

"Call off the guards and the patrol car. We can utilise them better now we know there's no danger." The brigadier rose and thumped him on the shoulder. "What a family, Watson, what a family. I don't envy you, man, and that's the truth." A small pause. "At least we can put the issue of Captain Smit and his wife to rest, hey?"

*Bloody hell.*

"Yes, sir."


Julie woke up in pain. For one sweet moment, the physical ache in her limbs and torso had overshadowed the ache of mourning.

She checked the bathroom mirror, standing on tiptoe to see more than just her face and neck. The places where her body had made contact with the white Mercedes were pulsating purple hills, but Julie dismissed them with a shrug. Her school uniform would hide them. And Danny had promised not to tell Mom, as long as she told him everything she knew.

She hadn't.

"Mom." Danny touched her shoulder. "I need to talk to you in private, please."

His expression was severe. What'd happened to his customary heart-splicing smile? Annette led him to Gordon's study. Not for the first time, she was struck by how little of her late husband had rubbed off on this room.

"What is it, Danny?"

"I'm worried about Julie. The attack on her last Wednesday..." He trailed off.

Annette squeezed his hand. "Don't worry about that. The person who did that wasn't after Julie."

"The alternative doesn't make me any happier, Mom."

Since when had Danny started using concepts like "the alternative"?

"Don't worry," she repeated. "That person wasn't after me, either. I promise."

"Mom. Julie knows something and she won't say what it is."

*She's not the only one.*

"You don't want bread in the morning, Annette. A glass of orange juice is all a lady needs to get her going till lunchtime."

Annette loaded butter onto her knife and spread it in a thick blanket on her toast.

"And you should really get dressed, or at least put a robe over your night clothes."

For years, she'd dressed according to Gordon's rules and tastes. Now he was no longer here, should she fall back straight under her mother's thumb? "I happen to like dressing like this, too."

Hester shuffled into the morning room. "Madam Annette. This was under the milk bottle."

*This* was another envelope. With Gordon no longer there to require fresh milk, Annette usually forgot to bring in the bottles, leaving the task to the maid or the gardener.

"Thank you, Hester. Please put the note in one of the sandwich bags the children use for their school lunches. The police will come and get it later."

"Dusting for fingerprints," her mother said. "The police should really do something about this nasty business."

"Which nasty business, Mother? The murder or the anonymous letters?"

"Both."

The hypocrisy repulsed her. "Oh, Mother. Why pretend? You wrote the letters. You're the only one who calls Julie *Julie-Ann*. Including the hair-tie was heavy-handed, too. It's not as though a stranger could have walked into her room and grabbed one."

"I did it for your protection. The police would've arrested you two days after the murder if I hadn't thrown off their suspicions."

Two days after the murder was the day Mother had meddled with Beth's breastfeeding. Annette examined her heart. Gratitude level: zero.

Her mother was still talking, "The extra police protection can't hurt. That incident with the knife in church—"

"That was me."

"I beg your pardon?"

Annette wasn't sure her mother's remark was meant as a rebuke for interrupting or a request for clarification. "I was trying to protect Danny and Julie from the police, just like you were trying to protect me. All we've done, though, is create confusion, pile on more work for the police."

"For Trevor, you mean."

Annette took another bite of her toast, savouring the sinful sensation of melted butter on her tongue. Trevor must have worked that one out, she realised, as she watched the police car parked outside her garden grunt awake and leave.

Jones raised his head when Watson returned from the brigadier's office.

"A woman called you twice, Captain. Said she'd try again at ten o'clock."

Watson looked at his watch. 9:59.

"Did she say she had important information about Gordon Pretorius' murder?" he asked without an inch of hope.

"She did not."

"Do you? Have important information about the murder?"

Jones grinned. "As a matter of fact..."

The phone rang.

"Damn it," exploded Watson, stamping his foot in a sudden rage. He had no idea why he was in such a foul temper. Oh, wait, would it have anything to do with the woman he loved being threatened with arrest for murder?

The phone kept ringing.

"Shall I answer it, sir?"

Watson picked up the receiver. "Watson."

The office door closed silently behind Jones.

"I just phoned to let you know something." Charlene paused, giving Watson a chance to speak, and when he didn't, she continued. "We've talked it over, Frik and I, and we've decided to give our marriage another chance. So this is it," her voice snagged. "Goodbye."

He drew a big breath. "Good—luck."

"You know things could have been different, Trevor. If only you'd wanted."

"No," he said gently. "They couldn't have."

Charlene was silent for a moment. "You have to let it go," she spoke at last. "Soweto wasn't your fault. Heck, it wasn't even your fight. They were demonstrating against being taught in Afrikaans and you don't have a drop of Afrikaans blood in you.

You were following orders you didn't believe in."

His fingers were going numb. "Nothing good ever comes of following orders you don't believe in."

"Stop blaming yourself."

"Just like that?"

"Yes."

"Easier said than done, Char."

"No. It's just as easy. Say it with me: *It was beyond my control*." She waited. "Trevor?"

He took a big breath, exhaled. "One day, perhaps."

"Let Hester give Beth her bottle, Annette. It's a maid's job. That's why you have her."

Annette kept on walking, walking away from her mother, walking towards her baby. "No." The word came out confident. "That's a mother's job. That's why Beth has me. To look after and to hold and to love her."

"Nonsense, my child. Our maid did everything for you girls and you're not worse off because of it."

As if on cue, Hester appeared on the terrace with a bottle of formula.

Annette took the whimpering Beth out of her pram and felt a line the girth of a baobab tree connecting her to her tiny warm body.

"Thank you, Hester, I'll do it. Chicken for dinner tonight, please. It'll just be me and the children."

"Very good, Missus." Was that a smile on the maid's black face? "I'll strip the guest bed straight away."

Annette settled down, baby and bottle in her lap. "Mother," she said, "it's time for you to move back into your own house."

Watson stared at the makeshift Pretorius case board on the wall. A panel of cork with index cards didn't look as glamorous as the spectrometers at BRAVO, but as the brigadier had said, technology had got them precisely where they were with the case today. Nowhere.

He turned to the constable. "What's the big breakthrough you mentioned earlier?"

Jones scratched a pimple on his neck. "I think a man did it, sir."

"How do you figure?"

"It's just that—can you imagine Mrs. Pretorius hammering a nail into a door and then filing its head into a spike? Or connecting a hose to an exhaust pipe?"

Watson couldn't. He could imagine, and had imagined, Annette doing a number of exciting things, none of which involved hammers.

"It's not impossible," he said. "But I get your idea, Constable. Ladies don't like fiddling with cars and they don't know a spanner from an Allen key. Let's run with it. If a woman had planned this murder, she would have come up with a different MO. That particular poison would have worked just as well ingested. The murderer could've slip a pinch into the victim's food."

"But use poison at all?" Jones picked at his pimple some more. "Why not a gun? There's a personal firearm in almost every household. I checked everybody's gun permits, as per your order, sir. The victim had a .38 he kept on the top shelf in his walk-in closet. The professor carries his weapon in an ankle holster, Doc on his hip. Nick Haddow owns several guns, and he keeps them all in a safe, good chap. Lula has a firearm license and a .22, though she claims she's never even shot it at a range. Oh, and the secretary hates guns and doesn't own any."

"So if Sally wanted to kill Gordon Pretorius, she wouldn't have used a firearm."

"Neither would she have used anything that involved hammering and touching the exhaust pipe. She'd be too worried about ruining her manicure."

More to the point, thought Watson, Sally didn't have a motive. Why kill the man you're hoping to marry? Even assuming Gordon had ended the affair, a more appropriate response from the jilted girl would have been spilling the beans to his wife, or pinning the compromising pictures to the notice board in church.

Murder was simply too big a deal. Didn't Lula say something similar? *'Whoever killed him must have had an enormous motive, something bigger than life.'*

"Jones."

"Yessir."

"We're going to compose a list of all suspects together with their potential motives for killing Gordon Pretorius."

Jones didn't say, "Well overdue." Didn't need to.

Watson vowed never again to take on a case involving a woman he loved. Emotions and detective work were mutually exclusive.

After lunch, Annette's mother finally moved back to her own house. The older children came back from school and Annette had a snack with them while Beth kicked at the rattles suspended from her pram's frame.

"Homework," said Annette, relishing the normality of it all.

"Sure, Mom." Danny smiled at her with affection, pulled a pleading face. That was his tactic: agree then re-negotiate. "May we go for a swim first, please?"

The dry summer weather hung over his question.

"All right. Careful the pool water doesn't burn you in this heat."

Danny's laugh came from the belly, just like Gordon's all those years ago. "Good one, Mom."

With her mother out of the house at last, Annette could finish reading Gordon's letter. She found the place where her hand had started to shake before.

> *A few weeks ago I discovered that—contrary to my lifelong belief—my sister Lesley hadn't been stillborn. She was a healthy baby girl with curly black hair and dark skin. A coloured baby, Annette, in my family.*
>
> *For a long time my father couldn't accept she was his daughter, believing Lesley must have been the result of a rape or of infidelity on my mother's part. He gave*

*Lesley away to our maid, Rosina, whose family raised Lesley as one of theirs while Rosina continued to work for us, caring for my brother and me after our mom died, until she retired.*

*When my father had a breakthrough in one of his gene research projects, he launched a whole new way of proving paternity. I'm not sure why or how he found Lesley, whether he'd had contact with her all these years, but he performed the new tests and proved to his own satisfaction—or dissatisfaction—that Lesley was indeed his daughter. Her dark colouring must have been a genetic throwback, which implies both he and my mother had some black ancestry.*

Gordon's father, Annette remembered irrationally, had been rather swarthy of complexion. She had always attributed it to the hours he'd spent in the unforgiving sun.

*Non-white blood, Annette. I've made a few discreet enquiries and the fact does not re-classify us as non-white. We are not the only such family, and as long as a person looks white enough to pass, they can be White by law no matter their racial heritage.*

*Annette, nobody knows about it except you and me. Father never told a soul. Perhaps I should have done the same, shielded you and the children from this terrible secret, but I can't. I have a favour to ask you. Please find Lesley for me. Make sure she's provided for financially. I didn't mention her in my will for fear of a scandal, and so I'm relying on you to do right by Lesley. Please.*

*I don't have to ask you to look after our children. You are a loving and devoted mother, Annette, and I'd like to thank you for everything you're doing for them.*

*There is one thing you may not have realised, though. Julie is growing up fast. Too fast. She's*

*showing an unusual interest in Nick Haddow, and I'm
concerned because that young man has no judgement
and a warped sense of right and wrong. Please, I urge
you, beware of Nick and keep him away from Julie.*

    *Goodbye, Annette. Things haven't been right
between us, and should you wish to remarry very soon,
I'll be happy for you from beyond the grave, wherever
the Good Lord chooses for me to be.*

    *In the safe, you will find five thousand Rand to
tide you over while you're waiting for the inheritance
and the insurance payout to clear.*

    *Stay well.*
    *Yours,*
    *Gordon.*


Annette had no idea how long she'd sat there. Hester must have
taken Beth for her nap. The children must have returned from the
garden.

"Mom. Can we watch TV?"

TV. If there was something on TV, the time must be past
four o'clock.

"Mom, what are you reading?"

Annette snapped out of her daze. Astounding how being a
mother overruled everything else.

"It's just a boring document, and no to the TV. Homework,
remember?"

Julie scowled, "Oh, Mom!" and a gigantic claw let go of
Annette's heart. They were going to be all right. They would
survive the ordeal of Gordon's death and emerge stronger. About
the other matter…Gordon's disclosure—she had all the time in
the world to think about that.

The front door bell chimed and Annette heard Hester's
footsteps fading in the entrance hall.

"I'll get it," Annette called out. She turned to her children.
"Time for you guys to go upstairs. Danny, remember to practice
the piano."

\* \* \*

Jones took out a fresh piece of paper. "Sally Martins: no motive," he wrote.

Watson nodded. "Other than the one they all had: to prevent Gordon from going to the press about BRAVO's covert operations, but Sally is the one person in the office who's not directly involved. Also, she's such a self-centred young girl, I don't see her committing an altruistic murder."

"You think the murder was altruistic, sir?"

"If the objective was to stop Gordon from exposing BRAVO, then yes, I'd say the murder was an altruistic one. Patriotic even."

Even if the patriotism was misguided.

"I would say it was selfish, sir. A nation is too abstract an entity to feel any loyalty towards. People who oppose political change are simply trying to preserve their lifestyle."

Loyalty. Watson could write a thesis about the topic. "You feel no loyalty towards South Africa, Jones?"

"I feel oneness with the people, sir. South Africa's landscape and sun are in my blood. I was born here and here's where I want to die. But it only makes sense to feel loyalty and love for your country if the country is doing good things."

Watson nodded again. The boy was turning out all right.

"Lula Larsen's motive," he continued, "only the BRAVO one. Same for the professor, Doc and Nick. Incidentally, Nick had an additional motive: jealousy, because Gordon was screwing his girlfriend."

"And Ms. Larsen could have wanted the victim out of the way in order to progress up the career ladder."

Watson nodded. "Very good. Who's left?"

"Mrs. Pretorius," obliged Jones.

"Jones."

"Understood, sir. We also have Mrs. LeRoy. Mrs. LeRoy is an interesting candidate. Her motive would be to get rid of an abusive son-in-law. If Mrs. Pretorius were to get a divorce, she'd walk away with nothing, and Mrs. LeRoy would lose the house she's inhabiting. "

"Did you notice anything else about that scenario?"

"The ease of access to the victim's premises because she lives across the fence from them? Sir, the same argument applies to Mrs. Pretorius or one of her children…"

"Jones," Watson said again. His thoughts went back to the way in which the murder was committed. "Why wasn't Gordon Pretorius killed with a handgun? So much easier than poison."

"When we know that," Jones said, "we'll know who the murderer is."

He was wrong. By the time the day was up, Watson would know the murderer's identity before figuring out why a handgun hadn't been used.

Danny was climbing the stairs behind his sister when he heard the front door open with an elegant whoosh.

"May I come in? It's important."

Julie suddenly halted two steps above him. He bumped into her ramrod back.

"Shhh," she said before he got a chance to admonish her.

He whispered, "What?"

"Shush."

Danny looked over his shoulder. Nick Haddow. Julie's latest crush.

"Get a grip," he breathed the words straight into her ear. "He's too old for you. What is he, twenty-five? Practically a dinosaur."

Julie wasn't paying attention. Danny watched Nick follow his mom to the lounge. Julie crept back down the stairs.

"Come," she beckoned.

Annette didn't know what she had expected. But not this. Not Nick Haddow, briefcase in hand, in her lounge, standing over the cooling teapot.

"How dare you," she snapped. "Leave this house at once. I never want you near Julie again. Understood?"

Nick held up his free hand. "I've come to warn you."

"Warn me?"

"I'll get straight to the point. It's difficult for me to accuse a colleague, somebody whose achievements in science I admire so greatly, but——" he toyed with the briefcase.

But you're going to do it anyway, Annette thought.

"You see, after the——after Gordon's death, I implemented extra security measures in the lab. A hidden camera activated by the door of the poison cabinet, among others. I review the tape daily, and this afternoon I saw footage of someone helping himself to one of the phials."

"Who?" Did she really want to know?

"Doctor Monterra."

Julie tiptoed away from the lounge door.

"What?" asked Danny. If this was some silly game of hers…

She put her finger to her lips. "Go get Pappa's gun from the closet," she mouthed, gesturing towards the stairs, her hand the shape of a pistol.

"No way."

Danny had to admire his sister's mimicry. Julie's eyes opened very wide, her eyebrows shot up, her mouth jutted out in a direct command. "Do. It. Now."

"Hello, Watson speaking."

"It's Hester," he heard. "Please come at once, Captain. Madam Annette's in danger."

"Look, Hester, it's all right. Those threats in the letters…"

It was unusual for a black person to interrupt, so Watson knew the situation was serious when Hester broke in, "It's not the letters. One of the guests is here. He's the one I didn't see."

"Hey?" Watson was dumbfounded. The one she did *not* see?

"Please come now." The phone went dead.

Watson turned to Jones and relayed the conversation.

"The one she didn't see," Jones repeated. "The one she was paid off not to see? The one she thought she saw but didn't? The one who should have been somewhere and wasn't—"

*The one who should have been there and wasn't.*

The fateful Saturday evening was forever etched in Julie's memory. She hadn't wanted to go to Grandma's. She'd wanted to stay home and…Not sure what. Speak to Nick? Kiss Nick? Be near him?

She'd known better than to argue, but once at Grandma's, she'd spent most of her time glued to the binoculars. Nick arriving with Sally. Nick in Mom's garden with his hand under Sally's top.

All the men wore identical evening suits, so when one of them used the side door to enter the garage before dinner, she hadn't recognised him. From the back, it could have been anybody.

Now that she'd seen the back of Nick's head, though, she knew better.

Annette stared at the low table with the tea tray still on it. Three cups, a sugar bowl, an empty pitcher of milk, sandwich crumbs, a plate of biscuits, her silver teapot.

Nick's words flew to her across the table. "Gordon was planning to expose BRAVO. Our country is at war and it's our mandate to develop certain—substances—to be used on the enemy. If the international media got hold of this, the ramifications would exceed all the commercial and sports sanctions put together. Somebody had to stop him."

"And you think Doc…" Annette couldn't finish the sentence. Something was very wrong. She couldn't put her finger on it. Nick—how could she trust him after what he'd done to Julie?

Nick opened his briefcase. "I don't know. Just telling you what I saw."

Beth got fed up with kicking the rattles. "Whaaaaa," she uttered her first warning cry, the soft one that primed her lungs for the full onslaught.

Annette looked up. Across the table, she caught the glint of a syringe. Everything fell into place in that one flash of glass and metal.

She kept her face still as she got to her feet and hastily unbuttoned her blouse. Thank goodness she still wore her breastfeeding clothes every day, hoping Beth would latch on, hoping the milk would come.

"Please excuse me," she said, fighting with the bra's front clasp as much as with her own sense of modesty. "The baby needs to eat."

Nick's eyes fixed on the white lace of the bra. He had no idea Beth was now fully bottle-fed. Annette clenched her teeth and unhooked the front clasp. Didn't bother to control her expression. It wasn't her face Nick was ogling.

Her bare breasts pushed forward and out. Nick's jaw slackened, the syringe forgotten for a crucial fraction of a second.

*Attack. How?*

"Mom," she heard Julie's small voice in the doorway. "This is the jerk who killed my Pappa."

A fragment of Gordon's letter came back to her. *Beware of Nick. Keep him away from Julie.* Annette stopped thinking. Her hand found the teapot, and all by itself whacked the warm silver into the jerk's temple, the weight pitching her off balance. A miracle she hadn't toppled over into his lap.

Dazed, Nick scrambled to his feet.

"Get out, Julie. He has a syringe." Annette spoke with calm urgency. Her hand still clutched the teapot. Behind, she heard Julie's fast shallow gasps and Danny's slower, deeper breath.

A deep laughter filled the room. Objectively speaking, Nick had a sexy laugh. "*He has a syringe, Julie,*" he mocked. "Oh, dear me. *He has a syringe.*" He walked purposefully towards Annette and the children. "Relax. It's just evidence of Doc's guilt."

She hesitated.

Nick took another step.

The rays of the afternoon sun caught the metal of the syringe, and it glittered like a Christmas decoration. Images of Christmas in this very living room flooded her memory, Danny in his cars PJs, Julie emptying the Christmas stocking onto the carpet, Beth wide-eyed as they sang *Silent Night*…

"Take your thumb off the plunger," she said.

Nick kept walking. "Julie, darling, explain to your mom…"

Annette's blood surged into her brain. She hurled the teapot. It flew in a powerful arc straight into Nick's throat, slid impotently to the floor. He yelped in pain, but didn't stop.

To her right, Danny raised Gordon's gun.

Annette caught the movement with the corner of her eye. Grabbed the weapon. Heavy. Cold. Smooth. Her finger brushed the trigger. In the distance, she heard a car slam into a flowerbed and drive all the way up the path to the front door. The sound of the shot pierced her eardrums.

The sound of the shot pierced his eardrums.

"Freeze," Watson shouted even before he reached the front door. "Police."

Hurtling into the house, his official pistol cocked and pointing, he saw Annette's profile. She stood in the lounge pointing a revolver, her small triangular breasts—he checked again just to make absolutely sure—*ja*, totally naked.

Playing it back in his head later, Watson realised exactly why he had failed to spot the children standing shoulder to shoulder with her, until one of them said, "Mom, your blouse".

Annette turned and her breasts disappeared from Watson's direct line of sight. That's when he saw the body.

One glance was all he needed. He holstered his own weapon, took Annette's from her unresisting fingers, and discharged it into the ceiling.

"That," he said, "was the warning shot you fired when the intruder started advancing on you. The sun was in your eyes and you couldn't see his face, nor make out the skin colour." The last bit was crucial. As long as the authorities thought Annette had meant to shoot a black trespasser, she would get away with killing a white murderer.

Annette's gaze met his, empty and uncomprehending.

"You were out of your wits with fright because of the anonymous letters," he explained. "That's why you had the gun on you."

"Right," Annette said in her uncertain voice. "But the letters…"

Her pause told him she knew who'd written the damned letters.

"The letters," he repeated. "You took them seriously. You were scared."

He directed his gaze at Danny and Julie. Bloody hell. They were only children. He hesitated.

"We get it," Julie said. "Intruder. Warning shot first. He didn't stop. Kept coming at us. It was self-defence. We'll explain it all to Mom when she's feeling better."

"Do you guys want to talk about it?" he asked. "I can get a female police officer…"

Danny took this one. "Nothing to talk about. This creep killed my father and now he's dead too. An eye for an eye. Don't worry about us. What you need to do now is look after Mom."

That was exactly what Watson wanted.

When they were alone, Danny put his arm around his sister.

"How are you holding up?"

She stiffened in his embrace.

"Julie, I know you must be going through hell. He was a good-looking guy…"

A breathy sob escaped from her mouth.

Danny tried again. "Look, I know it felt special when he paid so much attention to you. It's okay to cry."

"You—don't—under—stand," Julie snivelled. "I—hate my—self. How could—I—ever—have liked—him?"

Danny knew there was nothing more to say, so he held Julie tight and let her cry out her first romantic disappointment.

# Chapter 16—Fourteen Years before the Murder

AFTER THE WEDDING night, Annette was too ashamed to go back to her parents. Her father had just spent the equivalent of three months' salary on the dress, the hall and the festive food.

What reason would she give, anyway? That the perfect boy-next-door, a churchgoer who supported the correct political party and all the correct causes, the one her parents had chosen for her instead of her high school love—that he—in bed—during—no way would she be able to think the words, let alone speak them.

That's not what she had imagined lovemaking to be. That's not how the teenage kisses felt with Trevor. Where was the passion?

Nevertheless, it was done now. Gordon was her husband.

Only the day before, she had vowed to love him for better and for worse. This was the 'worse' bit. Annette squared her jaw and got on with the business of loving, as per her wedding vow.

She had also vowed subservience.

"I don't like you in mini dresses," Gordon said when they returned from their honeymoon in the tropical paradise of the Seychelles.

Annette threw out all her minis.

"You are too bubbly," he told her a few weeks later. "Now that we're married, you must act more in accordance with your new position in society. Don't *ooooh* and *aaaaah* over chocolate pralines in public, it's unseemly. Better yet, don't eat much in public at all. A good hostess should be too busy with her guests to enjoy the food herself."

"I agree," she replied. "What a good idea. Thank you for pointing it out to me."

Polite, serene, subdued. A perfect wife curbing her appetite for life. Anything to please her husband.

At night, when he rolled away from her, satisfied, she bit her fingers to stifle the screams of frustration.

The night after they returned from their honeymoon, Gordon attended a special meeting of the Order of Unicorns.

As soon as he entered the candle-lit hall, he was led to a single chair in the centre of the floor. White powder crunched under his feet. Salt?

"Sit down, son."

Gordon sat.

His father's voice shook with emotion. "With your marriage, you have become a man. Today you become a trusted member of our order. Close your eyes."

Just in time. A wet thumb wiped a secret sign across his eyelids.

"Blessed be your eyes, that you may see the right path."

Gordon smelled wine.

"Blessed be your nose, that you may breathe only in your country's service. Blessed be your mouth, that you may speak for the good of the cause. Blessed be your heart, that you may be faithful in your works. Blessed be your hands—"

He felt a smooth, hard object in the palm of his right hand. Cautiously, he raised his eyelids and stared into the unseeing eyes of an ivory unicorn.

# Chapter 17—Tuesday, Ten Days after the Murder

ANNETTE LOOKED AROUND the grey, shabby room, so different from Gordon's lavish office at BRAVO. Strange how these two men, both employed by the government, operated in settings that were poles apart. Their directives, issued by the same regime, were totally different, too. Trevor's purpose was to catch killers. Gordon's—she didn't want to think about it.

"So this is where it all happens," she said. "All the detective work. The analysis. Sorting the chaff from the grain, Cinderella-style."

Trevor shot her a self-deprecating grin. "You mean, the paperwork. I don't sort chaff as a rule, I'm afraid. Cinderella is not my favourite fairytale. As a fantasy, it doesn't appeal at all."

"What does appeal?" When she realised the double meaning, she felt her cheeks grow hot. "That is," she spoke quickly, "if from rags to riches isn't your plot, there is always…"

She hesitated. Snow White had an evil stepmother, and stepparents were not something Annette wanted to discuss with Trevor just yet. Sleeping Beauty was full of sexual innuendo. Beauty and the Beast—no way. Even Puss in Boots could be grossly misinterpreted.

Her sick, twisted mind was to blame. Her sick, twisted mind, so unbecoming of a lady.

Trevor gave her a look. "I don't really like any fairytale. The

Brothers Grimm wrote horror full of violence and gore. Besides, I stopped believing in magic long ago."

Now, thought Annette. The time to tell him was now. Bring the magic back.

She couldn't.

"So," Trevor said. "Please make yourself comfortable on this unpadded wooden chair and let me have your official statement as to the events of yesterday afternoon."

Annette sat down obediently, and then, much to her own surprise, burst into long-overdue tears.

Trevor put his hand on her shoulder, large and strong and comforting. "What happened yesterday was really for the best, Annette. Believe me. The case—we would have had a hard time proving anything in court."

It was sweet of Trevor to think that's what was worrying her. Killing a man. Truth be told, she hadn't had a single qualm of conscience. Not over that. The weight on her shoulders had everything to do with BRAVO's work. How could the man she'd lived with for fourteen years be involved in such evil?

"I killed a man who killed a man who could potentially kill millions of innocent people." She dabbed her eyes with a corner of a tissue. "What does it make me? A hero? A monster?"

The policeman in him knew it wasn't quite as straight forward as that. Gordon Pretorius had wanted to prevent those deaths, which is why he himself had died—maybe. Or maybe Nick had just killed him over Sally. They would never know—now.

"Just let me sign my statement," Annette said. "I want to go home."

Home, he thought. A huge mansion with a huge swimming pool and two servants, like in a fairytale. And in the huge mansion, a boy was growing up, growing up into a soldier, to kill or be killed in the Bush War. Just like in a Grimm fairytale.

Somewhere in the police station, music was playing. Watson recognized the unmistakable sound of Bucks Fizz: *Something nasty in your garden's waiting patiently till it can have your heart.*

314

The name of the song came to him as a shiver ran down his spine. '*The land of make believe*'.

South Africa was that, all right.

"Forgive me?"

Lula turned to follow the voice. Her husband was hiding behind—literally—the biggest bouquet of roses Lula had ever seen.

Their fragrance beguiled and beckoned. She remembered their first date, the single red rose. "One day," he had said, "I'll be able to afford hundreds, thousands of red roses, to lay at your feet." He'd never fulfilled his promise. Until now.

"No." She was pleased with her tone. Cool. Unemotional.

Her husband, soon to be ex-husband, she reminded herself, placed the bouquet on the ground, turned as if to walk away, made a summoning gesture with his arm.

A small truck parked on the kerb came to life and drove onto their property. Two black men emerged with buckets of more roses and started lining the driveway.

"How about now?" he asked.

"No."

It had nothing to do with the airhostess, Lula understood suddenly. It had everything to do with the children she would never have and the foetus they had murdered before it became a baby.

Her husband made a puppy face. "I've been a fool, my darling. Such a fool."

At least something they could agree on.

She gave him a gentle push. "Go. Don't come back. Your girlfriend needs you. Soon your baby will need a father. And I," Lula laughed with relief when the realisation dawned on her, "I don't need you at all."

Entirely true. Although Lula knew she would always need a man in her life, she didn't need this one.

"Oh, and do leave the flowers," she called over her shoulder. Then she slammed the front door in her husband's face.

\* \* \*

"Patriotism leads to evil."

Jones said it and the words hung in the dusty air of the office, among the particles of Annette's perfume. Annette was long gone, her statement sworn and signed, but the scent of her lingered.

"Not patriotism, Jones. Politics. Politics is what turns a simple matter of loving your country into something sordid."

"You're saying politics killed Gordon Pretorius, sir?"

Good question. The more he thought about the case, the more he wondered whether Nick's motives were political at all, despite his perfect psychological profile for the job. Had Nick known about Gordon's plans to blow the whistle on BRAVO, or had the motive been pure revenge for stealing his girlfriend?

Watson could kick himself for not having spotted it sooner. "Jones. We need a tech team at BRAVO. Make that yesterday."

"What are we looking for?"

"Surveillance equipment."

"Mom? Can I ask you something?"

The light from the open fridge chiselled Danny's features into lines beyond his maturity. Annette's heart swelled. As usual, whenever one of her children was in the room, the rest of the world ceased to exist. She took in his serious expression, the t-shirt that fitted last week but was already too short today, the wedge of cheese as thick as his wrist.

"Sure, Danny. Anything."

"Why did you marry Pa?"

That was not the *anything* Annette had expected. She assumed it would be a philosophical question about taking a human life, or religion, or both. The previous day's events still hung in the air. Not for Danny, though. Evidently.

"That's a good question." Was Danny old enough to hear the truth? About how Annette hadn't wanted to rock the boat, lest her disobedience cause her parents to divorce? About how

Gordon had promised Annette she would go to university when she was his wife?

Not a good idea. No child should ever hear anything other than a love story about his parents. But Annette was done with lies. "Your granny told me to marry him. Said I was too young to know what love was and that he would make my life good."

"Boy, was she wrong."

Annette pulled her son into her arms. "Actually, Danny, your father did better than give me a good life. He gave me a fabulous life."

"For real?"

"A beautiful home and three beautiful children. For real."

# Chapter 18—Seventeen Years before the Murder

SITTING AT THE dining room table after supper, Gordon watched his father take apart his Luger pistol and check the chamber for a stray round. His movements were confident, efficient. So were his words, direct and to the point. "When will you get married, son?"

*Married.*

The word filled Gordon with dread. Marriage meant you became the head of your household, responsible for all the decisions and accountable for any misfortunes. Gordon didn't want to be the head of anything. He wanted peace and quiet and enough time to do his research.

"Gordon?"

"When I meet the right girl, Father."

His father shook the pistol's magazine to remove the follower. "She doesn't have to be perfect—*adequate* will do. Every successful man needs a wife. That's how the good Lord, in His wisdom, designed us." A faraway look clouded his eyes. "Trust me, son. We are not complete until we are joined with our other half."

Gordon nodded, unconvinced. He actually felt totally complete when alone.

"The Lord said, *go forth and multiply*, son. It's your turn to do God's work on earth."

Gordon had known this discussion would come and he had his arguments prepared in advance. "With respect, Father, I believe we've already gone forth and multiplied enough. The earth is overpopulated. We're killing off one species after another. Give us fifty more years the way we're going now, and we'll put elephants on the endangered list."

His father took out a small brush and began the laborious process of cleaning the gun parts. He worked in silence for a few minutes before he raised his eyes. "The day I'm forbidden to shoot an elephant trampling my crops or a Black trespassing on my property will be the day God turns His face away from South Africa."

Annette sat on the edge of her narrow bed, cringing with embarrassment. She didn't want to have this conversation. Her mother could talk about a spoon and make it sound embarrassing.

"Sometimes boys, wicked boys, will try to get their way with you. To make you do things you don't want to do. You mustn't let them."

Her thoughts rebelled. What if boys make me do things I want to do?

"A girl has to be pure on her wedding night, and your husband will be able to tell if you've let anybody touch you under the skirt, understand?"

Annette stared at a poster of the Beatles on the wall and nodded. How far one could go with a boy without compromising your virginity was a topic of every lunch break discussion at school. Were you still a virgin if you were to touch it? Were you still a virgin if you've never as much as kissed a boy but did horse riding as a sport? And would your husband really be able to tell?

"Some boys will make good husbands one day, others will not. Before you fall in love, ask yourself whether he's…"

Did all people know how to turn feelings on and off? What was wrong with her that she couldn't?

"This Trevor who walks you home after cheerleader practice, don't think I haven't noticed, he is not husband material.

His hair is too curly."

"Mother."

"Don't interrupt. It's not ladylike."

*If being ladylike means putting your brain in a cage and following the crowd, then to hell with being ladylike.*

Mother cleared her throat. "Now I'm not saying he's got a drop of black blood in him, and I'm not saying he doesn't. All I'm saying is, he's not for you."

*You're wrong, Mother. You're so wrong, it's not funny.*

To keep the peace in the house for her younger sisters' sake, she said, "Yes, Mother."

She had no intention of sticking to it.

# Chapter 19—Two Weeks after the Murder

"DAMN IT ALL, it still doesn't make sense," Watson muttered into the canteen air thick with cigarette smoke and the cloying aroma of today's chicken lunch.

He had just reviewed all the surveillance tapes they'd found at BRAVO. The next step was completing the case paperwork on Gordon Pretorius' murder and he could put the whole matter to rest.

In theory, this should have been handled weeks ago, but a new case had come along just then, a burglary that could have been staged in order to cover up a murder. Fortunately, no ex-girlfriends of his were involved, and Watson found himself operating with his usual clarity of mind.

The difference between the two cases was humiliating.

"You know, Jones, I just can't shake off the impression that I've been a bloody fool about the Gordon Pretorius murder."

"Sir?"

"Think about it. Pretorius died at a time most convenient for BRAVO. They couldn't have picked better if they tried. Gordon hadn't yet gone to the press, but he might have done on the Monday following the party. He managed to send some compromising information to his lawyer, but as you've seen yourself, it amounted to nothing. Without Gordon to back it up, the authorities squashed the story. The press had a field day anyway: an upcoming young scientist killing his married mentor over a piece of skirt young enough to be the mentor's daughter. It would only confuse matters to throw in allegations about the nature of the scientific experiments BRAVO was involved in."

"Sir, you said yourself nobody knew Gordon was going to spill the beans. He didn't have time to make the announcement..."

"That was before we saw the tapes."

The professor had a camera feed in every office. He knew about Gordon's affair with Sally. On the Friday before the murder, he must have watched Gordon shred those project documents and bind others into a parcel for his lawyer. He must have realised the implications.

"Consider the end result, Jones. BRAVO *doesn't* get exposed and continues functioning for the so-called greater good of our country. The window of opportunity was only three days: from the moment Gordon made up his mind to leave the agency to when he would have gone to the press. Three days, man. Two, if you discount the Sunday on which a religious person like Gordon wouldn't have acted. How lucky is that?"

"Very lucky. Do you believe in coincidence, Captain?"

He didn't. "Coincidence is the word we use when we fail to spot the real connection. Nick may have done the deed, but somebody pushed his buttons."

Annette refused to admit how relieved she felt to hear from Trevor again. He'd been busy last week. Busy at work, or busy avoiding her, she couldn't tell.

"You've cut your hair," he said as soon as she'd opened the front door.

The new look suited her, she knew. It went with the other changes, all part of a quick three-step guide into inventing a new you. Step one: change something drastic about your appearance. Step two: change something drastic about your behaviour. Step three—she wasn't sure there was a step three.

"Yes, I did," She couldn't help smiling at him, really smiling, not just going through the motions of being a good hostess. Her heartbeat made her feel as if she'd been running. "Do you like it?" The question was out before she could stop it.

*What did it matter whether he liked her hair?*

It mattered a great deal.

Trevor took his time, his gaze roaming up and down her silhouette. "It brings out your neck," he said. The last word came out huskier than the rest.

*Her neck. Did he remember? No, he wouldn't. Of course he wouldn't. Boys—men—never did.*

Their first kiss, his lips hot on her neck, shivers of pleasure all the way to her toes…Nobody else had ever kissed her that way…

She shook the memory off with a defiant toss of her chin-length bob.

"Can I offer you a cup of coffee?" she asked as they walked through the house to the swimming pool area. "Or a cool drink? It's a hot morning for March."

"You could offer me your opinion."

Warmth filled her chest. "My opinion? It's been a while since anybody asked. Whenever Gordon and I didn't agree, he made it his duty to persuade me that my opinion didn't matter." Another thought struck her. "Gosh, he was so much like my mother. Fancy that. I always thought girls were supposed to marry replicas of their fathers?"

"You have a chance to marry one now." Trevor took her hand in his and Annette felt the connection. Electric. Magical. Steady.

Trevor kissed her palm. "This is not how I imagined asking you. Dash it, Annette, I planned it all romantic and everything. Still, you have to rate it for spontaneity, so here goes. I love you. Will you marry me?"

The irony of it was—she wanted to. Her words scraped her throat raw. "Trevor, I'm sorry. Please understand. It's…"

"Inappropriate?" he interrupted.

*That too.*

"Too soon. I need to stand on my own two feet. Be my own person. Be free."

A smile darted across his lips. "I'm not Gordon."

*That alone might pose a problem for the children.*

Annette suppressed a sigh. "Speaking of Gordon," she hesitated, her embarrassment reaching uncharted peaks, "I still haven't done anything about..." her throat was so tight, it hurt, "about his last request. You know. His—sister." She couldn't look Trevor in the eye. "Please help me find her," she managed.

"Do you want me to leave right away, or can I get that opinion off you first?"

The straight face delivery caught Annette by surprise and she snorted with uncontrolled laughter.

For fifteen years, nobody else could make her laugh like that. They were fifteen long years.

His eyes combing the sparkling blue swimming pool, Watson suddenly remembered the chlorine stains on the front seat of the BMW. Another clue it had been Nick sitting in the car, Nick whose shirt got wet when Gordon's punch sent him into the water. He would have prepared the poisoned nail earlier, of course, after his walk with Sally in the garden, when he went outside again, alone this time.

All the evidence had been there for Watson to put together, yet he'd shut out anything that could have implicated Annette in the murder.

Time to live up to his reputation.

"Please think back to the party, Annette. In your opinion, did anybody act out of character?"

Annette's brows met at the base of her highly kissable forehead. Everything about her was kissable: the undersized nose, the curvy mouth, the slim neck...Damn, he should have kissed her when he'd proposed to her, kissed that spot on her throat that always pulsated with pure passion...

"Hmm, let me see. Well, Lula acted outrageous as usual, so nothing out of character there. Doc was charming and lovely," she smiled a faraway smile and Watson felt a stab of jealousy. Oh, how he wished it to be Doc, that silent instigator who had pushed the young, impulsive, oblivious Nick into committing murder for him.

"I'm sure he was," Watson muttered under his breath, "utterly charming, utterly lovely, utterly two-faced."

"Trevor?"

"Yes?"

"I love you. *You.* Doc means nothing to me."

She'd actually said it. Watson felt like punching up into the air shouting 'yes!' but that would have been childish.

"Yes!" He leaped out of his chair, pumped his fist up, lifted Annette into his arms, his lips searching out her throat long before settling on the plump mouth.

Her tongue tasted of promise and sin. She broke the kiss a fraction of a second before it was too late, before he carried the woman of his dreams indoors and made love to her on the thick carpet of the lounge.

"We can't," she said simply, and he understood. Her upbringing wouldn't allow her to go against social conventions. A woman like Annette didn't have sex out of wedlock, particularly with her husband only dead two weeks.

Still, it was many, many seconds later before he could concentrate on the case again. He repeated his earlier question.

"All the men acted like animals in the swimming pool," Annette said, her cheeks colouring. "They played chasing games with Lula and Sally, as though they were all teenagers. You wanted to know about acting out of character? Professor Adelbrecht sounded positively juvenile with all his comments about Sally's hidden treasures and the lucky man who'd get them…" she broke off.

Watson did a mental wince at the thought of Annette's husband getting Sally's *hidden treasures*. Another wince about a conservative sixty-something man cracking asinine jokes.

The same conservative man who'd told Sally's boyfriend to speak to Gordon on Friday, at the precise time Sally was seducing

Gordon in his office. And knowing Nick's new poison needed testing...

The pieces of the puzzle fell together at last. *When you have eliminated the impossible, whatever remains, however improbable* makes you want to bang your head in frustration. There was no way he would ever be able to prove it.

"I have to go," he said abruptly.

Annette flashed him a teasing smile. "Sure. Now that you got what you wanted from me."

"*Ja*, thanks. I really value the information you provided. Though a quickie would have been all right, too."

Her laughter was cut short with an abrupt, "What's going on here?"

Mrs. LeRoy stood three paces away from them, her chin shaking with anger. "I told you to stay away from my daughter."

"Indeed." Watson shrugged. "And I was a bloody fool to listen to you that time. It's not going to happen again. I've grown up and realised not all elders should be respected."

"Oh, you—you—you...Of all the impudent...Take your attitude, Trevor Watson, and get out of my house."

"Actually," Annette interjected, her tone as cold and as sharp as broken ice cubes, "this is *my* house. And this," Watson felt her small hand slip into his, "is my guest. Please go home Mother. To your own house. While you still have it."

Watson was blown away by the implicit warning in the last five words. This was a brand-new Annette.

He liked her this way, too.

# Chapter 20—Twenty-Nine Years before the Murder

GORDON HAD REHEARSED the ritual many times before his thirteenth birthday. Today, however, was the real thing, with candles and white robes.

"Who seeks right of entry to the Order?" intoned the Grand Master.

Gordon's teenage body shook with anticipation. "I do."

"Why do you seek it?"

"To fight for my country. To uphold her way of life and to preserve her as she is today." The reply, learned by rote, rolled off his tongue with conviction. "We need to protect our womenfolk from rape, we need to keep our houses safe and our children on the right path."

*What is rape, Father?* Gordon had asked when learning the words of the ritual.

It's when the blacks force white women to have their babies.

He shuddered at the memory.

"How are you going to serve?"

"I promise to serve with all my heart, with all my soul. With obedience and without reservation. So help me God."

"Brethren. I submit this boy to you asking to make a man of him."

Gordon didn't know what would happen next. The rite of passage demanded ignorance and blind faith.

A hood fell over his eyes, many hands lifted him up in the air. He didn't cry out when the needle pierced the skin of his foot.

For South Africa.

Mommy sat on the sofa, the thin line of her mouth scary.

"I didn't like your behaviour today, Annette. If you want friends, you will always smile. Show me your smile, no, not like that, I can see your teeth. Watch me when I smile, see, like this."

The three-year old Annette didn't understand big words like *behaviour*, but she understood smiles. Daddy smiled often and when he was around smiling came easy. Not so easy with Mommy around.

"I don't see you smile, Annette."

Annette tried hard to work her mouth into the perfect shape. "Can't, Mommy. My shoes hurt."

"Don't complain. Your shoes are pretty. It doesn't matter if they hurt. You shouldn't feel the hurt, you should be happy about the pretty things you have. No nonsense now. Smile, even if you don't feel like smiling."

The tingle in her eyes turned wet. "Mommy—"

"Young ladies don't argue. If you want people to like you, you have to look pretty and be nice to them. Pull up your socks."

The familiar tread of footsteps peppered the porch like a welcome summer rain.

"Daddy!" shouted Annette. "Daddy's home."

"Only maids shout, Annette. Young ladies listen."

"Yes, Mommy. Daddy, Daddy, look! Pretty picture! I made it."

Her father's reply was drowned by her mother's rebuke. "Don't boast, Annette. It's not nice for little girls to boast."

It not nice for little girls to feel, concluded Annette.

# Chapter 21—Three Months after the Murder

THE CORRUGATED-IRON shack held none of the primitive grace that marked the more traditional huts made of red mud and silver thatch. White man's civilisation had replaced the weather-insulated dwellings with scrap yard junk.

"You must be Lesley," Watson said to the caramel-skinned woman who greeted him at the door.

She lowered her eyes. "Please come in. Won't you have a cup of tea? I've only just brewed it."

He accepted the tin mug Lesley handed him with both her hands. She spooned in a glob of thick condensed milk. Of course: no electricity, no fridge, no fresh milk. Watson wondered how she had boiled the water. He guessed on a real fire outside, right next to the rough plank of a swing for her children.

"Is this your first time in Soweto?" Lesley asked politely.

Watson's heart darkened. "No." He didn't elaborate and she didn't press for details. The tea was strong, hot, and very sweet.

"You said you had news for me," she prompted.

He didn't know how to break it to her, so he recited the facts.

"Let me get this straight." Lesley opened and closed her fists in rapid succession. "You've come to tell me my mother is not my mother and my father is not my father? That the people who raised me and loved me are not really my parents?"

He waited.

"I'll tell you something," Lesley turned to him, her eyes like liquid chocolate. "They will always be my parents. More so than if I were born to them, because they had a choice whether or not to take me in."

What could his news offer her, anyway? Her biological parents were dead. Both her biological brothers were dead.

"Your sister-in-law would like to," he hesitated, thinking of the best way to phrase it. He chose the words from Gordon's letter to Annette. "She wants to do right by you."

"That's mighty big of her, recognising a coloured relative."

That's not what Gordon had meant. Had he? Annette was assuming he'd been talking about money. Would she welcome Lesley into her home? Would she let Danny and Julie visit Aunt Lesley in Soweto? "She wants to do what's best." Of that he was positive.

Lesley was silent for a long, long time. "My sister-in-law doesn't know what the best thing for me is," she said at last. "And neither do I. But I do know where I belong: here, with my people. My sister-in-law belongs with her people in her white suburb on the other side of life."

He inclined his head. "Annette will make it possible for you to collect your share of your father's estate."

"I spit on his estate."

Nothing more to say. Watson got up to leave.

"*Lumela 'mè!*"

A girl, perhaps Julie's age, ran into the hut and stopped abruptly when she saw him, a stranger, a white stranger in her house. Mistrust dulled her eyes.

16 June 1976 came back with unwelcome vividness. On that day, he saw mistrust in schoolchildren's eyes, too.

"That's my daughter, Ntabi," Lesley said. She added something in Sotho and the girl laughed, her dread dispersed.

All twelve year olds sound the same, he thought. For a moment there, he could have sworn it was Julie laughing. And no wonder. Julie and Ntabi were cousins, although their circumstances couldn't have been more different. Julie had a swimming pool in her garden, her own room, a bicycle, a TV. Ntabi had a plank for a swing and...Watson glanced around—not a single book or toy.

It could have been Julie marching in the protest that day. If her genes had worked out less fortunately, if her skin had been darker, Julie might have ended up in Soweto with Ntabi. Granted, they had only been six years old when the massacre took place. Still, the realisation rattled him.

"Will you do something for me?" he asked Lesley. "Will you take me to where the riots happened?"

*You have the right to remain silent*, that's what the police always said in American movies. This, however, was South Africa. The prisoner had no rights.

Jones knocked on the door leading to an opulent office in the centre of town.

"Good morning, sir. Please come with us."

"You must be joking." The man behind the desk looked authoritative despite his small stature.

Jones walked towards him and placed the steel bracelet on the man's right wrist.

"We'd like to ask you a few additional questions in connection with the murder of Gordon Pretorius. Sir."

"I demand to see your captain."

"The captain," said Jones, "is otherwise occupied."

Lesley's voice lilted in his ear. Soft. Matter-of-fact. "I remember the helicopters dropping crates of tear gas. I remember the Hippos spitting bullets at us."

Watson remembered the Hippos too. Anti-riot trucks. He had been driving one through a rain of well-aimed stones. The policemen inside the vehicle were supposed to fire real bullets into the stone-throwing mob.

Heroism came in different flavours, like chewing gum. Watson had experienced it first-hand, after he had turned the

Hippo around and drove it away from the demonstration before they could shoot. Some of his colleagues shook his hand in admiration of his courage to stand up to the regime, others called him a traitor. He didn't agree with either interpretation. To him, shooting at a crowd was just another crime, like murder. As a police officer, he couldn't go along with it. Almost got fired for his principles, except cops were quitting in droves post-Soweto. The sudden staff shortages meant he was allowed to stay on.

"This is where Doctor Melville Edelstein was killed," Lesley pointed. "Stoned to death by the rioting students. He did charity work in Soweto, loved us all as though we were his family. But on that day, all that mattered was the whiteness of his skin."

Of all the things she could have shown him, she chose that. Soweto's shame, the chink in her reputation as a heroic revolutionary.

"There was too much hatred here that day, too much fear. Everybody panicked. It was going to be a peaceful march." She changed the topic suddenly. "You're a policeman, aren't you? I could tell as soon as you walked into my house, even though you're wearing civvies."

Surely she knows, he thought, surely she realises...He waited for the blow.

"I was a teacher at the time," Lesley said. "When our leaders told us about the protest, I was all for it. It made sense to teach students in their native language, rather than in the language of—" she broke off.

"The oppressor?"

"The employer, the big *baas*, I was going to say. But you see, the language issue was not what the uprising was about. It all turned political. The leaders wanted to show the world how bad the apartheid regime was."

"They succeeded." Bile rose to his mouth.

Lesley humphed. "They failed. The world heard and did nothing. We're no better off. Nothing's changed, except that hundreds of families cry for their slain every day since."

Lesley and Annette were more alike than they knew, Watson

realised. They both saw war for what it was: a pointless loss of lives. Real victories weren't made on the battlefield.

"I've never entered the classroom since," Lesley's voice wavered. "I sent children to their death that day. Now you come here and tell me," she swallowed, "my biological parents were white."

Watson understood. For six long years Lesley had struggled with the overbearing feeling of guilt. Now that she wasn't black, the act of sending her students, her black students, to their death could be interpreted as double-crossing. A double burden.

"You acted in good faith, Lesley. You thought you were fighting for your Cause. What happened was..." he found the right words at last, the phrase came to him pliable and ready, "...was beyond your control. Say it, Lesley: *It was beyond my control.*"

Her gaze wavered like a wounded impala. She opened her mouth but no sound came out.

Watson stared at the spot where the first victim of the Soweto Riots had fallen. He whispered, "*It was beyond my control.*"

It didn't exonerate him, and yet a crushing weight soared off his chest. He followed it with his eyes as it drifted up to the deep pure blue of the African sky. "*It was beyond my control,*" he repeated. He touched Lesley's arm.

"Beyond my control," she whispered as the first tears rolled down her face.

Watson held her until she ran out of crying, then walked her back home. The streets of Soweto were not the safe streets of the white suburbs where children and women could wander unsupervised. How long before it all turned to custard, before the discontent in the black townships spilled over to the artificially utopian white neighbourhoods? How long before he again had to make the choice between orders and principles?

But for now, he was free of the demons. And when the time came to wrestle with them again, Annette would be there at the crossroads with him. He patted the folded drawing on a napkin he nowadays carried in his chest pocket. A good luck charm, even though he didn't believe in luck.

"What's the meaning of this?" asked the professor again, many hours later. The prison cell smelled of disinfectant, old urine and fresh sweat. "The case was closed months ago."

*Ja*, Watson thought. It had taken months to obtain permission to arrest this—this trash.

"You told Nick Haddow to speak to Gordon that Friday lunchtime. You knew he'd see Sally there. You also told him it was time to test the new poison for project Hydra. At the party, you provoked Nick into getting fresh with Sally and starting a fight with Gordon. You knew Gordon was clearing out his office and you guessed what that meant, particularly when the party invitation came along. You orchestrated it even though you did not issue a single order."

"That's absurd."

Watson shrugged. His body felt light as a helium balloon. "That's for the court to decide."

"The court? You don't have a shred of proof."

"We'll find it." He knew they wouldn't. Still, under South African law, they could hold the son of a bitch for weeks. "You will remain our—guest—while we keep on searching."

Adelbrecht's laugh echoed off the prison walls. "I've friends in places so high, you don't even know they exist. Be out of here as soon as I make a phone call."

"In that case," Watson turned to the door, "we'd better make sure you don't get to place that call."

"Can't believe Stuart died in Angola for the likes of you." Adelbrecht's hands shook. "He died for people like Gordon who didn't understand warfare and turned traitor, and he died for cowards like you who hide in a policeman's uniform instead of doing your bit on the border. Stuart was a true hero."

No, thought Watson. Gordon Pretorius was a true hero. He died fighting, without firing a single shot.

Immersed as she was in her part-time law degree at university,

Annette missed Trevor's company. They'd agreed to take it slow and she didn't want to miss him.

*Drat!*

Might as well not want to feel the sun's heat. Trevor was so different from Gordon. So—right.

"Mommy."

Annette reached out, found Julie's swimming-pool-cold fingers. The end of May was too wintry for recreational swimming, yet this year Julie refused to miss a day's training. She was focussed on winning the gala. She still wouldn't speak about Gordon, though Annette was sure the obsession with the swimming trophy was Julie's way of making her daddy proud.

She pulled her daughter closer. "What is it, honey?"

Julie nestled into her lap, all angles and sharp bones. Annette touched the top of the wet locks with her lips. A deluge of love washed over her body, overwhelming everything else. She wanted this moment to last.

"Mommy."

"I'm here."

"There was only one Pappa. I don't want another. Ever."

Just like that. No preamble, no space to negotiate. No other daddy. Julie's mind was made up. And she? What did she want? She didn't have to think about it.

"Mommy?"

"No other daddy, Julie. Ever. I promise." As easy as that.

That night, before she fell asleep, Lesley thought about her other daddy. Not the real father who had raised her, but the biological one who had erased her very existence from his life when he didn't like the colour of her skin.

She was almost sorry she'd lied to the cop. He'd looked so vulnerable, so out of place, so consumed by his own guilt, it would have been easy to confess her own crime to him.

Pieter Pretorius hadn't died by his own hand.

Pieter Pretorius had died by the hand of his own rejected daughter.

* * *

The Minister With No Official Portfolio was long back from his Mauritius holiday. Before he went to bed, he checked on his little daughter and tucked the blanket around her sleeping figure, because the nights were getting colder.

His wife, now in the last trimester of the pregnancy, snored softly in their marital bed. The minister kissed her forehead, mirroring the goodnight kiss he'd just given their daughter, tiptoed to his study and dialled a number.

"The damage?" he asked.

"Negligible at the moment. Adelbrecht's refusing to cooperate with the police."

"Good."

"He's asking for you."

The minister felt the first cold beads of sweat pool between his brows. "Not good."

Silence as the man on the other end of the line awaited instructions.

"Eliminate him," he said at last. "Make the soap in his morning shower particularly slippery."

"Understood."

# Chapter 22—Thirty-Seven Years before the Murder

THE HOUR WAS late, well past his bedtime, and the bedroom was as cold as only a Transvaal house can get on a cloudless pitch-black winter night. The five-year old Gordon couldn't fall asleep. The sound of his parents' arguing ripped into the silence of his room and slashed into the smokescreen of his composure.

Ever since the death of his baby sister—he hadn't even been allowed to see her—his parents were at each other's throats every evening as soon as Gordon and Stuart went to bed.

Today was no different.

"Just tell me the truth," his father bellowed.

Mamma's sob made Gordon want to run to her and hug her tight. He couldn't. Animal fear tied his feet together.

"Come on, tell me. Was it rape? Tell me which kaffir's responsible for the baby and I'll string him up by his balls."

More sobs.

"Serves me right for marrying an Englishwoman. A bloody darkie-lover."

"Scottish," Mamma's voice mixed with her tears. "My mother was Scottish. And my father was an Afrikaner just like you."

Gordon understood the words, but put together they didn't make any sense.

*Darkies? Baby? What was it all about?*

"I hate you," Father said to Mamma as Gordon's childhood started falling apart one brick at a time. "I used to love you but now I hate the sight of you. You've ruined my life." The voice twisted as it repeated, "I hate you, hate you, hate you. Why don't you just die?"

She did. A few weeks later Gordon and Stuart stood hand in hand at her grave, with Rosina and Rosina's baby daughter a few steps behind them.

"Bacterial infection," somebody murmured. "That's what's taken her."

Gordon knew better. Angry words had killed his mamma. One day, when he was bigger, he would make his father sorry.

Perhaps one day, he'd have the guts to kill him.

# Chapter 23—Two Years after the Murder

ON A QUIET Soweto street, a new school was opening its doors today. Annette parked her car in the scant shade of a thorn tree and rolled down her window. The morning air was hot and smoky from the breakfast fires, thick with the unmistakable smell of corn porridge.

Against the tin shacks of the township, the school built with Lesley's rejected inheritance stood out like a palace, its plaster still bright with newness, its roof straight, its windows glazed.

Julie pointed to the school building. "So they have computers?"

"Ten BBC Micros in a dedicated lab." Annette tucked a strand of her daughter's brown-red hair behind the small pink ear. The girl insisted on keeping her locks short. "The challenge is to find a tutor. Not many people know computers." Not many of those who knew computers were willing to set foot in Soweto.

"Danny and I can teach them, Mom. After school. Weekends."

Danny gave a thoughtful nod. "I know a few words in Sotho. *Morutisi* means teacher. *Dipuku* is books."

"More-tea-she," Beth repeated.

Pride squeezed Annette's throat. "That's a super idea, guys." She started the engine. Time to drive back. If Danny and Julie arrived late at their own school, their own white privileged school in which computers were nothing special, they'd earn detention at lunch and a pink slip in their permanent file. A double pink slip if the headmaster found out where they'd been this morning. And when Danny finished his education, he'd have the forced privilege to join the army and kill or be killed in the name of patriotic duty.

Annette blinked back the tears. In this beautiful land of gold, diamonds and sunshine, nobody was completely free.

# Note to the Reader

In the pre-1994 South Africa, a white woman was usually referred to as "madam" and a white man "master" by the black population. The custom, while racially prejudiced, had none of the sexual connotations often associated with the terms nowadays.

Also, Afrikaners are settlers from northwest Europe who established themselves in South Africa from the mid-17th century onwards. They were the white elite group during the apartheid era (pre-1994). Not to be confused with Africans, who are the native black inhabitants of Africa.

Chapter One of Colby Marshall's

# *Chain of Command*

Carved from the tradition of top-flight political thrillers, *Chain of Command* is a sizzling potboiler of a tale.

–Jon Land, best selling author of *Pandora's Temple*

The first chapter of this book will shock you–and the shocks keep right on coming. Colby Marshall has written a book that deserves to be called THRILLER.

– R.L. Stine, New York Times best selling author of *Red Rain*, *The Haunting Hour* and the *Goosebumps* series.

# CHAPTER ONE

## *Zero Hour*

## *California*

HIS HEART RATE never rose above sixty as he looked through the scope of his .50 caliber sniper rifle at the unfortunate soul caught in his crosshairs.

He kept his breathing even. He inhaled deeply, slowly, so he could hold his breath as long as it took when the moment came. Then, he controlled his exhale equally. Hold. Breathing when he pulled the trigger could affect the shot's precision. He had done this a time or two. Actually way more, but this one was different.

This one he knew.

Still, no reason to worry. Stick to the protocol.

He fixed on the target's head in the center of the scope. The perfect kill shot. Just the way the United States military taught him.

Beside him sat a cell phone, the prepaid kind you could pay cash for in any discount store so it couldn't be traced. Only one person had the number to this phone.

He sucked air into his nostrils, noting the feel of the air temperature as he watched the glowing face of the phone, the clock flicking in time from 8:59 to 9:00 PM. The phone vibrated against the cement. He turned it on and listened in his earpiece.

"You good to go?"

"Yep, have to go now. Target locked."

2

"On my three," said the voice.

It was important their shots go off at exactly the same time so the message would be unmistakable.

He heard the voice count it off at the other end of the phone. "One..."

His finger tightened on the trigger. His eyes bored into the skull of the man he was about to blow apart. He was lucky he still had a clear shot, but then again, the plan was perfect. Amazing something so incredible and horrible could be counted off in the same manner as ripping a Band-Aid off of a five-year-old kid's knee.

"Two..."

His finger tensed just the right amount and held there, ready to fire.

"Three."

As he squeezed the trigger, he heard the shot at the other end of the line. *A blast right on top of my own. That's a new one.*

Even as the recoil slammed his frame backward, he was already back on his feet and disassembling the rifle. He thrust the pieces into his case in less than thirty seconds, then ran down the stairwell, calm but rushed.

And he was right to be in a hurry. He'd not only just heard the gunshot that killed the President of the United States.

He had just executed the Vice President.

### Day 1: Early Morning
### Washington D.C.

The phone rang. The shrill cry of her mockingbird ringtone crowed in the air demanding an answer. Try as she might to ignore it, it wouldn't stop.

"All right, all right!" Fifty-three-year-old Elaine Covington rolled over in her bed and pulled the receiver to her ear. This had better be good.

"What?" she barked into the phone. The numbers on the clock

beside her four-poster bed read 12:44 AM. Who the hell would be calling at this hour, and what was so important they felt it warranted waking her?

"I'm sorry for the lateness of the hour, Madame Speaker," said the voice on the other line, tension seeping through his tone. His first words were too fast, his last too slow, as if he didn't know what to call her. "But it's an emergency. This is Bert Royal."

She knew him, though her staff spent more time with him than she had. There weren't many occasions when her position required her to interact with President Seymour's Chief of Staff. Elaine clutched the phone tighter as Bert spoke.

"The president and the vice president have been shot. Both are dead. Madame Speaker, you're the first Congressperson, um, former Congressperson to know."

Through the white hailstorm in her mind, the lists of what to do, what to say, in what order, and to whom battled for dominance. She had to get dressed, had to get out of this room, out of bed, damn it. "Give me ten minutes. No, make it fifteen. Get that new bimbo press secretary we just hired. Meet me at the office."

"No, Madame Speaker. I'm sorry. I've got orders to send a car with a special detail to take you to a secure place."

She swore. What her exact words were she doubted she'd remember. She agreed to be ready within the hour. Knuckles still white from clenching the phone, she dropped her cell back on the nightstand.

Elaine lay back on her pillow. Surely she was in the middle of a dream. A nightmare. Congress would assemble; she'd have to preside for hours over a debate about whether or not to attack the country responsible.

Suddenly, her eyes flew open. She sat up straight in her bed. She hadn't been asked to show up at the Capitol. She had been told she'd be taken to an undisclosed location where she would be debriefed.

It was as if she'd been slapped across the face the same way her grandmother smacked her once when she talked back to her at age ten.

President Seymour was dead.

Vice President Tifton was dead.

The Constitution dictated the next person in line.

Elaine Covington blinked twice. She was now the President of the United States.

Elaine's heart pounded as she was ushered into an unmarked black sedan. It sped through town without yielding to a single traffic light or stop sign and pulled into an underground parking garage. Other than that, Elaine couldn't tell where they were. She'd tried to follow the maze of turns the car made from the moment the Secret Service closed her inside, but she'd lost track. She only knew they hadn't driven too far, so they must still be in DC.

Two Secret Service agents hustled her into a dark corridor. The men on either side of her were supposed to make her feel safe, but somehow they only put her on edge. Sweat seeped into the silk blouse she'd thrown on underneath her charcoal gray suit. She fought to breathe evenly. To present a calm facade.

As she came to the end of the tunneled hallway, low lights streamed into the corridor from one side. The agents steered her inside the room, where she found herself standing face to face with President Seymour's Chief of Staff, the president's National Security Advisor, the Secretary of Defense, and a handful of other people she didn't recognize right away. A rip tide of whispers surged around the space. Nervousness crept up her neck like a wild electrical current threatening to catch fire.

Another person standing in the room caught her eye, though he was off to the side and not part of the general buzz of conversation. He stood next to the wall in his Navy uniform, alert. The briefcase he held was handcuffed to his wrist. Elaine's chest clenched, but somehow she swallowed the moan that threatened to escape her lips.

The nuclear "football" was a forty-five pound briefcase that held, in essence, the ability of the President of the Unites States to unleash a nuclear response to any threat to the nation. The briefcase, always handcuffed to a high-ranking military officer, was never more than a few feet from the president at all times.

And now, the power to detonate those weapons was in this room, only a few feet away from Elaine Covington. This was no dream. No action movie scenario. This was real.

The briefcase still held Elaine's attention when a voice reminded her others were in the room.

"Madame President," Ronald Garrety, the National Security Advisor, said.

The silver hair receding from Garrety's round face swam in Elaine's vision. Some part of her understood his words addressed her, but hearing him refer to her this way made it harder to pay attention to what followed.

"I know this must be a difficult evening for you, but we have much to discuss." He gestured to a chair across the table. "Please."

"Of course," she said, straightening her jacket. "Ladies. Gentlemen." She sat down, giving a nod to the two other Cabinet members who'd not yet spoken to her.

Elaine licked her lips. What would a president say?

"Do we know anything?" As soon as the words tumbled out of her mouth, her face burned with how stupid she sounded.

Bert Royal slumped in his chair. The short, dapper man looked for once like he had dressed in the dark, thrown on whatever clothes he'd worn the previous day. Bert had not only worked as President Seymour's Chief of Staff; he was also a good friend. This couldn't be easy for him, having to continue to do his job and act as if his emotions weren't all over the place.

The National Security Advisor shot a glance toward Royal, but then quickly returned to facing Elaine. "Not a lot yet," he said, "but our people are on it, covering it from every angle. Vice President

Tifton was killed as he was leaving an auditorium at the University of California, Berkley, where he spoke to some college students. President Seymour was shot getting into his car. He'd just returned to Washington from his trip to visit the region in Alaska hit by the earthquake." Garrety's eyes once again flicked toward Bert Royal, then back to Elaine.

"And other than that?"

"That's all we know. We know it was professional. Deliberate. The timing was too precise to have been a coincidence, so the two shootings must be connected. We're going to have to wait for further investigations to yield some results. At this point we have no leads. All we know is we're dealing with two sick bastards who are damned good shots."

"Terrorists? Foreign country involvement?" she snapped back.

"Given the plotting and precision of the attacks, you'd think so, but we can't be sure. No one has claimed responsibility. We haven't picked up on any communications, though we're watching that situation closely."

Bert Royal, who until now had been sitting at the end of the table, silent, finally piped up. "Isn't that unusual? Plenty of whack jobs should've lined up by now to tell us it was their brilliant idea to kill the president and vice president simultaneously."

"What that tells me," Garrety said, "is this wasn't an attack on the American way of life. These aren't your typical terrorists who want martyrdom and infamy. The killers wanted to get the job done without getting caught."

Garrety leaned forward, folding his hands on the table between them. "Most demented bastards who pull stunts like this want their names in the paper. They're proud of what they've done. Our killers aren't like that. They executed their mission and disappeared. Which means one of two things: they were guns for hire, or they have another agenda. Maybe both," he said.

"In other words," Bert said, "professional assassins."

"Exactly," Garrety replied.

Chain of Command is available from the Stairway Press website (http://www.stairwaypress.com/bookstore/chain-of-command/) and all online and physical bookstores worldwide.

Visit Colby online at www.ColbyMarshall.com

# STAIRWAY≡PRESS

www.StairwayPress.com